Dear Impostor

Nicole Byrd

J

JOVE BOOKS, NEW YORK

DEAR IMPOSTOR

A Jove Book / published by arrangement with
the author

PRINTING HISTORY
Jove edition / August 2001

All rights reserved.
Copyright © 2001 by Cheryl Zach and Michelle Place.
Excerpt from *Lady in Waiting* copyright © 2001 by Cheryl Zach
and Michelle Place.
This book, or parts thereof, may not be reproduced in any form
without permission.
For information address: The Berkley Publishing Group,
a division of Penguin Putnam Inc.,
375 Hudson Street, New York, New York 10014.

The Penguin Putnam Inc. World Wide Web site address is
www.penguinputnam.com

ISBN: 0-515-13112-1

A JOVE BOOK®
Jove Books are published by The Berkley Publishing Group,
a division of Penguin Putnam Inc.,
375 Hudson Street, New York, New York 10014.
JOVE and the "J" design
are trademarks belonging to Penguin Putnam Inc.

PRINTED IN THE UNITED STATES OF AMERICA

10 9 8 7 6 5 4 3 2 1

For Peggy LeGate and Ruth LeGate Foster,
two of our own favorite aunts, with love,

and for Bradley, of course

One

*H*e should have guessed that redemption, unlike a well-dealt hand of cards, would not be so easily grasped; perhaps heaven always lay two steps beyond hell's gaping door.

"There—'e's over there!"

Gabriel Sinclair glanced quickly over his shoulder. He had mingled with the last of the emerging theatergoers, hoping to lose his pursuers, but the gang of ruffians who had followed him halfway across London was not so easily shaken.

Gabriel stepped sideways behind a pudgy gentleman in an opera cloak, although his tall stature could not be completely hidden by the shorter man. The skinny woman who clung to the other man's arm looked up at him, flushed, and fluttered her lashes as she stretched her too-thin lips into a wide simper. Gabriel returned the smile without really seeing her. He had always had this effect on women; he hardly noticed anymore.

He was more concerned with escaping the attention of the roughly dressed men who hesitated at the edge of the thinning crowd—too many even for him to fight his way through. His own immaculate evening dress should have made him appear part of the tonnish men and women leaving the theater, but the sharp-eyed man with the scar on his cheek who seemed to be the leader of the gang was not so easily distracted.

"Nab 'im, ye brainless curs!"

Gabriel backed one step deeper into the shadows at the corner of the building, then turned and ran for his life.

But the alley was littered with rubbish and one drunken street-sweeper, who had evidently earned enough pennies to buy himself the solace of a cheap bottle of gin. Slumped against the theater's outer wall, he snored in drunken bliss, a strong odor of gin rising from his open mouth like mist on the moor, almost strong enough to obscure the otherwise prevalent stench of rotting garbage. His balding head reflected the dim light from the avenue's streetlamp beyond, the empty bottle was still cradled in his lap, and his coarse-fibered broom blocked the narrow alley.

Gabriel saw the dirty broom in time to leap over it, but he had to slow slightly; behind him, he heard a muffled curse and then a crash as his closest pursuer was not so nimble.

Gabriel grinned, but saved his breath for running. He was still not free of his stalkers. He covered several more yards, then leaped across a puddle of stagnant water. As his feet again hit the pavement, he caught a glimpse in the corner of his vision of a reflection in the dank pool, a dark shape moving behind him. He heard the splash of feet pounding through the water, followed by an almost indiscernible whisper of sound. He whirled in time to see the cudgel descending.

Most men would have died then and there in the refuse-strewn alley, but Gabriel Sinclair was not most men.

He dodged the blow easily, then caught the weapon at the bottom of its arc and jammed it upward hard against the villain's chin. With a grunt, the man fell. Gabriel pulled the club free of his attacker's suddenly slack fingers and struck the next ruffian hard in his stomach. The man bent double, cursing and gagging on his own sour-smelling vomit.

"Eat something that didn't agree with you?" Gabriel asked, his tone pleasant. "A spot of bad wine, perhaps?"

Warily, he eyed the remaining three men, who drew back

in alarm now that their victim held a weapon. Two of the men held only rough truncheons, but the leader, his eyes narrowed, pulled a long, evil-looking blade from his sleeve and stepped forward. The scar-faced man smiled, revealing rotting teeth, and shifted the knife with an ease that came of long practice.

Gabriel winced at a whiff of the man's foul breath. He watched the villain's eyes instead of the narrow, lethal weapon. Gabriel had not spent fifteen years living by his wits to no purpose—he knew when it was prudent to fight and when to flee.

Of course, Gabriel thought, *prudency has never been one of my virtues.*

He made one quick feint with the club, and the would-be assassin jumped back. Once more, Gabriel took to his heels.

He turned the corner and had traveled only a few yards when his path was blocked by a skinny man of almost his own height, who paced up and down in front of the theater's back entrance.

The other man, who also wore evening dress, tugged at his too-high neckcloth and muttered to himself as he perused a sheet of paper. "Aunt Sophie has white hair and a long nose. Cousin Mervyn has a fat paunch and thinning hair. No, that's Cousin Percival. Oh, hell's bells—I'll never pull this off."

Gabriel tried to sidestep him, but the man moved in the wrong direction, toward him instead of away. Gabriel skidded into the man, sending the paper flying into the air. Knocked off his feet by the impact, arms flailing, the other man sprawled across the wooden steps that led to the rear entrance.

"Pardon me!" Gabriel kept his balance, but barely, and he dropped the club. He glanced at the theater's back door, but it looked firmly locked. Then, even as the footsteps from the alley came closer, he heard the sound of horses' hooves.

A vehicle was approaching, not a hackney, which he might have hired, but someone's private carriage. To his surprise, it drew up before them.

"One of you the marquis of Tarrington?" the coachman called down to them both.

The man draped across the steps gaped up at the coachman, then waved his hand feebly. "Uh, that—that's him, right there."

Gabriel turned sharply to look down at the unknown man. "What?"

But the door of the carriage swung open in invitation just as he saw three of the ruffians turning the corner, their weapons held ready. And a fourth, one of the men he'd knocked down in the alley, stumbled after them, his expression murderous.

"Get in, if you please, my lord," the coachman called.

Gabriel was not one to turn down a gift from providence. He jumped into the carriage, slammed the door shut, and the vehicle pulled away. Through the window, he saw the gang members stare blankly at the departing rig.

"Another time, gentlemen," Gabriel called. Then, laughing, he leaned back against the thick soft nap of the velvet squabs. What a way to return to his native land!

Taking a deep breath, Gabriel relaxed for the first time since he had set out that evening for the exclusive gaming club that he had never reached. He had seen poor losers in his time, but never one to rival Barrett's murderous ire.

Of course, few gamesters had lost a stake the size of Barrett's last wager. An estate in the south of England—a landed property suitable for reestablishing the fortune of an impoverished younger son, a black sheep who had left England in disgrace years before.

It was the opportunity Gabriel had been waiting for—a way to return with dignity, with style, and to prove at last to his father, to his whole censorious family, that Gabriel was not the ne'er-do-well they all believed him to be. He had always vowed he would never return with his tail between his legs, in poverty and dishonor, begging for handouts.

He had been stroking the smooth mahogany panel of the door, and his long fingers clenched involuntarily into a fist. No, he would come back successful or not at all. He would show them he had survived, more than survived, triumphed! An estate of his own, with rents to collect and a handsome house to make into his home—it would change his life forever.

If he could just live long enough to collect his winnings.

Barrett, the disgruntled card player who had lost his own birthright over a hand of cards, had conceived of an ingenious if not terribly original way to wipe out his debt of honor.

Dead men could not collect their spoils.

But Gabriel did not intend to die for someone else's convenience. If that were the case, he would have given up long ago, in all those years of wandering, of card-playing, of existing on the fringes of civilized society, living by his wits, his charm, his handsome face, and his sharp mathematician's mind.

He looked out through the glass panes once more, absently noting changes in the London cityscape. Here was a newly refurbished mansion, there a new shop boasting elegant ladies' hats trimmed with tall ostrich plumes or delicate silk roses. The streetlights were more prevalent than he remembered on his first boyhood trip, glowing with the steady flame of gas instead of oil.

And he had changed, too, perhaps more so than the city, the country, he had left behind. He glanced down at his own sun-bronzed fingers—harder and leaner, surely, than the pampered white hands of the boy who, heartsick, had turned and walked away from his father's sharp-tongued disinheritance. The man who returned would establish his own place without seeking his father's blessing.

The carriage slowed to allow an old-fashioned coach to move out of its path, and Gabriel heard the coachman cursing from his front perch, and the other vehicle creaking as it rolled ponderously across the intersection. Shutting his eyes, Gabriel smiled. The curses sounded as lyrical as a Mozart overture—they were in English, after all, not French, not German, not Spanish, not even one of the polyglot dialects of the West Indies. And the smells of the street—manure and rain-washed brick and sweating horses—these were also the smells of London, not the spicy odors of a Tobago market or the sewage-laced stench of a Venetian canal. He was home again at last, and this time . . . this time, no one would drive him away!

The carriage moved forward again, and Gabriel wondered where the carriage was taking him. He didn't really care as long as it gave him a momentary respite from his attackers. Judging by their zeal, they had been promised a small fortune for his death—and considering what Barrett would save by it, Gabriel didn't wonder at his enemy's generosity.

And where was the real marquis of Tarrington? Still inside the theater, wooing some second-rank actress in her tiny dressing room? He would be annoyed that his carriage had picked up the wrong occupant. Why on earth had the driver not recognized his own employer? As to that, why did the man Gabriel had flattened confuse him for this Tarrington fellow? There were puzzles here, but Gabriel always enjoyed a good intrigue; he had spun enough of them on his own.

Now the carriage slowed again. It was stopping, this time, in front of an impressive mansion where a footman sprang to attention, ready to swing open the carriage door.

Now for the discovery, Gabriel thought. He had no real plan, but something would come to mind. It always did. With only mild anticipation, his heartbeat quickening just a little, he straightened his well-tied cravat and bent to exit the carriage.

To his surprise, when he stepped down to the uneven stones of the street, the footman showed no sign of recognition—or, to be more accurate, of nonrecognition.

"Your lordship." The servant bowed slightly and stepped back so that Gabriel could move toward the spacious house that rose before him, its tall windows glowing, showering shafts of light outward to brighten the darkness of the street. Already he could hear the sound of a pianoforte and the faint murmur of well-bred voices.

Gabriel ascended the broad steps with measured slowness. This was not the marquis's own residence, then, and there seemed to be a good-sized party going on inside. Was he here as a guest? Did this mean that he—Gabriel—could keep up the pretense a few minutes longer? Why not, he thought. He had always loved a good party.

He nodded to the liveried footman inside the doorway and paused to glance into the tall looking glass on the wall. He had lost his hat during the chase, but his dark hair was in place, his evening attire still immaculate despite his last mad dash through the littered alleyway. He flicked one almost invisible speck from his dark coat front, smoothed his lapel, then relaxed his shoulders and prepared to climb the staircase toward the next floor, where the sounds of chatter and the clinking of glasses could be plainly heard.

God, but he could use a glass of wine! Gabriel hoped that the master of the house, whoever he was, had a discerning palate and a good wine cellar; that earlier run for his life had left Gabriel with a dry throat and a giant thirst.

The other guests seemed to be already assembled; he climbed the wide staircase alone. At the worst, that meant all eyes would be on him when he entered the double doors, flung open to welcome the party-goers. At its best, perhaps he could hide amid the crowd long enough to enjoy a glass of burgundy, a brief respite before he was off again on the run. It had been his way of life for so long that it no longer seemed strange. Only this time, his purpose was not just another easy conquest or high-stakes card game; this time, he had a real goal—the estate that he meant to live long enough to claim. He had something to prove, to his father, to his brother, to his hawk-nosed great-aunts, and perhaps even to himself.

With these thoughts still simmering in the back of his mind, Gabriel composed his expression to one of well-bred indifference, with only the faintest hint of polite greeting. He stepped up to the doorway.

Without apparent prompting, the footman declaimed in echoing accents: "The marquis of Tarrington."

The chatter of conversation died as every face in the room turned in his direction, and at the very end of the room, an elderly lady raised her lorgnette to stare at him through slightly protruding eyes.

Gabriel waited for someone to cry out, "Impostor! That is not the marquis!"

Silence, still. He glanced quickly around the edge of the well-dressed crowd until one woman, standing a little apart, caught his gaze. His breath caught for an instant in his throat before exiting through slightly unsteady lips.

She was tall for a woman, slim but exquisitely formed, her curves evident beneath the soft folds of her blue evening gown. A pity it was cut a bit too high at the neckline; he was sure that her bosom was worth closer inspection. Her flaxen hair had been pulled into a simple but severe twist on the back of her head, and her perfectly shaped oval face was still as she gazed back at him through icy blue eyes. Her features were regular and classically beautiful, but it was the spirit inside those cool eyes that held him, that spoke of passions that even the woman herself might not guess at. Gabriel, who had not been called a rogue in seven languages without good reason, sensed heat beneath the frigid demeanor as surely as a beast scented danger.

But he had forgotten, for an instant, his perilous situation. He would not be here long enough to woo this vision, and he felt a flicker of disappointment. The instinctive flare of longing that had leaped inside him would have to be suppressed. A damnable shame, but there it was.

"So," the dowager with the lorgnette said, her voice loud amid the silence. "This is the mysterious fiancé you have at last allowed your family to meet."

It took all of Gabriel's prized sangfroid not to show his surprise; he blinked, but otherwise maintained his expression of polite indifference. Fiancé? His goose was cooked, then, and well sauced to boot. He was already rehearsing his escape route when the blond goddess spoke.

"Welcome, my lord," she said.

Two

Psyche Persephone Hill was not amused. The last half hour of her life had been insufferable. Her cousin Percy had been leaning over her shoulder trying to sneak none-too-subtle glances down her bodice, her slippers pinched, and her *fiancé* was late to his own betrothal party.

Smothering her irritation, she stepped forward now, gladly escaping Percy's goggle-eyed perusal, and approached the man who was going to change her life forever.

All he had to do was obey her orders.

Her maid, who had negotiated the terms with this second-rate, unknown actor, had said he was tall, dark-haired, and well enough to look at. Psyche had never doubted her devoted maidservant's eyesight before, but if this was what Simpson called "well enough to look at . . ."

Smoothing her tense face into a smile, she stretched out her gloved hands to the tall stranger in apparent affection. With each step she took, her skin tightened as if she were moving closer to a source of incredible energy—unknown energy wrapped in the benign familiarity of black-and-white evening dress. Looking up into the dark eyes beholding her with wary amusement, she felt a sudden unease. She had an insane urge to snatch her hands back before he could touch her. Suppressing the feeling, she moved steadily toward him.

He loomed even taller as she approached him. Rich black hair, dark eyes—a very deep blue, perhaps, not brown as she'd first thought—and unfashionably tanned features. Firm lips parted in an admiring smile revealed even, white teeth; a small scar marred the strong lines of his chin. Resolutely, she took the last step toward her future.

"You are late," she said, her jaw stiff with anger she could not afford to show.

One dark slash of an eyebrow rose. "My dear, I had no idea my services were needed."

Reaching out, he took one of her gloved hands, turned it palm up, and brought it to his lips. Caught off guard at the unexpected intimacy, she gasped when the heat of his kiss seemed to sear her palm. She snatched her hand back.

Were all actors this forward? No doubt he was accustomed to loose women, not to well-bred maidens who had particular reason to maintain their decorum. Psyche took a deep breath and tried to steady herself

Lowering her lashes coquettishly as her family would expect in response to her affianced husband's lovemaking, she spoke in low, hurried tones that did not match her compliant smile. "You know your services are needed, otherwise you would not be here. Now, behave yourself and you'll get what you want."

Looking up at her through thick, dark lashes as he rose from his bow, he grinned. "God, I love an eager woman."

Praying that no one else had heard his outrageous comment, she put her hand on his arm, and her fingers pinched hard through the expensive superfine of his evening coat. Were actors always this well dressed, she wondered in some corner of her mind. They must earn more on the stage than she had imagined. She hoped he was not more successful than her maid had said, or else one of her relatives might recognize him, and that would mean the end of her brilliant, supremely risky plan.

His only response to her pinch was a tensing of his biceps—were all actors this well formed?—and a slight narrowing of those incredibly beautiful eyes. Standing this close to him, Psyche was aware of a masculine smell of soap and fine scent and just the hint of street odors, as if he had been lounging too long in a back alley. That did seem more like some little-known treader of the boards. She told herself to relax; her assembled family were watching them both with intent, curious eyes.

She heard someone clear his throat. Psyche turned, the actor following her example, and they faced two men who glowered at them with almost identical expressions.

"This is my uncle Wilfred, my lord," she said quickly. "My kind guardian, who has looked out so zealously for my interests since the death of my parents." If the irony in her tone was apparent, no one seemed to take notice. "And this, of course, is his son and my cousin, Percy."

Neither man extended his hand, so her fake fiancé bowed slightly.

Both of the men who faced them were shorter than the actor on her arm, both barely tall enough to meet Psyche herself at eye level. Uncle Wilfred was gray around the temples, and his balding pate was already reflected in the pattern of his son's thinning hair. Both men, despite their well-cut jackets, revealed paunches that spoke of hearty appetites and sedentary living. And both round faces wore expressions of strong dislike.

"Never heard of this Tarrington title," her uncle said rudely. "Seems a curious thing, eh?"

"Indeed, our family is old, but sadly undistinguished," the actor agreed.

Psyche heard a titter of laughter from behind her, quickly suppressed.

Her guardian was just beginning. "And why should this family find you suitable for our beloved niece?" Uncle Wilfred demanded, his tone as rigid as the set of his shoulders.

"Because I will cherish her, make her madly happy, and sire many beautiful children," the actor suggested merrily, as if answering a riddle.

A wave of scarlet mottled Percy's plump cheeks, and his father frowned. "Don't be impertinent! We have long had other plans for our dear Psyche. In fact, Percy here—"

"Who has always been as dear as a brother to me," Psyche injected smoothly, knowing what was coming, "and has, I'm sure, only good wishes for my happiness."

"W-well, yes," Percy sputtered. "But, dash it, you know that I—that I—I'm not your bloody brother, Psyche."

"Please conduct yourself like a gentleman, Percy," her aunt Maris, standing nearby, snapped, staring hard at the offender. "We have no need for such language when ladies are present."

"No, Aunt Maris." Percy pulled out a handkerchief and wiped his perspiring brow. "Of course not, beg your pardon, of course, of course. But Psyche and I—we were always— Psyche, you know—dash it—"

She knew, all too well, and she didn't wish to hear his oft-rehearsed professions of love. She turned the man on her arm firmly toward the rest of the waiting family.

"This is my cousin Matilda," she told him, "and my aunt Maris."

The actor bowed to both ladies—heavens, but he was graceful. She wondered how he would dance, how it would be to waltz within his arms, and then pulled her thoughts sharply back. If all went well, she would never see him again after this night. He was here for a purpose, a singular purpose, and it had nothing to do with dancing.

He was saying something polite to her relatives; Psyche tried to pay attention.

"It is no wonder that Psyche is so well endowed with elegance and beauty," the man said. "I can see that her whole family is similarly pleasing."

Psyche stared at him, and Cousin Matilda looked uncertain, as if unsure whether he were making covert fun. Matilda was plump and round as a fatted partridge, her cheeks too ruddy for conventional beauty, and her neck too short. And Maris, staring at him in suspicion, was as thin and gaunt as an old turkey that had long outlived its appointment with the chopping block.

"You have lovely eyes, Cousin Matilda," the man continued, "as smooth and deep as a mountain lake."

Goodness, so she did; why had Psyche never noticed before? Matilda's eyes were the shimmering green-brown color of, well, of still, deep water, just as the actor had said. Psyche watched as Matilda flushed even redder with pleasure, and Maris nodded in stiff approval.

"Thank you," Matilda muttered. "You're too kind." And Aunt Maris allowed a rare smile to lift her lips and lighten her usual dour expression.

"Only observant," the man said, his smile relaxed.

If she didn't hurry him on, Matilda would be ready to marry him herself, Psyche thought wryly. Nonetheless, she glanced at the actor with more respect as she guided him toward the next group of relatives.

"That was generous of you," she said under her breath. "Matilda is not accustomed to compliments, but she's a very sweet soul."

"Every woman is beautiful," the man on her arm murmured back. "If one only knows where to look."

Was he gazing again at the curves beneath her gown? For some reason, his glances did not hold the same leering lust as Percy's covert appraisals always did, and she did not feel the same disgust. From this man, a woman sensed only genuine appreciation, and—

Psyche tried to pull her thoughts together. And that was the most dangerous flattery of all, she told herself.

The fraudulent marquis shared polite greetings with the other family members assembled for this betrothal party, and Psyche could sense a gradual change in the atmosphere as the women responded to his charm and the men found their stares firmly met.

At the end of the room, a white-haired woman sat stiffly in a large chair that almost gave the illusion of a throne— and Psyche, knowing her great-aunt Sophie, knew her placement was quite deliberate.

"Whatever you do, don't disagree with her!" Psyche whispered as she steered him toward the final and, aside from Uncle Wilfred, perhaps most formidable member of the family. "Be respectful. Say as little as you can, just as I wrote you."

"This is my great-aunt Sophie, whom I've told you so much about," she said, raising her voice again to a conversational level.

"So you're the man who has swept my prim niece off her feet." The older woman peered at him through her lorgnette. "Never thought it would happen. You've got a pretty face, but then, how much is that worth in the long run? Must be more to you than that."

"Of course," he answered, taking the hand she offered and bringing it to his lips as he bowed with the ease and grace of long practice. "Why else would my dearest Psyche agree to my proposal?"

"You're not after her fortune, then?" Aunt Sophie snapped, retrieving her hand from his grip.

"A sensible man is never averse to a fortune," he said, smiling.

This time Psyche bit her lip and waited for her aunt to respond with indignation and outrage. Instead, the older woman gave a snort of laughter.

"At least you don't make any pretense of it," she said. "I thought you might spout some romantic nonsense about her sky-blue eyes and her rose-petal lips, or other such bilge."

"Oh, I see more to her than her eyes and lips," Psyche's hired fiancé assured them both, his gaze deliberately dropping to her high neckline and the well-covered curves of her breasts beneath the pale blue silk of her gown.

Psyche blushed and tried to pinch his arm again, but his biceps were too firm; she knew he felt little pain, already prepared for her assault. Whoever this actor was, he learned quickly.

Aunt Sophie snorted again. "You might just do," she said, her tone surprisingly mild. "You might just do, Lord Tarrington."

Psyche, still seething with anger over this man's outrageous conduct, stared at her aunt in surprise.

It was going to work, against all the odds! She sighed in relief, remembering the desperate moment when she had come up with this far-fetched scheme.

It was because Cousin Percival had been even more clinging these past weeks since the Season had begun, dogging her every move. If she attended a party or a ball, he was there at her elbow. If she rode into the countryside for an al fresco outing, he was there, puffing along on a staid nag and urging the plodder unmercifully as he tried to stay the same course as his more adventurous cousin.

He glowered at other potential suitors and often grabbed her arm, despite her not so subtle attempts to shake him off, when any other eligible bachelor seemed too keen in appreciation of her beauty or too persistent in attendance. And his constant presence was taking its toll. The circle of admirers around her was thinning, and she knew that with every year, it would shrink even more.

It was not hard for Percy to make himself her shadow, despite all her attempts to discourage him. Of course he would receive invitations to the same social events—her father's family were of impeccable lineage, though mostly endowed with modest wealth. Only her scholarly father, with his penchant for strange experiments and new inventions, had managed to build up a large fortune, safely invested since the accident in government funds. It was a fortune that Uncle Wilfred had coveted even before the death of his brother, and now Wilfred and his insufferable twit of a son thought the answer to their greed lay easily within their grasp. All that was necessary was for Psyche to agree to marry her first cousin.

And that, despite an increasing desire for financial independence, she could not bring herself to do. When Percy took her hand, when she felt the limp, damp clasp of his fingers around her own, Psyche wanted only to push him away. She had never kissed him, but one glance at Percy's moist pink lips made her stomach turn at the very thought.

Even the emancipation marriage would bring from her father's too-strict will, which had firmly wrapped up her inheritance in trust till she was safely affianced, could not alter her distaste for her cousin.

And when, a fortnight ago, he had backed her into a prickly holly bush in the countess of Shrewsbury's garden, while music and the glow of many candles had flowed out from the ballroom windows just behind them, she had been driven to desperate measures.

"Please, Cousin," Percy had begged, trying to take her hand. "You know how I feel—"

"And you know how I feel, Percy. We've been through this a hundred times. I cannot marry you. I have no affection for you, not in that way," she'd answered him firmly, pulling her hand away.

But with a fortune the size of Psyche's only a marriage vow from his grasp, Percy could be incredibly persistent. "Oh, come now, Cousin, I know your maidenly hesitation is only proper, but it's time for you to listen to my avowal of affection. You're becoming an acknowledged spinster. You're five and twenty; this is—what?—your seventh Season. Better to accept my suit, or—fortune or not—you'll soon be at your last prayer."

"Percy, I am not at death's door just yet. And I am not being proper!"

"Of course you are," he argued. "You're always proper, unlike your mother, who—"

He must have seen the anger flare in her eyes, because Percy hastily altered the words he'd been about to say. "That is, I have every respect for your mother, but to go gadding about the countryside in that way, urging such shocking opinions upon decent women—"

"Percy, you were speaking about me," Psyche had been forced to remind him, only to regret her words even as he reached once more for her hand. She tried to move aside, edging away from the sharp-edged leaves that pulled at the fine silk of her gown, only to hit the edge of a stone bench.

The pain of the impact caused her knees to buckle, and she sat abruptly. Percy seized his chance.

"That's right, about us. Dear, dear Psyche, you must allow me to profess my undying love." To her horror, he knelt upon the damp grass, still holding tightly to her hand.

"Get up, Percy, at once! You'll make us the talk of the Ton," she'd answered sharply. "Anyhow, you're going to ruin your best pantaloons."

He winced at the thought of the damage he was doing to his formal costume, but refused to rise. "I don't care if people talk," he told her, his tone smug. "I want everyone to know how I feel about you."

Just as they already gossiped that her stingy uncle would never agree to any other suitor, Psyche thought with renewed frustration. What could she do to gain some measure of independence and yet not be tied for life to this milksop of a man? There seemed to be no other choice. What other admirer would approach her when Percy kept guard over her like a jealous dog over a bone. And yet—

Marriage to Percy would free her of the confines of the trust, she told herself, trying to find the willpower to agree. She doubted his lust would last long past the marriage bed, if her own lack of response had anything to do with it. And then she could take proper care of Circe. Except—

After marriage, her husband would control her income; women had no legal rights, of course. And Percy was just as tight-fisted as his father, No, marriage with her cousin wouldn't work, she told herself—in some relief, because her skin crawled at the thought of Percy pressing his body against hers. Even the grip of his hand made her uneasy. She tried again to pull away.

"Percy, I cannot marry you!"

"Why not?" He leaned closer, his lips pursed. Heavens, he was going to kiss her!

"Because I am already engaged!" she snapped, then stopped, almost as aghast as her cousin, whose eyes bugged out for a moment like a startled toad's. He released his grip on her hand and struggled to his feet.

"What do you mean, engaged? To whom? I don't believe it!"

"To the marquis of Cara—of Tara—the marquis of Tarrington," Psyche announced in desperation. "I met him on the Continent last summer when I went abroad with Aunt Sophie and my sister."

"You said you went to take Circe to see the great museums," Percy argued, his tone indignant, his expression of betrayal almost comical.

"So we did," she answered. "He's a great art lover, the marquis."

"French? You're going to marry a damned Frenchman?" Her cousin couldn't seem to grasp the news. "It's impossible; my father will never allow it."

"He's English, of course, he only resides on the Continent," Psyche responded, trying to think fast enough to make her spur-of-the-moment story credible. "And when Uncle Wilfred meets the marquis, I'm sure he will think him a suitable candidate for my hand."

"Never! I will speak to my father," Percy said in an ominous tone. "He will forbid it!"

But Percy had stalked away, leaving Psyche sighing with relief—as well as nursing a glimmer of an idea. The next morning she had sent a hasty note to Mr. Watkins, their family solicitor. He had received her in his dark-paneled office when she arrived, pouring tea into fragile china cups and announcing, "You know I cannot break the trust, my dear Psyche, as much as you wish it. Your father only meant to protect you—"

"Protect me? Whatever he wished, he has delivered me directly into Percy's damp hands," Psyche retorted. They had had this conversation a dozen times, and they'd combed through the thick pages of convoluted language which made up the trust just as many. "No, I think I have found a loophole!"

He handed her the cup, then offered a small plate with thin slices of lemon. "What do you mean?" His tone was cautious, but lawyers were certainly familiar with loopholes.

"Go to page six," she directed, sipping the hot tea, then returning the cup to its saucer and picking up her own much-thumbed copy of the trust. "Where it says that I will receive half of my inheritance when I become betrothed."

"Ah, yes." The lawyer flipped to the page she'd mentioned. "Your father wished to be sure you had ample means to buy your bride clothes and prepare for the nuptials to follow, being familiar with his brother's parsimonious—that is, his brother Wilfred's penchant for economy—"

"Yes, but now go to page eight. My uncle has the right to prevent an unsuitable marriage, but it doesn't say he has the right to forbid an engagement!" Psyche took a deep breath. It had occurred to her last night—a plan brilliant in its simplicity—as she'd tossed and turned, disturbed by Percy's increasing audacity.

The solicitor adjusted his glasses and reread the ponderous phrases of the document. "Perhaps you could interpret it like that, but—"

"I don't have to interpret it; that's what it says!" Psyche argued, pressing her hands together in nervous appeal.

"Even so, what good would it do to be engaged, dear child, if you could never marry?"

"I would have control of half of my funds!" she exclaimed, impatient with his slowness. "That's much, much more than Uncle Wilfred allows me now. I could hire proper art instructors for Circe; we could travel. I could do all the things that my uncle will not allow me money for!"

Freedom, she'd thought, closing her eyes for a moment as the solicitor pondered. It meant freedom from her cousin's close pursuit, freedom from her uncle's dictates.

"But it's pointless. No suitor would agree to such an arrangement, Psyche," the lawyer had pointed out, "an engagement without a marriage to follow."

"Oh, I think I know one who would," Psyche told him, knowing that her eyes were alight with mischief.

Mr. Watkins stared at her, his own eyes narrowing behind the spectacles. But after a short silence, he said only, "Take care, my dear girl."

Psyche had ridden home light with happiness. At last, she had found a way out of her legal cage. Her impromptu declaration to Percy would set her free. She would be engaged forever to this mysterious marquis who had sprung out of her imagination, and no one would be able to tell her, or Circe, what to do.

It was brilliant. . . .

Except that when Percy had shared her news, her uncle demanded to meet the man who had inspired this sudden, secret engagement. And that had seemed to doom her plan until she thought of hiring someone to play the part. All she needed was a fiancé of respectable appearance for one evening, then the mysterious marquis could disappear across the Channel again, and she would have access to her own money, for good and pressing reasons. . . .

It would all be worth the sleepless nights she had spent contemplating the details of her scheme. She'd sent her maid to the theater to find a suitable candidate to act the part, promising him the best part of her quarterly allowance. And Simpson had reported success.

True, Psyche had never expected her unseen employee to look or act quite like this tall, well-formed man with a face of such startling good looks. And if he acted this well, she could not imagine why he was not more successful—why, tonight she would have been willing to swear that he was a gentleman, indeed. But little matter, it had worked, her design had worked!

As Psyche applauded herself on the unlikely success of the most madcap plot she had ever envisioned, it occurred to her that this was more unconventional than anything her parents had done. The thought did not please her; she was in all things unlike her eccentric parents, she told herself quickly. Then her private musings came to a sudden halt.

One of her mother's brothers was inviting her hired fiancé to a party in two weeks. And had there been other invitations? Heavens, she must pay attention.

"No, no, he will be away again by then, will you not, my lord?" she interrupted hastily.

"What, leaving your wife-to-be already? We must properly welcome the new husband of our dear little Psyche. Eh, my lord, surely you don't wish to run back to the Continent in such haste."

"Not at all," the actor answered, smiling down at Psyche with a wolfish grin, his white teeth glinting as his lips pulled back just a fraction too wide, his eyes mocking. "I have no desire to crush my betrothed's sensibilities by leaving so soon." He leaned closer to the men as though confiding a secret. "She can't bear to be apart from me too long, y'know. Cries till her eyes are red and puffy, ghastly, really." He grimaced as if at the thought of Psyche with swollen features.

To her disgust, her male relatives nodded and looked in condescending pity at Psyche as if she might burst into lovelorn weeping at any moment.

Unbelievable! These men had known her all her life and had never seen her have hysterics. Yet they took the word of this insulting, arrogant—*actor*—as gospel truth.

Her mother had been right all along. Men did stick together with the mentality of a pack of mongrels.

"Why, I never in my life—" Psyche tried to put in, aware that indignant heat had flooded her face. She felt a light squeeze on her elbow, but it was a disturbing new thought that silenced her: Would this ruffian dare to blackmail her for more money—was that what this was about?

"And what's your given name, boy, if one may ask?" the older man continued.

The actor smiled again. "Of course, Uncle Octavius. We're all family here. My name is Gabriel Sinclair, marquis"—he glanced down at Psyche, now stiff with alarm—"marquis of Tarrington."

Three

*F*or Psyche, the evening, which had for a brief spell been sweet with the taste of victory, now took on the aspect of nightmare. Numb with shock, she listened to the spurious marquis cheerfully accepting invitations of all kinds from her hitherto hostile relations. Had they all fallen beneath his spell? What kind of monster was this man, this unknown actor whose powers she had so woefully underestimated?

When the butler announced dinner, Aunt Sophie went in with Uncle Wilfred, followed by a stately procession of elderly, higher-ranked ladies and their partners, and then the marquis escorted Psyche into the dining room. Here, despite the marquis's false rank, they were mercifully separated—had Percy bribed the butler?—but although she now had time to try to collect her scattered wits as she pushed at the food on her plate, Psyche found her ears straining to hear the cause of the merry laughter from farther down the table.

What was he telling them—what fanciful tales of travel and adventure? She could catch only snatches of the conversation, which seemed to be the liveliest and merriest of all those around the whole long table. Did thespians travel this much? No, his anecdotes must surely be merest fantasy.

And what happened when he was exposed—as every witty story made more possible? Psyche, who had never had a nervous fit in her life, wondered if she might break all precedence.

Her appetite was totally gone, despite the tempting portions that now covered her plate. Psyche pushed aside a forkful of sautéed mushrooms and found her stomach clenched into painful knots. Was this her punishment for departing from the safe and circumspect behavior to which she had always been so careful to adhere? She now deeply regretted her scheme; how had she thought she could pull this off?

As soon as the actor, who must be drunk on the wine the footman poured him, slipped up, he would be exposed as a fraud, and then so would the whole fallacious engagement. She would end up more firmly imprisoned in her uncle's power than ever, and she might be forced into marrying the odious Percy just to escape a major scandal.

Oh, what had she done? Psyche felt sick with apprehension. Circe would be helpless, too; she had failed her little sister, and she had left them both in danger of disgrace. All because of one reckless actor who would not sit meekly and play his part—or perhaps he played his part entirely too well.

The conversation at the top of the table had almost died, as more and more of her family listened shamelessly to the stories and jests that the man at the other end dispensed so easily, with such lazy charm. His comments were punctuated by bursts of laughter from the people lucky enough to be seated around him, and his stories received rapt attention.

Next to her, Percy stabbed at his roast pork with short, angry motions. "I cannot think why you would prefer such an obvious trickster—"

Psyche thought she might faint. "What are you saying?" she asked, her voice weak.

"I mean, it's obvious that charming manner is all a pretense. He only wants your money, Psyche. How could you be taken in by such a fortune hunter?"

Psyche relaxed a little. "That isn't true," she said, trying to sound as if she believed her own words. In fact, she was increasingly afraid his charge was more accurate than Percy guessed, and this actor was motivated not just by the payment she had promised him but by hopes of a larger gain. If not that, he was totally insane, throwing himself into the part like this, with no sense of the consequences to them both if he were found out.

"I cannot see how you could possibly prefer such a flibbertigibbet to your own cousin, whom you have known all your life." Percy slapped his fork down onto the table, his narrow eyes seething with outrage. He had a trace of gravy on his chin, and his neckcloth was now dotted with crumbs.

She stared at him and kept her voice even with some effort. "I know it's hard to imagine, Percy. You must consider a female's natural tendency to folly."

As always, irony was wasted on Percy. "I do think you've taken leave of your senses, Psyche, and I always thought you had escaped the irrationality of your parents."

She glared at him, and he changed his direction awkwardly. "That is to say, you've always shown the utmost respect for society's dictates, doing only what was proper and decorous, unlike—unlike some people. But this—this—well, he's almost a dashed dandy, Psyche. I really thought you had better sense!" Percy's voice was shrill with dismay.

Psyche looked back down the table toward her hired fiancé. The man showed no sign of dandyism; his evening dress was perfectly cut, his jacket a sober black, his cravat snowy white linen, his whole costume just what good taste dictated. He wore only one simple signet ring; he had no fobs or gold chains or diamond studs to flaunt his wealth or singularity of taste. Yet, he still stood out of the crowd—he really couldn't help it. His dark good looks, the tanned skin that should have made him look like a common laborer but somehow instead only emphasized the excellent cheekbones and rakish dark brows, the dark blue eyes that flashed with intelligence and wit. No, this actor might have escaped the attention of the masses so far, but he must have been acting inside a barrel to do it.

He seemed to have mesmerized her whole family. Or almost all—when her great-uncle Ernest, on her other side, leaned over the table, intent only upon his pudding, she turned her back on Percy's whining and listened once more to her fiancé's tales.

He was spinning some outrageous yarn about a game of cards in a gambling hell on some island in the West Indies— was that where he had acquired his darkened skin? Someone had tried to cheat him, and he had stripped the other man bare to the waist in front of a laughing crowd of gamesters to expose the extra cards the card sharp had tucked up his sleeves.

"And when I ripped off his shirt, a whole courtful of face cards tumbled out—queens and kings and knaves of all suits—and here was that rascal Antonio, trying to look as if he had no idea why his best linen shirt was lined with playing cards."

The table roared with laughter; the actor had made the tale a funny one. Even Psyche had to quench a smile.

But then one of her cousins, Mervyn, who, like Psyche's father, had a penchant for scholarship, cleared his throat. "Um, I visited Barbados when I went to the Americas last year," he said hesitantly. "I, uh, don't recall a club like the one you describe."

A silence descended upon the table, and Psyche felt the knots in her stomach tighten into one heavy iron mass. This was it; the idiot had embroidered one too many tale, and now the secrets would begin to unravel. They were done for!

The actor glanced at the young man who had had the nerve to question his story, something like respect in his deep blue eyes. Then he picked up his glass of ruby-hued wine and took a thoughtful sip. "It was in a somewhat unsavory part of town, Cousin; perhaps you did not dip into such depraved pursuits?"

But Mervyn, though his thin face looked a little pale beneath his spectacles, held his ground. "No, I saw all the island, I think."

Some of her relatives were regarding the marquis with obvious speculation. Psyche could see all the progress of the evening slipping away, like sand beneath a receding tide. Oh, what would she do?

Incredibly, her hired fiancé smiled. "It was located just off the main thoroughfare in Bridgetown, behind a small inn, and it was run by a—uh—female of dubious reputation and multitudinous charms. Her name was Nan; she had flaming red hair, and she wore peasant blouses and skirts of gauze so light that they sometimes revealed more of her delights than one might see at most society balls."

Mervyn blinked, and then a slow rush of scarlet colored his face, all the way down his neck past the slightly rumpled folds of his neckcloth. "Um, yes," he said, studiously avoiding the eyes of any of his female relatives. "I, um, I do seem to remember the—the lady."

The atmosphere at the table suddenly lightened. Several of the men chuckled, while the ladies either looked disapproving or hid their smiles behind their hands. Mervyn's brother taunted him, "And you said it was such an educational voyage, Brother!"

Mervyn blushed even deeper, if that were possible. "But it was."

More of the family laughed, though Mervyn's mother frowned in obvious censure.

Percy's nostrils flared with ire as he leaned close to speak to Psyche. His breath reeked of garlic and wine. "If that is the type of man you desire, Psyche, I am vastly disappointed. That you wish to give yourself, your future, and your fortune to such an infamous rake as this man surely is . . . Well! It seems I don't know you at all." Puffed up in self-righteousness, Percy chewed his roasted pork with bovine grace.

Psyche felt herself relax slowly, her muscles—which had been corded with tension—now easing. Her breath—which she had been holding almost unconsciously—slipped out slowly in a soft sigh. But when she spoke, her tone was sharp.

"I wonder, Cousin, if you are more concerned for my future or my fortune?"

Silverware fell to china with a clatter as Percy seemed to realize his tactical error. "You misunderstand me, my dear Psyche."

Feeling her situation pressing on her like a weighted cloak, Psyche turned away as a servant removed her plate. "I may be immoral, but I am not dim-witted." She raised one hand to stifle his protests. "No, Percy. I understand you perfectly."

It was a great relief when Aunt Sophie signaled to the other women that it was time to rise and leave the men to their brandy and odorous Spanish cigars. When Psyche followed the other women obediently out of the dining room, she could not help throwing one appealing glance back toward her fake lover, even as Uncle Wilfred was announcing, "Picked out this port myself."

Don't push it too far, she wanted to beg the impostor.

To her fury, Gabriel met her beseeching look with one of cool amusement. And, what was even more infuriating, one of those deep blue eyes dipped into a wink.

The nerve of that man! She was docking his payment for failure to follow her careful instructions. Seething, Psyche went reluctantly into the drawing room. And now that the women were alone, all the younger relatives drew close.

"Do tell us more about how you met him, Psyche," her cousin Matilda begged. "And how he was so thoughtful and so amenable to your every wish—"

Thoughtful? Amenable? The actor was making a mockery of her tales!

"It's the most romantic story!" Matilda continued. "I am so pleased that you have found a true love, not—not just a cousin who—"

"Who wishes to feather his own nest. But I never thought you would do anything so risqué as contracting a secret engagement," Aunt Maris said, her tone still unappeased. "I admit the man has charm, but what do you really know of him?"

Exhausted by the trials of the dinner and her own nervous qualms, Psyche was for once at a loss. While she hesitated, help came from an unexpected quarter.

"Leave the girl be," Aunt Sophie commanded. "Psyche, come and sit by me, child."

This was going from the kettle to the cooking fire with a vengeance, Psyche thought, trying not to show her apprehension. She sat down in a narrow chair next to the bigger armchair with carved crocodile feet that her aunt had as usual claimed—Aunt Sophie always took the most comfortable piece of furniture in the room—and waited, her throat tight, for the inquisition to begin. Her great-aunt had been shocked that Psyche had contracted a secret engagement while under her watchful eye on the Continent.

But her great-aunt surprised her once again.

"I no longer wonder what you see in him," Aunt Sophie said, raising her lorgnette and peering at Psyche with eyes that hardly seemed to need the aid. "I think he has charmed all the females of the family, even"— Sophie glanced across at Aunt Maris, who sat stiffly with her usual expression of peeved disapproval—"even Maris, though she will not allow her prune-face to unbend enough to show it. The men, now, the men will not be appeased by a handsome face and delightful manners. They will want to check out his background, your uncle Wilfred especially."

"But—" Psyche had to swallow her protests. Why was this so complicated? It had seemed like such a simple plan. "His . . . family is all dead, I believe. That is why—this is why he has gone abroad, to escape the memories."

"Indeed?" Aunt Sophie fanned herself and waved away a footman with a tray of ratafia. "No, go away, man, can't abide that stuff. Bring me some proper brandy, and not the poor stuff Wilfred brought. One of my own bottles."

When the servant had retreated, she went on, "He doesn't seem like the kind of man to run away, I would have said. Though there's something familiar about that name."

"Really?" Psyche asked, her voice faint.

"I can't quite grasp the memory, but it will come to me. In the meantime, don't risk your whole heart, my girl. He's a bit too smooth for my taste, marquis or not."

"It's not a matter of heart—" Psyche began, then stopped, appalled that she had been about to contradict her whole concocted tale of love at first sight.

"No, you just want to escape Percy, which is easy to understand," Aunt Sophie agreed, her tone matter-of-fact. "No one could fault you for that, no woman, at least. That is why I've kept my own counsel instead of ferreting out every detail of how you came to meet and engage yourself to this mysterious marquis. But tread carefully, or you might find that your escape is more dangerous than the fate you wish to flee from."

Psyche nodded, too dazed by the old woman's perception to try to argue. And Aunt Sophie would not have listened, anyhow. Psyche could only pray Uncle Wilfred was not so perceptive.

She was almost relieved when the men rejoined them, and she waited impatiently till she had the chance to pull her supposed fiancé aside for a moment of private conversation.

"Now—" She guided Gabriel toward one of the tall, slightly recessed windows on the pretext of pointing out the shadowy garden outside. "What else do you want?"

Gabriel's lips curled into a lazy smile. He looked her up and down, then reached for her hand, which she gave him reluctantly, glancing past him to the relatives who were bound to be watching the newly betrothed couple.

As he kissed her fingers, Psyche tried to repress an instinctive quiver. Her heart beating fast, she backed deeper into the window niche, instinctively seeking to put more space between them.

"My dear, this is hardly the place to tell you. I'm afraid your maidenly blushes—"

"Oh, don't try to gull me," she snapped, then, to her annoyance, realized that she was indeed blushing, caught using a cant term of which her aunts would not approve.

"You know what I mean. How much more do you want? How much money? I warn you, my funds are limited and you're not getting a ha'penny more out of me."

Gabriel glanced at her proper but well-cut silk gown, at the pearl ear drops that dangled from her neatly formed ears, the single strand of exquisite pearls that circled her white throat. He did not have to voice his skepticism.

She bit her lip and looked away. "I have money, but it's tied up in a ridiculous trust. Not until I am engaged will I have access to my own funds; Uncle Wilfred dribbles out my allowance as if I were still twelve years old. And I need more money!"

"Indeed." Gabriel remembered the thin man in the cheap evening dress at the back of the theater, the man he had knocked into a heap just before the carriage had appeared. The pieces were falling into place.

It was all blindingly clear. This was not a case of an arranged marriage, nor of a suitor whose embarrassing last-minute flight she was trying to cover up. He had even wondered if she might be with child. There was not, had never been, any marquis—she had made the whole thing up!

Gabriel gazed down at her with renewed respect. "What an ingenious fraud," he said, his tone admiring. "How on God's earth did you expect to pull off such a pinchbeck plot?"

She stood still, momentarily stunned into silence. He *admired* her plan? Admiration was the last thing she deserved for this outrageous, deceitful, unconventional scheme. What sort of man was he?

While he was obviously no stranger to deceit or depravity, if his dinner tales were at all true, this sort of business was the antithesis of all that Psyche was and hoped to be. Why, it revealed a disregard for convention that was exactly like something her parents . . . she quashed that thought and conjured up a mental image of Circe's earnest face instead. Her motives were honorable. She was sure the same couldn't be said for this rogue.

Gabriel watched her anger build; indignation had melted

her icy composure and sparked new vivacity in her clear blue eyes. He had to bite back a smile.

"I intended to do it with the help of a good actor, of course. Why do you think my maid promised you so much? And if you think to blackmail me into paying you more, you will be sadly disappointed. There is no more—that's the point—not unless I can pull off this deception."

She poked a finger into the folds of his cravat. "And if you sway too much from the plan, sir, I shall dock you accordingly. You shall have less money, not more!"

"Severe punishment indeed," he protested, his tone mock serious. "And unwarranted. Why, I have been the soul of propriety." He captured her hand with his own and tangled their fingers together. She hadn't replaced her gloves after dinner, and her skin was deliciously smooth and soft.

"Propriety!" she sputtered as she tried to pull her hand free. "Do you call kissing my palm proper? Do you call winking at me proper?"

He would not release her hand—the slim fingers, the sensitive palm that stoked the spark of longing inside him to a higher flame. He wanted more of her, not less. Instead, he brought it to his lips and kissed the palm again.

Psyche felt the quiver that ran through her whole body. His lips were warm against her skin, his breath a whisper that echoed deep inside her, stirring strange and unfamiliar feelings. Psyche took a deep breath, willing herself to remain calm.

"Sir, remember where you are!"

"I am enjoying the company of my fiancée, with her loving family all about," he retorted, enjoying the flush that anger brought to her cheeks. "And as for my payment being docked—I have never charged for a kiss before, though there have been those who have said that I should. Besides, it's not more money I want."

She blinked at him, once more biting that luscious smooth lower lip. "Then what?"

"Why, I merely want to throw myself into the role. I wish to be your fiancé, my love." He smiled sweetly as he again touched his lips to her bare hand, relishing the petal-soft skin of her palm. Was she this soft in other, more intimate places? He would love to stroke the ripe curve of her breast and show her what true confusion he could evoke.

At the moment, she looked flustered enough.

Psyche tried hard not to be distracted by the warmth of his grasp. Pulling her hand away, she stammered. "B-but—"

"Besides, I would call kissing my *fiancée's* hand an affectionate courtesy and nothing more."

"It was a shocking display."

"Shocking?" Laughter lurked in his eyes and at the corners of his mouth. "If a kiss on the hand shocks you, Psyche, you had better borrow your aunt's vinaigrette."

"Why?" she asked warily, eyes narrowing in distrust.

"Because this could very well send you into an apoplexy."

Moving far more quickly than she would have supposed someone of his infuriating indolence to be capable of, he wrapped one hand snugly around the back of her neck and pulled her forward. Their lips and breath mingled for only a moment, but the flood of sensation that his nearness caused overwhelmed her. It was surely the shock that had her standing so numbly instead of slapping his face as he deserved. Or maybe she had had too much wine. Yes, that must be the reason that she felt so overheated and dizzy. It certainly wasn't his crisp scent or the warmth of his touch. No other fumbling suitor's awkward attempts at an embrace had affected Psyche in this way.

Yes, it must be the wine, and not the sure, practiced kiss she had just received.

Gabriel stared down at Psyche's dazed expression with stunned consternation of his own. The innocent brushing of mouths should *not* have made his heart beat faster than his earlier chase through the London alleys. But insensibly, it had. He had only meant to steal a taste of the delectable confection before him. Now he found himself hungry for the whole feast.

Perhaps he would enjoy his role even more than he had first imagined.

Psyche took a deep breath and put both hands on his chest, pushing him back. She peeked around the heavy drapery, glancing toward the rest of their party, and was not a little relieved to see only a couple of the relatives still throwing covert glances their way. Even Percy was absorbed in pontificating to her uncles.

"Are you mad?" she whispered.

Gabriel shook his head. "I must be."

"You are the most shocking of libertines! You are—you are—" Searching unsuccessfully for a word worthy of her disgust, Psyche stepped out of the window alcove, hoping her face was not still flushed.

Gabriel followed slowly, an angelic grin on his dark face. She half expected him to hum a tune. It was all that was lacking from his innocent mien.

"Your behavior, sir, is . . ." she tried again.

"Improper?" he suggested.

"Yes!" she grasped the word eagerly. "Most improper. You are an unprincipled rake, just as Percy said, and totally lacking any sense of decorum."

Gabriel regarded her from beneath those dark slashes of brow. "Poor innocent Psyche, you really think that is the worst insult one can bestow."

"Of course," she said slowly, the confusion in her voice evident even to her.

"I hope you may continue to think so, sweetling." He smiled, a strange mixture of emotions visible briefly in the depths of his eyes.

Did he dare to offer her pity? "Save your breath and your smooth manners for my family, Mr. Sinclair. I have no need of them."

She turned in a swirl of silken skirts to leave him, but paused at a thought. Despite his improper behavior, she herself could behave correctly.

"I, at least, will be honest with you. That kiss just cost you five pounds!"

He chuckled.

Shaking her head, she turned to rejoin her family. He was mad, he must be. From across the room, Maris's ill-tempered voice rose. "Here, Psyche, show some discretion and rejoin the party. You promised to turn the pages while Matilda plays her latest tune."

Cousin Matilda, whose skill at the pianoforte was only moderate, flashed a silent plea toward her mother, but Maris ignored it. Psyche surrendered to the inevitable. She would be relieved to walk away from this impostor, she told herself, trying to believe it. "Behave yourself till we can talk further," she whispered to the infuriating man standing next to her. "No more tales of exotic islands, please!"

"Should I talk about Europe, instead, now that peace has reopened it to English travelers?" he murmured back, a teasing glint in his eyes. "I've had some amusing escapades there, as well."

"Dear God, no," she snapped. "Just stay out of trouble!"

"Psyche!"

"Yes, Aunt Maris, I'm coming."

She left him standing beside the window enclosure. Gabriel watched as she walked across the room—the girl carried herself like a queen, he thought—and took her place beside Matilda, giving her plump cousin a reassuring smile.

"I'm sure the new melody will be delightful," Psyche said, her tone warm.

He bit back a grin. She was not selfish though she did have a greed for money. Still, it was her own money she wished for, and that was better than most women, Gabriel reflected. Mostly, they wanted whatever their current lover could scrape up; he'd had his own pockets emptied more than once. This woman, despite her beauty, despite the passion he suspected lay well hidden beneath the cool surface charm, would be no different than the rest, and certainly, certainly she was not wicked enough to deserve a glimpse inside the dark secrets of his own heart. He tried to hold on to his usual cynicism as his gaze skimmed the room.

The rest of the family were listening to Matilda make a

brave effort at the pianoforte. Her mother, who must be tone-deaf, nodded in approval; the rest of the family bore it stoically, as if well accustomed to Matilda's musical talent, or lack of it.

When the first tune ended, there was a polite scattering of applause. Gabriel clapped, too, for Matilda's courage, if nothing else. "Very nice, dear," one of the women said.

Then Maris commanded, "Now the new ballad, my dear."

"Oh, Mother, I don't wish to sing," Matilda protested.

"Nonsense, you have a lovely voice," her doting mother insisted.

Matilda placed new sheet music upon the stand, and her fingers moved slowly over the keys. When the notes rose, and she added her voice to the melody, Gabriel winced despite himself. Matilda's singing was even less inspired than her playing. She had a thin voice, likely made more shrill by fear of her mother's disapproval.

He saw Matilda glance beseechingly up at Psyche, who had been standing beside the instrument turning the pages of the music. At once, Psyche added her voice to the song, keeping her own singing low, not attempting to drown out her cousin. But her pleasing alto added depth to the sound and gave her cousin's thin voice a much needed embellishment. This time, when the music died, the applause, which Gabriel joined heartily, was louder.

Matilda flushed with pleasure. As the two singers began another tune, Gabriel's thoughts wandered. She had heart, this ice maiden, despite her outer coolness. He was sure Psyche had other passions as well, hidden deep within.

But as alluring as she was, that was not why he had played for time, deciding to draw out this dangerous role as long as he could. He glanced outside into the dark garden, where shadows cloaked the shrubbery. He could find no better hiding place than this, no more secure sanctuary from which to assert his claim and acquire his newly won estate. This was better than cheap rooms or equally cheap inns for escaping the renewed detection of the band of ruffians hired to kill him. He had no false hope that they would give up; every time he set foot on the street, he would be a marked man.

And the strange thing was, he suddenly realized that he had enjoyed the evening. The warmth of the family gathered here, the welcome he had been granted, it was the kind of homecoming he would never receive from his own kin. And despite the fact that the shower of invitations and cordial greetings had been given to the wrong man, to a fantasy fiancé invented for one sole purpose, despite it all, it had fed some empty spot in his heart. He allowed himself to remember the lonely boy who had ridden away from his father's house, with no one of his own blood ready to take his part. The pain was still there, though he had pushed it deep and had never allowed himself the luxury of self-pity. The Sinclairs had rejected Gabriel, and he had repaid the favor.

But to stand in a room where, eccentric or not, sharp-tongued or not, most of the people assembled showed real affection for each other, warmed some of the coldness inside him. He glanced at Maris, whose peevish expression had relaxed into a smile that reflected obvious pride and fondness for her plump daughter. No, he had lived with the old emptiness for so long that by now he was barely aware it existed—until he stepped inside a warm, candlelit room where women's voices rose in sweet melody.

Damn, he must have had too much wine! These were not the thoughts of Gabriel Sinclair, rogue and cardsharp. Even that slight excuse seemed unlikely, however, as cheap and badly chosen as Uncle Wilfred's port had been. Gabriel winced at the aftertaste that still lingered on his palate. If nothing else, he must repay Psyche for her accidental help by rescuing her from the threatened marriage with her cousin, who showed every sign of being as stingy and stodgy as his father. Whatever her faults, Psyche deserved better than the blustering, simpering Percy, of that Gabriel was sure.

As for the quirk of providence that had caused their paths to intersect—he had seen too many strange things in his travels to wonder much. Perhaps the universe owed him this, after cursing him with the incredible stroke of ill fortune that had caused him to be exiled to start with. Still, he could be thankful for Psyche's aid, and he would somehow manage to repay her.

When this tune ended, the two ladies left the instrument and gave way to another cousin, who played a piece with dogged correctness and little imagination. Psyche's attention was still claimed by her aunts, who chattered away, patting her hand and pinching her cheek as they talked. She glanced toward him occasionally, her brow knit slightly in concern.

Gabriel was content to stand on the sidelines and ease her anxiety. He waved aside an invitation to sit down to a hand of whist—these elderly uncles and aunts would be easy victims to his experienced knowledge of cards, but relieving them all of their pocket change would not endear him to his new "family."

He did exchange a few well-chosen stories with Mervyn, when the bashful young man found courage to join him and discuss his own travels in the West Indies. And when the guests began to depart, he joined his betrothed to say good night to all his new acquaintances.

Psyche said her good-byes, rigid with tension. Even though the accursed actor had toned down his behavior in the last part of the evening, she would still be glad to see the last of him. He could not mean his threat about remaining in her life, she told herself, her heart beating faster at such an alarming thought.

She wanted only to see the last of him, and if her fraudulent fiancé demanded more money—well, it would depend on the success of her stratagem; right now, she had only her small allowance—nothing like enough to satisfy a real villain. Perhaps she had miscalculated badly, putting herself into this handsome rascal's power.

Percy and his father were the last to take their farewells. "I have not given my consent to this marriage," Uncle Wilfred reminded them both, his tone savage. "I would not plan the honeymoon just yet."

"And you haven't seen the last of me," Percy grumbled as he bent awkwardly over Psyche's hand, clutching it too tightly. "I know you will regret this impulsive commitment, Cousin, and I will be nearby, willing to forgive you, despite the scandal that a broken engagement will necessarily bring."

"Your magnanimity does you justice," she answered gravely, trying to pay attention. She was too aware of Gabriel's presence so close to her to concentrate on Percy.

The actor raised one dark brow. "I hardly think that will be necessary," he said, his tone smooth. "I'm sure you will grow to love me as one of the family, Cousin."

Percy glowered, and Uncle Wilfred snorted.

"Oh, get on with you, Percy," Aunt Sophie said. "My feet are aching. You may complain another day."

The two men left with no more farewells, and Psyche breathed a sigh of relief when she heard them clomp down the stairs.

Aunt Sophie glanced at the two of them. "You may say good night, Psyche," she said, "but five minutes only, and do not shock the servants."

She slowly climbed the staircase to her own suite of rooms, and Psyche took a deep breath. Two footmen waited at the end of the hall, but no one was within earshot.

"Thank God that's over," Psyche said, keeping her voice low. "I will get you the purse of money that my maid promised you."

Gabriel smiled, but his eyes held a dangerous glint. "Oh, no, my dear. Did you forget what I said? I am your fiancé, and I'm not leaving. I will be your guest, of course, since the marquis resides on the Continent. And you would not send your beloved to the cold, unaired sheets of a hotel, I'm sure."

"You can't!" Psyche gazed at him in horror. "It wouldn't be proper."

"You have a chaperon," he pointed out smoothly. "It will

be most proper. No one could dare consider being indecorous with Aunt Sophie in the house."

Of course she had a chaperon—an unmarried female would not live alone—and between her aunt and a houseful of servants, she should not be in any actual physical peril from this stranger. But to have him underfoot, meeting her family every day, with every new encounter a chance for exposure . . . Psyche felt herself go rigid with alarm.

Before she could think of an argument, she heard a slight sound overhead and turned to see her sister leaning over the rail of the next landing.

"Is this the actor?" Circe called, blunt as usual. "He's very nice to look at."

"Circe!" Psyche despaired of ever teaching her little sister to guard her tongue. "Be silent!"

"Why? And why is he not leaving?"

"I am staying to perfect my role, of course," Gabriel told her, eyeing the child with interest. She was as unlike her beautiful big sister as anyone of such close blood could be. Circe was thin and undeveloped still, with straight brown hair, escaping from its braid at the back of her head, and green eyes that regarded the impostor with straightforward curiosity.

"Of course," the child agreed, to his surprise. "Any artist would wish to perfect his creation."

"Circe, go to bed! I shall talk to you in the morning." Psyche sounded past all patience.

"Good night, my love." Gabriel reached for his spurious fiancée's hand, but she snatched it back. He bowed to her, instead, then turned to the footman hovering by the door. "You may show me to the best guest chamber."

Obediently, the servant led him away. Gabriel left Psyche standing beside the staircase, her face burning with anger. He knew the bent of her thoughts, her outrage and frustration, but it could not be helped. Outside lay danger and an assassin's knife. Inside—perhaps danger waited inside, as well. Gabriel remembered the smooth curve of Psyche's neck, where it led into the tempting dips and hollows of her shoulder. But the temptation must be resisted. He had a life to reclaim, and by God, he meant to do it.

Shaking with fury, Psyche watched the actor climb the steps. He was taking shameless advantage of her situation. Yet, she needed him—he was now the man her whole family believed to be her fiancé—and she could not expose him herself, nor throw him out, at least not just yet. A few days, that was all, and she would find a way to rid herself of this insolent intruder.

If she felt a flicker of regret at the thought, that was only a trick of her overstretched nerves. Surely, it was.

A few days of this pretence, Psyche promised herself. Then Gabriel Sinclair would be shown the door, and she would never suffer his presence again.

Four

A clatter of carriage wheels in the street outside the town house woke Psyche too early. She blinked at the pale clear sunlight peeking past the heavy draperies and turned her head, ready to slip back into sleep.

But something was wrong. It nagged at her half-aware consciousness, keeping her from sinking back into peaceful slumber. Then memories of last night flooded back, and Psyche gasped, sitting upright in her bed.

That man! That impostor, who had dared to take over her brilliant scheme, who had so coolly and without conscience walked into her home, was now doubtless sleeping easily in her best guest chamber.

If the actor hadn't fled in the middle of the night with a tablecloth stuffed with her best silver, that is. . . . On the whole, she would be relieved if he had, Psyche thought, her mood grim. Getting rid of this dangerous poseur who had stepped into his role with a too complete dedication would be worth a few pieces of silverware.

By now further sleep was impossible. She lay back against the smooth linen sheets and pulled the covers up to her chin, wishing she could hide her face beneath them as she'd done when she was a child frightened by bad dreams.

But Gabriel was no nightmare, vanishing easily into wisps of fog when sunlight hit. What on earth was she going to do about him? How could she get rid of him . . . because she must, as soon as possible, before he slipped and revealed to anyone else—to Percy and her uncle, especially—the falsity of her invention.

Psyche lay wide-eyed in her bed for over an hour, trying to come up with a foolproof scheme to undo the damage that had already been done, but she found her mind strangely blank. If only all her relatives had not met him—yet, that had been the whole point of the betrothal party, after all, to show that her fiancé did exist, to give him a face and a form. And now the marquis of Tarrington was real, to her family, at least, and the illusion must be maintained, or she would be once more in Percy's power. She thought of Percy leaning closer to kiss her and shuddered. Marriage with Percy—no, anything but that!

Unable to lie still any longer, Psyche reached for the bell rope and rang for her maid. When Simpson appeared, she brought a breakfast tray with its steaming tea and warm toast into the bedchamber, carrying it across the room to place carefully on the bed.

Psyche reached to pour herself a cup, then paused. There was something else on the tray—the early mail. But it was overflowing the confines of the tray, threatening to spill into her empty teacup and crush the brittle toasted bread. Psyche blinked in surprise, then picked up the top of the pile.

"What on earth . . . ?" She broke the wax seal and unfolded the first sheet. An invitation to lunch, extended to her—and to her newly pledged fiancé.

"Oh no!" Psyche groaned, ripping open the wax seals on several other notes and gilt-edged sheets. All the same—apparently everyone in her family was eager to entertain the charming marquis. What would happen when the rest of her acquaintance heard about this good-looking rascal who was aping his betters? It would only get worse.

She glanced at her maid, and the older woman grimaced. "I'm sorry, Miss Psyche," Simpson said. "When I went to

the theater, I made it clear to this"—she lowered her voice—
"actor person exactly what he should do. And I never said
nothing about him staying the night. I couldn't believe it
when I went downstairs and all the servants were chattering
about him staying here! I don't understand it."

"Nor do I," Psyche admitted. In the back of her mind, she
thought of the bold glimmer in his eyes when he looked her
up and down. The spark she had felt between them—no, no,
it didn't do to think on that. Besides, the man must know
that it was impossible! There was no way for a lady of quality and a low-born actor to form any real connection. It had
to be a baser motive. If he hoped to blackmail her . . .

"I think he means to hold out for more money," she told
her maid. "And since I told him I will have no extra funds
to give him unless this scheme works, he is waiting to see if
my uncle releases the purse strings."

Simpson still looked anxious. "He didn't seem the type
for blackmail. I never would have thought he had that much
gumption, miss," she worried aloud. "Trying to pretend to
be something he's not . . ."

Despite her worries, Psyche smiled. "But that is what actors do."

Simpson's lips tightened. She had served the household
since her young mistress first put up her hair and lengthened
her short skirts, and she could afford to be blunt. "But that's
onstage, miss. This is very different."

"So it is. We shall just have to put up with him for a day
or two until I can think of some way to rid ourselves of this
threat. In the meantime, try to dampen any suspicion that
may arise in the servants' hall."

Simpson hesitated.

"What?" Psyche braced herself. Trouble already? Curse
the man!

"Wilson has disappeared."

Psyche frowned. "Which one is Wilson?"

"The new under-footman, miss. He was the one who took
the actor up to his bedchamber last night. And"—Simpson's

voice sank into an ominous whisper—"he hasn't been seen since!"

Psyche bit her lip. Strange ideas whirled in her head for an instant, but she pushed the wilder notions aside. There was no reason for the actor to murder an innocent servant. Was there? Had the actor let his guard slip, said something that gave too much away, and had to get rid of Wilson to avoid . . . no, the cool ease with which the impostor had handled her family all evening would not have cracked in a few brief moments with a house servant. Then what?

"There's a logical reason," she said aloud, trying to convince them both. "There must be. Wilson will turn up."

She prayed it were true, and her scheme had not harmed an innocent person. Psyche pushed the tray aside. Her appetite was gone. "I must get dressed and go downstairs to see what is happening."

With Simpson's help, she made a quick toilette. Dressed in a modest, pale blue, high-necked muslin day dress, hair pulled into a simple twist, only a few pale curls escaping the knot to soften its severity and frame her face, she headed for the formal rooms.

But the dining room was empty. She knew Aunt Sophie seldom ventured from her own room till later in the day, and Circe would have had her breakfast in the schoolroom. The morning room had a cheery fire, but it, too, was vacant, as was the larger drawing room and the library. Where on earth was the man? Was he lying in bed all day?

Simpson had departed to the servants' quarters, with orders to report to her mistress when—or if—the missing footman returned, but so far, she had not returned with any reassuring news.

Psyche lingered in the upstairs hall, trying to think what she should do, when she heard the sound of the bell. It could not be the footman; he would return to the back door, of course. As she was in no mood for any callers come to congratulate her on her recent engagement, she hurried into the drawing room, of half a mind to tell the butler to say that she was not at home.

But when their aged butler, Jowers, puffed his way up the staircase and opened the door to the drawing room, she had no time to deny herself because the caller was right behind.

"Psyche!" her cousin Percy said, his face already flushed with strong emotion. "I must speak with you!"

Wonderful, just what she needed to make an already unauspicious morning even worse.

"Percy, this is not a good time."

Her cousin didn't seem to hear. He stormed into the room, pulling off his hat and gloves and almost thrusting them at the butler, who bowed and left the room. "I've been at my club, talked to everyone I could find, and no one—I mean, no one, Psyche—has heard of this Tarrington title. How do we know this fellow's who he says he is?"

"Oh, Percy, don't be ridiculous." Psyche found that her hands had tightened into fists. She made a conscious effort to relax; she must not reveal her own alarm that Percy was already checking on her story. "He told you himself that it was an obscure title."

"But a marquis, Psyche," Percy insisted. "Marquises don't sprout on every hedgerow, y'know!"

"Of course, not, but—"

"I think—" he interrupted, but she raised her voice and tried again.

"Percy, this is none of your affair. It's my life and my business. I must insist that you stop this interference and allow me to be the one to—"

"Not my affair?" Percy glared, his slightly protruding eyes opening even wider than usual. "Certainly it is. If your male relatives are not the ones to protect you—to protect a female from her weaker wit and too sensitive emotions, who would? It's for your own good, Psyche. Just ask my father."

She had no wish to bring Uncle Wilfred into this any more than he already was. "My uncle should respect my wishes."

And yet she knew how likely that was! Percy ignored the statement as unworthy even of answer. Percy continued to pace up and down on the carpet, his too tight shoes squeaking a little, then he turned quickly to confront her. "There's something smoky here, and I want some answers! I must speak to him myself, man to man. What is his direction?"

"I don't know," Psyche said before she thought, then put one hand to her lips, aghast at her slip.

"You don't know? What do you mean? Doesn't the fellow have a town house in London?" Percy's frown deepened.

"No, I mean, I told you, he has been living abroad."

"Smoky itself. Why would an Englishman leave his own country, except to escape debts or a scandal," Percy said, with unexpected shrewdness. "He's after your money, my girl. Didn't I say that already?"

"No, he is not," Psyche protested, but her voice sounded shaky even to her own ears.

"And if he has no residence of his own, which hotel is he frequenting? He must have told you!"

"Ah, he—he is staying here," Psyche said weakly. Her stomach clenched with nervousness, and she couldn't think; she felt more and more afraid that the charade would be exposed and all would be lost.

"Here?" Percy looked scandalized. "Aunt Sophie allowed this?"

"Of course, he is my fiancé, Percy. And no one could question my aunt as a suitable chaperon."

Percy grunted. "Still, not quite the thing. However, at least he's to hand. I wish to speak to him." He reached for the bellpull and tugged it vigorously.

"No!" Psyche said, thinking wildly for an excuse—any excuse. "You can't. I don't think he has risen."

But this time, the butler appeared in the doorway too quickly. She hoped he had not been outside listening to their argument.

"Jowers, take me to the chamber of that accursed marquis," Percy demanded with the ease of one long acquainted with the family servants.

The butler nodded and turned, and Percy strode after him. Psyche, furious to have lost control of the situation, was reduced to running along the hall after them.

"I will not allow my guest to be harassed, Percy!"

But he wouldn't listen. Psyche felt her heart beat faster. Was it over before it had begun? Her precious plan seemed in shreds already.

When the butler led them all to the guest floor and indicated the chamber, Percy plunged forward, pushing open the door after only the briefest knock, not waiting for any permission to enter.

From outside in the hallway, Psyche heard a startled exclamation—Percy's, she thought—and then a roar of outrage.

Had Percy attacked the actor? Or—remembering the missing footman—had the actor attacked Percy? Was someone being murdered? Psyche couldn't help herself—she ran into the room, only to stop abruptly just inside the doorway.

"What do you mean by this, sir? Are you some savage, to insult my cousin's household in this fashion?" Percy was demanding.

Psyche gasped. The actor sat in a large wing chair facing the window; he had apparently been reading the newspaper. But the reason for Percy's shock was obvious. The man was completely—bare-as-a-newborn-babe—*naked.* At least he appeared to be naked, except for the happy coincidence of the newspaper.

God save the *Times*, Psyche thought a trifle hysterically.

Gabriel had turned slightly to meet Percy's gaze, and his broad shoulders and chest were quite uncovered. The newspaper he had lowered covered his torso below the waist, but she could see a glimpse of muscular legs and bare feet.

Psyche felt her cheeks burn. She had never seen a man unclothed before. This was shocking, most improper. And if one corner of her mind couldn't help noting that the man's form was just as well made and as pleasing as his face, if she noted the breadth of his shoulders or the muscular arms—well, she smothered those dreadful thoughts immediately, of course. After one last lingering glance, she averted her gaze and studied the figured carpet beneath her feet with great concentration.

"No, indeed," Gabriel's voice was as calm and controlled as if entertaining au naturel were an everyday occurrence. For all she knew it probably was. Unprincipled wretch! Psyche risked another quick glance to glare at him, noting absently the faint stubble that marked his chin and lower cheeks. Even that did not mar his incredible good looks.

"I simply have had a slight accident with my apparel. When the servant brought me a cup of tea this morning, he took away my evening clothes to be brushed and pressed. Until I rose, I didn't know that my other luggage had not reappeared."

"B-but—" Percy stammered, still obviously flustered.

"I sent the footman to the hotel to fetch them last night," Gabriel continued smoothly. "But according to the other servants, he doesn't seem to have returned."

This brought Psyche's head erect again, and anger pushed aside any remnants of embarrassment. "You sent my footman out into the street alone at such an hour! How dare you?"

"It didn't seem an outrageous request," Gabriel said, his deep blue eyes mild. "I gave him a handsome tip to run the errand."

"But so late at night!" Psyche was still outraged. "Don't you know that the streets of London are always dangerous? There are footpads and robbers and—and—I don't know what."

"And you shouldn't," Percy interrupted, frowning at his cousin. "A lady should have no knowledge of such things!"

"Oh, don't be a fool," Psyche shot back, irritated at Percy, too. "I'm not a half-wit, Percy."

Gabriel spoke at almost the same time. "I have lived abroad in much more dangerous climes; I suppose I didn't think. If your servant has been injured, I certainly regret the fact." He sounded concerned, for the first time, and a little of Psyche's anger faded.

Percy shook his head as if to dismiss such insignificant concerns as a lowly footman.

"You've explained away your lack of proper attire glibly

enough." Percy bristled about, reminding Psyche of nothing so much as an angry hedgehog, "But I should like to hear you explain away *this*!"

Gabriel looked around him as if expecting something to magically appear. He smiled. "I'm afraid I am at a disadvantage. I don't know to which *this* you are referring."

Percy colored and fisted his pudgy hands.

"This, my lord, if indeed you may be called by that honorific, refers to the fact that you are a fraud! No one has ever heard of you. Your title is nonexistent, your name is unknown, you are a complete mystery."

He sounded even more pompous than usual, but Psyche found herself holding her breath to hear the actor's response.

But Gabriel appeared delighted. "How lovely."

"L-lovely?" Percy stammered.

"Yes, everyone will appreciate the novelty and I shall be all the crack. Soon, all the young bucks will be pretending not to know one another. We shall all be mystery men."

Psyche could not stop the giggle that escaped her trembling lips. Too late, she clamped her hand over her mouth. Percy stared at her, aghast. Really, she could not feel more annoyed with herself than he was. Ruthlessly, she squashed down the glimmer of admiration for the actor's audacity.

"I demand that you leave this house at once, sir!" Percy swung back to confront the impostor once more. "Sitting around in the—in the—without any proper garments at all! I will not have you compromising a lady of quality whose reputation is unblemished."

"Really?" Gabriel's deep blue eyes focused on Psyche, and she hoped that she was not blushing. "Not a glimmer of blemish, not even the tiniest blot? My dear, I fear you must have led a sadly tedious existence up to now. I'm so glad I came into your life to add that spark of controversy without which we should all perish of boredom."

"I beg your pardon—" Percy sputtered, but the actor transferred his gaze to her cousin, and Gabriel's blue eyes seemed to turn a steely gray.

"Besides, I rather think that I am the one who should be

concerned about protecting my fiancée—her person and her reputation—against any danger, imagined or real." His tone was cool, and Percy seemed to wilt slightly, his narrow shoulders drooping.

But Psyche felt a surge of warmth that took her by surprise. She had been alone for so long. Despite the presence of her extended family, her life had never been the same since the death of her parents. Since the accident, she had felt unprotected, vulnerable to all of fate's twists and turns. She had been forced to face the world alone, to fend off Percy's unwanted advances and her uncle's mercenary matchmaking, to look out for herself and her sister. That such a man would be her protector . . . to have a champion who would be at her side against all foes, take her part against any—then she shook herself mentally. This was all an illusion! The man was an actor, he had no interest in her, no reason to protect either her good name or her person.

Yet the feeling had, for an instant, soothed a hurt inside her which had been sore for too long. He must be an excellent actor, indeed, she told herself. But she must not forget that his talent was for make-believe, and his concern merely for her purse.

"I—I—" Percy obviously knew that he had lost command of the situation, even if he were not quite sure how. He struggled to regain his composure, drawing on his moral indignation to refuel his all too righteous ire. "I insist that you take your baggage and get out—"

"But I have no baggage, that's the problem," the actor interrupted to remind him helpfully. "I hardly think even you would wish to put me out in the street without a stitch or a scrap to cover myself."

"Hardly proper, Percy," Psyche murmured, her tone mischievous. "And surely that would not reflect well on me."

"No, no, but—" Percy blinked, seemingly at a loss. But he also, as Psyche knew only too well, always felt constrained to have the last word. "I shall demand that the servants return your evening dress and then you can be on your way! And as for this ridiculous engagement—"

"Percy!" Psyche interrupted, her voice icy. "You will not tell me what to do, or whom to marry."

"It must be ended immediately," Percy continued as if he had not heard her; he didn't even glance her way. "I shall speak to my father again."

"Your father has no power to forbid the engagement," Psyche snapped, forgetting the actor for a moment as she turned to glare at her cousin. "I shall have half of my funds as soon as my solicitor can act. We shall go to the courts, if necessary!"

"You wouldn't," Percy gaped at her. "Think of the talk—the scandal—"

"Then Uncle Wilfred should not try to interfere," Psyche told him coldly. "I will have access to my own money."

"But the marriage itself—*that* cannot take place without my uncle's blessing, and you know he will never give it." Percy stared at her, obviously perplexed.

"One step at a time," Psyche said, taking a deep breath to calm herself. Percy would never understand, but that hardly mattered. If she had more funds to tap, her current position would be more tolerable, and Circe would have the art lessons her talent deserved. They could travel again, go to the Continent and escape Percy's annoying and increasingly persistent courtship. She would have her life back and, most of all, precious freedom. When this actor disappeared once more into obscurity, she would remain happily engaged to her creation, the illusive and nonexistent marquis. She would not allow her backward-thinking uncle to control her forever.

"This marriage will never take place," Percy repeated, his tone grim. "In the meantime, I shall speak to the servants about this—this man's evening clothes." He stormed out of the room, so incensed that he apparently had forgotten that he was leaving his cousin behind, alone in the lion's den.

Psyche knew she should leave at once; this was most improper. As to that, Percy was in the right. But she needed to speak to the actor without any witnesses. Her missing foot-man—

Gabriel was regarding her gravely; his gaze now harder to read. The roguery that had glinted as he baited the slower-witted Percy had faded, and some other emotion—one she was afraid to name—glinted behind the dark blue eyes. "I apologize for my lack of attire," he said. "And I would not remain sitting while you stand, except that if I stood in the present circumstance—"

"No, no," Psyche assured him hastily, taking a step backward despite herself. Her voice sounded strained with the fear that this unpredictable man might do exactly that. "*Please* don't get up."

The actor bit back a smile, and Psyche's surge of embarrassment faded as her irritation returned. "As soon as you are decent, we need to talk."

The amusement in his eyes only deepened. "I shall refrain from stating the obvious and say only that my time—among other things—are yours for the asking, my lovely Psyche."

"You are overgenerous, sir. The only thing I wanted from you was your time. And I only paid for one evening's worth."

He leaned back comfortably in his chair. "Consider this an encore, my dear."

Trying to remain calm, Psyche clenched her jaw so hard that her teeth ached. "Your presence is no longer wanted, and do not call me dear!"

"As you wish, lovely Psyche."

"Or Psyche. I gave you no leave to call me that, or any of your other endearments." Her usual cool composure in shreds, she gestured wildly, pointing to the door of the suite. "I demand that you leave. I cannot afford this charade to go on."

"I am not charging you by the hour, dear Psyche." He regarded her with thoughtful interest.

"Don't call me that!" She almost shrieked. "I told you, I cannot afford—"

How fascinating that such an icy beauty should burn a man with temper, he thought. If only there were not more at stake here, if only he could afford the time to woo her as the passion that lurked beneath her cool facade deserved.

"Nor can you afford for it to fail."

He had spoken slowly, calmly. His control shamed her. Forcing a breath past her tight lips, she took hold of herself "No. I cannot fail. My sister and her future mean more to me than any little"—she looked significantly at Gabriel—"or large annoyance. But don't forget who you are, or rather who you are not, Lord Tarrington."

He shrugged the broad, tanned shoulders that she had tried not to notice. Where had he lived, for the sun to have so darkened his skin? She pictured him on tropical beaches, or in dense jungle, then pushed the images away. She had no time for fanciful daydreams, not now; she must hold on to her resolve, not be distracted by any blackmailing impostor, no matter how pleasant-looking he might be.

"Perhaps I do not need your title, Psyche." He ignored the widening of her eyes just as he continued to ignore her commands. A pity she hid her marvelous shape beneath such prim gowns, he thought as he watched her take a deep breath. "Perhaps I have a lofty title of my own."

Psyche rolled her eyes. "And maybe Zeus will ride down from the sky on a lightning bolt and zap my uncle and Percy on their"—she looked pointedly at his lap—"newspapers."

Gabriel just managed not to cross his legs at the thought. "I am only here to aid you, my dear Psyc . . . Miss Hill. We are working together toward a common goal, if you would remember."

"Are we?" She had regained her control, and her voice was cool. "Besides," she went on, remembering her additional grievance, "it was very thoughtless of you to send my servant on such an errand, at a time when few honest men are on the streets. You should have waited till the morning."

"True, but then I would have been in just such a fix as I find myself." Gabriel's all too charming smile flashed, and she felt its force despite all her resolution. She must not waver. He would not beguile her out of her anger.

"But now he is missing, and I am concerned for his

safety," she went on stubbornly. "My mother always taught me that the poorer classes deserve just as much consideration for their welfare as those of more affluent means, and I am sure that she is—was—right."

Was it respect she saw in his eyes? Most of the Ton would have thought her as mad as her unconventional parents for voicing such a strange notion.

"I hope he has been only temporarily detained," Gabriel agreed, his tone this time more serious. "I had best go and check on him myself. I will look a little strange in evening dress, but that cannot be helped. As soon as the man brings back my clothing—"

That reminded her again that she should not be here, alone in his chamber. She would start just the type of gossip she was so eager to avoid, and what on earth would Aunt Sophie say? "I will tell them to send up your clothing at once."

He nodded, his smile flashing once more. "And the next time I greet you naked in my bedchamber, I promise—"

"There will be no next time!" she interrupted sternly, afraid to hear the rest of his statement. The man seemed determined to shake her usual calm reserve. But before she left his room, she needed to inform him of something.

"I decided last night after you so rudely invited yourself to stay here, that it was only reasonable to deduct room and board from your fee. I'm sure you would agree." With a decided nod, she turned before he could do more than give a husky chuckle. Leaving the room in haste, Psyche released some of her irritation by slamming the door behind her.

When she turned, she stopped abruptly. Simpson stood in the hallway, her expression distressed.

Now what? "Yes?" Psyche demanded, then took a deep breath and modulated her tone. She would not be so petty as to take out her anger on her servants. "What is it, Simpson?"

"It's Wilson, miss," her maid answered. "I think you'd better come."

Five

*P*syche put her hand to her lips. "Is he—" She had a sudden vision of the hapless footman's body, found sprawled in an alley, his throat cut and his pockets rifled.

"He's shaken, miss, and has a fearful bump on his head, but—" Simpson began.

Psyche didn't wait to hear the rest. Relief easing the tension that had stiffened her shoulders, she headed immediately for the stairs. She hurried down several flights of steps and on through the door that led to the servants' quarters. When she reached the main servants' hall, she found a cluster of maids and footmen surrounding the no-longer-missing servant. He sat slumped in a wooden chair. When he saw her, he jumped to his feet, but then swayed and collapsed into the chair again even before she spoke.

"Sit down, Wilson. Are you all right?"

The rest of the servants made way for her, and she saw that the housekeeper, Mrs. McNilly, was wringing a clean cloth over a basin of vinegar water she had brought to the table beside him. As Psyche watched in concern, the housekeeper gently washed the large purple swelling on the side of the footman's head. He had other scrapes and cuts, and his livery was ripped and torn and covered with mud.

"Are you all right?" Psyche repeated. "Do you need to see a surgeon?"

The footman shuddered. "Oh, no, miss. Don't need no one bleeding me. I been through enough, I 'ave, lying cold and senseless all night in a dark alley."

Despite her concern, Psyche had to hide a smile. "Very well."

"Looks like no bones broken, Miss Psyche," the housekeeper told her, dabbing at a bit of dried blood on the man's face. "He's very lucky indeed. Set upon by a whole gang of footpads, 'e was."

"Tell me what happened," Psyche said.

The man rolled his eyes. "All I did was go where 'is lordship tol' me, to the inn down by the docks—shabby place it were, miss—and ask for his bags. 'E gave me a coin to settle his account and another for me—which they took from me." The footman's tone was bitter. "Nicest bit of coin I've 'ad since—"As if remembering this was not the person to complain to, he stopped abruptly.

Psyche pretended not to notice. She knew that their servants were well paid—her parents had never stinted on household economy, nor had she—but she could understand his disappointment over the loss of his unexpected largesse. "Who attacked you?"

"It 'appened after I left the inn, miss," the servant told her. "I 'ad his lordship's carpetbags—he don't seem to 'ave no trunk, maybe it ain't arrived yet—and when I turned to 'ead back toward Mayfair, all these men—musta been a 'undred of 'em—swarmed out of an alley and jumped me. 'Ad no chance at all to defend myself." He shuddered, remembering, and several of the younger maidservants shrieked in shared alarm.

The last thing she needed was a housemaid having hysterics. Psyche spoke firmly. "You are very fortunate, Wilson, to have escaped with only minor injuries."

He nodded, shivering again. "Last thing I remember, a bunch of sailors came out of a nearby tavern, miss, singing and swearing, and likely they scared the thieves away. I woke this morn with my 'ead 'urting that bad—I'm sorry about 'is lordship's things, miss. Guess those footpads thought 'e might have money or jewelry in 'em. I 'ope he don't 'old me accountable. . . ."

Psyche had forgotten about Mr. Sinclair's luggage. She looked around and saw two carpetbags, much slashed and ripped, lying on the floor nearby. Poor Wilson had been true to his trust, bringing back what was left of the luggage. But the bags had been ripped inside and out; she could see a scrap of a once fine linen shirt hanging out through one of the slits. The thieves had either been disappointed in what they sought, or very thorough indeed in searching for valuables.

"Someone must have heard you asking for the marquis of Tarrington's cases," she said thoughtfully. "It's really too bad."

"But I was very private, like," Wilson argued. "'Is lordship tol' me and I was careful, just like 'e said. He weren't even staying there under his title, miss, but under 'is Christian name."

Psyche raised her brows. Since Gabriel hadn't heard of his "title" until she had bestowed it upon her fictitious fiancé, that was no surprise. The other servants looked a bit shocked, however. "He was doubtless being discreet until he could find a more refined hotel," she said. "He has been out of England for some time, as you know. However, someone had better take this up to his lordship and allow him to see if anything here can be salvaged. And take back his evening clothes; he must have *something* to wear." She remembered the naked man upstairs, sheltered tactfully under his newspaper, and tried not to blush.

One of the footmen jumped, as if remembering that he was remiss in his duties and hurried away. Again, Psyche pretended not to notice. Her mother had been an excellent manager with her household staff, and she had taught her daughters that, for everyone's benefit, there were times to be vigilant and times to turn a blind eye.

Psyche looked down at the wounded footman. "Don't

worry about the loss of your own money," she said kindly. "I'm sure that when his lordship hears of your ordeal, he will replace your coin, and likely even increase it." She would make sure of it, she told herself.

Wilson brightened at once. Then, as she was about to turn away, he said timidly, "Um, miss, if I might be so bold . . ."

"Yes?" She looked back, her mind already engaged once again with the bigger problem of ridding herself of an unwanted fiancé.

"You won't—won't 'old me responsible for me ruined livery, will you, miss?" he asked anxiously.

It took her a second to realize what he meant. Servants were provided with household livery as part of their compensation and received new clothing once a year, but they were responsible for the upkeep of their uniforms.

"Of course not," she said briskly. "Jowers will see to getting you a new set of livery right away; you certainly can't be seen abovestairs in such a state."

The elderly butler nodded.

"Thank'ee, miss," Wilson said. He settled back into the chair to accept the ministering of the housekeeper and several maids, happy enough now in his role of the brave, abused victim.

Psyche returned to the main floor, thankful that her servant would recover. It had been most thoughtless of the actor to have sent the man out so late at night, but perhaps Gabriel had really not considered the dangers. Likely, the thespian was accustomed to the peril of the streets and had come to consider it simply another fact of life. Psyche sighed, recalling her mother's lectures on social systems and understanding the world of the underclasses.

As she entered the morning room, she remembered the stack of mail. She would have to decline three luncheon invitations, since her "fiancé" had no clothes to wear, and she herself was too distracted to leave the house and make polite conversation. Sighing, she headed toward her bedroom and the small desk littered with notes and cards.

In his chamber, Gabriel had groaned when he saw the

damaged bags. The footman who brought up his luggage had also detailed, with much colorful embellishment, the story of Wilson's return and of the attack he had suffered. Gabriel, who had just pulled his best linen shirt from the bag and was frowning at the slashes that now rendered it useful only for the housemaid's rag bag, forgot about his clothing. He turned and listened with all his attention.

"They jumped him outside the tavern, after he had collected my things?"

"Yes, milord. If there's aught missing from the bags, it really ain't his fault, milord."

This household staff's loyalty to each other was commendable, Gabriel thought. In his own father's house, the staff were so browbeaten they would have sold their own grandmother to have escaped censure from their overbearing employer. But he pushed that thought away. He never cared to think about his father.

"No, of course not," he agreed. Fortunately, he had left no money in such a rowdy inn, which had been chosen only for its cheap rates, and the note turning over ownership of the estate Barrett had lost during the card game—which must have been the thieves' true target—had been tucked inside his evening jacket, but still . . . he rummaged through the bag and sighed.

"Milord?"

"My gold stickpin is missing, of course. I thought I had it well hidden, but—it can't be helped." It was a trifle, worth only a few pounds, but he had valued it for other reasons. As usual, he pushed the deeper emotion away and focused on the needs of the moment. "Tell Wilson I shall see him presently when he has recovered and offer him my—um, condolences."

The servant nodded in complete understanding. "I'll tell 'im, milord. I know 'e'll be most appreciative."

Gabriel rummaged through the bag again. "Damn!"

"Milord?"

"They took my ivory-backed razors." Gabriel fingered the rough stubble that covered his chin and cheeks. In all his years of wandering, despite his poverty, his sometimes desperate straits, he had maintained his personal hygiene religiously. Perhaps at times that had been all that reminded him of what he had been, what he still considered himself—a gentleman.

The servant looked sympathetic. "May'ap I can do something about that, milord. Miss Psyche's father—his set of razors might still be put away, for sentiment sake, like. I'll ask the housekeeper if she could oblige."

"Thank you," Gabriel told him.

When the footman left the room, shutting the door behind him, Gabriel smiled grimly. Despite his losses, they had still been very lucky. He realized, more than any of them, how fortunate the footman was to still have his throat uncut and his head in one piece. Gabriel had not expected the band of ruffians to be so intelligent as to detect another man coming to fetch his cases.

On the other hand, the servant's livery had likely caused remark in such a lowly inn. It was too late now to regret his actions. Fortunately, the servant would heal, and Gabriel himself must deal with the loss of his wardrobe. With precious few coins left to spend, that was enough of a blow. Gabriel winced at his own pun. He had to replace his ruined wardrobe sufficiently to be seen outside the house without attracting comment, he had to engage a competent attorney to assure the legal transfer of title of the estate he had won, and he had to replenish his almost empty pockets. And for that, he would have to return to the gaming houses, while still escaping notice of the gang hired to kill him.

"I think," he muttered to himself, "it will be a most intriguing week."

In a short time, the footman returned with an engraved leather case and a brocade robe hanging over his arm. "The 'ousekeeper found a set of razors, my lord, and also a robe. Ain't no more of the late master's clothes as would fit you. And I took the liberty of ordering the maids to bring up 'ot water for a bath. Your evening clothes will be here shortly, as well, but your, um, drawers are still wet, milord; the laundry maids put them into the wash."

"I should like a bath very much indeed," Gabriel answered, keeping his tone calm with some effort. A warm bath in a clean tub—it reminded him forcibly that he was in a real home again, not just another grimy second-rate tavern or inn. This was luxury indeed, almost worth the repeated attempts on his life. Bless Psyche for offering him this haven, this moment of ease that reminded him of all he had lost, and all he meant to reclaim. Even if her offer was a bit involuntary. . . .

Grinning, he pulled on the robe, picked up the set of straight razors engraved *H. H.,* and followed the footman to the large bath, where the water emitted pleasant waves of warmth, and fresh soap and clean towels waited nearby.

"Do you wish me to shave you, sir?" the footman asked, his eyes glinting. Did he have ambitions of becoming a valet? It would be a step up for him, more money and more status. He seemed more intelligent than the poor fellow Gabriel had sent to retrieve his belongings, and Gabriel certainly had no man of his own. It wasn't a bad idea, Gabriel thought.

"I'll call you when I'm ready," he said aloud. "What's your name?"

The man bowed slightly; he had a lantern jaw and mild, intelligent brown eyes. "Brickson, milord." He left the dressing room and pulled the door shut behind him.

Gabriel dropped the thick robe and stepped into the tub, sighing as the water swirled around his legs. It had been a long while indeed since he had had a proper bath, not a dip in a stream or a quick wash from a cracked basin. He sat down, and the warm water enveloped him like the security he had lost years ago, the stability he would have sworn he cared nothing for.

Laying his head back against the hard curved rim of the copper tub, Gabriel found that he could relax completely, let down his guard as he never could in an inn or even some friendly harlot's bedchamber. In this house, he felt at home.

And that was ridiculous, he told himself sharply. It didn't do to let down his defenses too far. He had dangerous enemies outside the house, and he had a sharp-witted, albeit beautiful, adversary within. Psyche would have him out of this house as quickly as she could.

Except that Gabriel did not mean to go, not yet. He relaxed a moment longer in the gentle warmth of the water, then reached for the soap.

Psyche spent an hour writing quick but polite refusals and worked her way through most of the stack of mail. Then a sudden thought made her reach for the small calendar in her desk drawer, and she gazed at the dates, feeling a rush of dismay.

Oh, no! How could she have forgotten? She would send a note of apology—no, no, that wouldn't work, either. Psyche put one finger to her lips, chewing absently on the edge of her nail, then when she realized what she was doing—a childish habit—pulled her hand away. Oh, dear, oh, dear.

She would have to speak to the actor again. Perhaps by this time he would at least have his clothes on!

She made her way back to the drawing room, but found no sign of the man. Frowning, she pulled the bell rope and waited for Jowers to appear. "Where is the—my fiancé, do you know?"

Jowers, despite his slow pace and seemingly slow wits, somehow remained aware of everything that happened in his household. "I believe he is up in the nursery with Miss Circe, miss."

Psyche drew a deep breath. What on earth—? "Thank you, Jowers."

The butler nodded and withdrew, and Psyche almost ran toward the stairs. To leave her innocent little sister alone with a man of whom Psyche knew nothing—nothing except that his audacity and lack of respect for his employer knew no bounds—this she could not allow.

After a leisurely bath, Gabriel dressed in his evening clothes, forgoing the comfort of his smalls beneath—it wouldn't be the first time. He recalled one lady whose bedchamber he had left so hastily that he'd barely had time to pull on his outer clothing—the lady's husband had been pounding on the locked door, as he remembered, uttering grave threats toward the welfare of any strangers found inside. But his jacket and pantaloons had been brushed and pressed, spots of mud removed, and he himself felt much better after a bath and a shave. He brushed his damp hair into place and thought about what to do before venturing out into the street. Now that the footman was safe, Gabriel was in no hurry; his attire would look slightly less strange if he delayed his errands another few hours. And it was vital that he attract no unwanted notice.

On the stairway, he turned away from his own chamber and climbed another flight, till—by the simple expedient of opening several doors—he found the nursery chamber. His "employer's" younger sister stood at the end of the room, in front of an easel. It was placed beneath a high window, where the light would touch the canvas, and Gabriel's curiosity stirred. He came forward slowly; the girl was very intent on her brushwork, and he did not want to startle her.

"Hello again," he said.

Circe looked up at him, then put down her brush and drew a paint-spattered cloth over the canvas, hiding the scene beneath.

Gabriel had been curious about her work, but he accepted the silent rebuke with a nod.

"Hello," the child said. "Are you looking for Psyche? She isn't here."

"No," he answered, making his bow as he would to an adult. "I came to meet you properly."

Circe curtsied in return, then asked, "Why would you do that?" Her large green eyes met his gaze without blinking.

She showed none of the awkwardness or shyness he would have expected from a child her age.

He felt a stirring of interest in this unusual young lady. "As your future brother-in-law, it is only polite for me to address you properly."

She smiled suddenly, and her whole face changed. The too serious look that she usually wore vanished for an instant, and he saw another side of her, playful and free. Just like her older sister, this child had more to her than met the eye.

"Ah, but I know it is all a hum, the engagement, I mean," she said very low. Gabriel realized that an older woman sat in the far corner of the room, nodding over a lapful of knitting wool.

"But that does not mean that I should be rude," Gabriel retorted, his tone teasing. "We must keep up the pose, you know, not forget our lines."

"I suppose not," the child agreed. "It is like one of your plays, yes?"

"Indeed," he agreed. "And besides, you are an unusual young lady. I think I should *like* to know you better."

She considered that for a moment, then nodded in apparent agreement. "Would you care for some tea? The maid brought it up for me a while ago, but I was too busy to stop while the light was good."

"I apologize for interrupting you at your work," he said, giving her one of his best smiles. He expected her to display the usual polite denials or even a shy flirtation. He was ready to reply to her reassurance that his presence was far better than any silly painting. But she flattened his over-puffed ego like a sharp knife slicing into a soufflé.

She shrugged, apparently immune to his charm. "It's all right; the best light has gone."

Suitably chastened, he followed her to a battered round table, where Circe took a chair and poured out the tea. Gabriel sat down across from her and accepted a cup; the liquid was tepid, but he sipped politely, looking in interest at the child whose interests made her so different from the average young miss. Instead of a head full of fashion and shopping and romantic yearnings, she seemed to care only for her art.

"What are you painting?" he asked, his tone polite.

She narrowed her eyes at him over her own cup of tea.

"If you wish to talk about it, that is," he said, afraid she would retreat again into careful silence.

"If you really are interested—" She stopped, studied his expression, then seemed satisfied and continued. "I made a study of French villages when I visited the Continent with Psyche and Aunt last year. Our visit was too brief, but I did get some watercolors done that I was—almost—happy with, and I sketched more scenes."

"I would love to see them," Gabriel said.

Circe didn't answer. "Would you like a macaroon?" She offered him the plate.

Gabriel accepted his put-down and took a biscuit. It was light and sweet, and he nibbled it, watching her. "So you enjoy watercolors?"

She sighed. "I do, but I should really like to try oils, only it's very slow, trying to learn on my own, and we haven't been able to find a decent teacher. Young ladies are expected to dabble in watercolor, you see, but oils are for serious artists. Oils suggest more avenues to fully express one's work. Mr. Turner achieved his *Avalanche in the Grisons* by applying his paints with the use of a palate knife—is that not intriguing? I should so like to expand my skills." For the first time, her tone sounded forlorn.

"That is too bad," Gabriel murmured. At her slightly suspicious glance, he said, "No, I mean it. I can see that it matters to you."

Circe's narrow shoulders relaxed just a little. "Yes, and in addition, I am interested in landscapes, not portraits or still-life sketches, and that is not considered quite the thing, either. You know what Sir Joshua Reynolds said about the object of painting."

Gabriel didn't, but he tried to maintain an air of intelligent interest. "Yes?"

"He believed that painting should not copy nature but idealize it. And he preferred historical subjects, the 'grand style' that would elevate the observer's spirit, though mind you, he did enough portraits, too, but that was for bread and butter. But personally, I don't see why an artistically pleasing vista cannot do the same—elevate the spirit, that is!" Circe observed, with more passion than she had so far displayed.

"Quite right," Gabriel agreed, fascinated by her zeal, if not by the topic.

"But it's most unfair; even if I could be admitted to the Royal Academy School, which I can't, as I'm female"— Circe sighed—"landscape painting is not taught. One must apprentice to another artist, but finding a master who will take a girl . . . well, it's enough to make one quite downcast."

Gabriel stared at her clear eyes, sparkling now with the depth of her feelings. "But you will not give up," he predicted, and was rewarded with the child's sudden brilliant smile, which always vanished almost as soon as it appeared.

"No, indeed!" Circe agreed. "We are hopeful, Psyche and I, that on the Continent we might find a painter—poor, perhaps, in need of a paying student—who would be more open-minded. My mama always said that females should be allowed to exercise their talents just as men do, you know. Most people find that view shocking." She paused to observe his reaction.

Gabriel smiled quite genuinely. "I have traveled enough to be, perhaps, more open in my thinking. I see no reason why a talented woman should not express her genius fully."

Circe flashed another wide, dazzling smile.

He had a sudden increased understanding of how Psyche must feel about this adorable, if quite different child. No one was left to nurture her incredible spirit, or to protect her from the confines of a conventional existence, except her older sister. Psyche must feel the burden of her responsibility; no wonder her facade was so cool and her shell so hard to penetrate. She had assumed the weight of a parent's responsibility at too young an age.

"Someday," he remarked, "I hope you will allow me to view your work. These macaroons are excellent, by the way."

When Psyche reached the nursery suite, she hurried inside. To her relief, she found Circe sitting at the round table where Psyche herself had once conducted tea parties with her dolls. The actor sat across from her, and they were both drinking tea and eating macaroons, Circe's favorite treat.

"Circe, what are you doing with this—this man?" Psyche demanded, her tone too sharp. "Where is Telly?"

"Here, miss, did you need me?" The governess, Miss Tellman, sat up with a jerk; she seemed to have been napping in her chair in the corner of the room.

"No, that's all right," Psyche said, her tension fading a little. But her eyes were still narrow as she turned back to the actor. "And what is your purpose here?"

"I thought I should pay a courtesy visit to my future sister-in-law," Gabriel said, exhibiting his usual lazy smile.

"That's ridiculous," Psyche snapped, then pressed her lips together before she could give too much away. Circe knew all about her scheme, but Telly did not, and the elderly governess was not above a little judicious gossip with the other servants. "I mean, I appreciate your sense of the proprieties, but—"

"I thought it was very nice of him," Circe said, with her usual direct gaze turned toward her sister. "He didn't forget me or ignore me, like *some* people, just because I'm not out yet, or wearing long skirts."

"Oh, Circe," Psyche's anger faded into contrition. "You know I always think of you, dearest."

"Oh, not you," Circe explained. "I meant Percy, who never seems to think that *my* life will be altered beyond bearing, too, if he should marry you. In fact, it would be hideous, living with Percy and Uncle Wilfred."

Psyche needed no reminding. She would never leave her sister behind if or when she should marry; Circe needed her too much. And when her sister leaned forward and whispered, "It's a *game*, Psyche, we're pretending, just like a play," Psyche surrendered to the inevitable.

"Have a cup of tea, Psyche," her sister added, playing the role of hostess with aplomb. "It's cooled a bit, but it's still very nice."

"Yes, thank you," Psyche agreed, drawing up another chair. Her sister, at twelve, could be alarmingly mature one moment, and very much a child the next. Psyche could hardly blame Circe for being curious about this impostor, but she did not like his association with her sister. After all, she knew next to nothing about him or his past.

It seemed that Circe did. "Lord Tarrington," her sister said carefully as she passed the cup of tea, "has traveled extensively, Psyche. He was telling me about some French paintings he has seen."

Psyche tried not to show her surprise. If Circe had talked to the actor about her painting, she must have decided he was worthy of trust. Circe hated above all things being patronized, and her painting was not a hobby, although since their parents had died, only Psyche and perhaps Telly really understood the passion and the talent that this young girl revealed. And child though she was, Circe had a keen instinct for judging people's characters. She had always detested Percy.

Psyche stared at the actor who sat so at ease at this nursery table, sipping his tea; the man continued to surprise her.

"I told him of my interest in oils, Psyche," Circe told her sister. "He feels that I should be able to study the use of oil, and also landscaping, just like any young painter."

Another surprise, that Circe should be so open so quickly. "And so you should," Psyche agreed.

"When I was in Spain, I viewed some remarkable scenes by El Greco," Gabriel said thoughtfully, reaching for another macaroon. "His study of Toledo—quite striking. Two hundred years old, of course, but a definite mood to his paintings. I agree with Circe that landscapes should be more than mere studies of topography."

Circe beamed, and Psyche's mood softened even more. Circe had so few people to discuss art with seriously. She hated adults who tut-tutted and told her not to neglect her needlework and pianoforte, which would be more important to a young lady of fashion, after all. How did this actor know anything about art, anyhow, or was it all just another illusion, a clever fiction he was spinning for her sister's benefit?

Seeing the sparkle in her younger sister's eyes, Psyche almost didn't care.

The man seemed to sense the direction of her thoughts. "I fear that I am ignorant at art compared to your sister," he said to them both. "But I know enough to appreciate genuine passion when I see it."

Psyche was pleased again, both by his candor and his seemingly honest appreciation of her sister's talents. "Yes, she cares deeply about her work. That is why I'm trying to find her the right instructors."

Circe had smiled, but now she frowned just a little. "I keep working on my own, but it's difficult. That harbor scene I did at Calais wasn't too bad. But I'm still trying to capture the special quality of sunlight from behind a cloud, you know, not quite opaque, but that faint shimmer. . . ." Circe's voice trailed off as she looked away from them, as if envisioning an image visible only to her artist's eyes.

Psyche felt a wave of love and protectiveness wash over her as she gazed at her remarkable little sister. She vowed silently, as she had done so many times before, that Circe would not be pushed into a stifling pattern, forced to conform to the role of society maiden interested only in finding a husband. Circe had gifts that must be exercised, be allowed to grow, or something in her spirit would wither and fade, and Circe would bear the loss and the pain forever. And she had already lost enough. . . . No, Psyche would protect her. She would find the money they needed—her own money, for heaven's sake, her parent's inheritance, meant for just such expenditures as this. Her freethinking parents would have understood Circe's special needs; Uncle Wilfred did not.

"You care about your sister very much, do you not?" the actor said quietly.

She shifted her gaze to meet his. "Yes, I do. And I would allow no one to hurt her," she answered, just as low.

He smiled. "I promise you I would never injure a child."

But he could, willingly or not, if this imposture were exposed. Psyche's fears returned with a rush. "I have bad news."

He raised his brows and waited, his expression composed. She admired his lack of panic, Psyche realized in one corner of her mind.

"I had accepted an invitation to a party tonight, before—before I knew you would be here. I mean, I thought my *fiancé*—you—would have to return immediately to the Continent," she tried to explain, aware of the governess sitting a few feet away. "And now if I send regrets, when Percy will have told everyone that you are staying here, it will seem too suspicious.

"At least," she went on, "you do have evening clothes! But something must be done about the rest of your wardrobe." She bit her lip. Which tailor could provide proper raiment on short notice?

Simone would know. She would send a note to her modiste immediately. "Nothing too flashy, of course, nor too expensive, and then there's the bootmaker and the . . ."

Psyche suddenly became aware of the stares directed at her. Telly's round face was stunned, Circe's interested, and Gabriel looked a bit askance.

"Oh, dear. Was I speaking aloud?"

Circe nodded gravely. "Yes, Psyche."

Gabriel shifted uncomfortably on the little chair. "I assume you were talking about me?"

"No, this is for my other naked fiancé." Psyche rolled her eyes. "Of course I was speaking of you."

Circe giggled into her teacup.

Telly gasped, "Miss!"

Psyche frowned. "He has to have clothing, Telly. What's so improper about that?"

"But you shouldn't—young ladies don't discuss male attire, Miss Psyche. You know that." The older woman sounded distressed, and Psyche relented.

"I'm sorry, Telly." She turned to the actor to explain. "If I am improper, it's not because of lack of trying on our dear governess's part."

Gabriel smiled. "I don't find you improper at all, my dear Miss Hill. In fact, I find you quite perfect, just as you are."

Psyche felt a moment of warmth, then she steeled herself against his charm. The man was an actor, the man was an actor. She would have to embroider the phrase on her handkerchief and keep it within constant view.

It was so easy to relax and enjoy his sweet phrases. She had to remember that he was not sincere, that this was all a facade. She no longer wondered that he was not better known; she was beginning to think he had practiced his lines in ladies' chambers more often than on the stage. With his incredible good looks, he would have had sufficient chance. . . .

But this was accomplishing nothing. Since her parents' death, Psyche had learned to act, not just contemplate. She pushed herself back from the table and stood.

The actor stood, too, politely, and she thought she saw a moment of disappointment in his deep blue eyes. Was he truly sorry to see her go? No, it was likely another pretense.

"I am going out," she announced. "I will be back soon. We will leave for the party at eight, after a light dinner; they will have a late supper at the soiree."

His answering smile was twisted but she wasn't sure how much he knew about the social life of the Ton. It was not something an unknown actor would have had the chance to participate in. And with Telly in the room, she couldn't speak more plainly.

"I will be ready," he said, casting a sardonic glance down at his apparel. Since the evening attire was the only outfit he owned not in shreds, he was certainly prepared to go out.

Psyche almost laughed, then bit back her giggle. He might think she was making fun of his predicament, and she wouldn't hurt anyone's feelings through ridicule, not even this impertinent thespian. But it really was ridiculous.

"Psyche," Circe put in. "I could use a new pad of drawing paper, please."

"Of course." Psyche nodded. "I shall see you later, dearest."

The actor bowed, and Psyche inclined her head, then turned and hurried out. Sometimes she could almost regret that their engagement was not real. His attention was so unwavering, his regard so—no, no, she mustn't even consider such a thing. It was a game, she must remember, only a pose. It would all end soon.

Six

*T*here was nothing more satisfying than a successful shopping trip, Psyche thought, tugging off her kid gloves as she strode up the steps of the town house and through the open door that Jowers held. She had purchased Circe's drawing paper and picked up a few new brushes that Circe had ordered. Thinking only how delighted Circe would be at the sable brushes, she barely noticed Jowers's strange expression as her new entourage followed her through the door.

She had also called at the boot maker, glove maker, and, of course, Simone's establishment. Simone had been only too happy to give Psyche the name of a tailor. Between Aunt Sophie, Circe, and the many gowns Psyche needed for the Season, Simone made a tidy profit from the females in the Hill family.

While ensconced on a rose-colored silk settee, Psyche had sipped her tea and sighed appreciatively over the new French fashions. Now that that scourge Napoleon had at last been vanquished, trade was flourishing and the English could again enjoy their beloved French fabrics and designs. Not that some hadn't been smuggled in even during the war years, but Psyche's parents had frowned upon that practice.

Psyche had also slipped on for a final fitting the new gown she was to wear to the Forsyths' party that evening. It was a dream of a gown, icy blue in some lights, silver in others. The short sleeves were banded with a delicate, filmy lace and still more lace flirted with the low, square-cut neckline. The fitted bodice clung to her figure, then the skirt flowed smoothly over her hips and ended in a train that was a swirl of filmy fabric. Experimentally, Psyche twisted back and forth and watched herself in the looking glass. The fabric glimmered with each movement of her body. If for just a moment she allowed herself to imagine Gabriel's powerful arms guiding her through the swing and swirl of a waltz, or imagined the feel of his rough cheek against the smoothness of her own, or his warm breath against her cool lips as he leaned in for another forbidden kiss . . . well, no one but she would know of her foolishness.

After Simone had checked the fit of the new gown and pronounced it perfect, Psyche had left the shop with Simpson following behind her, carrying the dress. One more stop to gather her last needs and she had returned home in a glow of satisfaction. As she handed her reticule and gloves to a footman, she finally noticed poor Jowers.

She had never seen the poor man so distracted. Of course, as he held the door open for the last of the arrivals, he did have to duck to avoid being hit over the head by a very large bolt of black silk.

"Miss, excuse me. Who are all these men and what am I to do with them?"

"Why, they are here to assist me, Jowers."

Psyche pressed herself against the drawing room door to avoid another bolt of fabric.

Jowers tried to draw himself up in affront but had to stop to help one of the men lift a clumsy package of trimmings over the threshold.

"Miss, I am most sorry if you feel you must go elsewhere for assistance, but I assure you that our household staff is—"

Distressed, Psyche cut him off. "Oh, no, Jowers. Don't

worry yourself. These men are tailors and they are here to create a new wardrobe for Lord Tarrington. As you know, his clothing has met with an unfortunate accident."

"Oh, yes, miss. I see." An uncertain look crossed Jowers's wrinkled face. "But, miss, are you certain that Lord Tarrington wishes this kind of assistance? It has been many years since your father died, but surely things have not changed so much—"

Psyche paid scant attention to his worries as she directed the team of tailors into the foyer. "Jowers, where is Lord Tarrington?"

"He is in the yellow salon, miss."

"Perfect!" Psyche turned and waved the men down the hall toward the large room. "This way, gentlemen. Follow me. Your client is right this way."

"But I really don't think this is how it is done," Jowers finished weakly.

With enthusiastic vigor, Psyche threw open the salon doors and found her fiancé studying her mother's portrait over the fireplace. He was sipping coffee from a pale green and cream Sèvres cup, but his arm stopped midway to his mouth at the sight of Psyche and her tailors.

Absolutely dumbfounded, Gabriel stood motionless with his cup poised ready to drink. Psyche paused with her hand on the doorknob, directing what appeared to be a small army into the room—or, more accurately, *straight at him.* The gang of tidily dressed men rushed to Gabriel's still figure and swarmed around him. One little monkey of a man actually reached up and nipped the cup out of his hand. Gabriel was so shocked by this audacity, he didn't even pound the man as he normally would, had a stranger been so familiar with his person.

"There he is, gentlemen." Psyche waved a slender arm in his direction. "He will need morning attire, riding attire, daytime attire, something suitable for staying at home, and, Henri," she called to a small, wiry man who Gabriel took to be the leader of this group, "Henri, I think he would look marvelous in a deep claret."

Henri, in an eager rush to please his new benefactress, swung a heavy bolt of velvet her way. With an easy grace Gabriel had to admire even in his current state, she evaded the bolt before fingering the material.

"Oh, yes, Henri. That's just lovely."

"*Oui*, mademoiselle. And the midnight blue for another jacket," Henri suggested in his thickly accented English.

Psyche looked around for the midnight blue and found it spread with a pristine white-on-white patterned silk over the settee. She sighed with pure female appreciation for the rich fabric. "Oh, definitely, Henri. Simone was right, you have marvelous taste."

"Thank you, Mademoiselle Hill. With his coloring, we will stay with the deep, jewel colors."

They turned with narrowed eyes to scrutinize Gabriel, rather as they would a plump stewing chicken, he thought.

"Why, yes, monsieur. He does need bold colors."

"And minimal embellishments. He does not need the usual masculine trimmings."

"Right again, Henri. You have such an eye."

"And no padding around the shoulders. Monsieur has been blessed with very wide, thick shoulders."

Psyche looked away and chewed her plump lower lip. "Ah, really? I hadn't noticed."

Liar, Gabriel thought, pleased that she had. With a dreadful fascination, like a mouse hypnotized before a snake's approach, he watched Henri preen under Psyche's approval. One of Henri's assistants was busy unrolling the claret and midnight blue fabrics for cutting, another was setting up the thread and scissors and other tools, and yet three more were buzzing around Gabriel like annoying pests that Gabriel longed to swat. He had a measuring tape around his neck, another around his chest, and a third man was measuring his—damn it!—inseam. Gabriel kicked at the man, who had just gotten a wee bit too personal.

Gabriel's temper began a slow steam.

Unknowingly, Psyche caused him to boil over.

"And Henri, Lord Tarrington will undoubtedly need some personal items, as well."

Impertinent female! She just barely blushed.

Henri nodded with understanding. "*Oui*, mademoiselle. I have some excellent flannel that I use for just that purpose."

Psyche's brow wrinkled in disapproval. "Oh, flannel? I much prefer cambric. White, I think."

It was Henri's turn to blush. "*Oui*, if the mademoiselle prefers cambric . . ."

Psyche gasped with the realization of what she had just said and what it implied.

"Oh, no, I have no preference. Why, I don't care in the least what his . . . what they're made of," she babbled uncertainly. "I wouldn't even mind if he didn't wear any—oh, no. I don't mean that, either."

Gabriel suddenly felt seventeen years old again, when another woman, another commanding beauty, had dressed him and manipulated him. In a sensual daze, he had allowed it, been flattered by her attentions. At first. But Gabriel was no longer that boy, and he had had all he could bear. The sensation of being controlled, decorated like a china doll for someone's amusement, came flooding back, and it released emotions he'd thought long forgotten. He took a deep breath.

Psyche was still floundering desperately to cover her gaffe. "I mean, of course, that *I* don't mind *what*—"

"Miss Hill, I am beginning to think you have no mind." Completely ignoring the eager assistants and their efforts, Gabriel strode over to Psyche and Henri.

She drew a deep breath. "I should expect a little gratitude!"

"It's gratitude you want? All right, I'll give it to you."

As he loomed closer, Psyche drew herself up, her expression guarded.

"Thank you, Miss Hill," he continued, dark brows low over angry eyes. "Thank you so much for inviting these men to break my solitude, thank you for inviting them to touch me intimately without my permission, thank you for deciding what color and fabric my small clothes should be!"

He whipped his head back to face Henri. The little man flinched at his angry tone.

"By the way, I want cambric, not white, black.

"And I suppose I should thank you for not choosing pink and unmanning me even more than you have," he added, turning back to Psyche.

Psyche's brilliant blue eyes glittered with angry and embarrassed tears. She too looked at the poor tailor.

"Wool, Henri. Make them out of the cheapest, roughest wool you can find. And dye them red!"

"Red! You minx!" Gabriel didn't know whether to double over in laughter or to flatten one of the men who was still trying to measure his legs. Clenching his fists at his sides, Gabriel demonstrated what he thought was a herculean effort to rein in his temper. Again, he turned to Henri.

"If you do not call off your lap dogs, I shall put your pins and needles to very imaginative and uncomfortable use."

The Frenchman paled. He nodded quickly and whispered, "*Oui*, monsieur. At once."

In rapid French, Henri spoke to his assistants. He did not soften Gabriel's words, and the men leaped back from Gabriel's person with almost comic speed. One of the men even flew across the room to the collection of pins and stood blocking them with his body. They all glared at Gabriel suspiciously as if expecting him to attack them.

However, Gabriel moved in the opposite direction. In a few furious paces, Gabriel flung open the door and gestured to the men. "Now that your services are no longer needed, you may leave. Immediately," he clarified as the men reluctantly gathered up their tools and fabric.

Henri looked at Psyche with doubtful hesitation. "Mademoiselle?"

Gabriel glared at Psyche as if daring her to contradict him.

Damn the man! She was in an impossible position. Henri thought that Gabriel was her fiancé and that this was all a gift to him. She could not defy him without flaunting society's conventions. And she could hardly force him to accept a gift if he did not want it. There would be talk, and it would leak into the Ton through someone's valet or dresser.

Forcing a calm she did not feel, she smiled at Henri. "Lord Tarrington does not wish for your help at this time, but I am sure that later he—"

Gabriel's deep, infuriating voice cut her off. "*He* will find his own tailor when *he* decides."

Psyche smiled through clenched teeth. "Yes, precisely."

Henri's expression grew dim and disappointed. Psyche could imagine what this large commission would have meant to him. She could not bear to let the eager little man walk away feeling so deflated. The men had gathered all their belongings and were trailing down the foyer toward the front door. Psyche stopped Henri with a light touch on his arm.

"Lord Tarrington may not need your services, but one of my footmen is in sore need of new livery."

Henri's face brightened.

It cheered her so, that she continued. "In fact, all my staff could use new livery. Discuss it with Jowers on your way out. Good day, Henri."

Henri was positively beaming as he bowed his way out of the salon and down the hall.

She stood with her back to Gabriel and watched the men leave.

In a moment Gabriel spoke to her, the fury replaced by puzzlement. "That was exceedingly kind of you."

She turned slowly to face him. He stood there looking so comfortable, so infuriatingly right in the opulent surroundings, that Psyche could hardly believe that he had not been to the manor born. But his actions—his actions had been so arrogant, so blatantly haughty—

He was acting more and more like a real marquis every moment.

"And exceedingly unkind of you," she snapped. "Henri

is trying to establish himself as a tailor to discriminating gentlemen."

To her surprise, he did not sputter or redden or spit out an indignant denial. He simply nodded. "Yes, but if Henri's own too wide lapels and eye-catching waistcoat are any hint of his taste, I really think I should prefer another tailor. That does not mean that your good intentions do not deserve mention. I should not have lost my temper."

Psyche suddenly felt the way she had when she was a child and had spun around and around until she was dizzy and then tried to walk in a straight line.

"No denials?" she asked incredulously.

"No."

"No professions of superiority?"

"When I am just a lowly actor?" he asked with self-mocking calm.

"Quite true." She nodded seriously.

He laughed as if he could not help it and then sobered. "I was unforgivably rude, and I apologize."

"You what?" Her voice was shrill. Never since her father died had Psyche heard a man voluntarily admit wrongdoing. She had become so accustomed to Percy's blustering and Uncle Wilfred's autocratic ultimatums that she had forgotten that a man might still be found who took a woman seriously, who listened to her opinions, who—

"I apologize," he said easily.

"You admit you were a beast?"

"Unequivocally."

Psyche sank into a nearby chair upholstered in sunny yellow. "This is beginning to be fun."

"Oh, no, my dear Psyche. Don't get too comfortable. You have a bit of groveling to do yourself." To her discomfiture, he came and rested on one knee in front of her.

She turned her head to avoid those knowing blue eyes.

"Nonsense, I would never need to do such a ridiculous thing."

He smiled wickedly. "I would be happy to show you the fun we could have on our knees, my love."

She should have been scandalized. She *was* scandalized, but curious, too. What on earth did he mean? Puzzled, she turned back until her aloof gaze met the warmth of his eyes.

He read her perfectly and laughed again. He reached out and took her chin between his thumb and forefinger. "Apologize, Psyche. I never took you for a coward."

"I am no such thing! I would certainly apologize should I need to."

His steady gaze spoke for him.

"I do not need to apologize. I was helping you!"

"I felt," he said slowly, "like a poor, weak excuse for a man. Hell, I felt like no man at all. I felt like a paid doxy being outfitted for the pleasure of her buyer."

"But that's what you are," she burst out, unthinking. If she had not been so unnerved by his proximity, she would have thought before speaking. But it was too late; the words were out.

Suddenly, all his open warmth vanished. Although he did not physically move, she felt the sudden distance yawn like a chasm between them.

And she realized what she had said.

"Of course you are not weak," she said lamely, wondering how she could repair this. "And you are no . . . 'doxy.'" She stumbled over the crude word. "But you are an employee, and it is my responsibility to clothe you during the time you're here. All my servants receive uniforms. . . ." Her reasoning sounded weak, even to her own ears.

Smoothly, he stood and crossed back to the fireplace. He tossed back the rest of his by now cold tea. The expression on his face told her he wished it were something stronger.

Shame washed over her. Who was she to talk of kindness? Had she not just attacked a man where he was far more vulnerable than his coffers?

She rose, uncertain if she should approach him. Oh, if only she had someone to ask about men, how to handle them, what to do, what she should say. Her elderly maiden aunt would be no help, and Circe was only a child. If only her mother were still alive. . . .

Psyche remembered what her mother had always said about her father. "My dear, your father has become a great man. But he could never have done so had I not been beside him, believing in him." Psyche remembered the easy and open affection the two had shared.

Her mother had wanted Psyche to find such a partner, a man she could stand beside and believe in. Psyche did not know why, but it was suddenly imperative to make this man, this impostor, forgive her.

Carefully, she walked to stand beside him. He was not looking at her but at the fire crackling cheerfully in the grate.

He spoke before she could.

"It is true that I am poor, that I have none of the riches that should be mine." He faced her, lines she had never noticed etched deeply beside his mouth. "But I have my pride, Psyche. I have held on to it through all these years, and I will not have it taken from me."

Psyche opened her mouth to protest, but he put up one hand to stop her.

"It may be a vain virtue, but I have precious few. I will let no one, not even you, rob me of that. There was a time when I allowed myself to be led, but never again, Psyche. You cannot take that from me; I have already been stripped of too much."

He turned away from the mantel and walked out of the room. Psyche watched him go, feeling somehow that she had just made a terrible mistake.

He went up to his bedchamber and rang for Brickson, asking first for a glass of brandy while he composed himself—he had never meant to say such personal things to Psyche. Why did the woman get under his skin so easily? Her cool beauty, her too controlling attempts at assistance—she seemed to slip past the guard he had erected so carefully over the years. . . . He must be more vigilant.

No woman had controlled him since he had left England;

he had been savagely wary of his independence, had prided himself on keeping a cool head. Oh, he had certainly given in to his passions, when the opportunity presented itself, but never—never since Sylvie—had he allowed a woman to cloud his brain or rule his actions.

The memories of his youth were still too painful. Perhaps it had been his innocence, his awareness of his ignorance in matters of love as well as drawing room society that had led him to allow his first lover to take over so much of his life.

Brickson brought the brandy; by this time, Gabriel was regaining his usual calm. Psyche had been right about one thing; he must have a new wardrobe. A short conversation with the footman Brickson, who still swelled with pride at the chance to take over temporary valet duties, had given Gabriel the names of the most highly regarded tailors and bootmakers. Evidently, Gabriel had been correct in the man's ambitions; Brickson knew a great deal about male fashion.

"Some of the military gentlemen prefer Shultz, milord, but Weston is favored for evening and day wear by the most discerning," Brickson explained, his tone serious. "And as for bootmakers, there's a shop on Bond Street. . . ."

So Gabriel went downstairs and donned his hat and gloves. When Jowers hurried up, the butler asked, "Do you require a carriage, milord?"

Gabriel thought for a moment. He would have walked, but at midafternoon, his attire was still most incongruous, and he had no wish to attract attention. "Will it inconvenience the ladies?" he asked.

Jowers blinked, then said, "Um, no, milord. The ladies have no plans to go out this afternoon."

"Very well, then, yes," he said. And he rode to Bond Street in luxurious ease in the family chaise, with its thick squabs and carved wood inlays.

Gabriel was ushered in to the tailor's establishment by a courteous underling, although the man gave his outfit a curious glance. He was left to wait in a small but well-appointed anteroom until the great man himself came in.

"Milord." The tailor bowed slightly. "Welcome to our humble establishment."

"Thank you." Gabriel acknowledged the salute. "My luggage has had a sad accident, and my clothing is in shreds. Therefore, I am in urgent need of your assistance."

The man nodded slowly. "Yes, milord. I regret that I am not familiar with your family. But I would say"—he looked closely at the jacket that Gabriel wore—"that this attire is French made?"

"Yes, indeed." It was a discreet but reasonable question. Englishmen retired to the Continent when they could not pay their bills and the duns became too urgent. "I have been living abroad for some time, but when I inherited the title— an obscure one, to be sure, but still, bearing its own responsibilities, it was best that I return." He might as well take advantage of Psyche's story, Gabriel thought cynically. "And since my betrothal to Miss Hill, I must have a wardrobe suitable for the many social engagements that must follow."

"Miss Psyche Hill?" the tailor asked, his tone sharper.

"Yes, indeed," Gabriel agreed, "I am most fortunate to have secured her regard."

"Ah, allow me to offer my felicitations," the other man said, bowing again even more deeply. His expression became much more genial. As the fiancé of the wealthy Miss Hill, Gabriel's status had just increased enormously, not to mention the tailor's odds of seeing his bills paid. The man snapped his fingers, and an assistant materialized at his elbow, measuring tape in hand. "Let us just take your measure, milord."

Some time later, Gabriel found himself in an inner room, wearing a thick velvet robe and waiting for the assistant to return with his clothes. There had been measurements galore, and discussions of fabric and cut, although, happily, not as uninhibited as with the hopeful tailor that Psyche had recruited. "I see that his lordship favors the latest French style," Weston had said, "but I must point out the advantages of the British cut. . . ."

Now Gabriel relaxed in a comfortable chair with a glass of port; the port was only mediocre, but the prospect of a new and elegant wardrobe was certainly pleasing. His "engagement" to Psyche had developed unforeseen advantages. He would not, of course, allow her to incur his expenses. As soon as he got into a decent game, he would reline his empty pockets and pay his bills. Then, when he took control of his new-won estate, he could forget the hand-to-mouth existence he had endured for so long. . . .

When the door opened again, he didn't bother to look around, expecting the assistant. Instead, a new voice said, "By all that's holy—Gabriel, is that really you?"

Gabriel stiffened in instinctive alarm. If his deception was discovered now, he could say good-bye to his new clothes, to his pose as the fiancé of a rich young lady, and he'd end up on the street with only one set of raiment to his name. He turned very slowly, and then, despite himself, smiled.

"Freddy!"

"It is you! Came in to tell Weston to run me up a couple new coats and thought I was seeing a ghost, don't y'know!" The young man before him had changed very little since the days they had been up at Oxford together. His thin blond hair, pale blue eyes, and round face, which always looked a trifle foolish in expression, had made him the brunt of many a joke by his peers, first at Eton and later even at university.

It had been Gabriel who had stood up for the smaller boy, fighting at his side against bullies who chose to make fun of his small stature and less than stellar wits. But the Honorable Frederick Allen Wyrick III had a good heart, and he was very loyal to his friends. And he did not, apparently, forget them.

"Haven't set eyes on you in—what?—well over a dozen years?" Freddy was saying. He had paused in the doorway in surprise; now he rushed into the room and grabbed Gabriel's hand to shake it vigorously. "That business with the woman—bad business, what, but not your fault, I was sure of it. . . ."

"You were the only one, then," Gabriel said, his own voice grim.

"Should have come to me, Gabriel," Freddy said, a bit shyly. "My father might have kicked up a fuss, but I would have stood by you."

Gabriel could not help but be touched by his friend's sincerity. "Thank you," he said solemnly. "I am glad to know that now, even if I did not know it then."

"Went abroad, did you?" Freddy continued, his expression curious. "That's what I heard, anyhow. And now you're back! Dashed glad to see you, old man."

"And I to see you," Gabriel told him, quite honestly. It had been a very long time since he had encountered a friend from his school days; he had often wondered if he would ever see friendly faces from his past. But the timing now was not the best—

The door opened again, and the assistant put his head in the door. "Milord, here are the coat and trousers that we were making for Mr.—for another client; we have adjusted them to fit your measurements, milord. They will allow you to be seen until your other items are ready. We will send your own garments back to Miss Hill's town house."

"Thank you," Gabriel said. In the corner of his eye, he saw Freddy frowning in bewilderment.

Fortunately, his friend waited until the man had left before asking, "You have the title, Gabriel? But—your father and brother, um . . ."

"It's Tarrington," Gabriel explained. "The title, I mean."

"What?" Freddy looked bewildered, as indeed he might. "But—"

"It came to me through a cousin's death," Gabriel said quickly. "A distant connection, actually."

"But your father, your older brother, wouldn't they be—"

"Um, normally, yes. But there are special circumstances having to do with my grandmother's second marriage and that disgraceful affair with the vicar's nephew—we don't like to talk about it, Freddy, you understand."

"Right-o," Freddy agreed, though he obviously didn't; he still looked puzzled. "Whatever you say."

Good old Freddy. He might not be the brightest twig to fall off his family tree, but he was unfailingly loyal; Gabriel felt a rush of affection. "I have to be back for dinner, but we have time for a quick drink first. Have some of the tailor's regrettably insipid wine, and let's catch up on old times, eh?"

"Just the thing," Freddy agreed with enthusiasm. "But not this rot—it'll ruin your palette if you're not careful. Tell you what, let's walk down to my club and I'll introduce you to some nice chaps."

That wasn't what Gabriel had in mind at all; he was supposed to be staying out of sight. But he couldn't push even Freddy's credibility any further, or the bubble might burst. Do the normal thing, despite strange circumstances, that was the surest way to pull off a scam. He knew that from past experience.

"Very well, but it will have to be a quick drink. I have a solicitor to see this afternoon."

"Ah, the new inheritance." Freddy nodded wisely. "Tedious, all that, but worth it in the end, eh?"

"I certainly hope so," Gabriel said, with feeling. "Just let me get dressed." He reached for his hastily put-together new garments.

"Not bad, under the circumstances." Freddy looked at the navy blue, severely tailored coat with a critical eye. "Not quite up to Weston's usual standards, perhaps, but considering your plight . . ." He brushed his own immaculate lapels absentmindedly. Freddy had always been a neat, almost prim little boy, which had only aggravated the bullies' attentions. However, judging from his own outfit, he had grown into a man with excellent taste, Gabriel thought, hiding a grin.

"Feel for you, old chap, all those years abroad. Nothing worse than being without decent English tailoring. . . ." Freddy patted his schoolmate on the shoulder and aimed him toward the door. "But you're back at last, and Weston will soon have that taken care of. Let me advise you about the best bootmakers, and as for shirts . . ."

This time Gabriel did laugh as he walked out side by side with his old friend.

Seven

He returned to the town house in good time for the evening meal. Jowers met him at the door, nodding in approval of the new coat and trousers. Gabriel handed over his hat and gloves and a handsome new walking stick he had acquired—the news of his "engagement" to the wealthy Miss Hill had a wonderful way of procuring unlimited credit, he had discovered to his amusement—and thought he detected a look of distinct sympathy in the butler's eyes.

"Did my evening clothes and my new shirts and neck-cloths arrive?" he asked.

"Yes, milord, they have been taken up to your chamber," the butler assured him. "You have just time to change before dinner, milord. The ladies are in the drawing room having a glass of sherry."

Gabriel nodded and proceeded up the staircase to his room; he found the footman/valet Brickson there, waiting to assist him in changing his clothes. Gabriel donned his own evening dress—the harried tailor had had no time to effect more miracles of assembly, but there was a new evening coat on order, in addition to morning coats, riding habits, street clothing, shirts, even underwear and nightshirts—as Brickson stood ready to assist. Then Gabriel took a clean neckcloth from the servant and arranged it with a careless ease into his own signature style. He had had aspirations of dandyism as a lad, he remembered, smiling a little now at his own folly. Perhaps that was one reason he and Freddy had hit it off as small boys, both with precocious vanity and big aspirations.

Gabriel could have cringed when he remembered some of his and Freddy's "costumes." They had considered themselves all the crack in their heavily ruffled shirts, garishly colored waistcoats, and ridiculously high shirt points. What had finally cured him of the high "ears," as the shirt points were called, was a very nasty eye infection that poor Freddy had suffered from a scratch inflicted by one of the starched points. Gabriel shook his head in bewilderment. How had he ever thought all that fluff was manly or attractive? Thank God for Sylvie. If she hadn't taken him in hand and discreetly guided his taste and taught him a bit of restraint . . .

His fingers stumbled for a moment on the folds of his cravat, then regained their normal dexterity. He would not think of her at all, let alone with gratitude. Sylvie had been a woman of many talents, he thought cynically. She had skillfully controlled him in a manner that appalled him to remember. By turns needy and demanding, she had played with his youthful passion like a puppeteer with an amusing new toy. He had thought her all that was lovely and womanly and had offered her all his naive passion. In return, she had destroyed his life.

No, he thought in disgust. They had destroyed each other.

Of course, enduring a scandal and then exile, running for his life, surviving by his wits, had taught him that life held much more important decisions to be made than the color of his waistcoat or the arrangement of his cravat. But, Gabriel thought as he gazed at the results of his efforts in the looking glass and gave an approving nod, he still liked to be pleasingly attired. When he finished, Brickson dusted the shoulders of his black coat with a soft brush and stood back, the valet's expression admiring.

Gabriel hid his smile at the man's pride and nodded his

thanks. "No need to wait up for me," he told the man. "After the party, I may escort the ladies home and then go out again for, um, other entertainment."

The man nodded, his expression revealing no surprise. "Good luck, milord, with the dice or the cards or any other game of chance you might engage in."

Gabriel grinned. "No ladies of the evening, Brickson, if that's what you're thinking. A man engaged to Miss Hill would be mad to pursue dross when he has a vision of pure gold before his eyes."

Brickson blinked, and Gabriel saw the slight lift of his lips before the servant regained a suitable expression of impassivity.

Leaving the man to chuckle in private, Gabriel descended the steps. He found Psyche and her sister in the drawing room—Circe was allowed to eat dinner downstairs with the family when they had no company, he had discovered—as well as Aunt Sophie, who was sipping a glass of deep-colored wine. No uninspired sherry for Aunt Sophie, Gabriel thought, suppressing his own grin.

"Good evening, ladies," he said, making his bow to Aunt Sophie, as befitted her senior status, then to Psyche and Circe in turn. Gabriel had already turned with the intention to pour himself a scotch when Psyche's appearance registered on his suddenly befuddled brain.

Gabriel jerked back to face her, not even caring that he stared. He also chose to ignore Sophie's snort of laughter and Circe's wide-eyed look of surprise. He ignored all save for the vision of angelic loveliness that stood before him. In a gown of silvery blue, Psyche glowed.

No, he thought, searching for the right word in his mind. She shimmered.

Her golden hair was twisted atop her head into a mass of curls. The silky fabric of her gown fitted tightly to ripe breasts and slim arms before skimming rounded hips and long, long legs. Diamonds glittered at her ears, neck, and hair. White gloves encased her arms to above the elbows with yet more diamonds encircling her delicate wrist. He had never seen such lush beauty in such an angelic guise.

No, angel wasn't the right term for his Psyche. An angel wouldn't respond to such obvious admiration with cool, cautious eyes, or prim, rigid posture. His Psyche was too proud, yet too full of passionate promise beneath her conventional veneer, to be anyone's angel.

And when the hell had he started thinking of this willful chit as *his*?

He strode to where she stood waiting, took her gloved hand in his own, and—just to wipe the carefully distant look from her face—he pressed his lips against the inside of her wrist. He watched smugly as her lips parted on her indrawn breath.

At this moment, he could have cheerfully scrapped his new estate or even his famous luck to take this gorgeous creature back upstairs to his room and strip her of her gown, her diamonds, and her precious manners. Want was a grinding ache in his gut as he stared into her accusing eyes. No angel could glare at him with such demanding authority . . . no angel, but— Normally, Gabriel would have laughed at such fanciful thoughts. But he had an alarming suspicion the joke was on him.

"You are aptly named, dear Miss Hill." He kept his voice low and intimate and did not step away from her, remaining close enough to see her pulse flutter nervously in the hollow of her pale throat. "You are a goddess, to be sure."

Long golden lashes dipped to hide her reaction to his words. Psyche did not answer. He suspected she was not so much flustered as wondering gravely what his new game was. He grinned. He couldn't help it. He was starting to understand her and, strangely enough, it delighted him.

Her curtsy was slight, and her expression cool. "I hope you had better luck with the tailor of your choice, milord."

"Indeed I did," he told her. "You were most kind to try to help me, but some things a man really must do for himself."

"Such as acquiring his own title?" Psyche had recovered

her usual chilly poise; she murmured to escape the attention of the others.

"Actors are accustomed to trying on new names as easily as new suits," he returned, keeping his voice low, too. "It's a skill that I am perfectly comfortable with."

"I daresay!" Her eyes flashed dangerously, and he thought he might have baited her sufficiently; no need to elicit, over such a trifle, the passion that he knew bubbled beneath her icy demeanor. There would be more appropriate times to evoke a spark from Psyche—and more appropriate places, he thought, with a glance toward the fascinated Sophie and Circe.

Sophie downed the rest of her drink in a healthy swallow and set the crystal goblet down on the little piecrust table at her side. "Psyche," she said, coming to her niece's rescue, "go see about dinner. An old woman could wither away waiting for her supper in this household."

Gabriel saw the relief in Psyche's eyes as she turned from him to obey her aunt's orders. But, to Gabriel's pleasure, Jower's arrival prevented her from going far.

"Dinner is served," Jowers said from the doorway.

Gabriel offered his arm, and after a slight hesitation, Psyche tucked her hand into the crook of his arm. It was only a polite gesture, the sort offered to the merest acquaintance, but with Psyche, it was so much more. He was acutely aware of her, standing so close, the slightest scent of rose oil that drifted from her skin, the faint rustle of silk from her gown; they all inflamed his senses and made him wish fervently for a brief time alone with her.

"I hope Cook has made that caramel pudding again," Circe said, innocent of the currents that swirled beneath the surface. She waited politely for Aunt Sophie to pick up her walking stick.

Reminded of his duties, Gabriel offered his other arm to the older woman, who waved him away.

"Do better at my own pace," she said. "Come along, Circe."

"And keep your appetite for the food, sir," Psyche muttered to him as they led the way into the dining room.

"Of course. What would make you suspect otherwise?" Gabriel had mastered his moment of longing, and his tone was innocent, but she continued to watch him suspiciously as she took her seat at the table.

With servants in the room, dinner conversation was confined to superficial topics. Psyche chatted about people he might meet at the party.

"And you'll likely also meet Thomas Atkins, the second earl of Whitkin's son; his wife has dark hair and—"

"Good heavens, child." Aunt Sophie shook her head as she motioned to the footman for another helping of sauce. "Do you intend to list every member of the Ton currently in London? You'll put us all to sleep before we e'er reach the party."

"Oh, sorry," Psyche muttered. "I just—just wanted to give Lord Tarrington some idea of what to expect."

The fact was, her stomach was in knots the closer they came to his public debut in front of England's elite. It was all very well, as she had told herself earlier, to remember the excellent acting job he had done in front of her relatives. After all, her maid had coached the man for several hours, given him extensive information on who was who and who liked what and which topics to avoid. Now he would be on his own; she'd had no time to prepare him properly, and she'd always heard that an actor was nothing without his lines. What if Gabriel froze totally, and said something so gauche that he put not just himself but Psyche and her whole family to shame?

She'd just hoped to give him some pointers. The man himself had a rather sardonic gleam in his deep blue eyes, so she wasn't sure if he appreciated her good intentions or not, but if even Aunt Sophie was noticing, she'd better be still.

Yet when Psyche reached for her glass of wine, she saw that her hand shook; she took a deep breath. They would get through this, they would, she would be there, she would guide him, they would not be exposed, humiliated. . . .

Gabriel watched the signs of his employer's agitation and hid a smile. Worried about his first public appearance, was she? He had his own reason for anxiety, but he kept it under control. He'd listened with careful attention to her catalogue of expected guests. A few of the names were familiar, but as he had spent little time in London before his exile, he did not feel in any imminent danger of his unmasking. There might be other schoolmates among the Ton, but not all, surely, would have as keen an eye and memory as Freddy.

Afterwards, Circe said good night to her sister and stopped to regard Gabriel seriously. "Enjoy the party," she told him. "But be on your guard."

"Why on earth would he need to do that?" Aunt Sophie demanded, her eyes narrowing.

Circe blushed; she had obviously not meant her aunt to overhear. "Only that Psyche says there are gossips who will fall on any suspicious—I mean, will make the worst of any unusual remark."

"I'm sure Tarrington has braved more dangerous gales than a bunch of windy old hens with too much time on their hands." Their aunt sniffed. "Off to bed with you, child."

Circe nodded and slipped out of the room, but Gabriel felt Psyche's anxious gaze on him. Gabriel felt only a mild sense of anticipation; but then, he always enjoyed a challenge. "Shall we go, my dear?"

The footman had brought Psyche her cloak; she arranged it around her shoulders and pulled on the gloves she had removed to dine. Gabriel had as yet no cloak—that was on order, too—but the evening was mild, and he had procured hat and gloves during the afternoon. He helped Aunt Sophie into the carriage, then turned to take the hand of the younger woman.

Psyche hesitated a moment before allowing him to take it. Even through the thin gloves he could feel the warmth of her fingers, the spark that seemed to flash between them when they stood so close—suddenly he was eager to reach the party; even a small affair was likely to have dancing, and he hungered to hold Psyche in his arms, to pull her even closer and—

"Milord?" Psyche said, her cheeks looking suspiciously warm.

"Yes." Giving himself a mental shake, he pulled himself together and assisted her into the carriage, climbing in to sit on the other side. It was not as satisfactory as sitting beside her, but at least he could gaze at her countenance, shadowy in the dim streetlights and the glow from the carriage lamps outside. The light played across the planes of her face, her sculpted cheekbones and firm, stubborn jaw. As if aware of his stare, she looked pointedly out the small pane into the street outside, astir with evening traffic.

"Hope Sally has better fare at this party," Aunt Sophie was grumbling. "Her pastries are a disgrace; she should fire her chef." In a rare show of affection, she patted Psyche tenderly on her arm. "Not every household had such a fine manager as you, my dear. Sally would do well to listen to you more often."

Gabriel watched as Psyche's expression softened with surprise and then pleasure. She took her aunt's hand in her own and pressed it gently. "Thank you, Aunt Sophie."

The old woman squeezed back before loosening her hold and clearing her throat. Her voice was extra gruff as if to make up for her momentary lapse into sentimentality. "Pish posh. It'll be a good thing when you are married at last, Psyche, then I can sit at home in front of my own fire instead of gadding about like some social nitwit."

Psyche's lips spread into a fond smile. She knew her aunt too well to be offended. "But you like Sally and her husband, Aunt."

"I like them better when the weather is dry, and my bones cease aching," Aunt Sophie retorted.

When they reached the street where their hostess lived, a jostle of carriages and chaises suggested that the party was not so very small. After a short wait, their carriage was able to approach the entrance, and Gabriel got out to hand the ladies down. This time his touch on Psyche's hand was brief and she avoided meeting his gaze. But perhaps she was only watching her step; the street was muddy and littered.

Inside, a line of guests waited to climb the staircase and enter the drawing room. Gabriel could hear the chatter of the guests already assembled, and someone tuning a violin. After the ladies removed their outer garments and Gabriel surrendered his hat, they too mounted the stairs, slowly because of Aunt Sophie, who was puffing by the time she reached the top. Psyche managed to whisper in his ear, "You must remember to greet our hostess first, thank her for allowing you to come without a proper invitation, and—" She bit off the rest when Sophie glanced at them with suspicion.

Did she think he was a total simpleton? No, she was trying to assist the hireling she thought he was.

The footman, with only a glance, announced their names to the room, and there was a stir of heads turning. Their hostess hurried forward to curtsy to Aunt Sophie.

"Damned crush," the old lady said. "Find me a comfortable chair, Sally. I'm not as young as I was, you know."

"Of course, dear Sophie," Sally Forsyth said, smiling. "Here, my man will lead you to a comfortable seat and fetch you a glass of wine."

When the older lady had been tended to, Sally reached to take Psyche's hand. "Psyche, my dear, at last we get to meet the mystery man! I'm all agog."

Psyche managed an appropriate smile, but it was hardly necessary. Sally had already turned to regard the man beside her with frank appraisal. "My dear Lord Tarrington, welcome."

Gabriel bowed over her hand. "It was very kind of you to allow me to come without a proper invitation," he said on cue. But Psyche had not instructed him to smile just so, his blue eyes glinting with that slight hint of mischief—as if he and Sally were engaged in some delightful scheme together—that was so irresistible.

"I am only too happy to meet you," Sally told him, her face aglow under the impact of his easy charm and handsome face. "This is not a grand affair at all, but indeed, as dear Psyche's fiancé, I would not wish you to miss this chance to meet some of her other old friends."

"Nor would I," the actor agreed readily.

Psyche gritted her teeth. He was following instructions, she would give him that. And his manner was smooth, but his luck couldn't last. He had to slip up eventually, reveal his low origins or his bogus background, and then where would she be? Oh, if only he had disappeared after the family dinner, as she had originally planned.

Yet she was also aware of the glances of the women around them, the hint of envy in their stares, and it wasn't so bad, she knew in her heart of hearts, to be seen with such a charming, handsome, quick-witted man, after having had only Percy at her elbow for so long.

As if her thought had conjured him up, like a bad fairy, she saw her cousin making his purposeful way through the other guests to join them. She stifled a groan. But by the time he approached her, she had her expression under control.

"Good evening, Percy," she said, her tone courteous. "You remember Lord Tarrington, of course."

Gabriel made a polite bow. But his attention was still claimed by their hostess; Sally continued to chat with Gabriel, her expression animated as she neglected the newest arrivals shamefully. She was standing too close to him, too, Psyche noted, almost leaning on his arm. Just because Sally was married to her staid, boring, balding husband, did she think she could forget all propriety? Really, the effect this man had on women was scandalous. Psyche should have added a warning to Gabriel about too particular attention. Perhaps she should go over now and—

But Percy was still talking. "Hard to forget him," he said, with only the barest nod to her fake fiancé. "When you have broken my heart, disregarded my long-standing passion—"

Psyche decided to affect a sudden deafness; Aunt Sophie did it all the time and it seemed to soothe the old woman's nerves amazingly. "Where is Uncle Wilfred? I sent him a letter about the engagement settlement. . . ." she began.

It worked; Percy was distracted. "Father is at home. His gout is acting up. Anyhow, need to speak to you about that."

"My housekeeper has an excellent beef jelly that might be of help. She would be glad to send you the recipe—" Psyche said, her tone innocent.

"No, no," Percy interrupted impatiently. "Not about the gout! I mean the engagement, of course, your engagement. Let us step aside for a moment."

"If Uncle has any questions, he should be speaking to my solicitor. Percy, let go of me. I have no desire for any tête-à-tête—" But to Psyche's alarm, Percy had a firm grip on her arm and he guided her toward the corner of the room. Psyche had to fight to keep her expression civil. She needed to stay near Gabriel; what if he made some awful blunder?

"What is the matter with you?" she demanded. "Let go of me at once, and for that matter, stop being so rude to my future husband."

Percy snorted, an inelegant sound that reminded her of a dyspeptic pig. "He is an impostor, Psyche."

"Don't be silly," she protested, but she felt a quiver run through her; she had to steady her voice with an effort. "You have a bug in your bonnet, Percy, and you must let go of this silly idea. Just because you don't know of Lord Tarrington's family—"

"But nobody else does, either," Percy argued, his face turning redder and his cheeks swelling with emotion until she thought he might burst. "No one I asked has heard of any Tarringtons. And, Psyche . . ." He paused for dramatic effect, but she refused to play along.

"I think I need some lemonade, Percy. Would you be a dear—"

"I've inquired of everyone I know, and nobody—nobody—Psyche, has heard of this supposed title!" Percy told her, his eyes wide.

But Psyche had been prepared for this.

"Oh, tosh, Percy. So his family is not well known. That means nothing at all."

Percy's face turned even redder with frustration.

"Yes, well, nonetheless, Psyche, I beg you to reconsider. The man is only after your money."

"But, Percy, I thought you believed me to be beautiful?" Psyche gazed at him, her eyes wide.

He was immediately flustered. "Of course I do, no doubt, no doubt, but—"

"And sweet and womanly and properly chaste, did you not tell me that so many times?"

"Course I did, but—"

"So how can you doubt that Lord Tarrington would love me for myself, Percy? After all, you were not motivated solely by my fortune when you pursued me, were you?" she asked, her voice utterly guileless.

"Um, no, no," Percy said. His expression was perplexed; he had been outmaneuvered and he didn't seem to see how it had happened.

"Then if you could love me for myself alone, I'm sure another man could. I know you will be prepared to wish us happy, as will my uncle, eventually," Psyche said coolly.

"No, no, Psyche, you misunderstand me."

Percy waved his hands in the air. She took advantage of his moment of agitation to slip under his arm and hurry back toward the heart of the party.

"Psyche, wait!"

Ignoring her cousin's plea, Psyche looked about. There was Sally; she had finally released her bogus lord and stood talking to two elderly women. Where was that man now? She needed to be close by, to offer him guidance if he faltered. She would find him chatting with another pretty stranger, no doubt, Psyche thought crossly. Really, the man had no shame.

However, when she located Gabriel, she saw that he was standing by a side table, holding a glass of wine and conversing amiably with Aunt Mavis and Cousin Matilda.

Cousin Matilda looked flushed with delight, and even Mavis had unbent under Gabriel's masculine allure; her usual scowl was replaced by a slightly bemused expression, as if she wanted to smile but was afraid of looking foolish.

"Ah, there you are, my dear. I was just telling Cousin Matilda and Aunt Mavis how you had so unkindly deserted me," Gabriel said as Psyche approached them.

"I deserted you? You were practically attached to our hostess," Psyche snapped. "I was in the kitchen fetching a cleaver to separate the two of you."

Matilda looked alarmed, and Mavis gave a twisted smile. "Fighting already, are you?" her aunt demanded. "Should think the two of you were already married."

Psyche blushed. The last thing she meant to do was to sound jealous. "Of course not," she said. "I didn't wish Gabriel to be monopolized, that is all. Sally is a sweet thing, but a bit of a flibbertigibbet."

"No, she has not your keen wit, my dearest," Gabriel agreed. "But of course I did not wish to be backward in expressing my appreciation to our hostess."

As she had instructed, the wicked glint in his eyes reminded her.

"Yes, but you also don't want to keep her from her other guests," Psyche said, her tone still tart.

"Certainly not," he agreed, his expression unrepentant. "And there are so many agreeable ladies and gentlemen here that I need to meet, and all, apparently, friends of my darling Psyche."

He was obviously baiting her again. The thought of him talking to everyone at the party sent a spasm of alarm through her that Psyche could barely hide.

She almost said a word, learned at the age of thirteen when she lingered in the stable eavesdropping on the hostlers, that would have made her aunt swoon. With difficulty, Psyche smoothed her expression and held her tongue. Drat the man for always managing to upset her so easily.

The musicians were tuning their instruments—the dancing was about to begin. She looked up to see Gabriel watching her, as if he understood perfectly the turmoil of emotions that ran through her mind. She pressed her lips together firmly. He would not continue to provoke her, she would not allow it. Someone had to keep a clear head tonight!

"We must have the first dance, my dear—"

But she had so much to instruct him. "Ah, no, why don't we sit at the side and talk for a moment—"

"I thought the first dance would be expected of us," he said. "Newly affianced lovebirds, you know."

Psyche bit her lip. He was making fun of her. But he was right, of course. Still, one lucky guess did not mean that he was competent to be left alone in this veritable jungle of social niceties. She could not relax her guard.

He bowed to the other ladies. "Later, I will request the pleasure of your hand, Matilda, in one of the round dances."

Blushing with pleasure, Matilda nodded. Gabriel grasped Psyche's hand and was leading her through the crowd to the portion of the big room where the dancers were taking their places.

Psyche gave him a quick, anxious glance.

"Yes, I do know how to dance," he told her gravely before she could express this newest worry, and Psyche relaxed for an instant until another thought struck her.

"You will have to do it now, you know," she whispered as they took their places in the form.

"Do what?" He made his bow to her and moved out into the first set of steps.

"Dance with Matilda!" she whispered again.

"Of course. Did you think I would say such a thing and then deliberately break my word?" His glance at her was quizzical and slightly wounded.

She almost blushed, feeling guilty and not sure why. She was only trying to help him, as much as herself. She had no way of knowing if he understood the careful code of conduct practiced by polite society, at least well enough to maintain his pose. His manners had seemed smooth enough at the family dinner the night before, but he could hardly realize all the subtleties involved in his assumed identity. An actor he might be, but how could he, after all, have had the chance to study the upper classes that closely?

They circled another couple, and when Psyche could

safely speak again, she muttered, "I didn't mean—that is, I don't—"

But the dance had separated them again, and he looked at her with a smooth smile that made her moment of anxiety seem foolish. He did not care what she thought of him, why should he? This whole thing was merely another acting job, extended only from his greed, his desire for a heavier purse. That hurt she thought she had glimpsed in the depths of his deep blue eyes—she was being too fanciful, Psyche told herself.

She stopped trying to talk and concentrated on the dance. The man was graceful, she would give him that; he had the controlled grace of a swordsman. No doubt he had studied fencing in order to act Shakespearean tragedies. The thought led to another, of what Gabriel, with his perfect face, would look like dressed in old-fashioned garments, Elizabethan hose that clung to his muscular thighs . . . and then she blushed at the direction of her own thoughts.

Good heavens, what had come over her? No wonder sensible women lost every vestige of their wits when Gabriel smiled at them. She was no longer angry at Sally. No man had the right to so handsome a face, to such masculine beauty. And to have broad shoulders and well-sculpted arms and legs, to have that irrepressible wit dancing in the deep blue depths of his eyes, to be intelligent and articulate and . . . and yet to be a total fraud. It was too bad.

Musing sadly on the inequities of the universe, Psyche finished the dance in silence. When the music ended, she made her curtsy to her partner, and he held her hand a moment too long before releasing it.

"Did I displease you, my sweet Psyche?" he murmured. "You are very quiet, of a sudden."

She sighed. "Of course not. I'm just a bit on edge. Let us find a couple of chairs so that I can instruct you upon—"

But they were interrupted once more. Sally was walking toward them. Psyche bit back her words and stood very straight. This business of living a lie was downright exhausting; one had to be ceaselessly vigilant.

"Sophie is asking for you, Psyche," Sally said brightly. "And I have several people who are anxious to meet your fiancé."

All female, no doubt, Psyche wanted to say, but she controlled herself with an effort. She wanted to grab him by the superfine of his coat and keep him beside her. Instead, she had to settle for giving Gabriel a warning look, then she headed toward the side of the room.

She found Aunt Sophie sitting comfortably in a wing chair, chatting with several other older ladies. "There you are, child," her aunt said. "I wanted you to greet some old friends of mine."

Psyche schooled her expression to one of polite interest. She could not forget her own manners because of her concern over the actor and how long he could maintain this pretense.

"And besides," her irascible relative added, "doesn't do to hang on that young man of yours like a lovesick mooncalf, no matter how fair his face or pleasing his form."

Psyche stiffened, meeting the old woman's sharp-eyed gaze. No indeed, she could not make a spectacle of herself, nor stir up just the suspicion she was trying to avoid. So with this not so subtle encouragement, she turned her attention away from the party to chat with her aunt's friends.

It was a quarter of an hour before it seemed natural to excuse herself and return to the mass of guests. Where was Gabriel? She located him in the midst of a bevy of young ladies, all flushed and laughing, smiling and fluttering their lashes at her supposed fiancé.

Had they no sense at all, Psyche thought, irritated despite herself. Could she interrupt them, or would it seem too pointed? As she hesitated, she found herself next to the mother of one of the young things. "I'm amazed that you did it at last, Psyche," Mrs. Monnat said as she sipped a glass of wine.

"What?" Psyche frowned. "Did you think me so on the shelf that I had no hopes of finding a husband?"

"Not at all, child," the matron said, laughing a little.

"With your fortune, you could always find a match. But I thought you would never shake off that odious cousin of yours long enough to make a connection with another eligible gentleman."

"Oh." Psyche relaxed. "It wasn't easy."

"And to find such a charming fellow, with such a way about him—you will be the envy of all the other single ladies. He is so much more engaging than your poor cousin."

"Your Lucille seems to think so," Psyche said wryly.

Lucille's mama smiled, and her tone was matter-of-fact. "She has enough sense not to fall for a betrothed gentleman, and he is such an accomplished flirt, the practice will do her good. She is still a bit shy, not much at ease in society, and she has nothing like your dowry to tempt the more practical of men. Not that we aspire for a marquis, of course, but I should like to see her happily settled."

Psyche felt ashamed. "Lucille is a delightful girl, and I'm sure she will find someone who deserves her."

"Thank you, my dear, I hope so," Mrs. Monnat agreed, fanning herself.

They watched the group together. As the musicians struck up another tune, Psyche saw that Gabriel was excusing himself to the ladies clustered around him. He walked to the side of the room, rescued Matilda from a group of older ladies, and led her to the dance floor. Matilda looked flushed with happiness, and Psyche felt a surge of unexpected pride. He had not forgotten; she was both relieved that he was—so far—conducting himself properly and pleased for her plump, sweet-natured cousin's sake.

Sally joined them in a swirl of silken skirts. She said, her tone half-serious, "Gracious, Psyche, he is scrumptious! I am so envious of you I could spit!"

Psyche smiled again, but this time she felt her lips stretch a little too wide as the tension returned. If they only knew the truth, she thought, suppressing a quiver of anxiety, no one would be envious. Instead, she would be the laughing-stock of the Ton. And Percy would have her firmly in his power. *Oh, please*, she thought, glancing again at Gabriel and the grace with which he moved through the dance, *please don't betray us*!

"I thought this was only going to be a small party," she said to their hostess, her tone almost accusing.

"Oh, it began that way, but you know how it is," Sally answered. "You invite Cousin Georgia, and then you have to invite her odious son, and then the son's promised wife, and then her parents, and . . ."

Psyche listened to Sally chatter on until the dance ended, then she saw Gabriel bow to Matilda, escort her off the floor into a group of young people, and in a minute or two leave her with a callow youth whose neckcloth almost obscured his chin. How Gabriel had managed to get the shy Matilda in conversation with a gentleman her own age, instead of stuck in the corner with the matrons as usual, Psyche had no idea, but she admired him for it.

He was approaching their little group. At last, she could take him aside and give him more lessons in deportment. Gabriel bowed to her and the other women. "If you would permit me, ladies," he said. "My fiancée has promised this dance to me."

She had done no such thing. "No, no," she said. "Let us find a quiet spot, I have so much to say, and—"

"The chat can wait," he said, smiling at the others, but his tone was unexpectedly firm. "This time, you shall listen to me, dear Psyche."

And somehow Psyche found herself being led to the dance floor once more, and this time, Gabriel was putting his hand on her waist and pulling her so close, so close. . . .

Psyche found it hard to catch her breath. "I don't—I mean, I'm not—"

"You are allowed to waltz; I asked Aunt Sophie earlier," Gabriel cut off her first flustered attempt at an excuse. "You are not a blushing novitiate in her first Season, but a sophisticated lady who is quite at home on the dance floor. And I have had enough instruction for this evening, if you please."

"I was only trying to assist you," Psyche said, then

wished she could take back the words. She had been thinking mainly of herself, admit it. But surely he did not *want* to fail.

But at the moment, social niceties seemed to be the last thing on Gabriel's mind. His grip was so firm, his arm so strong, there was nothing for her to do but be swept along as they circled the dance floor.

It was a strange feeling. Of course she had waltzed many times, with many partners, including the stumbling Percy, who always clutched her too tightly and tended to step on her feet. But no one else had given her this feeling of no longer being in control, of being guided smoothly and with consideration, but most definitely directed. The independent and strong-willed Miss Hill should have been bothered by the new sensation. She was, Psyche assured herself. She was most bothered indeed.

Except it was such an unexpected change of mood that it felt almost a relief, to relax for just one moment, to let someone else be in control for just a little while. . . .

What on earth could she be thinking? It was the effect this too smooth actor had on all the women who came too close to him, and she refused to be another. She must be firm.

Except it was hard to be firm when he spun her about with such practiced ease. Never had she felt this way about any other dance partner, but Gabriel leaned so close, with his immodest good looks, his clear-eyed gaze, the dark blue eyes, which always seemed to hold a fire in their lapis depths that suggested so much smoldering passion. . . .

She shook herself mentally; this was not the way a proper young lady should think. She refused to fall under his spell. The man was not just an actor, he must be a magician as well. With great effort, she pulled her gaze away from his face and instead looked down at his well-tied neckcloth.

"I call it the Sinclair," he told her lightly. "I invented it when I was up at Oxford and had aspirations to be the next dandy, cock of the walk, and all that."

"What?" She was startled enough to once more meet his

eyes. That was a tactical mistake. This time, those clear blue orbs seemed to have captured her within their lucid depths, and she could not look away. Her throat felt dry. "What are you talking about?"

"The arrangement of my neckcloth, of course. I thought you were interested in male fashion?" He was gently teasing, but she blushed in earnest at the reminder of their earlier dispute.

"I was only trying to help," she said, her tone dignified. "Just as with my—my advice in social matters—"

"I know that, and I should not have lost my temper," he agreed.

"Is that why you asked me to *waltz*?" she demanded, feeling suddenly irritable herself. "So that you could torment me with such reminders?"

"No, my dear." He turned her, pulling her even closer. "I asked you to dance because I have been praying for a waltz since before we set out for the party."

"Really," Psyche began to demur, "you're too—"

"Because I have ached to hold you in my arms," Gabriel finished, his tone caressing, "and if I must play the part of your lover, you must allow me the indulgence of a little loverly solicitude."

She could not speak. He was teasing her again, of course, but still, his eyes were so warm, his expression so intense, and the music swirled around them like soft waves in a southern sea, carrying them away from the crowded room, away from the hum of conversation that competed with the thin strains of the tune. Perhaps some far part of her mind tried to warn her: the man is an actor; you cannot believe a word he says.

But for this one moment, this lyrical moment as they swayed together, so close that she could catch the smell of clean linen, blended with a masculine hint of musk and warm skin, Psyche's usual self-control deserted her. Even more strangely, she did not attempt to regain her customary armor. She gave herself up to the sure guidance of his hand on her waist, felt the pressure of his grip on her other hand,

and allowed herself to forget everything except this momentary enchantment. Yes, he must be a magician after all.

When the music stopped, it was hard to come back to reality. They stood still for a moment as the tune died, and she felt strangely loath to step out of his arms. Gabriel gazed down at her, his expression hard to read. Psyche only hoped her own bemusement was not evident to the curious eyes that surely watched them.

"Thank you for the waltz," she said at last, her voice husky. "You are—you are a fine dancer." And a better actor than she had ever suspected, she thought sadly.

"You inspire me," he said, his voice low.

Her heart tripped once, twice in her chest. She knew it was nothing but empty words; he had danced gracefully with Matilda, too, but still, he moved her. She suddenly wanted so much to believe him, wished that the attention he gave her was sincere. If only—

If she had needed a reminder of harsh reality, it came too soon.

"This man is a fraud!" someone called in ringing tones.

Eight

She felt Gabriel stiffen. Psyche jerked, turning to see who would dare to make such an accusation in front of the whole party.

It was Percy, of course.

"You must rethink this foolish entanglement, dear Cousin," he said, lowering his voice. But everyone was watching them, and a buzz of curious conversation floated around the room.

"Percy, how could you!" Horrified at Percy's display and, worse, what he might reveal, Psyche clutched Gabriel's steady arm. She kept her composure only with the greatest effort. She could feel her stomach clench and her throat go dry as more and more of the guests turned to regard them. The chatter in the rest of the room was fading as people strained to hear, and even the musicians seemed to play more softly.

Percy regarded her, his goggle eyes bright with single-minded zeal. "I cannot allow you to be taken in by this impostor," he repeated, raising his voice again so that the curious matrons and portly gentlemen standing at the corners of the room would not miss a juicy morsel of this brewing scandal. "I have spoken to all my friends—"

"That must not have taken long," Gabriel commented.

Percy blinked in surprise, but plunged ahead "—and no one has heard of this man, or his so-called title. It is all a hum, and I must save my dear cousin from this lecherous parasite."

Psyche swallowed hard against the angry bile that rose in her throat. She thought she might be physically ill right here, and it only needed that to become a complete disaster.

"You doubt my credentials, sir?" Gabriel demanded, facing Percy squarely. His tone was as icy as any that Psyche could manage. She had to admire his steel.

Percy paled a little, but he held his ground. "I do."

"Perhaps you and I should step outside and discuss this privately," Gabriel suggested. He smiled, and Psyche thought of a wolf baring his fangs. Despite the desperate situation, for an instant she almost—almost—felt sorry for her cousin. Then common sense reasserted itself, and she thought, no, she wasn't sorry at all. She wanted to see him torn into little pieces.

But Percy was shaking his head. "No, no," he said. "Have no intentions of being manhandled by a would-be fancy man like you."

The murmurs in the crowd around them grew louder. Gabriel's smile faded, and he looked even more alarming.

"I had other alternatives in mind," he said quietly.

Percy shook his head again. "No, no, can't call me out if you're not a gentleman, no obligation for me to answer to someone not of my own class. And—"

"Is it necessary for me to take you by the neck and shake the life out of you, like the pathetic little coward you are?" Gabriel demanded, his tone clear and penetrating, even though he did not raise his voice. He took one step forward, and Percy backed away.

Percy had flushed, his composure at least cracked. "I am only stating the obvious, sir—or whoever you are. I refuse to say 'my lord' when—"

"My name is Gabriel Sinclair, lately marquis of Tarrington," Gabriel said, in ringing tones. "And if anyone disputes my name, my reputation, my very honor, they should be prepared to face me and present proof of their accusations."

"But—but no one has heard of you," Percy stuttered. "And—and—"

"Gabriel, ol' chap, what's this?" a new voice said. "What's this little beetle accusing you of, anyhow?"

A new figure appeared in the doorway; he must have just arrived, though Psyche had missed the announcement of his name, if the stunned footman had even remembered to declaim it, considering the rising tension in the ballroom. He was a young man with natty evening clothes, pale hair, and a round face. He was also the very embodiment of correctness.

"This idiot thinks I am not who I say I am," Gabriel said. His tone was noncommital, but she saw that the tension had left his shoulders.

"Why in blazes would he think that?" the newcomer demanded. He turned to peer at Percy as if he were some inferior form of animal life. "We were up at Oxford together, don't y'know? Knew him at Eton before that. We were grubby little schoolboys together."

This elegant young dandy had never been grubby in his life, Psyche would have taken a vow on it. But just now, she felt both intense relief and almost equal confusion. Oxford? Eton? No actor could have attended . . . Who was he? Had the actor hired another actor to—no, no, that didn't make sense. How would Gabriel know just when he would have need of a character reference. And anyhow, Psyche thought this young man's face was familiar. Surely she had seen him before. Frederick, Freddy something, was that it?

"Freddy, you are a brick," Gabriel said with affection. He put one arm around his friend and turned him away from Percy, as if the man were not worthy of any further argument. "Come and meet my dearest wife-to-be."

Psyche, in greeting Freddy, barely heard Percy say desperately, "No, no. He—he must be an impostor, too—"

"Oh, Percy." Sally had come up to scowl at him. "I've known Freddy Wyrick since I was born. His family and mine go back together two hundred years. Now will you kindly disappear into the woodwork and stop trying to ruin my party!"

How had Gabriel managed to summon up a friend from a nonexistent earlier life? Psyche greeted Freddy Wyrick with a charming smile, but her mind still raced. There was some simple explanation of this, she was sure. In the meantime, she smiled at him with such warmth that the young man blushed.

"Gabriel, you always were a lucky dog."

Then Freddy paused, and a look passed between the two men, as if he had said too much. What had caused the flash of pain that crossed Gabriel's face, brief but unmistakable? Psyche felt as if she were trying to solve a puzzle that was missing half its pieces; she had no hope of deciphering all this.

Around them, the hum of conversation had resumed, and another dance was being played. But Psyche found she had no more appetite for gaiety. She still felt sick from the stress of Percy's accusations. When she saw Aunt Sophie signaling to her from the side of the room, she excused herself to the two men and hurried to her aunt's side.

"Percy is even more of a fool than his father," Aunt Sophie said, her tone cross. "He will make us all the laughingstock of the Ton. I wish to go home. I've had enough of this nonsense for one night."

Psyche could hardly agree more. "I will tell the servant to fetch our cloaks." She did so, and made her farewells to their hostess.

"I'm sorry you're leaving so early," Sally said. "And shame on Percy for being such a poor loser—for your hand, I mean."

Psyche made a face of disgust. Sally didn't know the half of it.

"I wish he would go stick his head in a well," she muttered, still angry at Percy for precipitating such a scene.

"We all have nuts on the family tree somewhere, even if the tree is supposed to grow apples." Sally laughed at her own wit. "He'll get over it in time, you know. Don't let him spoil all your fun. Lord Tarrington is—"

"I know: scrumptious," Psyche said, giving her friend a kiss on the cheek. "But right now, I'm still suffering from indigestion à la Percy."

To her annoyance, Gabriel had vanished. She found him at last in the card room with Freddy, talking to a group of gentlemen and apparently quite at his ease.

"Aunt Sophie is fatigued, we're about to take our leave," she said, smiling at them all, then she retreated to the hall and waited for him to join her. He took his time shaking hands and saying good-bye, she saw from the doorway. Finally, he clapped Freddy on the shoulder and made his way to her.

Aunt Sophie was waiting for them in the anteroom, as a maid adjusted her cloak about her shoulders. "About time," the older woman said, her tone shrill. She clutched her cane and allowed Gabriel, for once, to give her his arm.

When they climbed into their carriage, Psyche saw that the older woman looked drawn and her face more heavily lined than usual. The scene with Percy had taken its toll on her nerves, too, though she would never admit it. Psyche felt a wave of guilt. It was inexcusable that she had not realized what she would be letting her family in for, when she dreamed up her impossible scheme. She had been selfish and shortsighted to ever start on this perilous course. And now she was committed, at least until she could persuade the fake lord to quietly disappear.

"I'm sorry, Aunt," she said quietly as the carriage jerked a little over the rough stones of the street.

"Whatever for?" her aunt demanded, sounding more like herself. "You didn't make Percy an idiot, did you?"

Psyche laughed weakly.

"We must blame his father and his mother, poor timid thing, for that. His tantrums are bound to cause talk, of course. Next time you start up a secret engagement, missy, you might consider that fact."

But beneath the tart tone, Psyche saw that the old lady

looked at them both with something suspiciously close to approval. "Still, the two of you made a fine pair on the dance floor, quite a picture."

The man sitting opposite them nodded in acknowledgment of the compliment, and Psyche knew she was blushing. But her aunt wasn't through.

"They're saying it's probably some obscure Irish title, you know," Sophie said to Gabriel. "Since no one knows it. Poor coin, but if that's the worst they say of you—the rational people, I mean, not Percy with his bee-infested bonnet—you'll survive."

"Thank you, ma'am," Gabriel said. "I hope I do."

Not half as much as Psyche did. She drew a deep breath and tried to relax as her aunt repeated several scandalous tales she had gleaned from her contemporaries, remembering to laugh in the appropriate places and gasp in others.

Only after they were home, and Aunt Sophie had ascended the staircase, did Psyche pause to speak quietly to Gabriel.

"I must commend you, too."

"For making a fine picture on the dance floor?" Something in his tone suggested that he did not care to be reminded of his masculine beauty.

"No, of course not. For keeping your head in such a tight spot."

"I've been in worse," Gabriel said.

He seemed to refuse to allow her to say anything positive, and Psyche, after all the inadvertent insults she had flung at him earlier, was determined to be fair. "And for being a better actor than I suspected. . . ."

"It's easy to put on other people's titles, other people's lives," Gabriel said, his tone suddenly cynical. "Easy to look people in the eye and lie. Actors do it all the time."

"Oh, I see," she said, though she didn't, but taken aback by the sardonic grimace that could not really be called a smile.

"Of course," he said. "It only takes a complete absence of conscience. And that is a lack I am most familiar with."

Psyche threw up her hands in exasperation. "Really, this is too much! You're—"

"A rogue, a scoundrel, a man without scruples?" His tone was mocking, but his eyes flashed, and his lips—his lips were parted, and he was leaning forward.

Whatever she had planned to say was lost against the firm lines of Gabriel's mouth. With an easy efficiency, he swept her close, his arm hard around her waist. The forbidding wall of his chest pressed against her so tightly she could feel the imprint of his coat buttons against her tender flesh. She resisted the unexpected, uninvited kiss. But when she struggled against him, when his lips softened and the kiss gentled in contrition, she was lost. Just when she would have separated her lips as he seemed to demand, he thrust her away from him. Brushing the back of his hand against his lips, he smiled with self-mockery.

"Go ahead and dock ten pounds for that kiss. And don't wait up, dear Miss Hill," Gabriel said. "I shall be back very late."

After the confrontation at the party, and then Gabriel's scathing remarks—just see if she didn't dock him those ten pounds!—and brief but unsettling kiss, Psyche went up to bed with a pounding head. Her mattress seemed stuffed with rocks for all the repose it provided her, and it took hours before she fell asleep. Percy's shrill accusations echoed in her head over and over, and she couldn't forget the look of strain on Aunt Sophie's face.

Why had Psyche ever thought she could pull off this crazy scheme? Only Gabriel's skill and glibness had saved them so far. She really did feel a sense of gratitude toward him, or she had until he'd reminded her that he was entangled in this plot for far different and more nefarious reasons. Yet when they had danced, he had seemed so . . .

It was almost daylight and the first bird was trilling outside her window when she finally shut her eyes.

She slept late into the morning, having left orders with her maid the night before not to be awakened, and when she finally opened her eyes, Psyche could tell by the golden tint of the light slipping past the draperies at her windows that it must be almost noon.

Yawning, she rang for her tea, and once more considered last night's horrible scene. If every outing with her fake fiancé was going to be like this—oh, curse Percy, anyhow. The rest of her family and acquaintance might wonder about the so-called secret engagement and Gabriel's sudden appearance, might whisper behind her back, and it was inescapable that they would suspect that Gabriel was marrying her for her money, assuming it could ever be pried out of Uncle Wilfred's tight fists. But no one else except Uncle Wilfred and the omnipresent Percy would have dared to challenge Psyche openly. Percy had not yet given up hope of gaining her fortune for himself, that was obvious.

Castigating Percy occupied a few satisfying moments until Psyche remembered Freddy's fortuitous testimony. How on earth had Gabriel managed that trick? Simpson appeared with a tray, and Psyche sighed and turned her thoughts to more practical matters. "Is the actor up yet?" she asked.

"I haven't seen him, miss, but Jowers said that he was up in the nursery having a cup o' tea with Circe and Tellman," Simpson said. She placed the tray carefully on the bed, fluffed the pillows behind Psyche, then went to pull open the heavy draperies. Sunshine poured into the room. The day was even more advanced than Psyche had suspected.

This unexpected friendship between the actor and her little sister was puzzling. Circe was usually a little shy and not drawn to new acquaintances. Last night Psyche had thought with horror that her earliest impression must be correct: the actor had no morals whatsoever. Yet why did Circe regard him with approval? Perhaps her sister was simply too young and inexperienced to recognize a total reprobate.

Psyche had better dress and get upstairs. She should try to discourage Circe from spending time with this unprincipled man. She could simply forbid her, of course, but Circe had a mind of her own, and while she never argued with her older sister, she had a habit of simply going ahead with whatever course seemed right to her, without considering the consequences. Perhaps, Psyche thought, sighing, it was a family trait.

Simpson laid out a sprigged muslin day dress, white with touches of blue, and threaded a blue ribbon through Psyche's golden hair to hold back the tangle of curls from her face. It softened the classical lines of her face more than her usual smooth knot, but Psyche found that she approved. Anyhow, she had no plans to go out and with luck no one would call. She wanted only a day of unalloyed peace.

When her toilette was complete, Psyche went out into the hall and turned toward the upper floors, but she never made it to the nursery. Before she could ascend, she heard a knock at the front door, then voices as visitors came into the house.

Oh, drat, Psyche thought. *If that's Percy—*

She had a good mind to deny herself, but, knowing her cousin, he would come upstairs and search her out, and she did not wish to have another argument with him in her sister's presence. Reluctantly, she went down to the morning room, a smaller and more intimate chamber she often used for family visitors.

But it was not Percy. Instead she found Cousin Matilda and Aunt Mavis already seated on the silk-covered settee.

"Good afternoon, Psyche," Mavis said. "I trust you have recovered from the pleasant exertions of last night. Jowers has informed me that dear Sophie wishes to rest in her bedchamber today."

It was more likely the wily woman wished to avoid visitors. "Yes, thank you, Aunt Mavis."

Her aunt's tone had been unusually mild. She must have come to gossip and see how Psyche was holding up to Percy's accusations—and her observations were sure to be shared with half a dozen of her closest friends, so Psyche must not allow her aggravation to be known.

"It was a lovely party," Psyche said at once. "With only

a minor annoyance or two, mostly to do with my mutton-headed cousin."

Matilda giggled. "Percy can be difficult at times."

"Pigheaded, mulish, slow as any ox . . ." Psyche ran through the animal kingdom swiftly. "Oh, do let us talk of more pleasant topics. Did you enjoy Sally's party, Matilda?"

Her cousin's round cheeks flushed delicately. "Oh, yes. It was so nice to be asked to dance; your fiancé has the most lovely manners, Psyche. After he danced with me, he introduced me to Mr. Stilton, who asked me to dance next, just fancy! It was a marvelous evening. I do believe Lord Tarrington has a kind heart, too, beneath his excellent polish."

Another innocent deceived by his smooth charm. Psyche smothered a sigh. Matilda was hardly worldlier than Circe, despite her more mature years. Psyche would not try to disillusion her, but . . .

"Not that he needs it much, with such a handsome face," Aunt Mavis added with something of her usual tart tone. "However, it will make your marriage easier, Psyche. With any luck, he won't flaunt his other conquests beneath your nose."

"Pardon me?" Psyche stared at her aunt in astonishment.

"You don't expect a man who looks like he does to be faithful, do you?" Mavis met her gaze calmly.

"Oh, Mama," Matilda protested, blushing again.

"I think you're being most unfair." Psyche couldn't help defending her bogus betrothed. "You don't know that he will be an unfaithful husband."

"Don't be naive. Most of them are." The older woman sniffed and needlessly smoothed a graying hair back into her coiffure.

Psyche bit back an angry rebuttal as she suddenly perceived the hint of sadness beneath her aunt's cynical tone. She took a deep breath. What had Mavis's own marriage been like, before her husband's death? She felt a rare moment of sympathy for her acid-tongued aunt. "I think some husbands may be constant," Psyche said quietly. "I believe my father was. I will continue to hope that my husband will be, also."

Mavis lifted her brows. "But if not, don't make a fuss about it—doesn't help. Pretend not to notice, that's my counsel."

In some twisted way, Psyche thought her gruff relative actually meant this to be helpful advice. She was spared having to devise a reply by the butler's return. Jowers had brought a tea tray as well as a plate of scones. Psyche performed the elaborate ritual of pouring tea for the ladies and waited for her aunt to take a sip. By then, happily, the conversation meandered into less dramatic topics.

But not for long. They were discussing Miss Lelleman's sad choice of pale orange trimmed with yellow for her ball gown when another guest arrived. He stomped into the room unannounced, looking even more affronted than usual.

"Percy!" Psyche could have groaned with frustration. "What are you doing here?"

"Do I need an invitation to check on my beloved's welfare?" her cousin demanded, stripping off his gloves and moving forward to grab her hand.

Psyche evaded him by hastily snatching her teacup from the small table before her. Deprived of his object, Percy stopped awkwardly before her with his arm still outstretched. Matilda couldn't quite stifle a small giggle. Psyche sent her a warning glance before glaring at Percy.

"I am *not* your beloved, and haven't you caused enough trouble? That scene last night was unpardonable!" Psyche told him hotly. "How dare you subject me, all of us—the whole family, Percy, and you with your much-vaunted pride of family—to such gossip?"

"Badly done, Percy," Aunt Mavis agreed.

"I put your well-being even above the sanctity of the family name, Cousin Psyche," Percy assured her gravely. He gave her a prim smile, as if waiting to be thanked. "Is that not proof of my devotion?"

Gratitude was not the emotion that flooded through her. Psyche wanted to wring his neck. Indeed, he looked much like a plump peacock in his bright purple coat and gold-patterned waistcoat. She wished he could be served roasted and stuffed, like any minor course at the dinner table.

"I would like you to keep your mouth shut," she told him.

"Now really, Psyche—"

"At any time, but certainly in such a public venue. I don't need your advice, or your help in managing my private affairs. I don't know how to state it more plainly." Psyche met his affronted gaze with an icy look of her own.

"Now, now," Percy repeated, sniffing. "If that is all the thanks I can expect to receive—"

"It is," Psyche assured him.

"Then I will not trouble you with my company—"

"Good—I mean, good bye, Percy. You know the way to the door."

"But not until I have spoken again to this pretender marquis," Percy finished. "I have given Jowers a message to ask the man to join me. I will await him in the library, and we will have a private conversation—or perhaps confrontation—there. It is just as well that ladies will not be present as I mean to be, ahem, forceful." Percy puffed up with manly self-importance.

"As you were last night?" Psyche demanded. "Percy, you will not harass my fiancé. I forbid it!"

He ignored her and made a dignified retreat. Psyche had no doubt he would indeed retire to the library and wait for Gabriel there; she could only hope that the actor would be up for yet another difficult session. She would like to be there, Percy's scruples regarding a female's nervous frailties notwithstanding. If only her other guests would leave. . . .

She turned back to Aunt Mavis and Matilda. Her cousin looked worried, but Mavis seemed grimly amused.

"I always said Percy was an idiot," Mavis said calmly, reaching for another currant scone. "I blame it on the black cat his mother saw while she was increasing. Bad luck from which he could never recover, you know."

Matilda looked faintly scandalized.

"I don't think we can blame Percy's peculiarities on a

cat," Psyche said, straining her ears—was that the sound of a door shutting?—what was going on? How could she hint away her relatives so she could go check on the men? "He's very much like his father, you know, and despite what he says about his solicitude for my welfare, you know he's more concerned with the well-being of my fortune."

"True," Mavis said, flicking a crumb off her lap. "He does not wish for anyone to waste it, anyone except himself."

Matilda laughed again, and Psyche steeled herself not to turn toward the hall and listen openly. What was happening? She distinctly heard a male voice raised, though she could not make out the words. Had the two men actually come to blows?

The door opened, but it was Jowers who looked inside. "Ah, miss, if I could have a word?"

"Of course," Psyche said quickly, delighted to have an excuse to leave the room. "Aunt, Matilda, please excuse me for a moment."

"Really, Psyche, you must train your servants better," her aunt said crossly, but Psyche was already hurrying toward the door. She shut it firmly behind her and faced the butler in the hallway.

Jowers had already turned toward the front of the house. "There is a—a person who is creating a disturbance, miss, and I don't quite know what to do with him."

"What kind of person?" Perplexed, Psyche gazed at the man's strange expression.

The butler huffed a little, his cheeks very red. "Your *other* fiancé, miss."

Nine

Psyche thought she could not have heard the words correctly. "What?"

"Um, that is what he says. Obviously a lunatic person, miss," the red-faced butler said. "I have called for extra foot-men to assist me in expelling him"—the elderly servant looked affronted to have to admit his own physical weak-ness—"but one is off on an errand, and another in bed with a toothache, leaving only Wilson, who's rather small him-self. And the madman is so insistent—"

"Good heavens." Psyche stared, unable to imagine who this man could be. She had expected the problem to be with Percy.

"We'd better not leave him alone, miss. Lord knows, he may try to murder the whole household."

"Indeed!" She hastened after the butler down the hall and into the main foyer to find a thin, narrow-shouldered man in a cheap morning suit pacing up and down, while Wilson, the footman who had already come to grief once this week, watched him nervously.

"G-greetings, Miss Hill," the man stammered.

"How do you know my name?" she demanded, shocked to be greeted so by a stranger.

"Of course I would know the n-name of someone so n-near and dear to me," the man said.

Psyche felt her head spin. He *was* a lunatic; Jowers was correct. What could she do with him? Should she humor his delusion? She had heard that this could be the safest course for dealing with madness.

"Ah, I see," she murmured. "I suppose you would. I'm sorry to say that I don't—forgive me—remember your name just now."

Turning her head toward the butler, she whispered, "Fetch the marquis, Jowers. He will assist us. Wilson, go and roust the other footman from his bed, toothache or no!"

Jowers headed for the stairs, and Wilson, stepping quickly as if happy to be out of this potentially dangerous situation, retreated to the back part of the house toward the servants' stairwell. This left her alone with the madman, but he was slight of stature, and Psyche, though she felt her heart pounding, kept her expression calm. So far he had made no threatening moves.

Indeed, the man now gave her a formal bow, sweeping a trifle too low. "I am, of course, the m-marquis of Tarrington, your humble servant, ma'am."

"So you say." Psyche thought frantically. How?—What?—the impostor had an impostor? Had the whole world gone mad? This was her punishment for defying every rule of decorum. The universe had turned against her.

"I must ap-pologize for missing the b-betrothal dinner," he went on, stammering. "But I was, uh, s-suddenly taken ill and—"

Psyche was distracted by the sound of a doorknob turning; she jerked her head to see the library door begin to open. Oh, no, not Percy, not now!

She darted forward and grabbed the lunatic's hand, pulling him toward the small book room next to the library. The man was thin, and she was able to push him inside the room before he could catch his breath.

"Stay here and don't make a sound!" she hissed, shutting the door on his look of astonishment.

When she turned back, Percy was in the hall. "I thought I heard the marquis announced. Where is he?"

"He's not here yet, Percy; you are mistaken. Please wait in the library," Psyche said, maintaining her poise with the greatest effort. "I will inform you when he comes down."

"Tell the man to hurry up about it," Percy grumbled, but he returned to the library. Psyche sighed with relief to see the heavy oaken door shut. Now, she must sort out this quagmire before—

The book room door opened, and the little man peered out. "Miss Hill, we really must speak about the terms of our engagement—"

But now another door was opening, and Psyche waved her hands at the madman. "Not now; shut the door!"

Mercifully, he did. Matilda peered out of the doorway of the morning room. "I'm sorry, Psyche, but Mama says will you be much longer because she's got more to discuss with you, and—"

Psyche sped across the foyer to speak softly to her cousin. "I have a problem, Matilda, there's no time to explain. But please, please, keep your mother inside the room and keep the door shut."

Matilda's eyes widened. "Of course, if you wish it, Psyche, but—"

Psyche pushed her back inside. "Now make some excuse to Aunt and close the door."

Her cousin disappeared, and Psyche turned back toward the book room. She had to get the lunatic out of the house, out of sight before he stirred up more suspicion on Percy's part and made her situation even more dangerous than it already was.

She had reached the middle of the foyer when she heard someone behind her. By now so agitated that her nerves were thin as paper, Psyche whirled, but it was only her own maid, Simpson.

"Miss, is everything all right? Jowers came past me looking most agitated and muttering that we could all be murdered in our own house!"

The book room door opened again, and the little man peeked out. "Miss Hill?"

"Shut the door!" Psyche almost shouted. He disappeared once more, but beside her, Simpson gasped.

"Miss, you can't treat him like that, no matter how annoyed you are at his avarice, wishing for more money for his role. People will notice, and—"

"Not now." Psyche didn't have time to try to decipher this strange remark because she was trying to watch all the doors at once. "I'm waiting for the actor to help rid us of this madman who claims to be the marquis of Tarrington. Percy must not see him."

"But, miss, that *is* the marquis of Tarrington."

"What?" Psyche felt the room whirl again, and her maid reached out to steady her. "What are you talking about?"

"I mean, that's the actor I hired to play the part, miss," Simpson explained, touching her employer's head as if wondering if she were feverish and delusional.

"It can't be," Psyche said, her voice weak. "Haven't you seen . . ."

No, in the last two days her maid had had no reason to be in the same room as the fraudulent lord. But if this were the actor . . .

"Then who is *he*?" Psyche whispered to her servant as steps behind them announced the arrival of Gabriel Sinclair. He gazed inquiringly toward her.

"You have need of me?" he asked. "Your butler is almost incoherent, poor man. He muttered something about the house being invaded by a lunatic, but surely that is not correct?"

"I have no idea, miss." Simpson stared at the tall man before her.

"Oh, my God." Psyche felt as if she could not get a breath. "I think I'm the one who has lost my mind." She wanted to sit down, but there was no time.

Doors were opening again. Aunt Mavis peered out from the morning room, pausing only to look back for an instant over her shoulder. "Be quiet, Matilda, I shall be right back.

Psyche," she said, facing her niece again, "your household is very poorly run. You must take your servants in hand, my dear. I've rung the bell rope three times. Matilda is faint and I need smelling salts. She doesn't want me to leave her side, but—"

A small shriek interrupted from the depths of the morning room.

Good God! Had the madman attacked poor Matilda? But no—he couldn't have gone past without her seeing, Psyche thought wildly.

"Mouse?" Mavis jerked to look. "What do you mean, you see a mouse beneath the settee cushion?" She hastened back inside the room to defend her daughter from the wild beast.

"Shall I fetch the kitchen cat?" Simpson inquired.

"I don't think—"

"You're going to set the cat on the lunatic?" Gabriel inquired with interest, as if this conversation actually made sense.

Now two doors opened at once. The small man in the cheap suit looked stubbornly out of the book room, and Percy emerged again from the library.

"There you are," Percy said. "I wish to have words with you, sir."

But Gabriel was regarding the madman with surprise. "You?"

"Who are you?" Psyche demanded, turning on Gabriel. "You told me—"

But it was the stranger who answered, in a voice much too loud, as if to bolster his fading courage. "I am the m-marquis of T-Tarrington."

A moment of stunned silence, then everyone spoke at once.

"Is this a joke at my expense?" Percy thundered. "Who is this man?"

"What does he mean, Psyche?" Aunt Mavis had apparently frightened away the fictional mouse; she had entered the hallway again.

The small man looked flustered, and Psyche herself was dumb with shock. This man—this man was the actor her maid had interviewed, prompted with information about her family, and hired to play the part? This skinny, thin-shouldered man with the badly cut suit, who could not even declaim his supposed title calmly—he would never have been able to withstand her relatives' scrutiny, or stand up to Percy, or carry off the whole untruthful scheme. She shuddered at the thought of what a debacle her betrothal party would have become if this timid, stuttering actor had been by her side.

But then where had Gabriel Sinclair come from?

Everyone waited for her to speak, but it was Gabriel who answered, his voice calm.

"He means that he is the marquis of Tarrington's"—Gabriel glanced at the cowering little man—"secretary. He's a bit shy, poor fellow, and easily rattled, and he does have a slight speech impediment. But he's very good with my letters and such."

"Poor man," Matilda said from behind her mother. She had apparently recovered from her assumed vapors and had been unable to resist the urge to peek at the commotion in the hallway.

Psyche took a long deep breath. Percy shrugged. A servant, even one of more distinction than ordinary household staff, was beneath his notice. "No matter about him. I wish to speak with you, Tarrington."

The little man opened his mouth, but quelled beneath the look that Gabriel gave him. "I will be right with you, Hill. Let me just speak to my secretary and give him the instructions he has doubtless come to collect."

"Be quick about it, then," Percy grumbled, but he turned back into the library and shut the door.

Gabriel put his hand on the little man's shoulder and guided him firmly back into the book room.

"I see you are recovering," Mavis was saying to her daughter, who flushed slightly at her mother's words. "I think we had better take our leave, Psyche. Matilda needs a healing tisane and a long quiet repose."

Psyche crossed the hall to give her cousin a hug of genuine gratitude. "Thank you," she whispered into her ear, then, releasing her, added, "I hope you are soon recovered, Cousin."

"I'm sure I will be," Matilda replied, her eyes glinting with the success of her ruse and her pleasure at Psyche's approval.

Psyche saw them out, hoping that the concoction that Matilda was now fated to consume was not too nasty in taste. But she had more essential matters on her mind. Jowers was hurrying up. She managed to smile at him.

"It's all right," she said. "He was not crazy after all. He just has a slight, um, stammer that makes him hard to understand at times. He is the marquis of Tarrington's secretary."

"Oh," Jowers said, his expression smoothing. "I'm sorry to have alarmed you for nothing, miss."

He had no idea. "It wasn't your fault," Psyche said soothingly. The butler turned away, and Psyche motioned to her maid. They entered the book room together to find the two men standing a few feet apart, as if taking each other's measure.

"Now," Psyche said, her tone icy. "I want to know just how this has come about, and I want to know everything!"

A pause, while the two men eyed each other, then the thin little man swung to face Psyche, as if hoping for a more receptive audience.

"She"—he gestured toward Simpson—"she hired me to play a part, miss, at a private party. Promised me twenty quid, she did."

"Yes, but you never turned up to assume your role, did you?" Psyche pointed out calmly, her voice cool. "So why should you be paid for nothing?"

The man blinked. His eyes were a pale hazel. His features were regular, but he had an unfortunate spotty complexion. "Ah, um, that is . . ."

"Why didn't you come?" Simpson demanded, then blushed. "Begging your pardon, miss, but he promised!"

"He lost his nerve," Gabriel put in. "I met him by accident at the back of the theater, and when your carriage pulled up, he told the driver I was the marquis of Tarrington."

Which meant, Psyche realized, suppressing a shiver, that this man knew that Gabriel was an impostor. If he were intelligent enough, he could hold that knowledge over their heads like the Damocles sword it was. They must be very careful.

Gabriel met her gaze very briefly; he knew the danger, too. She could tell from the slight narrowing of his eyes.

"I got a bit nervous, you see," the actor was saying. "And anyhow, I thought I would get the part of Iago in the next production at the theater, or at least one of the lords, but th-they gave the part, all the parts, to someone else."

Psyche wasn't surprised. "You'll forgive me for asking, but do you have much experience on the stage, sir?"

"Green, Thomas Green, at your service." Green gave her a low bow. "I've played over half a dozen parts, miss. I played the second murderer in Mac-b-b—the Scottish play, and a footman in the last but one farce. And would have done much more, but I have this stammer—but only when I get nervous, you see."

"And do you get nervous before you go onstage?" Psyche couldn't help asking.

"Always," the little man answered sadly. "That's why I only get small parts, and lately not so many of those. But anyhow, you promised me a nice sum, and I'm short on my rent, and me landlady's threatening to toss me out into the street. So I'm here now, and I want to play the part."

Psyche bit her lip, and it was Gabriel who answered.

"We really don't need you any longer for that role, I'm afraid," Gabriel said. "Since I was forced to step in when you didn't keep your appointment."

Green blinked, and his dismay seemed tinged with belligerence. "B-but—"

"But we can offer you another," Gabriel added quickly.

The little man brightened. "What is that?"

"You will be my secretary," Gabriel explained. "You're the son of a clergyman, recently engaged in this post, and you've never been onstage in your life. You are unfailingly loyal to the marquis of Tarrington, who is me. Can you do that?"

"Of course," the actor said, puffing out his chest. "I will be the p-perfect secretary, sir—milord. No one will ever know different."

Psyche swallowed hard. Perhaps it was better to keep this man under their eye, but somehow her original plan, which had seemed so simple and foolproof, just kept getting more complicated. Who was going to turn up next? Six white horses and a fairy godmother?

"You will be paid according to the original agreement, with enough for your lodging right away, and I will give you a job to do—that is, you can read and write, can't you?" Gabriel paused to inquire.

"Of course!" Green looked wounded. "How else d'you think I could learn me lines—*my* lines?"

"Yes, of course." Gabriel didn't seem too impressed. "While you are here, your job is to keep your mouth shut as much as possible. Don't talk to the servants. Remember, as a secretary of good family, you're above them in class, so don't lower yourself to gossip."

He glanced over his shoulder and winked toward Simpson, who sniffed. As if she should care about this poor excuse for an actor turned secretary, her expression implied. Psyche had a mad desire to giggle.

"And what is my task?" Green asked, fingering his shabby hat, which he still held in his hands.

Gabriel walked across to the bookshelf. Some of the less valuable books that had overflowed the library's crammed shelves—Psyche's parents had been great readers—had been put into this smaller room. He picked up a faded volume and flipped open a page.

"You can sit here, in this very comfortable, warm

room"—he nodded toward the fire in the hearth—"and Jowers will see that you have your meals on a tray—excellent cook they have here, too—and all you must do is copy this for me."

The actor had glowed at the thought of food and easy surroundings, but he frowned a little at the page Gabriel held out. "But this is a collection of sermons."

"Yes. I'm thinking of a career in the church after I leave this role," Gabriel said, his tone perfectly serious.

Psyche turned another giggle into a cough with the greatest of difficulty. If there were anyone less suited to becoming a man of the cloth . . .

Simpson rolled her eyes, but she maintained her usual dignified silence.

Green eyed the book, and the pen and ink and paper Gabriel had now unearthed from the small desk drawer. I suppose I can do it. I, uh, I'm not a very swift writer, my lord."

"That's fine; there's no rush," Gabriel assured the man. "And I will suggest that Jowers bring you a glass of wine, just to help you relax and get into the role."

Green's expression looked positively blissful.

"We will leave you to it," Gabriel said. He held the door open and motioned to both women to exit. Outside, he nodded toward the footman hovering nearby. "Bring my secretary a glass of port, if you would."

"But only one," Psyche added. "We don't need a drunken, um, secretary on our hands."

The footman nodded and left to fetch the wine.

"No, that would not be wise," Gabriel agreed. "We want to shut his lips, not open them."

Psyche did not return his smile. There was still a great gulf of misconception to cross. "Simpson, you may leave us," she said.

The dresser nodded. "Yes, miss," she said, and her glance at Gabriel was both speculative and pitying. No one liked to cross Miss Hill when she was in *that* mood.

Simpson retreated. The footman had disappeared. For a moment, they stood alone in the hallway.

"Now," Psyche said, her voice grim. "You—"

The door to the library opened. She had forgotten Percy.

"I demand to speak to Lord Tarrington," her cousin said, in his usual self-important style. "I have waited long enough—"

"And so have I, for a little peace in my own house!" Psyche snapped. "You have nothing to say to Lord Tarrington, Percy. I can manage my own affairs."

"But, Psyche—"

"Leave us, Percy. Now!"

"If you need assistance to the door, I should be happy to help you find the way," Gabriel suggested, his blue eyes glinting with mischievous anticipation.

Her cousin eyed the other man's stature and muscular build with alarm. "No, no, I would not lower myself to—" He frowned, looking affronted. "Yes, well, when you realize the error of your judgment, Cousin, when you need help with this fortune-hunting libertine—"

"Out!" Psyche shrieked, at the last vestige of her patience.

Percy sniffed and turned toward the outer door, pausing only to pick up his hat and gloves from the hall table. "You'll be sorry," he muttered, determined as always to have the last word.

Psyche ignored him. In a moment, the front door closed, a little too hard, and Psyche drew a deep breath. "Let us retire to the library."

Gabriel walked across the hall and motioned for her to enter, then followed her into the room. Psyche walked across the floor, glanced down at one of the comfortable chairs that her father had chosen for his own use, then paced up and down instead, too agitated to sit.

Gabriel shut the door behind them. The silence was balm. Just to have Percy out of the house seemed to make the atmosphere lighter. Psyche drew a deep breath and swung to face this man of mystery who had somehow become so entangled in her innocent—well, almost innocent—pretense.

"Who are you?"

Gabriel's lips lifted, but his eyes were shadowed by emotions she could not begin to decipher—she felt a moment of real trepidation. What kind of man had she allowed so unknowingly into her life?

"That depends on whom you ask," he said, his voice quiet.

"Spare me any more riddles." She waved away his words. "Why on earth did you take up the pose of my fiancé? Are you an actor, too, or—or what?" She was almost afraid to hear his answer.

"I have been many things," he said.

She was about to lose patience yet again. She found that her hands had clenched into fists. "Just tell me the truth!"

"I have earned my living for the last decade at games of chance," he told her, his eyes oddly distant, his tone matter-of-fact.

She gazed at him in horror. "A gamester?"

He met her gaze squarely. "Yes."

And she had introduced this man to her family, allowed him to meet her little sister! "You are a cheater, a dishonest—"

"I never cheat!" Gabriel answered quickly. She seemed to have penetrated his unnatural calm at last. "That is, unless my opponent cheats first."

"And you were down on your luck and in need of a few pounds to get you into your next game?" It began to fall into place. "How fortunate that you should come across an actor with a bad case of stage fright." No, Psyche thought, shaking her head in confusion. There were still pieces of the puzzle that did not fit. "But what about Freddie Wyrick? How did you convince him to pretend to be your old schoolmate?"

He gazed at her steadily, his aspect hard to read.

Slowly, Psyche felt her legs turn weak. She sank into the chair behind her. "It was not a ploy; it's true. He *was* your schoolmate." Images of Gabriel—his smooth manners, his impeccable speech, his graceful dancing and socializing— flashed through her mind like scenes from a play. And she knew with a dreadful certainty—

"You are well born, are you not?" she almost whispered.

"You are disappointed that I am not a lowly thespian? Being of good birth is somehow worse than aping my betters?" he asked, his tone light. But his eyes were dark with those emotions she still could not read.

She felt a spasm of distaste cross her face. "What's worse is that it means," she explained, putting her jumbled thoughts together, "that your passion for gaming was so extreme that you lost your own inheritance—"

"No, I did not lose my position in life over gaming. I gamble only to survive," he told her, his calmness somehow convincing. "Not for the thrill of it."

"Then, if excessive losses did not cause your fall, the only other reason—there must be some terrible scandal—"

The expression on his face stopped her. Oh, God, what was it? What had she stumbled upon?

"I have committed sins enough, Miss Hill," he said, his words barely audible. "I do not need to march them out for your inspection. I will play my part for your benefit, and my own, then I will leave this house as soon as possible. And you need never see me again."

He turned and left the room with a swift economy of steps.

Psyche raised quaking hands to her forehead, her mind aswirl with new implications and a headache of monstrous proportions.

Ten

*P*syche rubbed her temples and grimaced at the pain. She took a slow breath, still chilled from the tone of his voice, the look in his eyes. What had he done? What had *she* done, letting this man into her house, giving him access to her young sister, her elderly aunt? Oh, dear, oh, dear. She must find some way to deny him time with Circe—yet how was she going to explain it to the governess? To Circe, for that matter! Her little sister could be so headstrong.

She stood up, her knees still rubbery, and headed for the staircase. She climbed two flights, and despite her wish to stop in her own bedchamber and climb into bed, pulling the covers over her head, forced herself to climb another flight to the nursery level and check on her sister. She glanced into the schoolroom, finding it tenanted only by her sister and the governess, both absorbed in a French lesson. Circe was reciting a French poem, her expression abstracted, as if her thoughts were elsewhere.

Psyche smiled in relief. No doubt the best light of the morning had waned, and Circe had agreed to put aside her brush and canvas for a while. She slipped out again and did not disturb them. She descended to the next landing and retreated to her room. She would lie down for just a while and shut her eyes, and perhaps when she woke, this would all be merely a bad dream . . .

She spent the rest of the afternoon in her room, somehow sure that Gabriel was also in retreat and would not trespass over the bounds of propriety. She replayed their last interview in her mind; she thought she had sensed hurt inside him, hidden somewhere deep. There was that look in his deep blue eyes—the way they darkened when emotion stirred within him—though one had to look close to tell. He had perfected his insouciant pose over the card table, after all, playing for stakes higher than she could imagine. So she was probably wrong. Who was she to think she could see through this trickster, this impostor, this professional liar?

It must be as she had first thought: he was simply out for the money, the free garments—no, he had rejected her offers of tailor and shirtmaker. . . . Then perhaps he thought he would enjoy a short respite in a house of good reputation, while he waited for her uncle to release half of her fortune so that he could be better paid than the original sum Simpson had promised—no, no, Simpson had promised that money to the little actor currently scribbling away in her book room. Nothing made sense. She could not find the logic in any of this.

Oh, Lord, what a tangle. Psyche shut her eyes again and tried to think of other times. Good times, before her parents had been killed, and she had been thrust into this impossible position, with her inheritance controlled by her uncle, with her person subject to Percy's unflattering courtship. She searched for a good memory, and a scene came to her, all of them playing lawn bowls in the garden beside their country house, her mother laughing, her father's eyes bright as he claimed victory, and a smaller Circe shrieking as she challenged his roll. . . . Psyche relaxed and drifted into sleep. But then the picture changed to the wide pasture and the calm day when her father had tried out his latest toy, the hot air balloon with the new valve he was in the process of perfecting. And how he had, at the last moment, cajoled his wife, laughing but nervous at the prospect, into the basket with him.

They had floated up, up, just over the trees, and then suddenly the balloon dipped too low—her father seemed to be having trouble with the controls—then a gust of wind sent the balloon careening toward a tall oak. Her mother's face was pale—even from that distance Psyche could see how pale her mother looked, and how she turned to gaze down at Psyche, her expression anxious, her mouth open in words that Psyche could not hear. . . .

Psyche tried to push away the vision, but she was deeper into sleep now, and she could not prevent the images from unfolding, as they had troubled her slumber so many times since that terrible day. Her father shouting, the balloon suddenly seeming to collapse into itself, her mother's scream, Circe shrieking from behind her. Psyche herself had been unable to yell or speak or move; she stood as if cast in stone and watched the balloon fall to earth, the basket dipping on its side and the two figures inside cast out like rag dolls, limbs flailing, to plunge toward the hard ground.

They all ran frantically, Psyche and her sister, Tellman, the other servants, and Psyche dropped to her knees as she reached out to embrace her mother, to steady her father's crumpled body. But it was too late. Her father had been dead when they reached him, his neck snapped. Her mother had lived until the next day, but she'd never opened her eyes, never spoken to her daughters again.

And then it was only Psyche and Circe, and the horde of sympathetic relatives, and the shock of their father's will.

Psyche forced herself up from the nightmare, struggled to wake, and found her cheeks wet with tears. She missed her parents so much. It was so hard to go on alone, to bear all the responsibility by herself. Perhaps that was one of the reasons she struggled so hard to maintain her control over the household, over everyone's actions, over her own deeds. If she were unceasingly proper and took no risks, perhaps danger would never swoop out of a calm, blue sky and destroy her life all over again.

And she was not the only one who had nightmares; she knew that Circe sometimes awoke in the middle of the night screaming, and her little sister no longer climbed up to the attic to paint in privacy. The view from the tallest window made her stomach clench, Circe told her sister, and she had fetched her paints and easels back down to the schoolroom. They all had scars from the tragedy.

Sighing, Psyche went to wash the tear tracks from her face and then rang for a cup of tea. She could not go down to dinner looking woebegone. She owed it to her sister to maintain a pretense, at least, of calm. Besides, she knew in a distant corner of her mind that the rigid self-restraint she had prescribed for herself was a shield, a barrier against further hurt. No one would breach that wall of propriety, no one. Psyche could not bear to be so wounded again. Nor could she allow Circe to be hurt once more. She would guard her sister from any contamination from this man with the shadowed past. Somehow, she and Circe would come out of this darkness, and someday, they would be whole again. To see Circe painting happily with a suitable instructor, to be free of Percy and his wiles—Psyche drew a deep breath and steadied her ragged emotions. She would not give up, no matter how convoluted her quest for freedom seemed to become.

When Simpson brought the tea, Psyche drank it slowly, and then it was time to change for dinner.

"Have you been up to the nursery floor, Simpson?" Psyche asked as her maid laid out an evening dress.

"Miss Circe is just fine, miss," Simpson told her immediately. "Tellman told me that man ain't been up there at all today. In fact, Miss Circe was asking about him, but Tellman set her to parsing verbs, and your sister got so distracted she didn't ask again."

Psyche nodded, and perhaps her relief was too obvious, because her dresser added, "Don't you worry, miss. We'll keep an eye on that—that man. We won't allow him to get too familiar with an innocent child."

"Thank you, Simpson. But you haven't said anything to the other servants to give away the imposture?"

"Oh, no, miss." Simpson looked hurt. "I know better. But the rest of the staff are alert, and they know I don't trust him yet, so they'll take their cue from me."

Psyche nodded as Simpson brought out a pale pink silk gown with a embroidered trim of tiny rosebuds around the modest neckline and filmy sleeves. For a moment they were both silent making sure the underslip slid over Psyche's head without disturbing her hair, then Simpson fastened the long row of tiny buttons on the back of the bodice. Psyche glanced into the looking glass. For tonight, she had returned to her usual simple, severe twist at the back of her head, with no frivolous curls around her face to suggest a feminine weakness that a ridiculously good-looking male might try to exploit.

"Don't you worry, miss," Simpson repeated. "We'll be on our guard, we will."

Her longtime servant's loyalty made Psyche's throat tighten, and she nodded. "Thank you."

When Psyche went down to dinner, she found everyone very quiet. She and her sister and her aunt, and Gabriel, sitting in elegant solitude on the other side of the table, shared an almost silent dinner.

"Thought you were going out to the theater tonight, Psyche?" her aunt demanded, dipping a spoon carefully into her turtle soup.

"I sent a note telling Lady Carre I was indisposed," Psyche said, avoiding Gabriel's eyes. "How is the soup?"

"Needs a bit more pepper, I think," her aunt said, and fortunately, she did not pursue the question of why her obviously healthy niece had canceled her evening's plans, launching instead into the possible benefits of a new recipe for stuffed hare.

Afterwards, Gabriel sat down with her aunt in the drawing room and showed her a new French version of solitaire and made himself agreeable to the older woman. Aunt Sophie seemed to relish his consideration, and Psyche told herself she should be pleased that she did not have to contend with his unwanted attentions. She played games with Circe, and her sister went up to bed soon after dinner. Psyche sat down with a book, occasionally glancing at the other two from the corner of her eye.

What was he up to now? She didn't trust this new air of serious domesticity. Was he deliberating avoiding her, or was he currying favor with her aunt for some diabolical scheme of his own? She hated second-guessing the stranger. It was bad enough to have to doubt Percy and her uncle's motives. She was tired of people who were not what they seemed!

She turned a page quickly, trying to also turn the directions of her thoughts, but found that she had no idea what she had just read. She was glad when Jowers brought in the tea tray. She poured for them all, and when the tea had been drunk, she could say good night to her aunt and to Gabriel.

He bowed. "I wish you both a pleasant night."

"Not likely, with my bones aching the way they have been. Too damp this spring by half," the old lady grumbled. And perhaps her words obscured the fact that Psyche had no answer for him at all.

Or perhaps it didn't. It seemed to her that the actor—no, the gamester—missed very little.

The next day was Sunday, and the three women went off as usual to church. Gabriel excused himself due to the deficiencies of his wardrobe.

"But surely," Circe argued, "God would not care if your new coat has not yet arrived." Her face had fallen when she found that Gabriel was not accompanying them.

"God would not, my dear," Gabriel told her solemnly, "but your neighbors might speculate as to my awkward situation, and they would gossip. I would not wish to bring any shadow upon your sister's reputation, you know."

"Quite right," Sophie said, nodding in approval. "You can always spend the morning in quiet contemplation and prayer."

Gabriel's brows rose, and his lips threatened to turn up, but he controlled his expression at once. "Of course."

Psyche frowned at him; the man had no shame at all. "We are going to be late," she said. "Come along, Circe, did you find your prayer book?"

They hurried out. After the service, they returned to Sunday luncheon, then Aunt Sophie retired for her usual afternoon rest. Psyche took her sister out for a stroll in the park, determined not to allow her to spend any more time than necessary with the impostor.

"Aren't you going to ask Gabriel to come with us?" the child asked, turning her clear green eyes disconcertingly upon her older sister.

"Um, no." Psyche pulled on her gloves, avoiding her sister's gaze. "I'm sure he would think such an excursion very tame."

"But it's a lovely day," Circe pointed out. "You could ask him. . . ."

"We must hurry," Psyche said. "You will want to see the daffodils in the clear light. It's threatening to cloud up, you know."

The artist in Circe pushed away all other concerns. "Oh, yes, you're right," she said, and they proceeded out the door.

That night, Gabriel went out right after dinner and had not returned when the ladies retired. Where did he disappear to at night? She knew from Simpson's grumbling that he often went out until the early hours of the morning. But where? It was too much to hope that he would lose his nerve and depart her life for good. She should be so lucky, Psyche told herself fiercely. No, Gabriel would never lose his nerve, she was sure of that. No doubt he visited one of the gaming halls that well-bred gentlemen stooped to frequent, where fortunes were routinely won and lost. What would people think of her "fiancé" if they saw him at such a place?

Aunt Sophie would say she was being too prim—plenty of noblemen and men of class were addicted to their cards and dice, she knew. But still, it made her toss and turn for some time, wondering what quagmire Gabriel might pull them into next. And if, in some corner of her mind, a logical little voice reminded her that she was the one who had originally conceived this scheme, she refused to listen. When she had dreamed up this plot, she had envisaged an actor who did what he was told—not the infuriatingly independent Gabriel, who was forever doing something unexpected.

On Monday, the little actor, who had been given Sunday to himself, returned to take his seat at the desk in the book room and resume his slow copying of the sermons Gabriel had assigned him. It was ridiculous, but it seemed to keep him safely out of the way. As far as Simpson could detect, the servants had no suspicions.

But on Monday, Gabriel left the house early, and Psyche found herself worrying again. When at last he returned, well past lunch, wearing a new dark blue coat of excellent cut, with an equally fine new white shirt and perfectly arranged cravat, his tan pantaloons hugging his well-muscled thighs, she could see that he had been back to the tailor. The new clothes were being completed, it seemed. But he also carried a sheaf of papers under his arm. Was this more masquerading?

"Where have you been?" she demanded.

Gabriel raised one brow. "Were you bereft at the loss of my company, Miss Hill? I had rather thought that you were actively desiring my absence."

Psyche bit her lip. She would not blush at his ridiculous assertions. She nodded toward the papers he carried. "I only thought—"

"I had business with a solicitor, Miss Hill, as well as with my tailor. I had, um, pressing business matters to discuss with him."

"Another title to assume?" she suggested, her tone icy. It was impossible to believe his statements, now that she knew that he did have something to hide. An even worse thought came to her, and her eyes widened. "You are not wanted by the authorities?"

His smile turned cool. "No more than usual."

Her breath seemed to snag itself in her chest. Psyche thought she might actually be ill. "What have I done?"

"You ridiculous chit." Gabriel sighed. "Stop baiting me and use your very fine mind." Exasperated, he threw his papers down on a table and strode to where Psyche was standing. With the crook of his finger, he raised her chin and looked into rebellious blue eyes.

"I am not a wanted man. My consultation was about a— a most prosaic legal matter." That was not completely true, but the disdain in those beautiful eyes was hard to bear. Sometimes he wanted to kiss her, to penetrate that icy shell that hid the passion he knew lurked beneath; and sometimes he wanted to shake her, to tell her that he was no reprobate to be treated like the family skeleton who has inconveniently fallen out of the closet. And then he remembered the disgrace that he carried, and he knew that the bones were rattling close enough. "If I had been wanted by the courts, would I have come back to England?"

"I see." She steadied her breathing. "In fact, you are a paragon of virtue?"

"Not precisely, but I keep my word, Miss Hill, and I will honor our agreement—"

He was standing too close; flustered, she stepped back. "We have no agreement."

"Of course we do. I will be your fiancé long enough for you to escape the clutches of your cousin and uncle."

"And you will get a handsome sum as reward for your efforts?"

"That, among other things."

She wasn't sure she had heard him right. What else could he want? Then she saw that he was staring at the book she had tucked inside the fold of her arm.

"Why are you carrying about a child's book of stories?"

She flushed. Now he was prying. "It is . . ."

"And don't tell me it is for Circe. She is much beyond such simple reading matter. What are you up to now, Psyche, my love?"

"I am not up to—don't call me—oh, be off with you,"

she retorted. She retreated in sad disorder. To her relief, he did not follow her. Thus she was even more surprised and discomfited when, half an hour later as she sat in the servants' hall with three of the maids seated in straight chairs around her, she looked up and saw him watching her from the doorway.

Psyche flushed, but she looked down quickly so as not to embarrass the servants, who did not seem to notice the new arrival. "Go on, Lily, you are doing very well."

"'And then good King 'Enry married a Sp—'" The girl bit her lip, trying to piece out the word.

"Spanish."

"'Spanish pr-princess, K-K—'"

"Katherine," Psyche prompted.

"'Katherine of Ar-ar—'"

"Aragon," Psyche said gently, and the reading and history lesson continued. To her relief, Gabriel slipped away as silently as he had come. But when the daily lesson had finished and she returned upstairs, he was waiting in the drawing room, with the tea tray.

"What was that all about?" he asked.

"My mother, indeed, both my parents, believed in the education of women, sir," Psyche said, refusing to be embarrassed by his discovery of her odd habits. "I am simply putting these principles into action, in a very small way."

"By teaching your maids to read?"

She nodded, serious about this subject. "So perhaps someday they will not have to be maidservants, or at least, they can aspire to higher positions than scrubbing the kitchen pots and taking out the ashes."

He gazed at her, and she could not determine what he was thinking. "Not a fashionable pursuit."

"No." She reached for the teapot, once more in command of herself. "Tea, Lord Tarrington?"

There was the sound of a cane tapping on the polished floorboard of the hall, then Aunt Sophie appeared in the doorway. A footman held the door for her as she came into the room. While her aunt knew about her unconventional lessons with the servants—the footmen had lessons, too, when they wished it—Psyche did not often discuss the subject with her aunt, who was not as forward thinking as her nephew and his wife had been.

They spent another quiet evening at home, and this time, Gabriel sat down and played a nonsensical card game with Circe, making her laugh at his sleight of hand, until Psyche sent her sister up to bed.

"Just a few minutes more?" Circe pleaded.

"You will be too tired to paint in the first light of morning," Psyche pointed out, trying not to smile as Circe's expression instantly changed.

"You're right," she agreed seriously. "But it was most diverting, Gab—Lord Tarrington."

Gabriel bowed to her; he always treated her like an equal. How could this man be so wicked inside—he must be, he had said so himself—and yet be so considerate of a child and an elderly lady?

Aunt Sophie was also ready to retire. Gabriel said good night to the older woman, and he and Psyche followed her into the hall.

As Sophie slowly climbed the steps, Gabriel looked over and caught Psyche's gaze upon him, and the dark brows lifted.

"I was wondering why you are so courteous to my family," she said, "To Circe and Aunt Sophie. You do not have to be so obliging."

"Perhaps I like them," Gabriel said, his tone hard to read. "Or perhaps I have nefarious reasons of my own—that's what you're really thinking, is it not, Miss Hill?"

He stepped closer, and she braced herself, she would not succumb to the charm that had disarmed so many women. She did not have to ask about his past conquests; their multitudes were easy to read in his offhand charm, his unspoken assumption that women would melt at his merest glance. Just because those dark blue eyes had a gleam in them that made her stomach weak . . .

She was a modern woman. Her mother had always noted

that logic and reason were not solely male attributes, that women could be educated and sensible, just like men. Psyche took a deep breath, then wished she had not. She could smell his masculine scent, the odor of new clothes and soap and a subtly male scent of tanned skin warm beneath his shirt. . . .

She pulled her thoughts back, giving herself a mental shake. Logic and reason, she must remember, logic and reason, both of which commanded she have as little as possible to do with the reprobate who had lost his own status in life due to some unnamed scandal that still pained him. And what on earth could shame such a shameless man? The offense must be nefarious indeed, and she should—must—keep her distance.

Perhaps he was simply a good actor, after all, an impostor to his very soul. Certainly not a man whom she could trust, and yet now he had become the key to the fulfillment of all her hopes. She should never have undertaken this wild plot, but at this juncture she had no choice. She must see it through. But she would be prudent, she would be proper, she would not risk straying from the rules of decorum again.

One part of her mind knew that was ridiculous; hiring a man to pose as your fiancé was as improper as one could likely get. Yet Psyche clung to her sense of what was decorous as if it were a lifeline tossed to a drowning sailor. Above all, she would not succumb to the feelings that Gabriel could arouse in her, feelings that weakened her knees and made her breath come faster—never, never. She would master this situation, she would master her own irrational attraction, she would master him.

Gabriel's lips curved into a disconcerting smile, as if he could somehow read her thoughts. He stood there, candlelight glinting in the dark centers of his eyes, and watched her struggle with herself.

"Don't be too certain, my dear Miss Hill," he said quietly, "that you hold all the cards. I might yet have an ace up my sleeve."

Eleven

After dinner on Monday he went out as usual, hiring a hackney—he would not take Psyche's carriages into this kind of neighborhood—and making his way through the early darkness into the East End. When he alighted and paid the driver, he ducked under a low doorway into the cramped front room of what Brickson had assured him was the most infamous gaming hall in London. Almost immediately, the thick smoky haze left a tangible, nasty feel upon his skin. The air stank of sweat, both desperate and victorious. The taste of it all was gritty and sour. But he could taste something else, too—the feeling of familiarity that he had known in more than one country, more than one continent. He was at ease in this most incongruous of surroundings.

A tarnished mirror hung across from the door. He saw that his teeth slashed white in the heavy air. He hadn't felt so at home since he returned to London.

"Offer you a whiskey, milord?"

Gabriel looked down at the woman who had pressed herself against him. She batted gummy lashes over hard eyes. One hand clutched the neck of a half-empty bottle and the other was caressing his thigh. She smelled of gin and cheap perfume and unwashed flesh. Significantly, she glanced down at the cheroot nestled between her abundant breasts.

"Or would a discriminating gent like you prefer a cheroot?"

Gabriel grinned. "I'd bet the house you could offer every vice known to man."

"And a few unknown, milord."

The heavy rouge that coated her lips cracked when she smiled. He felt a mild disgust when her hand became bolder. Smoothly, he captured her wandering hand in his own and brought it up to his lips.

Her hard eyes melted at the unusual chivalry.

"Ah," he said, brushing his lips over her cracked knuckles to soften his refusal, "knowledge and beauty. Too much for a weary adventurer such as I."

With one deft movement, he plucked the cheroot from its snug display and clenched it between his straight teeth. He left in its place one of his last remaining guineas. Her shoulders hunched in reaction to the warm coin against her skin and a gasp escaped her at his largesse.

"Allow me the privilege of just observing you and enjoying the anticipation."

She sighed. "Oh, yes, milord. Whatever you wish."

Gabriel had turned to walk deeper into the hell when she called after him. "Just ask for Annie, should you be needing anything, milord. Anything." She pressed her knuckles to her cheek.

But he had already forgotten her. With an experienced eye, he observed the procession of little rooms which ran into one another. Faro, E.O., and hazard were all being played with varying degrees of enthusiasm. But in the back room, Gabriel found his game—whist. A number of young, foolish aristocrats with more money than sense sat at the tables. Their eager faces, so delighted at being out of the schoolroom, showed every trick as clearly as if they were spreading their hands open on the tables before them. The serious gamesters lolled against their chairs in varying degrees of bored superiority, looking as if each maneuver were purely whim. But their eyes never missed a thing—always weighing, always calculating the odds. All to relieve the foolish of the burden of their wealth.

Tonight, Gabriel shared similar ambitions. Any twinge of shame he might have felt for his prey had long been tempered by his very necessary need for survival. A man walking into such a place as this deserved to face the consequences. Gabriel was long past any crisis of conscience.

Or so he thought.

"Why, I'll be damned for a bastard of a whore. It's Sinclair!"

Gabriel winced, recognizing the voice of drunken excess. And drunken excess had no discretion.

Pretending deafness, he turned to weave his way back to another room and another game. But a hand grasped his upper arm and exerted pressure to pull him around. Surrendering to the inevitable with a sigh, Gabriel turned.

"By God, it is you, you bastard!"

The handsome young man swaying in front of Gabriel on very expensive heels wore a smile of delight such as only the very drunk can assume. He looked as pleased at recognizing an old acquaintance as if he had rediscovered America.

Gabriel felt a moment of pleasure, tempered sharply by the need for caution. He shook the hand off his arm and bowed slightly.

"David."

"Son of a bitch, I'm glad to see you." David Lydford, earl of Westbury, whose estates marched alongside Gabriel's onetime home, was ten years younger, but as a lad he had had a severe case of hero worship for the older youth. David had followed after Gabriel through the fields of the home farm as they shot birds and waded through cold streams when they angled for trout. And Gabriel had, mostly, been patient with him, teaching him to cast a fly, showing him how to gentle a horse. Neither of them had had loving fathers, and they had found solace in each other's company.

David had followed, puppylike, wherever Gabriel had led. Gabriel had thought about him during his exile, wondering what had become of the lad. David's lofty title had been thrust upon him at a very early age when his father had caught a fever of the lungs and died. David had once confided how his rake of a father had caught the sickness. The old roué had fallen ill after making love to his mistress in the garden fountain.

It seemed David had not forgotten their boyhood friendship, but he could hardly have chosen a worse time to announce their acquaintanceship to the world. They were drawing stares.

Gabriel sighed. He could not ignore David. The boy had grown into a man of stature, only an inch shorter than Gabriel himself, with chestnut brown hair and blue-gray eyes.

"David, I would be much happier to see you if you were sober."

David laughed raucously and pounded Gabriel's shoulders in a bear hug. "Don't tell me you've turned into a damned Puritan, you sotty ol' bastard. I won't believe it. Why, I learned everything I know from this man," he told a disinterested passerby.

Gabriel grimaced slightly and tried to avoid the whiskey fumes emanating from David's mouth.

"I've never been prouder, I'm sure," he said dryly. "And David, my legitimacy is not a subject to be bandied about a gaming hall. Please refrain."

Much to his discomfiture, David grinned and hugged Gabriel again. Gabriel straightened his lapels.

"'Course, I know that. Say!" David paused theatrically as a thought occurred to him.

Gabriel watched warily as David's alcohol-blurred eyes brightened.

"I need you!"

"And I need to find a game, David. So if you'll excuse me." Gabriel tried to loosen his hold, but David held firm.

"And David. Try to be discreet. I am not ready to announce my return as of yet."

"But that's what I need you for, Gabe." David gestured to the table behind Gabriel. "I lost my partner, and if you don't join me, I shall lose the very cloth that's covering my arse." David laughed with drunken delight, his tone unconcerned.

Gabriel glanced over his shoulder toward the table to which David had pointed. Surprise and shock sent him spinning to face it.

Seated at the table and idly fingering the enormous pile of markers in front of him was the last man Gabriel wanted to see—the man whom Gabriel knew to be a cheat, a thief, and, recently, a would-be murderer. It was the man who had lost his estate to Gabriel: Nathaniel Barrett.

Barrett and one of his ugly henchman sat at the battered table. Knowing how Barrett operated, Gabriel glanced around and found two other eager helpers behind David. Damn it, he had just delivered himself right into Barrett's dirty hands. He might as well have been bloody gift-wrapped.

"Why, Sinclair, of all the hells in London, you walk into mine."

Accepting this bit of unlucky news with characteristic composure, Gabriel stepped closer to the table and his greatest enemy. He should have asked his new valet not just the location of the most promising hells, but who owned them. Not that Brickson would necessarily have known. With practiced nonchalance, Gabriel swept up the pack of cards that were on the table and shuffled the thin sheets of cardboard.

"Oh, no, Barrett. This is turning out to be *my* personal hell."

If it were possible, Barrett's expression just got uglier. "You best be polite, my lad. I could have my men toss you out in the alley and cut your throat for good measure."

"No need, I assure you. I much prefer the refuse in here."

Barrett's man half rose out of his chair, but a motion from his employer had him sitting again.

"Got that, did you? You're brighter than I gave you credit for."

"Yes, yes. Glad we are all acquainted." David had been swaying happily and chugging another drink he had snagged from a passing barmaid. "Gabriel, sit down and help me win back my self-respect."

"Among other things," Barrett said, his eyes glittering with satisfied malice.

Gabriel's stomach turned over as sudden, sickening comprehension came to him.

"What things?" he asked tersely.

"Only ten, fifteen . . .'." David trailed off, squinting his eyes with uncertainty.

"Fifty," Barrett said decisively.

"Fifty thousand pounds," David finished blithely.

Gabriel jerked David up by his lapels and gave him a frustrated shake.

"You drunken idiot! You've been playing that deep with these nasty characters?"

David pushed himself away and attempted an expression of offended hauteur. "What's come over you, Sinclair? I often play this deep. I've seen *you* play even deeper."

Gabriel wanted so much to go on shaking David that he had to clench his hands to restrain himself. "Yes, but not with a man such as this, and not when I am the only thing standing between a sickly mother and ruin."

The hauteur disappeared from David's face. The young, proud features hardened into a mask of anger and hurt. Reminded of his responsibility, he seemed to feel it hanging heavy as a shroud.

"You would speak so to me, when I count you among my friends?"

"Oh, save your wounded sensibilities for later, you young fool." Placing a hand on David's shoulder, Gabriel shoved him down into a chair. "Right now, I'm the best friend you've got."

With grim purpose, Gabriel pulled up another chair and sat across from David. "Shall we play?"

Barrett nodded regally. "By all means. It would cap off my evening perfectly to retrieve what I was so reckless to lose before."

And just like that, because of some damned shred of honor that Gabriel hadn't been sure was still in him, he was risking his only chance at a future. Gabriel turned to look at David. *You had better be worth it*, he thought.

David reached out to grab another drink as it passed him on a tray.

"Oh, no, you don't." Gabriel took the glass from David's hand and then tossed it back himself.

"What the hell?" David exclaimed in disbelief

"Only tea for you, my friend. You're just drunk enough to be dangerous."

David sputtered indignantly, but Gabriel ignored him and turned to face his nemesis.

Barrett lolled easily in his chair as he watched the interplay between Gabriel and David. His fleshy lips curved into a smile. "It seems Fate has decided we shall have another game, Sinclair."

Gabriel met his gaze squarely. "Not Fate, Barrett. But rather you, taking advantage of a schoolboy who should be drinking milk and not the swill you serve."

Barrett picked up the deck of cards and sent them flying between his fingers. "He entered on his own power and imbibed on his own as well. He is the earl of Westbury and has no nursemaid with him."

David, who had been studying the cards flash past him with fascinated absorption, raised his head and said proudly, "Hell, no! Evaded them. Very cunning, you know."

"Who is cunning, David?" Gabriel asked with waning patience.

"I am, of course. I lost the annoying brutes. Don't need them bloody hanging about me. Am man enough myself."

It did not surprise Gabriel in the least that David's smothering mother had hired guards for her only son. And of course, it had only driven him to further excesses.

"Yes, indeed, Westbury," Barrett said soothingly.

"Grown men do not need nursemaids following them about and telling them what to do." He pushed his glass of whiskey—untouched—toward David. David reached eagerly for it but Gabriel swept it aside, adding the glass's contents to the already sticky floor.

"That's right, *earls* don't need nursemaids, Sinclair." David grimaced at Gabriel. "You know, I'm beginning to forget why I ever liked you."

"Because I never could resist a hopeless case," Gabriel drawled. "Lucky for you."

"This is all vastly entertaining," Barrett said, rolling his narrow eyes. "But am I going to win back what is rightfully mine or not? I doubt you have enough blunt to match David's losses—and my winnings—in this game, else."

"It appears I must play with my old friend here. But one game only, winner take all. And you will not recover what is now mine." Slowly, reluctantly, Gabriel reached inside his pocket and pulled out the deed that Barrett had lost to him weeks ago. He had never been without it. Swallowing the lump in his throat, Gabriel dropped it to the table.

Barrett and his henchman glanced at each other and laughed as if sharing a prime joke. The evil sound sent a cold shiver up Gabriel's spine and into the base of his neck. Barrett sat up to the table and dealt thirteen cards to each player, then turned up the last for trump.

Barrett, his henchman, and David all picked up their hands. Gabriel alone, leaning back in his chair, made no move to pick up his hand.

Barrett raised a furry brow. "Planning on joining us, Sinclair?"

Gabriel raised a finger in the direction of the doorway. Annie scuttled up to Gabriel, her short skirts twitching.

"Yes, milord?" she asked breathlessly.

"A light, please, Annie." Annie lit the cheroot swiftly, all eagerness. Gabriel puffed contentedly.

"Ah, the hands of a woman. So soothing, so clever, so . . . agile." He grinned at her through the blue haze of the cheroot. Annie smiled back, revealing her rotted teeth.

"Annie!" Barrett barked, "Fetch me a drink and a cheroot."

Annie didn't turn her head but kept gazing longingly at Gabriel. "Get it yer own damn self."

Barrett drew back his hand but stilled at Gabriel's softly spoken words.

"I'd think hard before striking a lady in my presence."

"I don't need to. Do I, Annie?" Barrett lowered his arm, running a hand over his oily hair and then resting it in a fist on the table.

Uncertain, Annie turned to Barrett.

"Annie knows who provides the means to care for her old granny, don't you, dear?" he continued. "And she knows who can remove those means."

The light that had shone briefly in Annie's eyes dulled. Quickly, she fetched what he had demanded and then faded into the corner shadows.

Barrett lit his cheroot and sighed appreciably. "Now, back to our game."

"I'd be perfectly amenable to that," Gabriel began. Barrett nodded with a grunt. "Providing we use an *un*marked deck."

Barrett glared at him over the tops of his hand. But he did not deny the cards were marked. With a snap of his fingers, a new deck was brought to the table. With insulting condescension, he broke the seal.

Barrett sucked in a deep draw and released the smoke in Gabriel's face. "Happy?"

"Almost," Gabriel drawled.

"What now?" Barrett snapped.

"Your men." With a flick of his cheroot, Gabriel indicated the men positioned behind him and David.

"What about them?" Barrett asked through clenched, yellowed teeth.

Gabriel spoke precisely, clipping the words. "Move them."

A jerk of Barrett's head accomplished the movement of the large men.

"Before they go," Gabriel added, "they can take the mirror with them."

Barrett nodded tersely. The men removed the large, tilting mirror that had been hanging on the wall behind them.

"Anything else?" Barrett asked, his voice heavy with hatred.

Gabriel shook his head, chiding him with mocking amazement. "Really, Barrett. Can't your efforts be more imaginative? Those tricks are positively elementary."

Barrett looked steadily at him. A droplet of sweat trickled down his pale forehead before disappearing into the heavy brow. Underneath, Barrett's dark brown eyes were shuttered, revealing little. But Gabriel knew in Barrett's mind, he was dying a particularly violent death.

"Let's begin." Gabriel grabbed the deck before Barrett's beefy hand could claim it. "I'll deal, if you don't mind."

With practiced ease, Gabriel's long, brown fingers dealt each player a new hand. He flipped over the last card. It was the deuce of spades.

"Trump," Gabriel declared as he added it to his hand. "Spades."

He gathered up his hand and glanced at Barrett, who glared at his cards, then at Gabriel. His death was getting more and more violent.

Gabriel assessed his hand and considered the trump card. Spades. Spades were used for digging. For digging graves. Gabriel met Barrett's evil gaze.

How appropriate.

The burly man on his left put down the queen of hearts. David threw down the jack. God, he was drunk.

"Don't waste your face cards," Gabriel snapped.

David blinked, his expression unfazed.

Barrett threw down the trey, Gabriel added the six of hearts, and Barrett's man scooped up the trick.

He continued to dominate the game for three more tricks. David was now frowning, but Gabriel's own expression was calm. In David's inebriated state, he might have forgotten that in whist, no points were given for the first six tricks taken; with the seventh trick, Gabriel would worry.

On the fifth trick, the thug threw down the six of clubs. David was either too drunk to try for the trick or else had a lousy hand; he put down the four. Barrett, his expression triumphant, placed the king of clubs on the table. Gabriel laid down the five and kept his expression even.

"Cards not going your way, eh, Sinclair?" Barrett taunted.

"The game's not over yet," Gabriel answered, his voice quiet. "David, try to pay attention."

David yawned and hardly seemed to notice when Barrett took the next trick.

"Skill will tell, Sinclair," Barrett pointed out, his tone arrogant.

"Skill did tell, the last time we played," Gabriel noted, but he felt a coldness inside him. David was in no shape to help his partner, and if Gabriel lost the estate back to Barrett, after all he had been through—no, he refused to think of defeat. The game was not over yet, and it was not too late to turn it all around.

Gabriel looked to his hand and prayed to that fickle goddess of luck who had smiled upon him so many times before. And in his mind, he kept careful count of the cards that had been already played, trying as well to gauge from the pattern of play what the other players were likely to hold. Gabriel had never sunk to tricks of mirrors or even to the signals he was sure that Barrett and his hired hand were covertly sending back and forth. He relied on his keen memory, his knowledge of strategy, and his understanding of his opponents.

Barrett, he knew quite well. He also knew his method of play—and how much he relied on trickery. So the next time Barrett's henchman reached up to scratch his ear or his nose or his chin, Gabriel lifted his glass of wine a little too fast and splashed the man.

" 'Ey, watch it," the man snarled, but he never finished his signal, and Barrett looked nonplussed. It was Barrett's lead, and he hesitated, but his partner was wiping his face with a grimy kerchief and seemed to have forgotten to signal his employer which suit to lead.

Barrett frowned, and at last led with the ten of hearts. From his smug expression, Gabriel knew the man was confident that all the higher cards of this suit had been played. Gabriel got rid of his last heart and held his breath as the man on his left added the eight. But David, unexpectedly, seemed to do something right. He threw down the five of spades. Trump. Gabriel tried not to laugh at Barrett's expression of fury as David took the trick. Another point for Gabriel and his partner.

"Have you no hearts left?" Barrett demanded. "Or are you too drunk to know what you're doing!"

"Nope," David said cheerfully. "I'm heartless, you might say." He laughed lustily at his own weak joke.

Barrett's partner looked guilty under the force of Barrett's glare. Their signals had gone awry. And the next hand was no better. As the man on Gabriel's left reached to make the usual signal, Gabriel, with casual nonchalance, stomped on the man's foot.

"Oww!" the man said, and he dropped the jack of clubs into the hand.

"Careless of me, so sorry," Gabriel said. Barrett fumed, David revived enough to throw down the queen of clubs Gabriel had been betting he held, and they took another trick.

David led with the ten of clubs, and Gabriel had the ace. He had control of the game.

Taking a deep breath, Gabriel smiled sweetly at Barrett's grimace. He held his cards close to his chest, and he played with consummate skill, for David's fortune, for his own future.

More tricks fell to Gabriel, or to David. But the score was too close; they could not afford to lose another trick. On the very last round, Gabriel knew there was an errant queen of diamonds lurking in someone's hand. Judging by Barrett's play, Gabriel thought it was his opponent's.

The rest of the room was very quiet. Barrett's face was drawn with tension, and his henchmen seemed afraid to distract him by even a cough. The smoky air was even thicker than usual, as if the tension could be felt from wall to dirty wall.

David put down his last card, the ten of diamonds, and yes, Barrett played the queen, smirking with triumph. But Gabriel had been hoarding the ace of diamonds. He laid it down slowly and heard a hiss of indrawn breath as Barrett saw his sweet victory waver.

It came down to Barrett's man. Did he have a diamond left, or would he trump the hand and win it all?

According to Gabriel's count of suits and cards played, there should be another diamond left. If he was wrong— they all waited, watching the fourth player, and the room grew even more still. Gabriel had been watching all night to make sure no one switched a card, and now he narrowed his eyes, watching the man's hands more than his face.

The man's expression was twisted into a nervous grimace, and he held the last card so tightly it was nearly crumbled in his hand.

"Play it, you idiot," Barrett barked.

Glancing at his employer, the man put down his card— the jack of diamonds. Barrett swore, his voice thick with anger.

"My trick, I believe." Gabriel smiled, and David whooped with glee. The game was theirs.

Gabriel reached across and caught up the all-important deed, tucking it safely back into his inner pocket. Then he took the crumbled IOU that had David's signature upon it and tore it into tiny pieces, afterwards scooping up the stack of coins that lay beside it.

Barrett's eyes glittered with an anger almost impossible to contain.

"Skill does come through, when the trickery is put aside," Gabriel told him. "I win again."

"Only if you live to walk away." Barrett spoke slowly, as if having trouble moving his jaw. He seemed rigid with fury.

Gabriel had considered that problem, too. David was drunk and unlikely to be much help. He glanced around the room, checking for quick exits, but the murky, hazy air obscured any easy answer.

"David," Gabriel urged. "We are going now. Get up."

David stood, swaying a little. "So s-soon? But we won. It was a g-great game. Wanna play another hand?"

"No. I have some very fine brandy you need to taste," Gabriel told him. "It's time to leave."

"Oh, right." David took one step and swayed again.

Gabriel felt stiff with apprehension. He would never be able to get them both out of here alive. And to give that rat Barrett the pleasure of winning, by fair means or foul—

He heard loud voices from the other room, then three large men pushed their way past a protesting servant in a dirty set of livery.

"Baker, what—what are you doing here?" David looked unhappy.

Gabriel was not. He took a long breath and felt his shoulders relax.

"Milord, you should not have escaped us." The man approached their table, the other two stalwart servants behind him. "Your mother will be worried. We've searched every hell in London for you tonight."

Against the wall, Gabriel saw Annie. The harlot had left the room some time ago, he realized; he'd been absorbed in the game and barely noticed. But her eyes showed a gleam of victory. Was this how David's guard dogs had been summoned to his—their—aid?

Gabriel flashed a quick smile of thanks, and she nodded, then slipped out of the room before Barrett should recognize her involvement.

"Your timing is excellent," Gabriel murmured to the first Westbury bodyguard. "His lordship and I were just about to leave."

The servant gave Gabriel a quick appraising glance and apparently decided he was acceptable. "Yes, sir, just as you say, sir."

"My old friend Gabriel," David said, looking more cheerful as he threw one arm around Gabriel's shoulders. "Got some scotch for me to judge, or was it brandy? Oh, hell, I'll try the scotch *and* the brandy. I've a fine palate, you know."

"Yes, indeed, we will go now." Gabriel signaled to the burly servants, who looked around at Barrett's men. Two of the ruffians had risen from their seats, and they seemed to be waiting for their employer to give the word.

But Barrett apparently knew a lost cause when he saw one. Two of the bodyguards held thick canes and the third had the unmistakable bulge of a pistol in his pocket. "So, you win tonight, Sinclair," he said. "But remember what I said: you still must live long enough to enjoy your earnings." Hs tone sent a wave of coldness down Gabriel's back, but he kept his expression even.

"I plan to," he said.

With David walking unsteadily beside him, and David's men guarding their back, Gabriel left the gaming den and strode into the darkness. But the night was past its nadir. Light touched the eastern sky, a faint glow just visible beyond the low rough buildings that lined this narrow street. In his relief, Gabriel thought that even the open sewer-laced ditches stank less than usual.

"David, give me your word you will not come to this part of town again," he commanded.

"Eh?" David stumbled over a loose rock, and one of the men grabbed his elbow. David angrily shook it off. The next time he stumbled, Gabriel put out his hand to stop the manservant. He watched David tumble forward.

"Let him fall in the mud," Gabriel told the servants, his tone calm. "It might teach him to think a little next time."

He reached over to pull the younger man back to his feet. David had hit his nose when he landed, and blood dripped upon his muddy evening dress. He smelled like a cistern.

"Bloody hell." David tried to wipe away the drops and smeared the muck even more.

"Don't drink so much, next time on the town," Gabriel

told him. David shrugged off his words, but this time, he kept his footing. Gabriel retained his own counsel. The lectures would have to wait till David was sober again. Right now, they had to get out of this neighborhood before Barrett called in the rest of his gang. So they hurried their steps and watched the shadows.

As David stumbled along, and the servants murmured among themselves, Gabriel walked in silence, chilled to the bone by the thought of how much he had wagered, and how close he had come to losing. Never again. He was rapidly losing all taste for gaming, he thought. No, he just wanted to claim his new estate and learn to manage it well. Show Barrett he was the better man—certainly he would be a better landlord. Show Gabriel's father that his younger son was not the wastrel he had proclaimed him to be, prove to him what Gabriel was really made of.

And maybe prove it to himself as well.

As they walked, the streets became gradually wider and less littered with trash. Behind them, the pale light grew stronger until at last the sun lifted its golden head over London's East End. Just as in Gabriel's life, another day and another new beginning had dawned.

He did not intend to waste it.

Twelve

*After the near escape at the gaming hall, Gabriel was reminded that he must stay inside as much as possible, out of sight of Barrett and his hirelings. But since he was also trying to stay away from Psyche and her family, he found himself so bored the next day that he wandered down to the book room to chat with Green, the ineffective actor, who seemed more than happy to put down his pen.

"Terrible 'ard this is on the wrists, me lord," the little man said, pushing back his frayed and slightly grimy shirt-sleeves to rub his forearms. "Don't know how these scribblers do this, day after day."

"Take a rest," Gabriel suggested. He rang the bell and when a footman appeared in the doorway, said, "Bring us two glasses of port, if you please."

Green brightened as the footman went away again. "Thank'ee, me lord, uh, my lord."

Gabriel wasn't surprised that the man had not found success on the stage. "You must live your role," he advised him. "Be a secretary, think as a secretary thinks, every minute of the day."

The little man gazed at him. "You sound like a man who knows, my lord. You acted a lot, you have?"

"In a manner of speaking," Gabriel agreed. He sometimes felt as if he had been playing a role for years, playing the scapegoat, the rogue, the scoundrel. Was that who he was? He wasn't sure that he knew. He'd been hardly more than a boy when he'd been sent away in disgrace, and since then, his role-playing had been largely a matter of survival.

The footman returned with two glasses of port on a silver tray. Gabriel took the glass the servant offered and sipped it while Green eagerly accepted the other glass, then the servant bowed and departed, shutting the door behind him.

"I never afore acted off the stage, so to speak," Green continued. "I suppose the lady 'as 'er reasons."

"And we would do well not to question them," Gabriel said firmly, nodding toward the fire on the hearth and the comfortable chairs set before the narrow desk. He lifted his glass; the wine was excellent. "There are advantages, after all, to this unusual venue."

"Oh yes, indeed, my lord," the little man agreed.

Gabriel put down his glass. "I will leave you to your work."

"If you say so, my lord." Green sighed and stretched his fingers, then once more picked up his pen.

It wouldn't do to linger here; the actor was too inclined to gossip. Gabriel left the room and hesitated in the hallway, not sure where to go. Gabriel had tried to tell himself he was only interested in sanctuary, in the long-denied luxuries of a vermin-free bed and a warm bath. But since he had begun to voluntarily exclude himself, as far as was reasonable, from the family, he had realized he had been enjoying something much more valuable.

The pleasure of Psyche's company and the constant beguilement of her charm, the open acceptance of a bright and unusual child, even Sophie's tart observations, which made him chuckle—Gabriel had allowed himself the illusion of being in the midst of family. It was a sweet fantasy, and he had relished it too much.

But he had seen the shock and revulsion in Psyche's eyes when she'd realized that he was not just an actor, that he had real sins in his past, which he had hoped she would never have cause to know. The disgust he had glimpsed in her candid blue eyes had chilled him, had wounded him, he who by all rights should be impervious to further scorn. After all, he had had enough of that for a lifetime. So he had withdrawn from them and had tried to stay as aloof as possible. He would not worry his lovely employer, nor bring that look of revulsion back to her face.

But he missed them. He could spend the evenings at a series of gaming clubs repairing his empty pockets, but the days were very long.

He wandered into the morning room, which fronted the street, and glanced out the lace-draped window. The sunshine was golden, and the street busy with carriages and the occasional tradesman's cart. A dandy with white-topped boots rode by on an elegant bay whose neck was just a little too short; on his way to Hyde Park, likely, to impress the ladies with his horsemanship.

A man in a brown suit stood in front of the house next door. He looked out of place, and Gabriel's gaze focused on him. Why did—

He heard someone call his name. Gabriel looked around toward the open door, but the doorway was empty. He realized that the sound came from above. He crossed the room and went into the hall, on to the staircase, and glanced up. Two landings over his head, Circe leaned over the mahogany railing.

"Come up and talk to me," she suggested.

He was tempted, but he shook his head. "I am conversing with my—um, secretary," he told her.

"Then I shall come down."

And expose her to two impostors? Even worse.

"No," Gabriel said. "I've completed my instructions." He took the stairs at a rapid pace, thinking that he would pay a brief visit, only.

On the nursery floor, he found Circe waiting. "Come into the schoolroom," she said. "We can sit down."

Her precocious poise made him hide a smile, but he did as she bade him, taking a seat at the battered round table.

"Where is Tellman?" he asked, looking over his shoulder for the governess.

"She went down to make me a tisane. I told her I had a headache," Circe told him.

Gabriel frowned. Psyche would not like that he was having a private conversation with her sister. "Perhaps I—"

"No," Circe said, taking her seat across from him. "Don't make an excuse. That's why I sent her away. I wish to talk to you. I don't really have a headache."

"No?" Gabriel tried not to laugh. When it came to plots and schemes, he would back Circe against any comer. "Then why the deception?"

"I wanted to know why you have been avoiding me. Are you angry at me?" Her clear green eyes studied his face.

Gabriel sighed. "Of course not."

"Then why haven't you come to see me? I enjoyed our conversations."

"As did I," he agreed. He would not lie about that, no matter what Psyche allowed.

"Then—?"

"Your sister does not think I am a suitable companion for you," he said simply. "And she is right."

"Why?"

Gabriel found this child's straightforward inquiry harder to answer than a magistrate's, and he'd had some experience with those august personages, too.

"Because I have—I have experiences in my past that make me less than perfect as an acquaintance."

"I know that," Circe agreed calmly.

He was startled enough to demand, "You do? How?"

She reached forward to touch his face, her touch light and impersonal. "Those lines around the eyes—the upstairs chambermaid, Jane, has the same. And the way your mouth clenches when you are disturbed—"

"Lines come with age, my dear," Gabriel protested, trying to laugh. "It means Jane and I are older than you, that is all."

Circe shook her head. "Not just age," she said. "Jane lost her husband to scarlet fever years ago. That's why she went into service, to support herself. She's happy here, mostly, but she still carries the sorrow with her. And I think you carry sad memories, as well. I should like to draw you, someday."

Gabriel was speechless.

"Lily, one of our laundry maids, is the same age as Jane, but she has eight brothers and sisters, and both her parents are still living." Circe paused, looking wistful at Lily's good fortune. "She visits them on her days off. Her father is a baker, and she has jolly times and brings me back fresh sweet rolls when she returns. And she likes her job, even though her fingers are always wrinkled from the laundry tub. She says she enjoys the smell of clean laundry, and she doesn't mind hard work—her arms are as well-corded as yours, you know."

Gabriel gazed at this extraordinary child, who saw with her artist's eyes so much more than anyone would expect. "A hundred years ago, you would have been in serious danger, you know. Witches were often thrown into the closest pond."

Circe flashed her wide smile. "But I have no black cauldron nor book of spells," she pointed out.

Gabriel was spared having to answer by Tellman's return with a tea tray and the tisane for her charge. The governess frowned when she saw Gabriel, but Circe cut off whatever rebuke the woman was about to offer.

"I shall drink it in just a moment, Tellman, thank you." Circe glanced back at Gabriel, who was silent, aware that he had earned the governess's frown. He should have avoided Circe, as he knew that Psyche wished. But Circe seemed to be just as determined as her older sister.

"I am going to show him my newest watercolor," Circe continued.

Gabriel knew that his brows had risen. Tellman's expression changed, too; she looked at her charge in surprise. "But, Miss Circe—"

"We shall have some tea in a moment," Circe said, her voice calm. "Would you like to see my painting?" She turned back to Gabriel.

He nodded. "Very much."

What had made her decide to grant him this token of her trust? He wasn't sure, but he rose and followed her to the far side of the room, where her easel stood beneath the largest window, looking out toward the back with its carriage house and stables and two large oak trees overlooking the back courtyard. The watercolor was covered with a cloth. Circe lifted it and stood back, waiting in silence for Gabriel to inspect her work.

He was prepared with words of praise and encouragement, as one would give any hardworking and hopeful student of the art, but the prepared sentences faded from his memory when he saw the picture.

He observed a park with trees in the background, and houses glimpsed beyond the budding branches. Early crocuses poked their heads through the grass, glimpses of yellow and white brightening the greenery. The sky was a soft blue streaked with patchy clouds. It was a simple scene, but light seemed to glint from the canvas, and he could almost feel the movement of the wind that stirred the leaves of the trees and bent the grass.

It was so far from the usual childish drawing of a schoolroom miss, so much more even than many of the landscapes he had seen framed on the walls of the big houses he had once frequented, that he stared for long moments in silence.

Circe spoke first, her tone tentative. "You don't like it?"

"I think it's remarkable," he said with total honesty. "Circe, you have a gift that is—that is unique." No wonder Psyche felt compelled to find Circe qualified instructors. This kind of talent needed to be succored, encouraged. He doubted that Circe would give up her art without a struggle, but if the insensitive Percy should become the child's guardian, if Percy should wear down Psyche's resistence and force her to agree to marriage—no, it would never do. Not just for Psyche's sake, but for Circe's, that marriage must be prevented. Gabriel was determined to do anything he could to prevent Percy from ruining two lives.

"I look at this scene, and I feel that spring is coming," he said slowly, gazing down at the paper. "The whole picture speaks of an awakening, of unfurling flowers and budding trees and freshening skies, and most of all, of hope returning."

Circe was pink with pleasure. "Yes," she said seriously. "That is indeed what it is about. You do understand. Perhaps when it is finished, I will give it to you, to hang on your wall."

He was unexpectedly moved. "I would treasure it, indeed," he told her. "Although I'm not sure I will have a wall to hang it on, at least for a while."

"When you and Psyche are married—" she began, then paused and glanced at Tellman, who had taken her usual seat in the other corner of the room. Circe lowered her voice. "Sometimes, I almost forget it's all in play."

"Yes," he agreed, forcing his face into an easy expression. This child was altogether too fey for his comfort. He must not allow her to see that he could easily slip into this daydream, too, and enjoy it altogether too much.

The door opened again, and Psyche looked into the room. Her expression immediately changed when she saw Gabriel.

Gabriel kept his expression impassive, repressing a quick flicker of guilt.

"Ah, there you are," Psyche said, making a quick recovery. "I would like to speak with you, Lord Tarrington, in private."

"Of course," he agreed, rising and making his bow to Circe. "I have enjoyed our chat, Circe. Thank you for showing me your watercolor."

It pleased him to see Psyche's grimace of surprise, although she mastered her expression quickly. He followed her out of the room.

"You didn't plague Circe to show you her work?" Psyche

demanded, looking worried. "She's very selective about who views her paintings."

"She offered," Gabriel answered, not trying to disguise his annoyance. "I would not harass your sister, my dear Miss Hill, nor do I enjoy being considered a threat to small children."

She had the grace to color. "I beg your pardon. I didn't mean—"

"Your sister has extraordinary genius," he added. "I understand now why you are so intent upon finding her the instruction that her talents call out for."

Psyche nodded, then hesitated a moment in the hallway. "Come with me," she said. "If you have seen her latest work, I think you should see more."

Not sure why this sudden change of heart, Gabriel followed Psyche up the steps until she came to the attic at the top of the house. Mystified, he watched her enter a cramped attic room and when she gestured, he came after her. She moved to a table and pulled out a portfolio from a stack of papers and boxes and untied the ribbon that bound it together.

"These were painted after the death of my parents in a hot air balloon accident." Her voice was controlled, but he could see the effort it cost her in the tightening of her lips.

He moved closer to see, and even in the dim light from the small window at the end of the attic, he saw that these pictures were darker, in both color and mood, than the one he had viewed in the schoolroom. He picked up the first and glanced at the next one, and the next. These scenes showed lowering black clouds hanging over grim, bleak landscapes of barren hills and empty lowlands.

"I see," he said after a long silence. "She has come a long way."

"And I do not wish to see her hurt again—"

"Farther, perhaps, than her sister," he finished.

Diverted from the cautionary warnings she had meant to repeat, Psyche frowned at him. "What do you mean?"

"I mean, dear Miss Hill, that you have the same anger

and hurt inside you, and you have had no method of relieving those poisons. Your sister at least has her painting. You
have only the responsibilities of looking out for your sister,
and the irksome task of fending off the noxious Percy."

He saw something in her face waver, and then the sheen
of moisture in her eyes.

"I . . . you are very perceptive, for a gamester," she said
slowly, blinking back the tears. "I suppose it comes from
reading your opponents, seeking to determine their moods
and weaknesses from across a card table so that you will be
able to best them."

Her tone was almost insulting, but he ignored it. He
would not be distracted this time. "Does no one understand
you?" he asked, keeping his tone light with some effort. "I
am sorry you have borne so much all alone."

She bit her lip, and the gesture made him reach forward
despite himself. He put his hands on her shoulders, only to
support her, only in a brotherly gesture of aid—oh, hell, why
lie to himself? He didn't feel the least bit brotherly toward
the cool beauty, no matter how genuine his sympathy for her
plight.

And she knew it. She glanced up at him, her blue eyes
wide with alarm. "I didn't bring you to this secluded
apartment for—that is, you must not misconstrue my motives—"

"Oh, your motives are pure enough, I'll give you that,"
Gabriel told her. "And you have hidden your passion deep
beneath that floe of ice that surrounds you. It may confound
the rest of the world, but I can see through it, dear Miss
Hill."

"Will you stop calling me that," she said in a flustered
tone.

But this time, she didn't back away. They were only
inches apart, and he could detect the rise and fall of her
breasts—too well hidden beneath the primly styled dresses
she habitually chose—and the pulse jumping in the vein in
her temple.

"What shall I call you, then?" he teased. "Psyche, dearest, beloved?"

"You do not have to carry your role of my fiancé to such an extreme," she argued, but her voice trembled, and they both knew that she was breathing quickly. Hell, so was he.

"It's no role, and for once in my life, I am not pretending." He leaned forward. The shock of lips meeting was like the spark of a tinderbox, and he felt a tremor run through his whole body.

Her lips were soft and luscious. She shut her eyes. For a moment, she stood very still, then beneath the hard, sure pressure of his kiss, her lips parted, and he could taste the sweetness of her mouth, the smoothness of her tongue as he taught her what a kiss should be.

He closed his eyes, too, and forgot the dusty attic around them, forgot the killers that awaited him somewhere on London's shadowed streets; he forgot—almost—everything except the way she stood in his arms, not quite leaning into him, but not rejecting his embrace.

When at last she pushed him away, she was trembling. "I— You can't— I am not one of your light women, sir!"

But he had learned to read women long ago, and he saw the uncertainty in her eyes.

He grinned at her. "I've had my fill of light women, my lovely Miss Hill. I've had high-born ladies and low, I've had sun-kissed beauties on tropical beaches who were happy to share my embrace. I've never forced a woman in my life, and I would not do so now. But at present I find that I have a hunger only for an ice princess with a heat beneath her careful primness that she may have kept concealed from the world, and even from herself, but not from me. Who, my lovely Psyche, is pretending now?"

She had to pull away, she had to put this arrogant libertine in his place. Hadn't he just admitted that he had loved many women, had seduced them, most likely—no, be honest. The way she felt just now, the strange yearnings he induced, those women had likely thrown themselves at his feet and begged for his kisses.

If Psyche had had no shame, she would have done the same. The tiny scar at the edge of his mouth, the way his brow furrowed when he narrowed his eyes, the keen blue-eyed gaze with which he seemed to look into her very soul—Psyche felt a hunger she had never suspected, a melting pain low in her belly that made his firm, seductive kisses almost impossible to resist.

Just for one moment to lay aside all the weight of responsibility and decorum—strange, she had never considered her sense of propriety a burden before—but just to escape it all and relax into his arms. If he kissed like this, what would his further caresses be like?

Shocked at herself, Psyche drew a deep breath. But Gabriel gave her no time to reconsider.

He leaned forward again, and this kiss lasted even longer, sent her heartbeat even faster, till she felt as breathless as if she had run up four flights of stairs. He pulled her further into his arms, and the hardness of his body, the firmness of his thighs as they pressed against her own softer limbs—she had never been this close to a man. Even in a dance, there was a proper distance between the partners. This was like a marriage bed would be, and if their sham engagement had been real, on that night of wedding bliss even the thin muslin of her skirt or his fashionably tight-fitting trousers would not separate them. There would be only warm skin against warm skin, and she would know how his hands would move across her body, accelerating this tumult of emotion inside her to new and dizzying heights.

A clatter from belowstairs pulled her out of this forbidden fantasy. Psyche jumped, and then forced herself to step back.

"I can't—I mustn't—" she stammered, then turned toward the doorway. "I'm needed belowstairs."

He didn't hold her back, as she half-feared he might, didn't protest, but his dark blue eyes gazed at her with a knowing that made her blush. He knew her feeble excuses for exactly what they were. This was not a man easily deceived.

Psyche hurried out of the attic, ignoring a red-faced maid on the next landing who was wiping up spilled tea and collecting shards of china from a broken teacup. She continued till she was in her own bedchamber. There she shut the door and leaned against it. She found that she was still breathing fast.

Why did this one man, this gambler, have this effect on her? She had encountered good-looking men before, charming, well-spoken men. She was familiar with all the most accomplished flirts of the Ton. But no one else had ever affected her like this, she admitted ruefully in the safety of her solitary chamber. No one.

That wicked twinkle in his lapis blue eyes, the grin that he didn't quite allow to lift the corners of his well-shaped lips, the slight arch of his dark brows, the hard-muscled arms that had held her so tenderly—oh, for heaven's sake! She would *not* think of him.

She walked across the room to her small desk and pulled out her journal of household accounts. Perhaps a listing of linen that needed to be replaced and complaints about the quality of the last canister of tea that must be returned to the merchant, anything as boring and commonplace as possible—perhaps these everyday matters would divert her thoughts from this sensual, wicked man.

But when she found that she was humming a tune beneath her breath even as she added up the staff s quarterly wages, Psyche bit her lip. How could she escape the power of his attraction when she could not expel him even from her thoughts, much less her life! She was so unnerved by the encounter in the attic that she stayed in her room until midafternoon, when the butler appeared to announce a caller.

"Who is it, Jowers?" she asked, dreading the return of her annoying cousin. If it were Percy, she would turn him out of the house!

"Madam Forsyth, miss," the servant told her. "She is waiting in the small drawing room. Miss Sophie is in the large drawing room with three callers, the Misses Baldwin and their mother."

"Thanks for the warning. Very well, I'll be right down," Psyche said. She put away her ledger and glanced into the looking glass to make sure she looked composed and serene and not as if she had been trysting in the attic, then made her way downstairs. She found her friend garbed in an elegant walking suit of green striped silk, perched on the edge of a settee, frowning at a print on the wall as if it offended her.

"So, you have not taken to your deathbed!" Sally exclaimed when Psyche came into the room.

Her words of greeting died on her lips. "I beg your pardon?" Psyche raised her brows in surprise. "Did someone say I was ill?"

"No, but I decided that must be the only explanation for your disappearance from all of your normal activities. Either that, or you have been closeted with your delicious fiancé, making passionate love even before the banns have been said—and by the by, when are you going to have them read, Psyche?"

Psyche hoped she was not blushing. "Soon, and don't be silly."

"Oh, I know Aunt Sophie would not allow any real lovemaking, more's the pity." Sally's bow-shaped lips drooped in an exaggerated pout. "But you have certainly been keeping close to home; you've turned down four social engagements in the last three days, and those are only the ones that I know about!"

"What is there that you don't know?" Psyche retorted. "You are aware of everything that happens in the Ton."

"Well, then," Sally said reasonably, "tell me why you are locking yourself up like a prisoner in your own home."

"I, um . . ." Psyche searched her mind for a convincing answer, but Sally shook her head.

"If I did not know your spirit, my friend, I would say that you are hiding out from your annoying cousin."

"I don't—" Psyche still hesitated.

"But you would not allow Percy to frighten you, I know

you wouldn't." Sally blinked her brown eyes in the manner that had captivated her numerous suitors, before she'd finally chosen her good-natured, stout-framed husband. He was fourteen years older than Sally, but he doted on his young wife, and Sally seemed content with her choice.

Psyche knew that this time, she was certainly red-faced. "It was very upsetting, having Percy accuse my poor fiancé of being an impostor. How can I allow Percy to harass Lord Tarrington in such a manner?"

"How can you allow Percy to drive you into hiding? You have more courage than that, Psyche, I know you do. Will you hide out for the rest of the Season?"

"But I must think of my husband-to-be, as well as myself," Psyche tried to argue, but she didn't quite meet her friend's accusing gaze. "Just because I have such lunatic relations, it is not fair to Lord Tarrington if I subject him to their denunciations."

"I would wager that Tarrington is not afraid of your hen-witted cousin," Sally argued. "Oh, thank you," she said as a footman brought in a tea tray.

Psyche poured them both a cup. Sally accepted the fragile cup and sipped, allowing Psyche a moment to try to pull her thoughts together.

"Besides, Psyche," Sally continued after the servant had left the room, "if you want people to believe Percy's mad accusations—"

"Of course not!" Psyche said sharply.

"Then you must not be driven into hiding," Sally finished, her smile triumphant. "You must continue about your normal social rounds."

"But if Percy makes a scene again?" Psyche picked up her own cup and peered into the brown liquid as if she might read her future there.

"Then you must face him down. I will stand by you, and your fiancé is up to the challenge, I am sure of it. Come along now, Psyche. There is an opera tonight."

"I never meant to go," Psyche pointed out. "Everyone

knows the opera is not my favorite, and Aunt Sophie says that all that caterwauling gives her a headache."

"Tomorrow, then," Sally persisted. "There is a delightful excursion planned for the afternoon to the countess of Sutton's estate. We have a large party going, and you must not cry off again; it would be too bad of you! I have had no fun at all at the last two soirees and as for Lady Kettering's afternoon card party, Lord, it was too boring for words."

Sally sipped her tea, and Psyche tried not to smile. Sally had never been bored a day in her life. She indued every party with her own infectious good spirits and high energy. But her concern for her friend was obviously genuine, and Psyche was touched.

And perhaps Sally was right. Would people begin to believe Percy's accusations if she and Gabriel remained at home, avoiding the normal social whirl? She could not have that, it would defeat her aim and make all her risks be for naught.

No, she must not be so craven, Psyche decided.

"Drink the tea, it will not answer for you," Sally said tartly. "And you are no gypsy, to read your future in the tea leaves. So, are you going tomorrow or not?"

"I will go," Psyche said, then repeated more firmly. "We will go."

"Good girl!" Sally said in approval. "Don't wear your new red pelisse, as I am wearing purple, and we will clash."

Laughing, Psyche agreed.

Thirteen

The next day was fair, the air warm, with only a light breeze lifting the ribbons on Psyche's hat as she walked down the steps. Gabriel took her hand as she climbed into the open barouche. Aunt Sophie was already enthroned upon the other side of the rear seat. Psyche sat down beside her aunt, and Gabriel took his place on the opposite side, facing them.

At first, he had been strangely reluctant to agree to the outing. "You should go," he'd agreed when she'd first broached the subject at breakfast, appearing in the dining room earlier than usual to find him sitting at the long dining room table and sipping a cup of coffee all alone. He had stood to make his bow and listened to her explanation, taking a moment before replying. "You should go. I'm sure you will enjoy the company of your friends."

Psyche had narrowed her eye. What was he playing at now?

"And you would not enjoy meeting more of my friends?" she asked, her voice a little cool.

"I thought you didn't want me to appear in public more than was necessary," he countered. "Your cousin—"

"Sally thinks we will only reinforce the effect of Percy's

suspicions if we stay too much at home. And I have decided that she is right." Psyche had lifted her well-shaped chin, as if daring him to argue.

The idea of getting out of the house, out of London, past the danger of lurking eyes and well-paid assassins, sounded too good to be true. Something nagged at him, but he brushed his misgivings aside. Who was being too cautious now? He had been sitting at the table, watching through the pane how the breeze stirred the ivy that grew up the stone and poked its green tendrils above the windowsill. He would like nothing more than to be out in the countryside on such a day, with this fair-haired beauty on his arm.

"Very well, I am at your disposal," he had told her.

Psyche nodded, and told him what time they would be leaving, then retraced her steps to the upper floor to make sure Aunt Sophie had had her morning tray and would be dressed in good time.

"Drive on," Psyche called now to the coachman. He flicked his reins, and the pair of matched grays set out at a decorous pace. Behind the team, the well-sprung barouche rolled smoothly across the paving stones. The street was crowded again on such an agreeable day, so they could not have made better speed even if they had wished. Aunt Sophie nodded at an acquaintance who rode past them in an old-fashioned coach. She did not care for excessive speed and would be pleased with the sedateness of their passage.

Psyche could not imagine that a man in his prime would enjoy such a stodgy pace, however. He would probably have preferred to ride. "I'm sorry we do not have a suitable mount for you in our stables," Psyche murmured to him.

Gabriel grinned at her, the slight lifting of the lips that always seemed to denote some mischievous thought. "I am well content," he told her.

She could not know the vision she made, Gabriel told himself. Today Psyche wore a pale muslin dress sprigged with green, and a paler spring green spencer over it, with a matching parasol that made her eyes seem as strongly blue as the cloud-free canopy above them. Her cheeks were flushed with excitement, and her eyes sparkled.

He also felt energized, free at last of his self-imposed sequestration, and he took a deep breath, savoring the odors of London, from the savory smell of the hot-pie vendor, and the sweetness of cherry blossoms in the park they passed, even to the stench from a steaming pile of horse manure that a street sweeper had not yet scraped aside to spare the thin soles of a pair of ladies about to cross the avenue.

He was back in England at long last. Soon, he would be the master of his own estate, and the old shame would be put aside. He would show his father that the patriarch had been wrong about the son he had turned out so unmercifully, to sink or swim all alone. Despite the odds against him, Gabriel had survived, and he was here, ready to retake his place in his rightful level of society. And when he did, could he dare to think of wooing a lady like the beauty who sat in front of him?

Psyche said something to her aunt, oblivious of his speculation. Just as well, Gabriel told himself. He had any number of obstacles to overcome before he could consider asking for anyone's hand, much less for someone as desirable as the wealthy and ravishing Miss Hill.

No, better be practical. But he was here now, and he could enjoy the day. The air was balmy, and the breeze just enough to refresh them.

He glanced over his shoulder at the well-chosen team that drew their carriage, then turned back to enjoy the vision of loveliness before him. The vision was gazing at the houses they passed by, a distant look in her eyes as if she did not really see them. What was she thinking, the lovely Psyche? How could she have withstood the charms of all the suitors her beauty, not to say her wealth, must have attracted? Percy and his father not withstanding, what was wrong with the men of London that Miss Psyche Hill was still unwed? But thank God for whatever ailed them, Gabriel thought. Otherwise, he could not have taken part in the fortuitous masquerade, could not have relished his odd role as a fiancé who would never become a husband.

He remembered that he had told himself to put aside these thoughts, and he turned his head to gaze at the houses that were becoming more scattered as they at last left London behind. The road was still dotted with carriages as other Londoners also escaped the city. A chaise followed them, and behind that, a shabby little gig that looked somewhat out of place. Soon the houses fell away and there was open land around them, cows and sheep grazing on green meadows, and birds flying up from the hedgerows as the barouche rolled forward, the team of horses clipping along at an increased pace.

He had forgotten how beautiful England could be in the spring.

"You are smiling," Psyche said, sounding almost surprised.

"Have I been so forbidding that you have never seen me smile?" He gazed at her, dark brows slightly raised.

Psyche bit her lip. She should have held her tongue. The barrier he always girded himself with was back. "Of course not," she said slowly. "I have seen you smile many times, but not like that. You looked—at ease, as if you were among friends."

"And why shouldn't he be?" Aunt Sophie demanded. "Don't talk nonsense, child. I am feeling warm. Did my maid put in the bottle of lavender water?"

By the time Psyche had located the bottle, and her aunt had sprinkled a fine lawn handkerchief with the scented water and patted her temples, Psyche had lost any chance at observing Gabriel unnoticed. For the rest of the ride, he remarked upon the tranquility of the countryside or listened politely to Sophie's stories of her childhood and the country house she had shared with her siblings and parents, but the unguarded smile did not return.

What had driven him away, Psyche wondered, not for the first time. If it was not gambling, what scandal, what transgression could have uprooted him from his own home, his native country?

The simplest method would be simply to ask him, but she had seen the reserve that deepened when she queried, even obliquely, about his past, especially about his English connections. Gabriel would not willingly disclose his iniquities, of that she was certain. But the notion that she might be allowing a dangerous man to have regular conversation with her little sister still bothered Psyche. As for herself, why, that was another matter. She could certainly take care of herself. Gabriel had been heaven-sent to take up the pose of her fiancé. It was merely a business arrangement, she assured herself. When she had her inheritance, she would make him a handsome settlement, and they would part.

For some reason, this thought did not cheer her as much as it used to, when she had wistfully dreamed of being free of her uncle's control and her cousin's courtship. Sighing, Psyche watched a lark rise into the blue sky, looking wonderfully free and untrammeled. Someday, she would feel that way again and it would be worth all the hassle and danger of scandal.

Perhaps, she thought, nodding absently to a remark from her aunt, Gabriel's scandal was not much more than she risked, herself. No, that couldn't be. Aside from the fact that he would have had no need to conjure up a fake betrothal, men could face down social disgrace much easier than women. Her mother would have said it was terribly unjust, but there it was. Psyche knew all too well that women must toe a fine line. Hadn't her own mother, the most chaste and honorable person of Psyche's acquaintance, been whispered about abominably just because her views on education and rights for women were so unusual?

She bit her lip and looked up to see her aunt frown. "I was right, then," the older lady said. "This scarf is too bright to have by my face. Do I look too pale?"

"No, no, that shade of lavender is quite lovely." Psyche forced her mind back to more mundane topics and discussed fashion with her aunt until they arrived at the countess of

Sutton's estate. Their carriage drew into the long driveway and made its way up to the house, where several other carriages were disgorging passengers.

Gabriel stepped down from the barouche quickly and helped the ladies out. Aunt Sophie saw a friend at once, and Psyche had only time to smile her thanks to him before she had to follow her aunt and make polite conversation.

They were all directed by a footman into the house, where the ladies paused to check their reflections in the mirror before going outside again to the formal gardens at the side of the house.

Aunt Sophie spoke to their hostess, then Psyche introduced Gabriel, trying not to blush as the countess, who was the mother of six rambunctious children and had grown somewhat stout, eyed the man on Psyche's arm with frank appreciation.

"You've done well for yourself, my dear," their hostess remarked with her usual lack of tact. "Much better favored than your chinless cousin. Well done!"

Psyche knew that her cheeks were blazing. "Thank you, Lady Sutton," she murmured.

"You should have very handsome children," the other woman continued, looking Gabriel over as if he were a prize bull.

Psyche had her hand tucked into Gabriel's arm, and she felt it shake slightly. Hoping he would not disgrace them both by laughing aloud, she escaped as soon as she could, giving way to other new arrivals, and they walked rapidly off toward the tables and chairs that had been set out on the smooth lawn.

She tried to draw her hand away, but Gabriel held it fast. "Don't be so cold, dear Miss Hill," he murmured. "We have, after all, a charge to fulfill—we must start those beautiful babies very soon."

"I think not," she said, her tone severe.

She retrieved her hand as a footman held out a silver tray and offered them their choice of slender crystal glasses filled with pale liquid. "Have a glass of champagne."

Not that he needed the sparkling wine to lift his spirits, Psyche thought crossly. For some reason, Gabriel seemed very merry. "Come," he said now, sipping his wine. "Let us go and admire the garden."

She accepted his escort through the thick garden wall toward the flower beds, but made sure to stop and greet everyone she saw, determined that people should know that she was out in company with her fiancé. Let Percy put that into his slanderous mouth, and she hoped he choked on it!

But taking Gabriel into company was not such a simple matter as she had imagined. Captivated by his looks and charm, the women, married or not, tended to flock around him.

"Miss Hill, we are so glad to see you out," said a woman Psyche barely knew. "I missed you sadly at the theater party Monday night."

"I was indisposed," Psyche said, trying to keep her tone even as the woman simpered and smiled at Gabriel. She could have said she had a trained monkey in her drawing room and the woman would hardly have noticed, Psyche thought.

Mrs. Cunningham joined them, with her two daughters, both of marriageable age and both, sadly, possessing a slight squint. "Miss Hill, so lovely to see you," the matron gushed. "Do introduce us to your charming fiancé."

"Lord Tarrington, Mrs. Cunningham, Miss Cunningham, and Miss Lavidia Cunningham," Psyche said obediently.

Gabriel made his bow to all three women. The two girls blushed and batted their eyelashes, and their mother beamed. What business did they have flirting with an engaged man, Psyche thought, irritated again. At least, as far as *they* knew, he was spoken for.

Yet another trio of ladies joined them. They were going to look ridiculous, Psyche thought. And how could these women have so little sense. Just because he had such amazing good looks, they had no idea of his character or his heart! If they knew what—

Someone tapped her arm, and Psyche looked around, frowning. It was Sally Forsyth.

"Do you wish an introduction to my charming fiancé, too?" Psyche demanded, grinning reluctantly as Sally laughed. She stepped back to talk to her friend and allowed the bevy of women to flock even closer to Gabriel, who appeared to accept the attention with regrettable calm.

"If you were not my closest friend, I would certainly try to cut you out," Sally agreed.

"I'm sure your husband would approve," Psyche said, her tone dry.

"Oh, my sweet Andrew would never notice," Sally said fondly. "He's sitting back there in the shade of an oak tree. It's too fatiguing to walk about in the sun, he says. Anyhow, he lets me do whatever I wish."

"Which is why you accepted his proposal in the first place, no doubt," Psyche noted.

Sally pursed her pretty lips into a playful pout. "Why, you fiend, to say such a thing. Just because it's—almost—true. I was having such fun being courted, I hated to give it up, you know. And the most passionate romances in the Ton, I have found out, occur *after* one has married."

Psyche was startled. "Sally, you wouldn't!"

"Of course not. I am very fond of my Andrew," her friend said. "And he's very generous with my dress allowance. But that doesn't mean one can't flirt. And if I ever did decide to stray, I can tell you, your husband-to-be would be high on my list."

"Yours and every other woman's within a stone's throw, from the look of it," Psyche said, as she glanced back at Gabriel, still surrounded by women. "I think I have unleashed a monster."

Sally's light laughter trilled. "Come, let us walk a little away from them. Otherwise, they will say you are jealous, and that would seem very provincial."

"I'm not sure he's safe to leave," Psyche protested, but she followed Sally toward another display of flowers and pretended to admire the showy blossoms.

"It's a heavenly day," Sally was saying, glancing up at the clear skies from beneath her wide-brimmed hat with its fashionable trim of ostrich feathers. "Oh, Lord, do look at Mrs. Tweaton's maize-colored turban. She looks like an overripe stalk of wheat."

"Hush, she'll hear you," Psyche scolded, but she laughed unwillingly. Sally was quite right. The thin woman with the green gown and the gold turban could have easily blended into a field of grain.

"I'm glad to see you relaxing, you know," Sally said, some of her native shrewdness showing in her expression as she let her usual frivolous mask slip a little. "You've been much too prim and sedate since your parents' death."

Psyche frowned and looked down, allowing her hat to hide her face.

Sally's voice was gentle. "I know it was a harsh blow, my dear. But if you can learn to enjoy life again, I will be most thankful for your new find." She smiled, and her familiar impish tone returned. "Not to mention that you've provided us all with a sinfully gorgeous man to brighten the social landscape."

"You scamp." Psyche ignored the reference to her parents. Their death was still painful to discuss, and Sally knew it, so the subject veered back to the inconsequential. When they were joined by a young sprig of fashion who seemed to be Sally's latest flirt, Psyche let the other two talk and allowed her thoughts to wander.

Had she really become too prim, too guarded, as Sally said? She remembered that Gabriel had remarked upon her sedateness. Irked, Psyche glanced covertly from her own perfectly stylish muslin gown to Sally's. Perhaps Sally's neckline was cut a bit lower, perhaps her bodice was a tiny bit more fitted. Did Gabriel really see Psyche as boring and staid? It shouldn't concern her, she scolded herself, but the reflection did not please her.

She roused herself to answer a query from Sally.

"What shall you be, Psyche? Mr. Denver, here, is coming as a highwayman." Sally dimpled as she gave the young man one of her best smiles. "Unless I persuade him other-wise."

"Um, I haven't decided yet," Psyche said, trying to find her way back into the conversation. What was Sally talking about?

Her friend seemed to read her confusion. "Our big masked ball, silly. My household has been all astir. I have been working madly on the plans for weeks."

"You mean your housekeeper and butler and the rest of the servants have been working madly," Psyche corrected, smiling as her friend made a face.

"No, no, I dictated the list of guests myself, and it was sadly fatiguing, let me tell you!"

"You poor thing," Mr. Denver said, gazing soulfully at Sally's pretty pout.

She gave him a roguish smile, then turned back to Psyche. "But what shall you be, my dear? My costume is a se-cret, you must not ask. Although, perhaps I will reconsider my plan. I could dress as Persephone, and perhaps Lord Tar-rington can come as Pluto, lord of the underworld."

"Why do you say that?" Psyche demanded, a little too sharply.

Sally blinked in surprise. "Why, he has that dangerous look, don't you know. Don't worry, it only makes him more attractive."

Psyche looked back at the crowd of women still hiding Gabriel's well-shaped form. Only the top of his head could be detected amidst the flock of nodding plumes and high-crowned hats.

"I don't doubt that," she agreed, her tone wry. "But if anyone should be Persephone, I think that should be me, Sally."

"Spoilsport." The other woman sighed. "Determined to keep him all to yourself, I see how it is. Just because you are engaged to be married to the man. . . . Oh, Mr. Denver, you must console my broken spirits."

The young man stammered an answer. "I sh-shall be only too happy to try, Mrs. Forsyth."

Sally might find this insipid twig amusing, but Psyche was bored with him already. She turned back toward Gabriel. Enough was enough. "Excuse me," she said to Sally and her young conquest.

The sun was warm. She unfurled her parasol and lifted it to shade her face as she strolled closer to the knot of feminine admirers surrounding Gabriel.

"Oh, Lord Tarrington," she heard a young woman simper, "you are so witty."

"Indeed," Psyche agreed, raising her voice just slightly. "And so perceptive. Perhaps you would enjoy a stroll among the rest of the flower borders, Lord Tarrington?"

He turned at once and smiled at her, a genuine smile, she would have sworn, then inclined his head to the rainbow of gowns that flanked him. "It's been a pleasure, ladies," he said. "But you must excuse me. I would not allow my betrothed to fatigue herself by walking the gardens without me."

He slipped smoothly through the throng of disappointed faces to take his place by her side, and Psyche felt a small thrill of satisfaction, which she pushed aside as unworthy. It was all a pretense; he didn't really prefer her company to any other lady's.

"Thank you for having pity on my feminine weakness," she said, her tone cool.

"I suspect you would endure the walk without me," he agreed. "But I might not have survived the gale of fluttering lashes much longer. I was in great danger of being blown totally away."

He sounded sardonic, not boastful, and she glanced at him in surprise. Did he truly not enjoy the adulation his remarkable good looks attracted? "I shall try to contain myself, then," she told him.

He grinned, and again, it seemed so genuine, such a moment of shared understanding between two—two friends. But again, she doubted her own perception. He was too smooth, he had outplayed too many opponents across a card table with a face impossible to read. And that did not count

the women he had lured to his bed. No, she would not be so
easily taken in.

"Shall we lose ourselves in the maze? I understand it is
quite famous," he told her.

"And how many ladies offered to escort you there?" she
countered, glancing at him through lowered lids. The Sutton
maze was a spot famous for stolen kisses and brief illicit
trysts. "No, thank you. I believe we shall be content with the
flowers."

They ambled toward the beds at the far end of the garden,
walking side by side but not touching hands. She felt a little
self-conscious, recalling the kiss in the attic which she had
tried hard to forget. Perhaps Gabriel was remembering, too.

"I shall not forget myself in public view, dear Miss Hill,"
he told her, his tone mild but his eyes teasing.

"I shall count on it," she retorted, holding her parasol
tightly in both hands, so that he had no excuse to take her
hand. She pretended to lose herself in contemplation of the
flowers. Pausing in front of a large row of tulips, she heard
Gabriel say, "They have even more in Holland. Someday,
perhaps, I will show them to you."

She looked up at him in surprise, and he seemed for an
instant nonplussed.

"Just keeping up our pretense," he said.

"But there is no one to hear," she pointed out, glancing
around.

"A good actor is always in character," he teased her, taking a step closer.

She turned away at once, and he fell silent. But how long
could anyone stare at a bed of flowers? After duly admiring
the rows of scarlet tulips, she found they had run out of garden. Not wishing to return and be surrounded by Gabriel's
throng of admirers, Psyche nodded toward the far doorway.

"Shall we walk amid the fruit trees?"

He smiled and held open the gate. They passed through
the thick stone wall that surrounded the formal garden and
made their way into the orchard, with its rows of flowering
apple trees. Psyche lowered her parasol. The blossoms made

a white canopy above them, dappling the sunshine into mottled shade. The scent was intoxicating.

Psyche felt wistful. It was a setting conducive to romantic thoughts. If her betrothal was not a sham, if their attraction was not assumed, she might lose all her sense of decorum here; a kiss beneath fragrant clouds of flowering trees would be impossible to resist. But, though the engagement might be a sham, she could not lie to herself. The attraction between them was not in the least feigned. She tried to ignore the temptation, but even walking sedately side by side she could feel the allure of his presence, the spark that always flowed between them.

And Gabriel, keeping his gaze studiously averted as he studied, or pretended to study, the blossom-decked trees, did he feel it, too?

Perhaps they should allow someone to see them holding hands, she thought. That was not so very bad. A kiss she could not allow; it was not proper.

"We should look like an affianced couple," she pointed out, trying to keep her voice suitably prosaic.

"Indeed?" He still studied the tree limbs.

"For the benefit of the rest of the party," she explained. The fact that they had left the rest of the party behind in the walled garden did not seem relevant, just now.

"Oh, I agree." Then he turned to face her, and she saw that dreaded look of mischief which always preceded his worst actions.

He put out his hands and grasped both her arms, and she shook her head. "Hand holding is enough, I think."

"Really? I don't find it enough for me, dear Miss Hill."

He pulled her gently forward, and she found herself only a few inches away. She put her hands up against the superfine of his coat and held back. She could not press against him like a servant girl kissing her footman beau in an alley. She was not that far removed from her sense of what was proper. But he lowered his head, and she found her reserve melting. Perhaps, just one kiss—

But he paused and turned his head away. She felt him stiffen.

Psyche straightened, putting more distance between them. "Is someone coming?" she asked, blushing at the exhibition she had almost provided for some gossip to relish.

He didn't answer, but she saw the tenseness in his shoulders.

"What is it?" she repeated, keeping her voice low.

"Nothing. I think." But he took her arm and quickened his pace, as if desiring to return to the company of the other party-goers.

Then Psyche saw a movement behind them, and she glanced over her shoulder. "There's a man peering around the corner of the wall," she said in surprise. "Not a servant, and certainly not a guest, he does not look very well dressed. He has a jacket of some kind of poor brown cloth and rough trousers."

"Yes, you're right. I'm afraid he's the same man I saw on your street yesterday," Gabriel said, his own tone grim. "He must have been keeping watch."

"He's a friend of yours?" Psyche asked, her heart sinking. What kind of vulgar people did Gabriel associate with? Was this his unknown past coming back to haunt them both?

"Hardly. The very opposite, in fact. I thought I had escaped them, but it seems I was wrong."

"Who?" Psyche demanded, not liking his tone. "Escaped whom?"

"Walk faster, Miss Hill. I have no wish to put you in harm's way," was his only—and not very comforting—answer.

They increased their stride, and Gabriel kept her hand securely tucked inside the crook of his arm, keeping her close to his side. She saw that he was walking at a slight angle back toward the garden and the rest of the guests, keeping his body between her and the stranger. She began to feel really alarmed.

"What does he want?" she asked. "If he is after our purses—"

"I'm afraid he may want more than that," Gabriel said. "Don't talk; we must make haste."

They were almost running. But the man behind them, with no need to keep up any pretense, sprinted after them. Psyche heard the rush of steps on the gravel path, coming closer.

"Gabriel?"

"Take my hand; we're going to run for it." His tone was grim, and his mouth pressed tightly together into a thin line.

She slid her hand down into his firm grip. She was frightened, but yet, with Gabriel beside her, not terrified, which she should have been. Who was this strange ruffian and what did he want?

She thought that Gabriel knew more than he was telling her, and once they were safely back amid the crowd, with servants and stout men who would thrust this intruder off the estate without ceremony, she intended to find out just what he was keeping from her.

"Run!" Gabriel directed, and they did.

They had increased their lead over the man in the brown coat, but then, just as Psyche was sure they would make the safety of the walled garden, another man stepped out of the wall's shadow, just ahead of them.

Gabriel muttered an oath beneath his breath. Psyche shivered with shock as they abruptly slowed their steps. Now they found themselves between two strangers. The closest man looked even rougher than the first; his clothes were grimy and his eyes narrow slits. His mouth was twisted by an old scar. Psyche swallowed hard.

"What shall we do?" Psyche breathed to Gabriel, whose brows were knit in thought. "If I scream—"

"They might not hear you," he responded. And she knew it was true. Even from here she could hear the high-pitched chatter from the crowd of party-goers.

"But if we both shout together," she urged, feeling a chill run down her spine. The men were coming closer, and they blocked the path to the nearest doorway in the wall. "Perhaps if we yell—"

But then she heard, like a wailing banshee, the strident tune of a bagpipe. The garden party's entertainment, and the special treat their hostess had hinted at in the invitations.

"Oh, bloody hell," Gabriel snapped. Even standing by his side, she could barely make out the words.

Psyche felt cold with terror. They were lost.

Suddenly she felt Gabriel jerk her hand. "This way," he mouthed. Then they were running again, but this time away from the sanctuary of the stone walls, leaving behind all hope of succor.

"Where are we going?" Psyche tried to say, but she bit back the words almost as soon as they left her lips. She needed her breath for their mad dash, and anyhow, she had realized their destination.

They were headed for the maze.

It was an impressive structure, eight-foot-high walls of thick greenery carefully trained into an intricate maze of twists and turns, with—it was said—only one correct path to the center, which held a lovely fountain and benches to refresh those who had persevered till they found the heart of the puzzle.

Gabriel pulled her inside before she could question the logic of his strategy. The thick hedges rose around them and blocked them from sight. Gabriel pulled her into a side turning almost at once, and then they ran several feet and turned again.

They came to an abrupt halt, and Gabriel gestured for silence. It was unnecessary. Psyche felt her head whirl, and she was speechless. The pipe music had paused, and in the brief stillness she could hear the sound of running, and a muffled oath, words in a Cockney accent whose meaning she could only guess and suspected that she didn't want to.

Gabriel had his head cocked, listening.

Psyche stood, stiff with fear, till she heard the men blunder past them, pushing against the thick unyielding walls of prickly shrubbery and cursing again when they found they could not push their way through, but had to follow its twists and turns like anyone else.

The thick bushes smelled lush and fresh, and the shade was welcome after their mad dash, but Psyche could take little comfort in their moment of repose. Her heart was beating fast, and she tried to take normal breaths.

Gabriel was mouthing something; she couldn't make out the words. She leaned closer, putting her ear almost against his mouth.

"Do you know the way in?" he was asking. "Is there any other exit?"

She shook her head twice, and his expression grew even more severe. His blue eyes were hard and looked almost black.

There was no sound from their pursuers. Where were they? "I've only been here twice," she was emboldened to whisper back. "And I don't remember the secret to the puzzle. Indeed, I never found it out."

He nodded, and they both paused to listen. Silence, then the wail of pipes rose again.

He motioned toward the way they had come, and she understood at once. If their pursuers had gone farther into the maze, perhaps they could slip safely back out the entrance.

With Gabriel leading the way, they walked, swiftly but as lightly as possible, and retraced their steps. Gabriel seemed to remember the way they had come, for which Psyche was thankful. She was already disoriented and was sure she would have taken the wrong turn.

The tall hedges towered around them, and there was nothing in the clear blue sky to guide them. A bee buzzed amid the leaves, but otherwise, she heard nothing but the whine of the bagpipes, which—muffled by the thick hedges—seemed strangely distant.

Gabriel paused at a juncture of passages, and with a tightening of his grip on her hand, indicated that she should stay back. She nodded her understanding. Gabriel bent slightly and peered around the hedge; apparently the way was clear because he tugged on her hand, and then they ran.

But they had gone only a few feet when a shout cut

through the background blare of the pipes. They had been seen! But they could still outrun the stranger—

No, one of the men was standing in the gap through which they had entered the maze. Gabriel swore, and Psyche suppressed a groan. She had hoped the rough-looking men were not clever enough to split up; perhaps they were more practiced at stalking than she had realized.

Just what in heaven's name was Gabriel embroiled in? If they lived through this, she was determined to find out.

Again, they were caught between two foes. But in the maze, there were ample opportunities to slip out of sight. Gabriel turned into a side passage, pulling her with him, and they ran, taking another turn, and then another and another.

"Oh no!" Psyche exclaimed as they skidded to a halt. This time, they had come to a dead end. If the man, or the men, succeeded in following them, they had no way of escape.

Gabriel looked around, as if seeking a weapon. But the slender twigs of the shrubbery, though strong enough when woven together in the thick walls of old greenery, would be little defense if taken one by one. And anyhow, the green branches would be hard to break, and they had no knife.

Psyche drew a deep breath, trying to stay calm. Gabriel had not panicked, nor would she. Her mother had had no patience for swooning, shrieking women, and neither did Psyche.

"What shall we do?" she whispered.

"Wait, for the moment," he whispered back, leaning close so that his breath tickled her ear. "And hope they do not find us here. I regret, dear Miss Hill, that I have led us into a blind alley."

She lifted her brows. "Luck is fickle, even for the most practiced gamester," she murmured.

She saw him, incredibly in this moment of danger, smile. "I do love your sense of the ridiculous," he said, lowering his face to her own.

His comment was so unexpected that she did not attempt to evade his kiss. His lips were as firm as ever, and he did not even seem to be breathing hard after their flight. His embrace soothed her, as perhaps he had intended. Her own pulse calmed in the pleasure of his kiss. This time it was not demanding but gentle, comforting. It seemed to say, "Do not fear; I am with you."

Not to face the perils of the world alone. For a moment, Psyche forgot her own trepidation; she wrapped her arms around Gabriel and pulled him closer. If she could stay here forever . . .

But she could not. The world awaited, not to say two dangerous men whose mission she could only guess. She pulled away from his embrace and said, loud enough to be heard over the bagpipe's wail, "I think we might try—"

Then froze, because the music had died away an instant before she stopped speaking. Had she been heard? Had their hiding place been exposed?

He gestured for silence, and they stood side by side, hardly breathing. Then he nodded toward the passage that had brought them to this dead end, and she followed, tiptoeing. When they neared the end of the passage and Gabriel slowed his steps to check out the intersection with the next corridor, she stood just behind him, still very close.

He leaned to look around the corner of the hedge, while Psyche tried not to make a sound.

A knife slashed through the bush beside them.

Fourteen

Psyche screamed, but the sound was lost in the blare of the pipes as the unseen piper began another tune.

The blade had come within inches of her throat. It was a large, rough-hewn weapon, and it must have been thrust with great ferocity to penetrate so far through the thick hedge. For a moment Psyche felt frozen with fear. She stared at the knife as if transfixed.

Gabriel straightened and grasped her shoulders, pulling her away from the threatening sharp edge. "Stay behind me," he ordered, his voice so grim that she hardly recognized it.

Then he turned away, and before she could protest this apparent rejection, she saw why.

One of the men had stepped around the corner of the maze. There was nowhere for them to retreat to—the dead end behind them blocked their passage—and she could hear curses as the second ruffian, pulling his knife from the thick hedge, tried to find his way back around to join his partner.

The other man held a smaller blade, smaller but still lethal, and his expression was set, his eyes devoid of any normal human emotion. It was the face of a man prepared to kill, Psyche thought, feeling cold all the way to her bones.

"Gabriel—" she whispered, then stopped, unwilling to divert his attention. He had put her behind him, and all she could see was the tenseness of his shoulders, but even the back of his head, as he watched the villain before them, revealed his alertness, his readiness.

Somehow, Psyche felt less afraid. She stood up straighter, preparing herself for the attacker's next move. She would not distract Gabriel by screaming or swooning or behaving like a fool.

The man jumped forward. Gabriel, unable to step aside and expose her, moved swiftly to deflect the blow. But she heard him grunt, and she feared that the blade might have met flesh.

Yes, she saw drops of blood fall to the gravel path. Gabriel was hurt!

Whatever her counterfeit fiancé had done, he did not deserve to be cut down like this, murdered by some nameless man when, with another person to protect, he could not even properly defend himself. Some distant part of her mind brought up her mother's voice, saying icily, "Why do men always feel that women are so defenseless?"

But what could she do? Psyche found that she was still clutching her parasol; it was frail and light, not much of a weapon. But still, the unexpected could startle, could divert attention.

Deliberately, she stepped to the side, away from Gabriel's protecting frame. He must have detected the movement from the corner of his eye because he muttered, "Stay behind me, Psyche."

She ignored him. The grimy man with the blade had his eyes focused only on Gabriel, and they had little time. The man's partner would find his way through the tangle of passages and be with them at any moment. She watched the villain carefully, and when he raised his arm again, she thrust with the furled parasol.

The assailant swore and shoved the delicate thing back. The spine cracked uselessly; she had never expected it to be an effective weapon. But she had given Gabriel his chance.

He sprang forward and with his left hand pushed the knife aside, then with his other fist gave the villain a resounding crack to the jaw. The man crumpled neatly.

Psyche gazed at the supine form. She had expected Gabriel to do something, but this was neat work, indeed. Such an economy of movement—no wonder men went to see bouts of boxing.

The fallen man moaned and tried to sit up. Gabriel kicked him in the stomach, and the man collapsed again.

"Come along," Gabriel commanded. He put his hands around her waist and lifted her bodily over the form that blocked the gravel path, then jumped over the villain. "We must run."

Run they did, pounding down the passages. Psyche hoped they would not meet the other man face-to-face as they twisted and turned and wound their way back—she hoped—to the entrance.

Again, Gabriel did not fail them. He led the way to the opening in the maze, and then they were outside again on the grass, panting, but there was no time to catch their breath. They raced across the empty lawn till they reached the stone wall of the formal garden, and only then did Psyche manage to say, "Wait."

Gabriel halted abruptly, leaning against the wall. "What? We should get into the crowd before they emerge from the maze."

"Yes, but we cannot go in like this." Psyche touched her hair, trying to tuck in the strands of hair that had come loose in their frenzied dash. "And you are bleeding!"

He glanced down at the stain of red that marked the white cuff of his shirt. "It's nothing, he barely marked me."

If that was nothing, she hated to think what he would consider a serious attack. "We need to talk," Psyche said, grim again. "I want to know—"

"Later," Gabriel told her. "We need to lose ourselves in the protection of the other guests." As he spoke, he had pulled out a clean linen handkerchief. He slid his arm out of the tight-fitting coat and pushed up his shirtsleeve. "If you would assist me?"

Grimacing when she saw the jagged cut, she wound the cloth around his arm. "You need to have that bathed," she worried.

"Later," he promised, watching her tie the handkerchief neatly so that it would stay in place. He pulled his sleeve down and then put his arm gingerly back into his coat, pushing the stained cuff up beneath his coat sleeve and out of sight. "Come on."

"I still look out of sorts," she protested, brushing a stray leaf off her skirt, and finding a lock of hair brushing her cheek.

"They will only think we stole a kiss in the maze," he told her and, taking her hand, pulled her firmly inside the garden.

With that thought in her head, Psyche had to face the curious eyes as everyone within ten feet, it seemed, turned to stare at them. There would be gossip aplenty about this little episode, she thought, trying not to blush. But the scandalmongers would never—she hoped—know what greater defamation they had missed.

She whispered to Gabriel, "Should we not send someone to apprehend those men? What if they attack the house?"

"With so many servants on hand, they will not risk it," he assured her. "Besides, what those men want is here. I'm sure they have taken to their heels by now and will be out of sight before we could raise an alarm."

She had to be content with that. To be truthful, she dreaded having to tell her hostess that her, Psyche's, fiancé had thugs stalking him. But she had to know what had caused this dreadful attack. What did he mean, "what they want"?

"We need to talk! Soon!" she hissed to Gabriel beneath her breath.

He nodded, but already, two women were crossing the grass to their side. It was Aunt Mavis and Cousin Matilda.

Psyche was thankful to see friendly faces. Well, one friendly face. Matilda was smiling bashfully, but Mavis frowned.

"Push your hair back into place, Niece," Mavis said. "Do you wish to be the talk of the Ton?"

"Come now, Aunt, if I may call you so," Gabriel said with his best smile. "Of course young lovers must steal a kiss now and then. I'm sure you remember how it was when you were first courting?"

Psyche was diverted by the thought of her sour-faced relative ever being young and giddy, but to her amazement, Mavis's expression wavered and her cheeks turned a pale shade of pink.

"Well . . ."

"You see, I was certain that you, too, have known the madness of first love. I've no doubt that you were a young lady impossible to resist."

Mavis frowned, as if suspecting sarcasm, and Psyche held her breath. Had he gone too far?

"You have the carriage of a queen," Gabriel said, smiling sweetly at her poker-stiff aunt. "And such expression in those lovely arched brows." His own dark brows rose a bit, and he smiled at the older woman.

How did he do it? He always found the most admirable trait. . . . If it was a ploy, it was a good one, Psyche thought, watching Mavis melt into girlish confusion. And if it was not just a parlor trick, this man had to have some goodness inside him, more than the surface charm, the incredible looks. But what about the scandal in his past, not to mention assassins in his present life? There was much here still to be unraveled.

"Oh, Mama, it's true," Matilda, always helpful, was saying. "You have beautiful brows. I wish I had inherited them, instead of Papa's bushy ones."

Mavis knew when she had lost the battle. She managed an almost benevolent expression. "I suppose I do remember," she admitted. "But Psyche, nonetheless, do push that lock of hair back into place. Discretion is still a virtue."

"Discretion is a necessity," Gabriel agreed. "Total abstention, however, is not."

"Lord Tarrington!" Matilda protested with a sigh. "You are shameless."

"I know," Gabriel agreed, as the corner of his mouth quirked with mischief. "It's one of my charms."

"Come along," Psyche said, afraid to let her roguish fiancé continue along this dangerous path. "Let us go and speak to our hostess. And I need to check on Aunt Sophie."

They all walked back to the top of the garden, where chairs and tables had been placed on the grass. They found Sophie chatting with several other older ladies.

"Ah, there you are," she said. "Psyche, the servants are about to serve lunch. Do find a seat, child. You keep disappearing, and it will cause talk."

"Yes, Aunt," Psyche agreed, only too glad to sit safely amid the crowd and enjoy the countess's ices and meringues and other light fare prepared for the outdoor luncheon. The countess had a French chef whose reputation, they soon discovered, was well earned.

But even as she munched on lobster fritters and crepes decorated with strawberries from the countess's glass hothouses and served with clotted cream, Psyche had to remember to maintain a pleasant expression. Her thoughts were not as sweet as the many confections that tempted her taste buds.

Why was Gabriel being stalked?

To her frustration, Psyche was unable to question him. For the rest of the party, they stayed safely amid the crowd. When the luncheon was cleared away, the party gradually broke up, and she called for their carriage, not even going up to the house but waiting by the driveway chatting to their hostess until it drove up. Then she and Aunt Sophie were handed in, and Gabriel took his seat opposite them, and the barouche drove off at a smart pace. She still could not speak of the issues that lay heavy on her mind, she had to listen to her aunt chat about gossip she had garnered at the party.

She knew that Gabriel was watching the road behind

them all the way back to London, but their assailants seemed to have been discouraged. There was no sign of them, and Psyche breathed a sigh of relief when they drove up to their own town house. They assisted her aunt down and saw her safely into the house, then Psyche turned back to Gabriel. "I would speak with you," she hissed beneath her breath. "In the library. At once!"

"Psyche, aren't you coming?" her aunt called from the doorway.

"Right away, Aunt," Psyche answered, but she threw a dark glance toward Gabriel, whose expression was guarded. This time, she would have the truth.

Aunt Sophie was fatigued from the excursion. Psyche offered her arm up the first flight of steps, and then handed her relative over to her dresser, when the maid hurried downstairs to assist her.

"You must take a nap, Miss Sophie," the maid said, looking in concern at the lines of weariness on her employer's face. "You've missed your usual lie-down."

"Nonsense, I'm barely winded. I shall just rest upon my bed and close my eyes for a moment, that is all," the older woman said.

"Yes, ma'am." The maid exchanged a knowing glance with Psyche. In five minutes, Sophie would be sleeping soundly.

Psyche leaned to kiss her aunt's cheek. "Just so," she agreed, and when Sophie disappeared into her bedchamber, she was at last free to turn and descend the steps. She paused only long enough to remove her own hat and gloves and spencer, which she had worn to prevent a chill in the open carriage, and hurried to the library.

To her annoyance, the room was unoccupied. She pulled the bell rope and, in a moment, Jowers appeared.

"Have you seen Lord Tarrington?" Psyche tried to keep her tone level.

"I believe he is in his bedchamber, miss," the butler said, his expression suitably bland.

"Oh." Perhaps he had gone up to change his bloodstained shirt, she thought. In that case—

"Packing," the butler added.

Psyche's mouth flew open, then she collected herself. "I see," she managed to say. "That will be all."

The servant blinked; any questions he had would not be answered this hour. As soon as he had departed, Psyche retraced her steps and almost ran up the staircase. She walked rapidly down the hallway to the best guest chamber and, after a quick knock, turned the knob and flung open the door.

It was true. Gabriel was folding his new shirts and placing them carefully into a worn carpetbag that sat on a stool in front of his wardrobe. The footman who had been serving as his valet was helping, his expression very glum.

"What are you doing?" Psyche demanded.

Gabriel looked up. He did not smile, as he usually did in greeting. Instead he glanced toward the servant. "Thank you, I will finish this myself."

The man bowed and disappeared into the dressing room, shutting the door carefully behind him. The door to the hall was ajar. Psyche glanced at it; she did not wish to suggest impropriety, but yet, she could not allow anyone to overhear this conversation, either. Sighing, she crossed and shut the door.

Gabriel watched her, a hint of his usual mischief in his tone. "If you wish a private moment to say good-bye—"

"I'm not in the mood for nonsense," she snapped, determined not to be diverted. "What do you think you're doing?"

"I'm leaving, dear Miss Hill. I would not wish to cause you embarrassment, and certainly not any physical danger. So I shall depart, quietly, and you can resume your proper and safe existence."

It was just what she had been ready to order him to do, and yet, illogically, she felt a burning anger that he would just give up and be ready to walk away.

"You have no right to leave!" she said hotly.

He raised those eloquent dark brows. "I beg your pardon?" He sounded genuinely surprised.

She wasn't sure she believed herself either, but she plunged ahead. "You made a promise to me, and I still do not have my money from my uncle; he must release it soon. You must stay here until he does, and until I agree that your employment is no longer necessary."

Gabriel put down the fine linen shirt and gave her his full attention. "But—"

"That does not mean that—that I don't still demand to know exactly what is going on. Why were those men following you—us? Why do they wish you harm?"

He frowned.

"The truth, not some fanciful tale," she warned him.

"Very well, but it will take some time to explain. I am not sure this is the right setting." He glanced at the bed. "I do not mind the servants gossiping, if you do not, but—"

Psyche flushed. This was quite a switch! He was thinking of the proprieties, and she was the one whose wits were wandering. Was the whole world going mad?

"I shall await you in the library," she said, trying to regain her dignity. "But I expect you momentarily."

And if you try to slip out, she thought, *I will—I will—I will never forgive you!* She turned and left the room quickly before he could discern her emotions. Outside in the hallway, she paused and tried to compose herself. She had been wishing him gone for days; she should have let him leave.

But her family, her uncle, the inheritance she was trying to secure—no, she did need him, for a while, at least. Then, when Psyche was mistress of her own funds, and Circe could be tutored properly, and they had funds to travel, then—

But she would not think of that just now. She went to the staircase and made her way down to the library, which was still unoccupied. She rang the bell rope and when Jowers appeared, told him, "Bring a tea tray for two, if you please."

He bowed and left, and she could see the speculation behind his bland expression. The servants would likely be wondering if the two of them had had a spat and then reconciled. So be it. She could not control their thoughts, and so far, the household knew nothing really damaging, except Simpson, of course, whose loyalty had been proven many times over.

Jowers brought the tea tray just as Gabriel appeared. He came into the room, nodding to her, and stood in front of the fireplace, waiting for the servant to put down the tray.

"I will pour, thank you," Psyche told the man. When Jowers had shut the door behind him, she ignored the tea tray, however, and stared at Gabriel.

He seemed to feel her gaze because he turned to face her. "What do you wish to know?"

"What do I wish to know?" she repeated, becoming annoyed all over again. "I wish to know why men with knives are following you, assaulting us both! Don't be a simpleton, tell me what kind of quagmire you have become involved in."

He folded his arms, looking for once almost defensive. "It started with a card game," he said.

Psyche shook her head. What else could she expect from an admitted gamester. "And?"

"I won an estate," he said baldly.

Psyche had heard of outlandish wagers before, huge amounts lost and won on a draw of the cards or a roll of dice. The concept was not unknown, but still, she blinked at his admission. "An estate?" Her tone was skeptical. "Is this another paper castle—"

"Like the marquisate you conjured up? No, my dear Miss Hill, the property is quite real, and it is mine, or will be, soon enough."

She shook her head. "What madman would bet his whole estate on a game of chance?"

"Someone who thought he was a better player than I. He was mistaken," Gabriel noted, his voice as chilly as her own.

"I've heard of wild wagers, but this is . . . And you mean to take it?"

"Of course I mean to have it. A man's gambling debts are

debts of honor, dear Psyche." He knew how to distract her, that was for certain. At the use of her Christian name, he saw the lights gleam in her eyes, and some of her reserve slipped away. "However, the loser, Barrett, is dragging his feet," Gabriel was forced to admit, "not wanting to hand over the property."

"So some debts are less honorable than others?" she suggested.

"Or some men," he countered.

She stared at him, as if still trying to believe the whole idea. Did she see him differently now? A man with property was a man to be respected, Gabriel thought, remembering his own elation when he had bested Barrett that eventful night in a smoke-filled Paris gaming salon.

"A nice little property in the south of England, the man said," Gabriel mused aloud. "With a manor house dating back a hundred years, and all the usual outbuildings. A spacious home park, and several farms with tenants paying rent."

"An estate for a gentleman," Psyche said, understanding dawning. "This was your means of returning to your homeland."

He nodded, and his glance held appreciation for her quickness. "Yes. I hoped to regain my birthright, if you would. I still plan to do so."

"But what does this have to do with the men at the maze?"

"Ah, yes, well . . ." He looked away from her for the first time. "It seems Barrett has hired a gang of ruffians."

"To do what?" Psyche asked, feeling goose bumps rise on her bare arms. She was afraid she knew the answer even before he spoke.

"To kill me, thereby—Barrett hopes—rendering the whole matter void."

Psyche shivered, then tried to be logical. "But that's nonsense," she protested. "Your heirs would inherit the property."

Gabriel's smile was grim, a bare lifting of his lips. "I have no heirs."

Her surprise must have shown. "No family at all?"

"None that would claim me," he said shortly, his tone even. But she caught a glimpse of the pain beneath the facade he struggled to maintain, and she felt a flicker of pity that she knew she dared not reveal. He had turned a little away again, as if through some instinctive wish to hide his face, and he stared into the embers of the fire.

He looked very alone.

Psyche knew about being alone, about making your way through life without an ally. And yet when her parents died, she had had an extended family of uncles and aunts and cousins whose support she could draw upon, even if some were more a hindrance than a help, so her experience had been nothing like his. Why had he been forced to leave England? There were still puzzles here, and it was still possible that he had committed some great wrong. Perhaps if she knew the truth it would horrify her, repulse her so much that she could never smile at him again, and it was for that reason that he was keeping silent.

But just now, all she could think of was the pain she felt in him, pushed deep beneath the cool charm and devil-may-care insouciance with which he usually faced the world. He was alone, and so was she. And he needed a friend, whether or not he would admit it.

"You can't go," she said, holding out her hand toward him. "I will not be bested by a poor loser with no honor, nor by his hired henchmen."

He looked up at her in surprise, and the light shining in the depths of his eyes made her glance away. She did not wish him to think—

"It is for my own benefit," she added hastily, dropping her hand quickly lest he misinterpret the gesture. "I mean, I need you here to keep up the pretense of the betrothal. I shall get my inheritance soon, or a good part of it, and by then perhaps you will have established a clear title to the property. So we shall both benefit. But you must stay."

Gabriel tried to keep his face impassive. Psyche fiddled with the lace trim on her bodice and did not meet his eyes. She could not mean—no, it was for convenience, as she said, for their mutual financial advantage.

But the warmth that had flooded him when she had refused to let him go—it filled a cold emptiness deep inside that he had lived with so long that he had expected it to be part of him forever.

Some small share of the old pain eased. There was still a great abyss of rejection and loss that he would carry with him always, but, like a sweet-smelling blossom drifting down to float on a dark woodland pool, something had been added.

Someone had held out her hand to him, and the look she had given him had been one of friendship, he was sure of it, not of an employer needing an actor to play a part, nor even of a woman lusting for his physical beauty and masculine energy. He had seen enough of those, and often enough had met their lusts with his own, with easy cynical charm and no emotion attached to those couplings.

With Psyche, it would never be that. With Psyche, he wanted something more, and the revelation shocked him. She would have no idea what urges, what needs she stirred within him, and he must not allow her to find out.

When this charade was played out, he must leave her. He had no right to possess such a lovely woman, to wish to hold such an untainted spirit, not when he carried with him the guilty memory of his destruction of another beautiful woman. He was cursed by his own sins, which would be branded forever on his soul, and he must bear them alone.

She was watching him.

"Very well," Gabriel said, and he found that his voice was husky. He cleared his throat and tried to give her his usual easy smile. "As long as you need me, I will stay."

Fifteen

The knowledge that there were hired murderers on Gabriel's trail could not just be ignored. That very afternoon, Psyche spoke to Jowers about hiring extra footmen.

"Big men, by preference," she told him. "And I want you to be extra vigilant about keeping the outer doors locked, and to watch for strangers who seem to be interested in the house."

The butler gazed at her with an unreadable expression, but his answer was spoken calmly. "Just as you say, miss."

She and Gabriel, sharing the tea at last, had also worked out a credible excuse over their teacups that would allow him to stay at home, out of sight and out of harm's way.

"I do not think you will be in any danger on your own," he told her. "It is me they are looking for."

Psyche nodded. "If I give up all my engagements, Sally will fuss. And it's true, it would cause talk."

So the next day she and Aunt Sophie went off to the theater unaccompanied by any male presence, and when a bevy of disappointed ladies came to their box after the first act to ask why the delightful Lord Tarrington was not with them, Psyche was ready with her answer.

"Alas, he slipped on a pebble during a walk in the countess's garden yesterday, and his ankle has swollen up dreadfully." Psyche smiled sweetly at Mrs. Monnat's Lucille.

"But he was walking just fine when he left," another young lady pointed out. "I watched him particularly." Then she blushed at her admission.

"I'm sure you did," Psyche said, her own tone dry. "No, it was not apparent at once, but by the time we reached home, his foot had begun to go black and blue. He has been advised by my physician to stay off his feet and to keep the ankle elevated."

"But there is Mrs. Forsyth's dance coming up soon," another young woman wailed. "He will miss it all."

"I'm sure he regrets that keenly," Psyche agreed.

Aunt Sophie plied her ivory-backed fan. "Not so much as the ladies of the Ton, I'll wager."

The young women around them blinked and reddened, and the raising of the curtain for the next act was a logical excuse for them to flee to their own seats.

"May have to lend you my cane to beat 'em off," Aunt Sophie said. "Marrying that scamp may be quite fatiguing for you, Niece."

Psyche grinned. "Do you think I should throw him back into the sea and wait for a better catch?"

Sophie grunted, an inelegant noise drowned out by a scattering of laughter from the spectators in the pit below as the actors in front began to declaim. "I doubt you will do better than Tarrington," she said, turning her gaze back to the stage. "If I were thirty years younger, I would have tried to snag him first."

Surprised, Psyche stared at her aunt. She had thought Sophie impervious to the most charming rogue. But Gabriel was more than that, and his allure was owing to more even than his remarkable good looks. It was the intelligence lurking beneath his laughing blue eyes, the kindness he occasionally exhibited, almost despite his own wishes, the way he spent time so willingly with a child or an older lady. It was—

Oh, what was the use in cataloguing Gabriel's positive

traits? He was not a permanent part of her life. He was only here for the interim until they both had their affairs in order. She must remember that. He was little more to her than the narrow-shouldered Mr. Green who still came every day to scribble away in her book room, playing the part of her fiancé's secretary.

Gabriel was an actor, too, in his own way, and she could not trust even what she thought she knew of him. As if her aunt could follow the direction of her thoughts, the other woman glanced across at her niece, her brows slightly lifted.

"Do you know anything about the Sinclairs?" Psyche asked, keeping her voice low. "Before they—he had the title, I mean."

Sophie pursed her mouth. "Not to speak of; I can inquire."

"Quietly, please," Psyche suggested. Sophie's cronies, older ladies with prodigious memories, were devoted in equal parts to long reminiscences and gossip both ancient and recent. She didn't wish to stir up any muck from the bottom of the pond, but if there was anything about Gabriel that she should know . . . and he was keeping something in his past a secret, something he was very much ashamed of. Even though he would be leaving soon, Psyche wanted to know the truth. At least, she thought that she did.

For the rest of the play, Psyche tried hard to listen to the actors onstage, but the drama played out there was so insipid compared to the drama of her own life that the flowery dialogue could not hold her attention. Her thoughts always returned to Gabriel, once again a virtual prisoner in her home, and how galled he must be to have to stay inside and out of sight.

After the play, a loud and occasionally funny farce was enacted upon the stage. During the scattered rounds of laughter and catcalls, Sally came across to speak to her. After greeting Sophie, Sally turned to whisper, "The ladies are gossiping about your stroll in the orchard yesterday. And now this sprained ankle—dear, dear. A stolen kiss is one thing, Psyche dear, but must you attack the man?"

Psyche's mouth dropped open. "Sally!"

"Just teasing." Sally giggled. "I know you wouldn't do anything so improper. Your life might be more entertaining if you did. If it had been me walking unobserved with your Lord Tarrington, now, it might be another story."

"If you don't stop saying such things, you will have no reputation left at all," Psyche observed tartly. "I only say this as your friend, of course."

"Of course," Sally agreed, but some of the laughter in her face had faded. "Amazing what hurtful things your friends can utter."

Psyche felt thoroughly ashamed of herself. "I didn't mean it, Sally. I beg your pardon. No one who knows you would think ill of you, it's just—just that you do have a tendency to make sport of serious matters—"

Sally waved her fan in disgust. "Lord, Psyche, you sound as bad as Percy! Don't sermonize."

"Your levity might be misconstrued, that is all," Psyche tried to explain.

"Like your exaggerated sense of propriety?" Sally gazed at her, her expression for once serious. "You never used to be so strict, Psyche. In our first Season, we were both dreadful scamps, and you were just as irreverent as I was. Only since your parents' death—"

Psyche brushed the words aside. She did not wish to discuss a painful subject. "I'm only trying to help."

"That kind of help I can do without," Sally snapped. "I have plenty of aunts and cousins of my own, not to mention my sainted mother-in-law! You are supposed to be my friend."

"I am your friend, and I apologize," Psyche said contritely. "I will not judge you, Sally. Please forgive me."

"Only if you promise to smile, and not be so dreadfully serious. You will get lines in your forehead well before your time," Sally warned, her tone severe.

That did make Psyche smile, and the tension between the two eased. They spoke of Sally's continued preparations for her masquerade ball and the costume she was having made for it, and of the new gown she had glimpsed at the dress-maker's.

Psyche tried to pay attention, keep her thoughts in order, but again they strayed to Gabriel. Frowning, she stared hard at the stage, where an actor waved his arms and bowed too low, losing his hat. The crowd in the pit below laughed and jeered.

Sally nudged her. "He's trying to be funny, you goose. Why are you making such a face at the poor man?"

"I'm, ah, just thinking that the lead actor is a bit disappointing." Psyche tried to sound convincing.

"Of course you are. You didn't hear a word I said about my new gown."

"It has silver-trimmed lace around the neckline," Psyche argued.

"Gold," Sally responded. "You see? And you were not watching the actors. You were a million miles away. You are not by any chance missing your handsome betrothed?" Sally plied her fan gracefully.

"Hush, I cannot hear the players." Psyche refused to rise to her friend's bait. "This actor is really quite amusing."

"You just told me how badly they were playing, so what does it matter?" Sally retorted. She rose to return to her own box. "Don't try to fool me, Psyche. I've tried all the tricks myself, plus a number your honest soul has never conceived of. Whatever your motives were for contracting this unexpected engagement, I know when you are in danger of losing your heart."

Startled, Psyche turned to stare at her friend, but Sally had lifted her long train to step back out into the corridor behind their box and didn't meet her gaze. It must have been only a frivolous jest, one of Sally's usual quips. Surely her closest friend did not mean to be serious.

Despite a few wayward thoughts, Psyche had no intention of falling for a man who was everything she most despised—a fraud, a gamester, a man with shameful secrets in his past. Even worse, in a way, he was a man who could not be depended upon to conduct himself with proper decorum.

And when her parents died, hadn't Psyche vowed that a conventional life, with no cause for gossip, no eccentricities to be whispered about, would be so much easier for everyone, so sweetly predictable, so much less cause for pain?

She must remember that hard-won pledge.

Gabriel paced up and down before the flames dancing on the hearth in the library. The chair set in front of the fireplace was soft, its leather upholstery smooth with age; the candles on the table burned steadily, their lights glinting off the glass panes of the bookcases. The glass of wine waiting beside his chair was mellow and rich to the palate, its ruby depths pleasing to the eye. Yet, with all this, he could not be at ease. The luxurious refuge of Psyche's comfortable town house had begun to seem more like a prison. It was ridiculous; surely, he could stay at home for one night.

Yet he was skulking at home like a wounded fox in its den, all because of that bastard Barrett. Gabriel wished that he could call Barrett out, but the man had no sense of honor—his treatment of the gaming debt was ample proof of that.

Gabriel had won the estate fairly, by his own skill at cards and a little judicious luck. Yet despite that, now Gabriel was the one who was chained to his fireside, while that villain crawled through the muck of London's seamiest gaming clubs, trying to repair his lost fortunes. It made Gabriel seethe with the unfairness of it.

Of course, he might not have been so discontented if Psyche had been at home, too. He had promised Psyche that he would stay inside, out of sight, protected. But Gabriel had spent the last fifteen years living a precarious, dangerous, *exciting* life, and it was not so easy, he was finding, to suddenly play it safe. It was boring. Not only that, it offended his sense of pride. If anyone should be frightened, it was Barrett, the miserable little coward hiding behind his hired thugs.

The more he thought about it, the more affronted he was by this whole arrangement. No, by God, he would not do it. When he was sixteen, he had done what he'd been told, allowed a woman to bend him to her will, to make all the decisions. But he also had sworn that would never happen again!

No, it would not do. Psyche would have to understand that some impositions a man could not bear. Gabriel took two long strides and rang the bell.

In a moment, Jowers appeared. "Yes, my lord?"

"Bring my hat, Jowers. I am going out."

The butler hesitated for an almost imperceptible moment before he replied, "Yes, my lord."

He disappeared, and Gabriel pushed back a momentary glimmer of guilt. He had promised Psyche, who he knew had only the purest motives—but it was his own safety he was risking, not hers, and he must be allowed to risk his own neck if he so chose. The important thing was that he was the one who made the choice; he *would* be his own man.

When Jowers returned, Gabriel donned his hat and looked over his shoulder as he headed for the door. "If Miss Hill returns before I do, tell her . . ."

"Yes, my lord?" Some flicker in the butler's impassive expression made Gabriel grimace.

"Actually, you don't have to mention that I have gone out."

"Yes, my lord." Amusement glinted for an instant behind Jowers's sober countenance.

"Not that I care—" Gabriel began, then realized that explaining himself to the butler was undignified. Oh, the hell with it, he told himself.

Yet, when the footman held open the big front door, Gabriel hesitated for a moment on the front steps. Beyond the flambeau's circle of light, the street seemed very dark. No carriages rolled past. It was late to be going out and early to be coming home again, and the rest of the houses along the street seemed to have turned their gazes inward.

Was he being a fool?

Probably. Gabriel grinned a little at the thought. Definitely. But he had tempted Lady Luck too many times to stop now. He saw no sign of lurking villains, so he set off down the steps with a determined gait. Still, he was not stupid enough to linger in the shadows. He walked at the edge of the street and avoided the darkness at the sides of the houses and the deep caverns of blackness that led into alleys.

Somewhere, he heard the distant tlot-tlot of horses' hooves and the clatter of carriage wheels rolling over paving stones. Then it was quiet again, and he could have sworn he heard the quiet footfalls of a solitary walker a few feet behind him.

Gabriel felt the hair on the back of his neck stand up, but he did not turn to look. He continued with a confident, steady gait, but his ears were attuned to the sounds behind him, and he felt like a cat, trying to see through the darkness, trying to listen for the rush of footsteps that would presage an attack.

He would be sadly outnumbered when it came; why had he done this? Was having one's freedom important enough to risk one's life over? It was just that he did not like to be manipulated, Gabriel told himself. He would not have his life ruled by others, certainly not by a cad like Barrett.

Gabriel's hands closed into fists as he heard a crackle, as of someone stepping on a fallen twig. The unseen stalker was moving closer. He should have brought a walking stick, anything that could be used as a weapon.

The sound came again, but Gabriel's pace did not slacken. He was nearing the intersection of the next street now, and his concentration on the man behind him almost cost him his life. He was listening hard for movement behind, but when the attack came, it was from another direction entirely.

Two rough-dressed men stepped suddenly out of the shadows just ahead of him. They were holding clubs, and Gabriel again clenched his fists, wishing for something with which to strike back.

His heart beat fast. He felt the rush of blood to his head and the almost uncanny awareness of every movement that came when one faced imminent death. Psyche would tell him he had been a fool to come out alone, and she was right. But it had been his choice, no one else's. At least the whole gang was not here.

Gabriel laughed. "What are you waiting for?" he demanded.

The first ruffian blinked in surprise and lifted his cudgel.

"Aren't you even going to make a pretense of asking for my purse?" Gabriel inquired, his tone easy. "You're new at this, aren't you?"

The bully paused, apparently confused by a victim who did not flee in terror, who seemed amused and spoke in conversational tones. "Um," he muttered. "As to that, 'and over your purse."

"No, you blockhead." The other man jabbed his companion in the ribs. "The man said we don't wait for nut'in'."

"But if 'e got blunt on 'im . . ." the first man argued.

Gabriel still listened for sounds behind him, but the third assailant seemed to be biding his time.

"Enough of this," he murmured. He stepped forward, straight toward the first man, who held the cudgel.

Startled by the unexpected actions of their prey, the man raised his club and swung, while his companion moved back to give his companion room.

But Gabriel jumped inside the rising arc of the weapon and hit the big man hard in the stomach. He fell forward, gagging. Gabriel had already turned to the second man, who lifted his own club. This attacker was more experienced, and he did not rush in, watching Gabriel with eyes that seemed pale in the dimness.

A sound from behind made Gabriel whirl to avoid being blindsided, but what he saw was so unexpected that he almost missed the movement of the second ruffian as he swung.

"Look out!" David Lydford, earl of Westbury, shouted.

Gabriel ducked, but the glancing blow caught him on the

left elbow. The impact sent waves of pain up his arm, leaving it momentarily useless.

David was grappling with the second ruffian; the first was still curled up on the street, groaning and holding his gut. David succeeded in grabbing the rough club. Pulling it away from the assailant, David pitched it aside.

Gabriel watched in exasperation as the younger man put up his fists in the elegant style of the best boxing saloons, dancing about lightly on the balls of his feet.

"Put up your hands, you cur," he exclaimed. "I will teach you to attack your betters!"

The second attacker looked disdainful. He reached inside his grimy jacket and pulled out a small but lethal-looking blade.

David hesitated, his eyes widening.

Gabriel took one long step, picked up the abandoned cudgel, and almost casually stepped inside the man's guard so that he could knock him neatly on the head. The man crumpled into a heap, the blade falling with him.

"Never throw away a weapon," Gabriel snapped. "And what the hell are you doing here, anyway?"

"Looking out for you." David sounded hurt. "I knew those men might try to jump you again."

"And you're playing nursemaid?" Gabriel could think of nothing more ridiculous.

The younger man flushed at his tone. "I thought it only fair. I owed you a debt for aiding me the other night, didn't I? Besides, we are old friends, after all."

"That doesn't warrant risking your own neck," Gabriel began, his tone angry. "And where the hell are your guards?"

David's young face turned sulky. "I escaped out the kitchen alley."

"You escaped—"

"Had to, don't you know? I am obliged to you."

Oh, happy days. Gabriel swallowed the sarcasm that rose to his lips. Now the boy thought he had to reclaim his honor. And to tell him how inane that was would only offend his sensibilities further, and the lad would put himself into deeper danger. Gabriel did not need this bantling's blood on his conscience, too!

Still, the lad did not lack for courage, Gabriel thought, as laughter rose inside him to replace his first surge of irritation. He swallowed the chuckle as well; he didn't dare to so much as grin. God forbid he offend the lad any further, or David might end up his bondsman for life.

"You do have a point," he said, his tone grave. "Thank you for your assistance."

David looked gratified. "You are most welcome." He inclined his head slightly. "If you like, we could drop into my club and have a brandy."

With some difficulty, Gabriel kept his expression somber as he nodded his acceptance. "Yes, this kind of exertion does make a man thirsty. In addition, you have suggested a recourse that was so obvious I hadn't thought of it."

David looked uncertain. "Which is?"

"You belong to a boxing saloon, do you not?" Gabriel suggested.

This time, David's frown was suspicious, as if he feared ridicule. "Yes, I do, and if you're intimating that I could put my time to better use—"

"Why on earth would I say that?" Gabriel raised his brows.

"My mother always complains—oh, nothing. What did you have in mind?"

"If you would be so good as to take me there tomorrow, as your guest, I have some business I would like to transact," Gabriel explained.

David still looked mystified, but he nodded slowly. "Of course, I would be honored to introduce you. Gentleman Jackson himself founded the establishment, and . . ."

Gabriel allowed the young man to rattle on, his attention only half on the eager discourse. He was still alert to further dangers from the shadows around them; they would have a quick drink at David's club, and Gabriel would return to the Hill town house. There was a time to be outrageous and assert one's independence, and there was a time to be prudent. He thought he had perhaps done enough of the former for one night.

But as he listened to the boy's rush of words, even with only half his attention, he was aware of symptoms of the same malady that had once beset a much younger Gabriel. David was starved for male company, male approval, and the lad's hunger touched Gabriel deeply. He would have sworn that those feelings were all behind him, all except a burning desire to prove to his father that Gabriel could surmount the exile to which he had been sentenced. His revenge would only be accomplished by his successful return to the life he had once known.

But if that were his only remaining emotion, why did he respond so keenly to the undertones he heard in David's words? Gabriel pushed the thought aside, but he no longer felt any inclination to laugh at the boy who walked beside him.

When they reached White's, David led the way proudly, introducing Gabriel to several fellow members. Gabriel shook hands and nodded to a couple of men he had met earlier when he had come here with Freddy. His old schoolmate was not here tonight. No doubt he had another social engagement, unencumbered by murderous assailants who lurked in shadows.

"We'll have to put you up for membership," David said after he had ordered the drinks from a footman.

"Yes, Freddy said the same," Gabriel agreed. "I should like that, presently." First, he would prefer to have his own name back, uncluttered by any false title, but he could not explain that reasoning to David. The thought of achieving membership in London's most exclusive male bastion, with no help at all from his father, amused him.

The footman brought their drinks and held out the tray. Gabriel took his glass and saluted David, as he would to an equal.

"To old comrades," he said.

David flushed with happiness, and some of the tenseness

that usually marked his body eased. "To a renewed friend-ship," he agreed.

They both drank. Around them could be heard the mur-mur of men's quiet voices, and in the next room, someone cursing over a bad draw of cards. The fire in the hearth crackled, and he sniffed the pungent smoke of Spanish ci-gars. Gabriel felt strangely at peace.

When Psyche and her aunt returned from the theater, Jowers awaited them in the front hall, along with one of the new footmen, a burly man with wide shoulders and steady eyes.

"Well done," Psyche said quietly to the butler as she glanced at the new servant. He seemed big enough to dis-courage anyone with thoughts of attack.

"Thank you, miss," Jowers said; and although his ex-pression was impassive, she was sure he understood her comment.

"Good night, Niece," Aunt Sophie said. "Do not stay up too long." She ascended the staircase with deliberate care, taking Psyche's acquiescence for granted.

"Yes, Aunt."

Psyche watched her aunt climb out of sight, then thought of the man she had left to while away the evening on his own. Had he been bored by this inactivity? Perhaps she should say something to him, just as a gesture of friendship, she assured herself

"Is Lord Tarrington in the library?" she asked Jowers after he had lifted her satin evening cloak off her shoulders.

"I believe Lord Tarrington is no longer in the library," the butler said. He paused, and Psyche waited for him to con-tinue. But the man was silent.

Psyche blinked. "Then where is he? Surely he hasn't gone up to bed already?" she said. "It's only half past eleven."

Jowers looked almost confused. "No, miss, that is—"

A door opened, and a familiar male voice said, "And how was the theater?"

Psyche relaxed. "Boring. That's why we came home early. What are you doing in the book room?"

"Just checking on my secretary's scribbling. His spelling is most inventive." Gabriel's lazy smile curled his lips, and his blue eyes brimmed with even more laughing mischief than usual.

"But he's copying from a book of sermons," Psyche pointed out. She couldn't hold back her answering smile. How could Gabriel always make her feel more lighthearted just with one lift of those elegantly curved dark brows?

"Then I fear we may need to purchase him a pair of spectacles," Gabriel noted. "Would you join me in the library for a drink before retiring?" He gestured toward the next room.

"Tea will be fine," Psyche said, her tone demure, but she was still smiling as she followed his motion and turned toward the library.

"A tea tray, then," he told the butler. "And a brandy for me, if you please."

There was a movement at the corner of her vision, as if a coin had passed from one hand to another, but Psyche paid it no mind. She somehow felt happier than she had all evening.

The library was serene, filled with the smell of leather and books and the glow of candlelight, although the fire seemed to be dying. She held out her cold hands to the fading flame. When Gabriel came into the room behind her, she glanced up and surprised a quizzical expression on his face, almost one of yearning. The man was full of surprises. And not all of them good, she tried to remind herself, but it was no use. She was still happy to be here in his company.

She remembered the reason she had wanted to see him. "I just wanted to commend you for being willing to stay in tonight," Psyche said. "I know you must be bored with the confinement."

His expression was impossible to read. "I don't deserve your commendation," he said.

She thought she had misheard. "I mean, I just know you would prefer—"

He waved her words aside. "Actually," he turned away slightly and gazed into the smoldering embers, bending to add a piece of coal from the scuttle, "I am more content now than I have been all evening."

She had been about to tell him not to bother, the footman would repair the fire when the tea tray was brought in, but she caught herself. He was not accustomed to being waited on; it was easy enough to see that. He had been on his own for a long time. She wanted to tell him that she realized how hard it must have been, thrust outside of his own social sphere, but she knew he would reject any sympathy, even from her. Perhaps especially from her.

Then she realized the meaning of his last sentence and she looked up, startled. She was afraid she might be blushing. "I—"

"You don't have to answer that," he said, and the reserve, the laughing mask that he usually wore to protect his deeper feelings, fell back into place. "Obviously, I am indeed bored with staying too much indoors. Hopefully, my solicitor will work through the tangle of legal maneuvering very soon, and I will no longer be a burden to you."

Psyche felt cheated. How dare he say such a thing, and then retract it in the next second? Of course, it could be true, he had not meant to imply—oh, drat the man. "No one hopes it more than I," she snapped, then bit her lip. "That is, I hope for your sake that the claim on the estate goes through."

"I appreciate your good wishes," Gabriel answered, his tone dry.

And the happiness Psyche had felt, the indefinable feeling that his presence had induced, had gone. She felt suddenly very tired.

A footman came in with the tea tray and Gabriel's glass of brandy. "I am fatigued," she said. "I don't believe I wish for any tea, after all. Good night, Lord Tarrington."

He nodded, accepting the dismissal. "Good night, Miss Hill."

They might as well be strangers, she thought bitterly as she walked out of the room. They *were* strangers, and it was foolish to think she understood him, that they shared any feelings of—that they shared anything except a mutual business arrangement.

When she reached her own bedchamber and Simpson came in to help her out of her evening dress, Psyche was silent.

"How was the play, miss?" her maid inquired.

"Insipid," Psyche said, knowing that her tone was peevish, but too weary to care. "And I have a headache."

Her dresser tut-tutted in sympathy. "I'll make you a tisane right away, miss."

Somehow, Psyche thought the healing draught would not be enough. She wanted . . . something else—and relief did not seem likely to come.

But she thanked her faithful servant and climbed into bed, pulling the smooth sheet up to her chin and blinking hard against sudden unreasonable tears.

The next morning the earl of Westbury knocked on the mahogany doors of the Hill town house before nine, a little heavy-eyed but his expression eager. David nodded carelessly to Jowers when he was admitted and then sank into a damask-covered settee against the foyer wall. Holding his achy head in his hand, he gestured to Jowers.

"Inform Gabriel I have arrived, won't you?"

If Jowers felt any amusement at the sight of the young earl, he was too well trained to show it.

"At once, my lord." Bowing, he walked smartly away.

As David waited, he held tightly to his head lest it finally roll off his head as it had been threatening to do since he had risen. At this point, he would hardly care.

"Are you ill?"

David jumped so sharply at the unexpected question that he had to take a few deep breaths to control the nausea. When he could speak, he looked around for the phantom voice. The salons on either side of the foyer were untenanted; his foggy mind could not think further than that.

Circe crouched down at the top of the landing, where she often sat quietly to survey visitors. An artist had to be observant, after all. She was about to speak again when Gabriel's footsteps rang on the marble foyer floor.

"Right on time, David," Gabriel said. He had been finishing his coffee and toast with marmalade in the dining room as he waited for David to arrive, hoping the young man would be out of bed in time to make his appointment. But apparently, a session at the boxing saloon was worth the lad dragging himself from his slumbers. Pulling on his gloves, Gabriel paused as he noticed the green tinge of David's skin. "Celebrated a bit longer last night, did you?"

"I'm never drinking again," David moaned, breathing deeply through his mouth.

"Oh, the promises of youth." Gabriel chuckled. "You'll learn."

David groaned. Was it necessary to speak so loudly?

"Maybe more painfully than necessary, but you'll learn." With callous unconcern, he pulled David to his feet and steered him toward the open door. "Let's sweat it out of you. Come along; I have to see my solicitor, Mr. Theobald, after we leave the saloon."

Circe watched silently as Jowers shut the door behind the two men. Slowly, she climbed the stairs to the schoolroom. The morning light would be striking her easel at just the right angle. Besides, she had much to consider.

By the time they had arrived at the boxing saloon, David was feeling much more the thing. Gabriel watched David's renewed enthusiasm as the lad bounded down the step of the phaeton and shook his head. Ah, to be twenty-two again.

After a few words with the doorman, the man bowed and opened the door for them.

"You'll find Jackson a real master of pugilism," David told him eagerly as they went inside. "And his instruction has merit. I am becoming much more practiced with my left hook."

"An accomplishment, indeed." Gabriel hid his amusement.

David led the way past a couple of young men in their shirtsleeves who were eying each other with measuring pugnacity.

"Here he is. Sir," David said eagerly, "I've brought the marquis of Tarrington."

The man who met their gaze was only of middle height but compact of body, with sharp intelligent eyes and a nose that had been broken more than once. He stared at the newcomer, his eyes narrowing.

"Hap' we have met before," he said bluntly. "Tho' thy wasn't any marquis then."

Gabriel smiled ruefully. "My misbegotten youth continues to haunt me," he agreed. "Hello, Jackson."

David's eyes widened. "You know him?"

"Gave me a good jab to the gut once," Jackson said.

"You sparred with him?" David looked even more impressed. "And you managed a hit?"

"I had a lucky punch," Gabriel said.

The other man grunted. "Lucky, my arse. And him hardly out of nappies."

"I was a bit older than that," Gabriel objected, but he grinned reluctantly. "I see you've come up in the world." He glanced around at the large open room.

"As have thy, me lord," the pugilist noted.

Gabriel made a face. "Ah, yes. Long story." And a subject he was happy to change. "Actually, I'm glad it's you. I have a somewhat strange request."

Jackson's eyes glinted. "Ah, me lord. Ah'm listening."

And Gabriel explained.

Sixteen

*A*fter a quiet lunch at home with Psyche and David, Gabriel felt sufficiently guilty about his near disastrous late-night foray to resist David's offer to visit his club. Instead, he stayed home while Psyche attended a tea party, but he was not as bored as he had expected. The house was quiet. Sophie had retreated to her room for her usual afternoon nap, and Gabriel sat in the library, drawing up plans for his future home.

Since he had yet to see the building, it was an exercise in futility, yet it soothed him that his solicitor swore that Gabriel was growing closer to the day when he could take possession. He had even acquired reading material on the most up-to-date farming methods so that he could be a reasonable and helpful landlord, not to mention the home farm that was likely attached to his property, which he would oversee himself. To think of having his own land, a piece of England that no one could ever take away from him—he felt a thrill of elation at the thought. And someday, he would be ready to bring a bride there, show her what he had done to the estate, how he had brought it back from its doubtless shabby state under Barrett's indifferent management to the shining success that he meant to make of it.

He could imagine it so easily. He and his bride would stroll the rejuvenated gardens hand in hand. The sweet, heavy air of twilight would surround them with the scents of blossoming roses. And he would tease her by tugging her hairpins out one by one until the golden mass fell in a fragrant spill over his hands. Then he would pull Psyche into his arms and into a darkened corner where he . . .

Gabriel shook his head to clear the sensual images from his mind. He could swear that Psyche's perfume and the scent of roses still lingered around him. He bent his head over his drawing and tried to ignore what his fantasy had implied. His future, hypothetical bride had an alarming tendency to assume the characteristics of his imperious, maddening, and lovely "employer."

No, he did not dare even imagine such an impossible feat. To clear his mind, Gabriel summoned up memories of his father, colored by Gabriel's own youthful vows of revenge. His father would know of his success. Even though the older man seldom ventured into society, he would hear of it. Gabriel would make sure that he did! And the elder Sinclair would recognize that the ne'er-do-well who had lost his birthright had triumphed, redeemed his disgrace, confounded everyone's predictions of an early and disgraceful end.

Someone cleared his throat respectfully at his elbow. Gabriel jumped. He had been so deep in thought that he had not seen the footman come up beside him. Damn, he had blotted his paper.

Gabriel picked up a piece of blotting felt and then glanced toward the servant. "Yes?"

"Excuse me, my lord, but you are wanted in the schoolroom."

That was not a summons one heard every day. Gabriel tried not to smile. What was the imperious Miss Circe up to now? "Very well," he agreed. "I shall come presently."

The footman bowed and retreated, and Gabriel folded his lists of necessary equipment and tucked them into a treatise on modern farming, which he placed in a desk drawer. He made his way up the staircase and found Circe seated on a stool by the window, while the governess worked on a stack of mending a few feet away.

"You wanted to see me?" Gabriel said, sending Miss Tellman an apologetic glance. She frowned a little, but she looked resigned. No one, it seemed, could control Circe when she was determined. In that way, she was much like her sister, Gabriel thought.

"You agreed to let me draw you," Circe said.

He blinked in surprise. "I don't recall—"

"Yes, you do," the child argued. She was wearing a blue smock over her day dress, and there were a few dabs of paint on its skirt. "I told you so the other day, you remember."

"I don't remember agreeing to sit for you," Gabriel pointed out.

"You didn't say no, and that's the same as a yes." Circe flashed him her quick elusive smile.

"Has anyone ever told you of your growing resemblance to your sister?"

An answering spark lit in her clear green eyes. "You and our good Telly would be in agreement, my lord."

"Hmm." Gabriel tried another tactic. "Your sister doesn't wish for me to talk with you, you know. I really should not stay."

"That's all right, you will not be able to talk. If you did, I could not draw your mouth properly," Circe told him, picking up her sketch pad. "And it's well shaped, too."

Effectively silenced, Gabriel gave up the fight. "Where do you wish me to sit?" he asked meekly.

"In that chair. Sit up straight and look toward the window. Put your hand on the book, so," Circe directed.

Gabriel sat down—the chair was shabby but comfortable—and assumed the pose that Circe ordered. He sat very still, and Circe's hand moved swiftly with her pencils and chalks. He found it harder than he had expected. In a little while, he found his arm going numb, and he tried to shift position just slightly.

"No, no," Circe said sharply. "Put your arm back the way it was."

Gabriel obeyed. "It may fall off before you are done," he commented wryly.

At first he thought that Circe was so absorbed that she had not heard, but then she responded, her tone low. "You only need one hand to hold the cards during a game, do you not?"

"I suppose," Gabriel agreed. "And surely I could learn to shuffle the deck with one hand—there must be a way. When I dance with your sister, however, I will be sadly unbalanced. If we find that I cannot perform the waltz at all, she will be most disappointed."

Circe giggled. "Silly. I am almost done." Sure enough, in another ten minutes, she put down her pencil.

"You are fast," Gabriel said. "May I see it?"

But she turned the pad away. "Not yet," she said. "I need to work on a few of the finer details."

Gabriel found he was disappointed, but he nodded. "Very well. Am I dismissed now?"

"Yes, but you must come back again," Circe told him. "To pose for me."

Gabriel felt a little hurt.

"And to talk," Circe added, as if she had read his mind. "We are friends, are we not? No matter what Psyche says."

The child was a witch, Gabriel thought, no doubt about it. He hoped that she never took up serious card playing. He nodded. "I am honored to be counted as your friend."

The luncheon party was rather dull, and Psyche left as soon as she could. She was just going up the steps to her own house when, with a clatter of hooves, Sally swept up in her carriage. The coachman pulled up the perfectly matched gray geldings, and Sally leaned out the window and waved to her.

"There you are," Sally called. "Come along, I'm going to the dressmaker's."

"I'm just getting home," Psyche protested.

"I know, I know, that awful luncheon. I begged off. Come along, this is much more important," Sally insisted. "Get in."

A footman hurried to hold the carriage door for her. Psyche shook her head, but she lifted her skirt and stepped up. Taking her seat, Psyche gazed at her friend.

"What is all this? Why is the appointment with the dressmaker so urgent, and why do you need me there?"

"Because yesterday Madam Simone told me that you have done nothing about a costume for my masquerade ball. Psyche, you wretch, it is tomorrow night! Don't tell me you have forgotten!"

"Of course not." Psyche tried not to look guilty.

"You are coming, you must come. I will hear of nothing else." Sally's bow lips fell into a practiced pout.

"Since there will only be four hundred of London's finest there," Psyche pointed out drily, "I should be sadly missed, indeed."

"I would miss you! You are my best friend, and I want you there!" Sally insisted. "Not to mention your perfectly dashing fiancé."

"The truth is out." Psyche grinned. "I will come, I promise, perhaps even with my fiancé, if his ankle is recovered."

"I will take him with or without a whole ankle." Sally's brown eyes held a wicked gleam, though her tone was demure.

Psyche refused to take the bait. "But why the abduction?"

"Because you cannot come without a costume," Sally insisted, waving her hand. "You cannot wait till the last minute, dear, and expect Madam to come up with a suitable disguise."

"Oh, that." Psyche shrugged. "I had thought a mask and domino would do, or I could find something in the back of my wardrobe—"

"To wear to my masquerade ball, the biggest function of the year!" Sally exclaimed, sounding genuinely horrified. "Psyche, how dare you—"

"It was a jest," Psyche said quickly, laughing. "I was teasing you. I am sorry."

"Very well." Sally fanned her pink cheeks. "As long as you take my ball seriously, I forgive you. However, the fact remains, you have done nothing about a costume."

"I've . . . been a bit distracted," Psyche told her.

Sally sniffed. "I know, I know, mooning over your perfectly divine—"

"Here we are," Psyche interrupted again as the phaeton slowed in front of the modiste's. "I will throw myself on Madam Simone's mercy and see what she can come up with."

"You're still not treating this with the gravity it deserves," her friend complained. "I have been planning my costume for weeks, Psyche!"

"But you are the hostess," Psyche said soothingly. "Of course you must have a grand costume."

"True, wait till you see it," Sally agreed, her frown disappearing. "This is my final fitting."

They were bowed into the dressmaker's shop and taken to the largest fitting room, where Madam herself hurried to wait upon them.

"Ah, Mrs. Forsyth," the seamstress purred. "It is turning out *très magnifique*; you will be sensational."

Psyche waited while Sally disappeared behind a screen. Two of the assistants aided her in disrobing and donning her costume. Psyche listened to the murmur of feminine voices and the rustle of heavy fabric. When Sally emerged, Psyche's eyes widened.

"It fits divinely," Sally pronounced, turning back and forth to gaze at her image in the looking glass. "My, these skirts are heavy."

"Good gracious, who are you going as?" Psyche demanded. "The queen of Sheba?"

"No, silly, Cinderella, after she has married Prince

Charming," Sally explained. "I had to have a dress fit for a fairy-tale princess, however. Is it not amazing?"

"I think I am likely to be blinded," Psyche murmured, as the assistants applauded, and the seamstress beamed—as well she might. Psyche gazed at the resplendent ball gown, which might well have paid the dressmaker's rent for a full year. Its huge golden skirts held two rows of scallops, all trimmed with gold embroidery, and the deeply cut bodice was trimmed with a row of Flemish lace that glittered with gold thread and sparkling gems.

"Surely those are not real diamonds?" Psyche murmured.

"Alas, no." Sally sighed. "Even my sweet Andrew might have drawn the line at that. But they are the very best paste, and I will have real diamonds in my hair and around my throat and in my ears and—"

"In other words, you will glitter from head to toe," Psyche noted. "You should be a marvelous sight."

"Oh, I do hope so," Sally admitted. "Andrew will be my prince, and dear little Mr. Denver is wearing mouse ears."

"Mouse ears?"

"You remember, the mice who turned into white horses to pull Cinderella's coach. And perhaps one or two more young men, too."

"Poor Denver." Psyche raised her brows, remembering the young man's rather narrow chin. He would look like a rat, she thought.

"I have planned this forever. But let us not forget—" Sally turned back to Psyche and looked her up and down. "What about your costume? Who shall you be, Psyche? Madam Pompadour? Cleopatra?"

"No indeed," Psyche said, beginning to get into the spirit of the game. "I shall go as Psyche."

"Dearest, no, you must have a costume!" Sally protested as she adjusted her long train and gazed into the looking glass again. "I insist."

"I shall, I shall." Psyche smiled. "The original Psyche." Her father's penchant for Greek legends might come in useful at last.

"Oh, of course." Sally's brow cleared. "You shall have to tell me the story again. I forget how it goes."

"Psyche married a mysterious young man of amazing beauty—"

"You've got that part right," Sally declared. "Tarrington is a cream puff, dearest."

One of the assistants giggled, then covered her mouth quickly when Madam Simone glared.

Psyche pretended not to hear. "But she was not allowed to see his face or know his name."

"Well, that was hardly fair. I would have peeked."

"She did, but then he was forced to leave," Psyche explained.

"Mm-hm." Sally's attention was wandering. "What a shame. Anyhow, what about the dress? You will need—"

"Something Greek, which should be simple for Madam's seamstresses to create on short notice," Psyche pointed out. "A simple tunic, it was called a chiton, as I remember from Papa's lessons."

"You are much too practical," Sally complained.

But Madam Simone nodded. "*Mais oui*, we can do it. And with Miss Hill's exquisite figure . . ."

Sally looked a bit less enthused. The dressmaker called her assistants, and they held a low-voiced consultation, while Psyche reassured her friend, "It will not be nearly as grand as your costume, of course. The Greek tunics were a simple sort of dress."

Sally was mollified. And presently, when Madam Simone pinned several lengths of white linen into a rough approximation of the finished costume, with a thin gold-colored belt around her waist, Psyche found that the Greek garb might not be elaborate but it was certainly revealing. She was momentarily askance at how much of her bosom the simple drape of the white dress exposed, and as for the glimpse of bare ankles below the linen . . .

Sally frowned for a moment, then laughed. "It will be worth it to see Percy's face," she pointed out. "You will need some gold-colored sandals, Psyche. I have a pair you can borrow that might be just the thing."

Psyche took a deep breath. She did look rather well in the simple gown. She gazed at her reflection. And she would be wearing a mask, of course, so not everyone would even know who she was. It was a liberating idea.

"And," she said aloud, "I believe I should do something about a costume for Lord Tarrington."

"Of course," Sally agreed.

Psyche only hoped it would be more successful than her last effort at dressing Gabriel!

The dressmaker delivered the costumes on Saturday after luncheon and Psyche wondered how to break the news to Gabriel. First she had to locate him. He was not in the library, nor was he in the book room, nor—when she sent a footman to check—was he in his bedroom. He never sat in the parlor, where Aunt Sophie's friends were wont to share hot tea and lukewarm gossip. At last she found him in the back garden, tossing acorns into a hat. The two stable lads who had been urging him on disappeared quickly when they saw their mistress approaching.

Psyche raised her brows. Gabriel looked as striking as ever, though he had removed his tightly fitted jacket to better his aim.

"Are you winning?"

"I always win," he told her, grinning. "Though I fear you have frightened away my competitors."

"I hope you have not won all their wages?" she asked, her voice cool.

His smile faded. "Miss Hill, I do not take money from children. We competed only to demonstrate our skill."

She waved at the cap full of acorns. "A notable accomplishment," she agreed, but this time her tone was easy. "Actually, I have a prize for you. I have found a way to release you from your isolation, at least for one night. Perhaps it will be more congenial than tossing nuts."

She detected a gleam of interest in his blue eyes. "How?"

"You will have a disguise."

His well-shaped brows lifted. "My dear Miss Hill, I am living my life in disguise. Have you devised a new title for me to assume?"

She blushed. "No, that is, Sally—Mrs. Forsyth—is giving a costume ball. It is to be a grand affair, and there will be a sad crush of people, everyone in costume. It's the perfect chance for you to leave the house and enjoy an evening out."

"And what am I to wear? Did you procure a mask and domino for me?" he asked.

"I—I have had a costume made up for you." To her chagrin, she could not keep from coloring again. Her cheeks felt hot.

He gazed at her steadily, but to her relief, did not comment on the last episode of tailoring she had tried to orchestrate. "And may I see this, uh, no doubt ingenious costume you have contrived?"

She bit her lip. "It's really quite clever. I'm going as Psyche, you see."

He was quicker than Sally. "The Greek goddess of great beauty? That is apt."

Good gracious, why could she not keep her composure? She felt her cheeks grow even warmer. "She began as a princess, I believe, and only became a goddess later."

"I stand corrected. And I shall be . . . ?"

This time, Psyche turned away and picked up a stray acorn so that he would not see her confusion. "You are going as Eros."

"Cupid?" She could not see his expression, but his voice sounded strangled. "You expect me to be Cupid? Psyche, if you have decked me out in hearts and gilt arrows, I swear—"

"No, no, it is quite unexceptional," she told him. "You will not be displeased, I promise. At least, it does have a quiver, but you don't need to carry the arrows or bow if you dislike the idea."

"No hearts? No pink velvet?" His tone was still suspicious. "No clouds of gauze to cover my, um, manliness?"

Her traitorous mind immediately conjured up the feel of his body hard against hers. Heat flushed through her as she remembered just what his tongue and lips had felt like as they had explored her own. Drawing a deep breath to clear her head, Psyche dared to lift her head and peek at his face. "Of course not. I would not expose you to ridicule. Although I have no doubt there will be every sort of costume there."

"No hearts," he asserted firmly. "No pink velvet. No gauze."

"But it's a very *manly* gauze," she teased, laughing at his expression of horror. "If you'd like to come inside, I will show you what we have done. My dressmaker had very little time to put it together, so I kept it quite simple."

"Thank heaven for that," he murmured.

She pretended not to hear and, remembering another bit of her mother's excellent advice, kept the rest of her laughter well hidden. He walked side by side with her, and when they had returned to the library, where she had left the costume, he lifted the cotton cloth that had protected it from dust and surveyed it silently.

Psyche held her breath.

"I suppose it will do," he agreed slowly. It was only a black shirt and loose-cut Russian-style trousers, with a blue satin sash, a quiver with fake arrows, and a long cape to wear over it all. "But about this sash . . ."

"You have to have a little color, or people will mistake you for a devil," she told him.

"Quite possible," Gabriel said drily.

"And I said no to wings, though Madame Simone said she could make up quite a nice pair with ostrich plumes and peacock feathers."

Gabriel seemed to shudder. "Very well, I will take the sash since you have spared me the wings. What about a mask?"

That she was most proud of. Psyche took it out of its wrapping and held it out for him to see.

"Ah," he said slowly. "I remember now. In the story, Psyche was not allowed to see her lover's face."

"It was her husband," Psyche corrected, biting her lip so that she would *not* turn red all over again—fair skin was sometimes a trial. "But yes, she was not allowed to see his features."

Gabriel held up the silk mask. It covered most of his face, with holes cut for the eyes, and allowed only a glimpse of his lips to show. Otherwise it was curiously blank—rather frightening, actually, Psyche thought, though she had not expected it to be fearsome when she had explained the idea to the dressmaker.

"And your costume?" Gabriel looked over his shoulder at her.

"You will see it tonight," she said gravely.

Gabriel nodded. "I cannot wait."

"I must go and dress for dinner. We will change into our costumes just after, and then leave for the ball," she instructed him.

Gabriel listened with amusement. He was becoming almost fond of her peremptory edicts. Good God. What was wrong with him?

She excused herself, and Gabriel watched her walk into the hall and gracefully climb the staircase. Perhaps it was because it was difficult to be annoyed with someone so kind. Not only had she been considerate enough to provide a means for a brief reprieve, she had taken his tastes into consideration when choosing his costume. So he had to wear a silk sash—it was a small price to pay for getting out of the house for one evening. And in the crush of people at Sally's ball, it should be easy enough to stay anonymous.

Humming, he picked up his coat and went upstairs to change.

Dinner was a quiet affair. Aunt Sophie had come down with a cough and had decided to beg off from the ball.

"Not that you will need me," she observed tartly. "And I doubt Sally will even notice my absence, the silly twit."

"Sally likes you!" Psyche protested. "And she's not really silly. At least half of her twittering is assumed."

"Humph." The older woman coughed, then recovered and took another sip of her soup. "Sally is well enough, and I will grant you she does have a sweet nature under her posturing, though she will never be as handsome as you."

"Why, thank you, Aunt," Psyche said, looking surprised at this unaccustomed praise.

"I would second that," Gabriel said, slicing his roast lamb.

Psyche looked down at her plate, but he saw that she smiled. He continued to gaze at Psyche across the white-clothed table, crowded with its silver trays and crystal glasses filled with red wine, its china dishes brimming with a bounteous feast, even though it was only the family at dinner tonight. Family. He shook his head at the thought. Already, he had become too accustomed to the role of Psyche's husband-to-be. He thought how much he would miss this easy harmony, this ease of friendship and laughter and goodwill when he would—very soon—have to leave this house, leave all these people behind. The thought was more painful than he would ever have expected, just a few days ago.

"I should think it would be nice to be beautiful," Circe said. Her tone was wistful.

Psyche looked stricken. "Dearest, you are very lovely." she told her sister.

"No, I am not," Circe argued. "I do not have fair hair. Mine is a most indifferent brown and it does not curl, and I do not have nice blue eyes and a straight nose. And I certainly do not have a bosom."

"Circe!" Aunt Sophie scolded. "This is not suitable dinner conversation. Is it necessary to send you back to the schoolroom?"

"I'm sorry, Aunt," Circe said. "But it is an accurate portrait."

Gabriel tried not to laugh, he did not wish to hurt her feelings. "Circe," he captured her attention although he kept his voice low. "All colts go through an awkward stage, you know, before they reach their full growth."

Aunt Sophie looked ready to issue further reprimands, so he hurried on. "What I mean to say is, you are not yet finished growing. I have no doubt that you will mature into a beautiful young woman. Then all the young men in London will have to guard their hearts."

"Do you really think so?" Circe sounded hopeful, and Psyche flashed him a quick look of gratitude.

"I am sure of it," Gabriel said.

"But Psyche will still be more beautiful." Circe poked a fork at her slice of lamb.

Gabriel turned his head so that the child could not see the wink he sent Psyche. "Yes, but by then, she will be old," he said gravely.

Psyche bit her lip to hold back a smile, and Aunt Sophie tried to turn a snort of laughter into a cough, with only limited success. But Circe brightened. "That is true," she said, and began to eat her dinner once again.

After dinner, Psyche went upstairs to dress for the ball. Circe lingered on the staircase. "I wish I could go to the ball. I should like to have a costume," she said.

"Your turn will come, I promise you," Gabriel told her. "Personally, I should be happy to donate one blue satin sash."

She looked hopeful, so he added quickly, "But I fear Psyche will not allow it."

Circe sighed.

"However, you could design a costume for the time when you are a young lady in your first Season," Gabriel suggested, trying to cheer her.

Circe looked interested at once. "That is true. I will get out my colored pencils."

Gabriel left her on the first landing and went up to change into his costume. He still thought a simple domino and half mask would have done as well. However, the fuller mask certainly did cover his face almost completely, and the

Cavalier-type wide-brimmed hat with the long plume that the dressmaker had included would hide most of his dark hair. He looked at the hat, which Psyche had sent up to his room after its late arrival, with disfavor. He didn't know which one was most ridiculous, the hat or that stupid silk sash.

Brickson was there to help him change, looking altogether too cheerful.

"Masquerades should be banned," Gabriel observed as he pulled off his neckcloth and slipped out of his evening jacket and white evening shirt.

"Yes, my lord," the manservant agreed. He held out the silk shirt, which touched Gabriel's bare skin like a caress. No wonder women liked silk lingerie, Gabriel thought. But he still felt foolish, and he felt even more so by the time he had on the whole outfit. "I look like I should be fighting Roundheads," he declared. "I can't see what is faintly Greek about this."

He went down to the landing where Circe waited patiently. "I'm going up to the schoolroom soon," she said, as if expecting a scolding. "But Psyche said I could see the costumes first."

He made a grand bow for her benefit. "My lady."

Circe giggled. "You look very fine, and the blue sash is quite nice."

He showed her the mask, and Circe raised her brows. "That is most eerie," she noted. "A blankness where the face should be, and only the eyes glinting through—very alarming."

"I hope the ladies will not all faint away," he said, playing along.

"If they have even an ounce of observation, they will know you by the set of your shoulders," she pointed out.

Gabriel shook his head. "I hope they are not all as perceptive as you," he said ruefully, "or my disguise will all be for naught."

At last he heard a soft step on the staircase, and he turned to see. The sight took his breath.

Psyche paused, her expression perplexed. "Is something wrong? Is it too much?"

He gazed at her for a long moment. "You look like a goddess, indeed."

Psyche shrugged her almost bare shoulders. "I feel very . . . exposed."

"You look as if you stepped down off Mount Olympus," he said with perfect truth, gazing at the simple white linen costume that showed off the swanlike curve of her neck, her white shoulders, the swelling curves of her bosom, even exposing a shocking glimpse of shapely ankles.

"You don't think it too revealing?" she asked, twitching her skirt a bit but only succeeding in revealing more of her well-formed leg.

Gabriel thought of all the men at the ball tonight, and how eager and lascivious their attention would be. Damn, he'd have to hang on her shoulder for the whole night to keep them away. Somehow, the idea did not displease him.

"I like it," Circe announced. "And your hair, too."

Her hair was pulled into a simple classical twist, with creamy white flowers tucked into the golden tresses. The color of her cheeks was heightened just now as they both stared at her. She was indeed a most stunning vision.

Gabriel tried to pull himself together. "Why did I not get a Greek costume, too?" he inquired.

Psyche bit her lip, obviously trying not to laugh. "When I looked into one of Papa's classical tomes, it appeared that a Greek man's costume would have left you . . . um, exposed, indeed."

Gabriel's own education came back to him. As he recalled, the male Greek warriors often wore practically nothing. "I, uh, can see how that might be impractical," he agreed with a grin.

"Besides, we wish you to be anonymous," she said. "I didn't want to make it too apparent that you were the other half of my myth. Also, the sable hue denotes mystery."

The clock chimed from the parlor, and Psyche motioned

to the footman for their evening cloaks. "It is time we were off. Circe, to bed with you."

Circe kissed her sister good-bye and smiled at Gabriel. "When I am a lady, you must save a dance for me."

"I would be desolate without your partnership," Gabriel agreed. They went, not out the front door, but toward the back, having agreed earlier that Gabriel must stay out of sight as much as possible.

In the back courtyard, a cat yowled from the shadows. Psyche grabbed his arm. "There! Did something move?"

Gabriel turned and narrowed his eyes. The dancing light of the lantern made it hard to see through the darkness. "It's nothing," he said, but they quickened their pace nonetheless.

In the carriage house, the coachman gazed at them in surprise. "Miss, no one told me you was waiting. I would have brought the carriage around just as always."

"We felt like a stroll," Psyche soothed him. Gabriel helped her into the carriage and then climbed in to sit beside her.

She was very much aware that Aunt Sophie was not with them tonight. He seemed to take up so much of the carriage, with his long legs, and his broad shoulders, and the very masculine energy that he exuded. She could smell his clean linen and the faint odor of shaving soap that clung to his tanned cheeks. A shame it was only a short drive to the Forsyth residence. Or perhaps a good thing, she told herself.

The carriage pulled out into the street, rocking a little over the uneven paving stones, and she put out one hand to steady herself.

Gabriel caught her hand and held it within his own. His grip was firm, and his fingers warm as they curled around hers. She felt the tension inside her, and saw that his eyes were dark with something more than his usual lazy charm.

"I'm all right," she said, settling into her seat, and tried to withdraw her hand. But Gabriel would not relinquish it. Instead, he used it to draw her closer. She held back for a moment only, before giving in and sliding next to him.

Turning her head, she opened her lips to scold him. But

Gabriel knew her too well—his mouth covered hers before she could utter more than a peep. His clever tongue moved with delicious slowness. It was a long sweet kiss. A shaky sigh escaped her when at last he began to nibble his way down her neck and over her exposed shoulder. She would have more gowns made in this fashion, she thought with a silent giggle.

All laughter fled when she felt the heat of his palm cup the heavy curve of her breast. Her shivers had nothing to do with the cool night outside the carriage and everything to do with the sensations his sure touch elicited. Uncertain what to do, she raised tentative hands to his wide shoulders. His warm breath against the curve of her throat made her bold.

"Oh, my lovely, lovely Miss Hill," he teased gently. "It's a very good thing you no longer have to dock my pay for my improper actions. If that were so, I fear that I would be about to lose it all. . . ."

Feeling just a little foolish at his reminder of her attempts at control, she hid her smile in the smooth fabric of his cloak and pushed all but his implied promise out of her mind. She wanted what he offered. All these incredible new feelings— she had never expected such pleasure.

Giving in to her curiosity, she slid her hands down his chest and under his cloak. The slippery silk covered the muscled planes of his chest and the steady thumping of his heart. Ducking her head, she pressed kisses against his tanned neck. Gratified when his heartbeat thundered against her hand, she leaned her face deeper into his shoulder. Drinking in the tangy, clean scent of him, she didn't notice when the carriage rocked to a stop.

David heard the sound of carriage wheels retreating as he hurried up to the Hills' front door, but he did not heed it. The Forsyths' palatial house was just four streets away, and already the street was full of carriages—the ball would be a crush indeed.

He rapped smartly on the dark wood of the door, and in a moment a footman pulled it open.

"I'm here for Tarrington," David said blithely.

The footman blinked. "I regret to inform you, my lord, that his lordship is out for the evening."

David shrugged and walked into the house, and the footman, looking surprised, gave way before him. "I know he's skulking about, but it's I, Westbury. Just tell him, will you?"

"I remember you, my lord," the footman protested. "But he is really not at home."

"I'll wait right here," David said. "He might need me, you see. Protection."

"I think I shall get the butler," the footman said. He retreated, looking vexed.

David stood alone in the front hall, but in a moment, he heard a clear voice say, "He's really not in, you know. You just missed them."

Who was speaking? The voice was vaguely familiar. David looked around, then up, and made out a small figure sitting on the first landing of the staircase. Her knees were drawn up to her chest, with her skirts pulled neatly down to hide any sight of her limbs. It was a child, a girl, a pale, stick-thin waif who looked down at him with a serious expression. One of the family, obviously—she was well dressed, though just as obviously not yet out. Too young anyhow, he told himself, this chit would still be in the schoolroom. But she would know where everyone was. He walked closer.

"Did he leave for the ball already?" David asked.

She nodded.

"Dash it—oh, I beg your pardon. I should have come a half hour ago."

"Are you on your way to the ball, too?" the child asked. She had a light clear voice that fell pleasantly on the ears. Too bad she was such a plain little thing, he thought, all big eyes and wide mouth.

"Yes," he said. "Not that I care much for such things, but

Tarrington might have need of me. He has enemies, you know."

"I know," the child agreed. "You have no costume."

"Oh, that's all right," David told her. "I have no patience for this dress-up nonsense."

"Psyche says that Sally will allow no one in without a costume," the child told him, her tone serious. "Her footman will give you a pair of mouse ears to wear."

"Mouse?" David thought he must have heard wrong. He'd only had one glass of wine with dinner, wanting his wits sharp, but— "What's wrong with the woman, eh?"

"It's because she's being Cinderella," the girl explained patiently. "You're not very familiar with fairy tales, are you?"

"Well . . . no." David frowned. He had to wear mouse ears? "Maybe I won't even go—no, dash it, I must. Promised Tarrington."

"And you likely have a sweetheart to meet?" the child prompted.

"Me? No, no," David told her. "Not into the petticoat line, too complicated."

"That's a shame," the girl said thoughtfully. "You have uncommonly expressive eyes."

"You think so?" David began to wonder if this child had had too much wine. Did children drink wine? Someone must have been drinking overmuch; it was the strangest conversation he had ever been part of.

"Yes, I do, and I know about eyes," she assured him. "And hands and mouths, too, of course."

He stared at her, slightly scandalized. "I think you know a bit too much about body parts for a schoolgirl."

"I considered you a bit foolish the first time I saw you, but now that I have observed you more closely, I think you will improve with time," she continued thoughtfully.

"Here now," David protested, wounded. "No need to insult a fellow."

"Yes, I think you should wait for me."

She nodded in apparent decision and raised her brows.

He noticed for the first time that her eyes were a clear lucid shade of green. Perhaps she was a fairy, a changeling, and not a little girl at all.

"Wait for you? Are *you* going to the ball as well?"

"I shall be eighteen in only six years," she explained. "Is that too long to wait?"

If he said no, she would likely turn him into a mouse, not just with ears but with whiskers and tail. David wondered how one dealt with a fairy bent on mischief. A bit of iron in the pocket, a silver cross? He'd have to ask the vicar on Sunday. If the shock of David showing up in the family pew didn't give the poor man palpitations.

"Is it?" Her tone was very serious.

"Oh, no, no," he assured her, backing away. "Wait, yes indeed. Expect I'd better be on my way, however. A good night to you."

"Good night," she said as he hurried toward the front door. "Sorry about the mouse ears," he thought she called after him.

A fairy child, no doubt about it.

Seventeen

Gabriel reluctantly raised his head when the carriage rolled to a stop. Psyche gave a soft sigh full of regret when he set her away from him.

He chuckled beneath his breath. "The footman may not understand ancient mythology, but a man knows *eros* when he sees it." He watched her lips part at his meaning. "And I don't wish him to see it. Do you . . . goddess?" This last he said quietly as he lifted her mask from the seat beside them and slipped it over her face. He tied the satin ribbons around her head and rejoiced in the kindling passion that lingered in her azure eyes. He had awakened this in her. He smiled, remembering that he was Eros, god of sensual love.

Perhaps there was something to be said for mythology, after all.

He had barely covered his own face when the door swung open, and the footman had laid down the steps. Alighting first, Gabriel turned and offered Psyche his hand. She waited a moment and then allowed him to help her down and lead her forward.

The street in front of the Forsyth mansion was crowded with barouches and chaises and every manner of vehicle, their lanterns flickering through the early darkness. Carriages discharged their costumed occupants, creating a crush of revelers on the steps.

Psyche hardly noticed. Her thoughts were still in the darkness of the carriage, still wrapped around the man who now clutched her unsteady hand with a tender gallantry. If only they might spend their lives wrapped up in each other, guiding each other, loving each other as fully as she loved him now.

With a start, she pulled her mind back from wild flights of fancy. She wasn't in love with him. She couldn't be.

They had arrived at the top of the stairs and Gabriel was waiting patiently for her to walk ahead of him. "Thank you," she murmured. Already she could hear music and laughter and the chatter of a large crowd of guests.

A servant took her cloak, while Gabriel retained his since it was part of his costume, and—Psyche hoped—would help obscure his wide shoulders and hard-muscled physique. For tonight, he must be safely anonymous.

Thinking of Gabriel, she had forgotten about herself. The feel of a draft on her bare shoulders, which, since the tunic had no sleeves, were now covered only by a narrow width of fabric, reminded her of her costume. Glancing into the looking glass on the wall, Psyche hoped she had not gone too far beyond the pale.

What had she been thinking? The fact that two passing gentlemen gave her long looks of appreciation did not reassure her.

Gabriel seemed to guess the direction of her thoughts. He offered her his arm. "You look divine, goddess," he told her, his eyes glinting with their usual spark of humor.

She understood what he was trying to tell her and smiled reluctantly. Very well, she was a Greek goddess, not the ordinary Miss Hill of tea parties and prim dresses. Tonight, she could hide behind her golden half-mask, and it made her feel strangely free.

As they climbed the wide marble staircase to the floor where the ball was held, she saw a menagerie of strange beings: a shaggy wolf in a red velvet tunic with whiskers glued to his cheeks; a round and merry Humpty-Dumpty who seemed well into his cups already; a demure shepherdess pulling a quite real, bleating lamb up the steps by its embroidered leash.

Wondering what on earth Sally's servants would think of cleaning up after a sheep, Psyche laughed and forgot her worries. Tonight was a step out of time, and she would forget about Miss Hill's concern with decorum. This evening, she was a Greek goddess, come down to play with mortal men and—perhaps—capture a heart or two.

She glanced toward Gabriel, wishing that might be true.

When they entered the ballroom, she found it bedecked with fanciful blossoms. Some of the flowers were real, and some must be contrived out of satin and silk, Psyche thought, for such oddly colored, glitter-bedecked blooms belonged only in a fantasy world. Gold ribbons were twined among the crystal chandeliers, and a wave of music rolled out to greet them, softening the shrill sound of many voices. The room smelled of perfumes and wine and flowers, and it was enough to make her hesitate a moment on the threshold. Perhaps they were indeed stepping into faerie land.

Certainly, the odd beings around them belonged in a storybook. Psyche saw Cleopatra walk by, wearing a stuffed asp around her neck, her arms glittering with jeweled bracelets that looked much more genuine than the snake. Her white linen shift was dampened in the French manner so that it clung to her body and showed more than a hint of the curvaceous charms hidden beneath. Psyche felt less uncomfortable about her own costume, which appeared positively Puritanical in contrast. Cleopatra accepted a glass of wine from a servant and turned to talk to a sea captain with a parrot on his shoulder.

A glittering vision of gold and diamonds floated up to them, and Psyche turned to greet their hostess. "Sally, this is quite marvelous! What a spectacle."

"I told you I've been laboring forever," Sally told them from behind her jewel-edged mask. "And do not call me Sally, tonight I am Cinderella."

It would be more accurate to say that Sally's servants had been working forever, Psyche thought, swallowing a grin, but she didn't contradict her. "Cinderella, meet Eros," she said instead.

Gabriel bowed over their hostess's hand. "You are a vision worthy of any fairy tale," he said, kissing her fingers lightly.

"And you are a most appropriate god of love," Sally declared, flicking her fan with practiced archness. "My, that mask gives me chills, darling. I adore it! You must come and dance with me—it is a royal decree. Andrew has already gone off to the card room. He says his corset is too tight and his crown is giving him a headache."

"But what about the guests still arriving?" Psyche asked in surprise.

"It's a masquerade, no one is being announced." Sally waved her fan airily. "Come along, Eros, and don't disappoint me."

Gabriel looked over at Psyche, his eyes glimmering with laughter. "I shall return," he promised, and then he led Cinderella off toward the dance floor.

Psyche noticed two women approaching. One seemed to be Queen Mary—she wore an antiquated dress with a wide ruff around her neck, and a gilt crown on her head. Her daughter was—well, she wore a crown, too. Psyche decided that perhaps it was the younger woman who was Mary Tudor, and the older who portrayed Katherine of Aragon. They were each trying to be some antique royal lady, that was certain.

When the older woman spoke, Psyche recognized the voice. It was Mrs. Fleming, and this must be her daughter.

"Is that you, Psyche?" the older royal demanded. "What an, um, unusual costume, dear."

"Do you like it?" Psyche asked calmly. "I thought I should live up to my name." She had regained her usual self-possession and did not intend to let this old cat . . . ah . . . queen upset her. She imagined the skinny matron as a cat, with whiskers glued to her cheeks like the wolf they had passed on the stairwell, and had to stifle a laugh.

"Is your fiancé here?" the younger woman asked, her tone eager. "The marquis?"

"Oh, I cannot tell you that, it is a masquerade," Psyche pointed out. "But you might just find him somewhere among the guests."

"Oh, look, Mother," the younger woman said. "The tall man in the Chinese emperor costume and the fake beard, I believe that might be him. Is it, Psyche?"

Psyche only smiled mysteriously, and the two women hurried off. "And good luck to you," Psyche murmured.

A man wandered up, wearing a drab brown coat, mouse ears attached to his half-mask, and, below the mask, a petulant frown. "Have you seen Madam Forsyth—that is, Cinderella?" he asked, his voice plaintive.

"I believe you'll find her on the dance floor," Psyche told him. "If you go and stand nearby, you can likely claim her for the next dance."

Brightening, the mouse hurried off.

A stout man dressed as a monk appeared at her elbow. "My dear goddess, your loveliness overwhelms me! No doubt you must be Venus, goddess of beauty. Perhaps you will favor me with the next dance?" He leered at her in a very unmonklike manner, and Psyche was reminded again of how revealing her costume really was.

"I'm sorry, that dance is already promised," she told him.

"Then perhaps you would like a glass of wine?"

"Goddesses subsist only on mead and ambrosia, didn't you know?" She smiled and stepped back. "Excuse me, I see a friend."

Actually, she saw a bevy of shepherdesses with crooked staffs and one rather stout king, whose crown was slipping over his bald pate.

"It just wouldn't behave," one of the young women was saying. "It kept stepping on my slippers and pulling at the leash. And it smelled—ugh. So I told the footman to take it away to the stables and give it some hay, or something. It didn't act like the poem at all."

Psyche smiled; so much for the sylvan peace of rustic glades. Then she did recognize a face beneath a half-mask.

"Matilda, is that you?" she asked. Her cousin's plump form was clothed, not unbecomingly, in a ball gown of striped lavender, her brown hair fringed with an arrangement of large silk flower petals. The young man with her was tall and thin and his costume was green. She wasn't sure who they were supposed to be, some kind of plants, perhaps, but they reminded her forcibly of Jack Sprat and his wife. She didn't say this aloud, of course.

"Psyche, you look beautiful!" Matilda was flushed and quite bubbly with excitement. "Isn't this the most wonderful ball? People will be talking of it for weeks."

"Sally will be happy, then," Psyche agreed. "Yes, I think it's quite marvelous."

"You know Mr. Stilton," her cousin added, blushing even more deeply.

"Yes indeed," Psyche said, making her curtsy. "How nice to see you again."

The young man bowed, his eyes widening just a little at Psyche's bare shoulders and brief tunic, but to his credit he turned quickly back to her cousin, speaking with a slight lisp. "We'd best head for the dance floor, thuch a crush, tho we can take our placeth for the next thet."

"Of course," Matilda agreed. "Will you excuse us, Psyche?"

"With pleasure," Psyche agreed, smiling to see her cousin's happiness. Long live the tall and thin Mr. Stilton-Sprat, she thought.

A young lady dressed as Mother Goose, with a wide hat and a toy goose under one arm, came up to her. "Miss Hill?"

"Yes," Psyche said. Her disguise was obviously not every effective. Next time, she would come as a Chinese concubine, she thought. Or a goose!

"My grandmother, Lady Serena, would like a word with

you, if you would," the girl said timidly. "She is sitting to the side of the room."

"Of course." Lady Serena was a contemporary of Aunt Sophie. Psyche would need to explain her aunt's absence and make a little polite conversation. At least it would deliver her from the monk, whom she saw eyeing her again from a clump of nearby guests, and a Cavalier in a blue cloak who was also assessing her. And by that time, perhaps the current dance would have ended, and she could reclaim her own escort. Psyche followed Mother Goose toward the side of the room.

She found Lady Serena wearing a sumptuous purple turban and a well-cut gown with a fichu tucker covering her wrinkled neck, her only concession to the masquerade a half-mask that dangled from her wrist. Even Sally had been unable to cow the formidable Lady S., Psyche thought, hiding her amusement.

"Hello, child, where is Sophia? I thought she would be here to amuse me with her wit," Lady Serena complained.

"My aunt has come down with a slight cough," Psyche explained. "She sends her regrets."

The old lady sniffed. "Not half the regrets that I have, stuck in this Bedlam of revelers with no one congenial to talk to."

Her granddaughter, looking meek in her Mother Goose disguise, tried to argue. "Now, Grandmother, you know that you have scads of friends—"

"Most of them in the graveyard!" Lady Serena interrupted sharply, apparently determined not to relinquish her role of martyr. "Anyhow, I wanted to tell you, child. Sophia asked me about a family, the Sinclairs of Kent."

"Yes?" Psyche's polite attention sharpened at once.

"I had something to tell her," Serena announced in sepulchral tones.

Gabriel led Sally through the intricate steps of the dance, amused by her skilled and lighthearted flirtation.

"You know that as your partner, I am the envy of all the other ladies," she told him.

Rule number one, flatter your gentleman friend, Gabriel thought. "You're too kind," he said, smiling down into her wide brown eyes until she whirled away from him.

"And I shall treasure this moment, since I know you will be occupied with your betrothed for most of the evening," Sally said, when next the dance brought them together.

Rule number two, show a hint of your attraction. "True," Gabriel agreed. They held hands briefly, then parted again.

"But I shall hope for another dance later, since even one's fiancé cannot expect constant attention," Sally added when they came back together. "It would be so provincial, don't you think?" She batted her long lashes.

He pressed her hand but kept his expression only mildly interested. *Rule number three, determine the amount of interest from the other party.* Sally could give lessons in flirtation, he thought. And he had always been an eager pupil, up to now. The woman currently on his arm was delightful, pleasing to the eye and soft to the touch and smelling of lilies, so why did his thoughts keep returning to the front of the room, where he had left Psyche too unguarded in her revealing costume? He was sure that men all over the ballroom were hurrying to flock around her. He wished the dance would end.

"I'm sure we will have another dance," he agreed. "If the crush of your other admirers permit it." He had seen more than one set of mouse ears among the guests. Then, glancing down into her caramel-colored eyes, he gave way to a mischievous impulse and added, "Or we could slip away to a secluded alcove, and I could teach you some of the mysteries of the East—lovemaking is something of an art in India, you know."

The brown eyes opened a fraction too wide, and Sally actually stuttered. "B-but—"

"A settee is not required," Gabriel added helpfully. "The

Kama Sutra lists over a hundred positions for the giving of delight, many of which—"

She gasped. "Oh, my. No, that is—my husband—he might notice—"

It was as he suspected—she was not truly serious; it was simply a game to amuse the hour. Since she was Psyche's friend, he was glad to know she meant no harm.

But Sally had regained her composure. "And, you wicked man, aside from my husband, we would have another obstacle to surmount before any such nefarious trysts should ensue."

"You fear that Psyche might discover us?"

"No, Psyche has a trusting soul. The problem would be closer at hand, I think. Secluded alcove or not, your thoughts would be on Psyche, just as they are now," Sally answered coolly. "A god of love you may be, my lord Eros, but I think your elusive heart may have at last been snared."

This time, he was silenced. It was just as well that the steps of the dance once more separated them. He could bow over the hand of a plump angel whose wings were wilting eiderdown all over the ball floor and avoid Sally's sharp eyes for a measure or two.

Psyche felt herself stiffen. "*What do you know about* them?" she demanded, then tried to soften her tone. "I mean, I will pass on the intelligence to my aunt Sophia."

"The Sinclairs?" the older lady sniffed again. "Or at least this branch? Most ungracious family. The father rarely leaves his estate and has no friends, he drove them all off years ago. His poor wife—"

"What about the son, Gabriel Sinclair?" Psyche had no patience for vague meanderings. "Do you know anything of him?"

"Oh, yes, a great scandal. Mind you, it happened years ago, but one doesn't forget such a thing." Lady Serena's words were slow and measured, as if she enjoyed Psyche's agony of impatience. "They tried to cover it up, shipped the boy off—he was not even properly on the town yet, still up at university when it came about—but whispers went round, don't you know?"

"What happened?" Psyche almost whispered. Her lips felt numb.

"He was having an affair with an older woman, the wife of a baronet, lovely little thing."

"Is that all?" Psyche felt an irrational relief—affairs among the Ton were as common as daisies in Hyde Park.

"Oh, no, dear," the venerable dame said, her eyes glinting with malice. "Not at all. When he decided to end it, the lady was distraught. Pleaded with him, they said. Threatened to make it all public and egg her husband to a divorce."

"Oh," said Psyche slowly. Affairs might be commonplace, divorces were not.

Lady Serena leaned closer and lowered her voice; her breath stank of sour wine. "The boy panicked, apparently. Afraid of his tartar of a papa, perhaps. At any rate, she died. They said he'd killed her."

Psyche felt as if she'd been struck. "He couldn't—"

"He was out of the country before anything could be done about it, and nowadays, few people remember. But you might want to ask him about it," the matron said, her tone smooth. "Before you wed yourself to a murderer."

Psyche wanted to escape, but her whole body felt frozen. She heard the woman beside her natter on, but the words flowed past her, their sense lost.

Gabriel a murderer? Oh, no, it was impossible. It had to be impossible.

"It was, no doubt, a moment of anger. Young men are so hotheaded," Lady Serena said, her voice still honeyed and still dripping with venom.

If Psyche didn't escape from this woman, she might become a murderess herself, she thought. Desperation gave her rubbery knees strength. She stood suddenly. "Excuse me," she said. "I see a friend I need to speak to."

"Of course, dear," the other woman said. "I know that the young are easily bored by the wisdom of their elders."

"So true," Psyche agreed. Giving the granddaughter a look of genuine pity, Psyche made her escape. But now her head pounded, and the room around her seemed a kaleidoscope of color and motion. She felt the room spin, and she thought she might pass out. Taking a deep breath, her steps a little uncertain, she walked on, determined to get away from that evil old woman.

Pushing past a couple of gypsies and a highwayman with a scarlet sash, she found another gilt chair unoccupied. Her knees had weakened again, and she sat more quickly than grace would dictate.

Gabriel a murderer.

No, it couldn't be.

Blinded by shock, Psyche looked around, not really seeing. She thought she might swoon, and she had never fainted before. She took slow deep breaths, trying to steady herself. She smelled cloying perfumes and strong wine and, from the highwayman, the faint scent of sweat.

"Are you all right, my dear?" a lady who might have stepped out of an Arabian night asked; her body was barely covered by the thin gauzy costume she wore, but her face was effectively masked by a scarf that covered all but her elaborately painted eyes.

A man in a kilt glanced her way, and two pirates, one wearing an eye patch, looked her up and down, their motives perhaps less altruistic.

"Yes, thank you," Psyche muttered. What could she say? *I have had a bad shock; the man who is my fiancé might be a murderer?* Except he was not really her fiancé, how could she think in such a way? It was too easy to enjoy Gabriel's easy charm, Gabriel's ready sense of humor, Gabriel's disconcerting habit of always understanding her. . . .

She had become so accustomed to his company in such a few days, and she had forgotten how little she really knew about him. He was an impostor, an expatriate with dark secrets in his past—he had said so himself. And then there was

the most disturbing thing—she was very much afraid that
she had fallen in love with him.

A woman in French court dress, with a towering powdered wig bedecked with a small gilt birdcage complete
with a real canary, sauntered by, and with her a Red Indian
in leather and war paint and—oddly—jeweled shoes.

Psyche felt her head spin again. Who knew what was real
anymore?

"Psyche, are you unwell?"

The voice was familiar, but she jumped anyhow.

Gabriel had returned to her side.

Was she speaking to a murderer? Hadn't she, once or
twice, glimpsed a steel-hard determination in his eyes?
Hadn't he admitted to sins that he did not wish exposed to
the harsh light of day?

But no, she couldn't believe it. Not Gabriel, with his
many small acts of kindness—Gabriel, whom her little sister trusted, who made Psyche's own heart quiver with his
barest touch.

"Psyche?" His tone was concerned.

"I feel a little—a little faint," she admitted, her voice
trembling.

"Would you like to step outside for some air? It's rather
close in here."

Psyche shut her eyes. It was true that the ballroom felt
too warm, and the odors of the heavily scented party-goers
were almost overwhelming. But to step outside onto the balcony, out of sight of the other guests—at another time, she
would have worried about gossip. Now she wondered if she
would be endangering her life.

No, that made no sense; it was impossible. But . . .

"I think I should like a little refreshment," she said, aware
of her roiling stomach.

Gabriel nodded. "I shall fetch it. Will you be all right
here? Should I send a maidservant to you?"

"No, just let me sit quietly," Psyche told him. Gabriel
turned and disappeared into the crowd.

He had barely gone when another young man came up to

her. For a moment, she thought it was Mr. Denver again, since he wore a mask adorned with mouse ears. But then Psyche saw that his coat was black and draped a better set of shoulders, and he had a more defined chin than the unfortunate Mr. Denver.

"Miss Hill?" he asked. "It is you?"

She recognized the voice. "Lord Westbury? Yes, it is I." Why had she bothered with the costume—she should have worn her name on a placard around her neck and be done with it, she thought crossly.

"Is Gabriel here? Such a crush, it's dashed hard—oh, sorry—to find anyone. I came along to your house to escort you both to the ball, but I was too late," David explained.

"He's here, he's just gone to get some refreshments," she told him. "He's wearing a black costume with a wide hat and plume."

"Ah." David nodded. "I shall see if I can catch up with him." Then he plunged into the crowd, too, and headed toward the refreshment tables. Or else vanished beneath a hillock, not to emerge for a hundred years, as seekers of faerie land were wont to do.

She wasn't sure anymore. A man in a Russian peasant costume walked past with a mermaid on his arm. A long blond wig covered the seashell top that hid her upper body, and her fishy tail dragged on the ground behind them. Psyche would have sworn the apparition even smelled of fish.

No more masquerades, she promised herself. Real life was difficult enough to comprehend without dressing everything familiar in exotic disguises. The scene around her was beginning to take on the aspects of a nightmare. She could find nothing to reassure her, to slow her pounding heart, nothing to ease the confused tangle of her thoughts.

Who was Gabriel, really? Beneath the costume, beneath the fake title, beneath all that was false and unreal—who was the genuine man?

And did her life, not just her heart, not just her ill-conceived scheme for financial independence, depend on knowing the truth?

Someone else walked up to her. She knew him by the heavy tread before she even raised her eyes to see the black-and-white Puritan garb that did little to disguise her cousin Percy. His mask had been discarded, and his expression was, as usual, peeved.

"Psyche, I need to talk to you."

This, at least, was quite normal, but she was not reassured. She felt the usual mixture of irritation and guilt that Percy always evoked, mixed now with a slight tendency to giggle. He made a worthy Puritan, indeed.

"How are you, Percy?"

He did not seem disposed for polite conversation. He plunged ahead, again as usual, into his own obviously already-thought-out speech. "I regret that I have neglected you for some days, Cousin, but I felt that I must express my displeasure at your current conduct."

Psyche hadn't really had much chance to think about his absence, and if she had, she would have given thanks. But it wouldn't do to speak such thoughts aloud. "I will make a note of your displeasure," she agreed gravely.

"But the time has come to confront this problem, Psyche."

"I'd really rather not," she said. "Let us talk about the ball instead. Is this not a fantastical setting?"

"My father has heard from your lawyer—"

"Sally's vision is really quite amazing—"

"And Father says he will not bend to such blackmail—"

"And the guests seem to be enjoying themselves immensely—"

"He cannot believe you really intend to parade our little family disagreement before the courts—"

"I'm sure the ball will be the most talked-about event of—"

"And he begs you to come to your senses and to rid yourself of this greedy Captain Fortune who means to have—"

"The Season—"

"Your fortune to squander—"

"Whereas you'd much rather squander it yourself?" Psyche finished for him.

The veins on Percy's forehead bulged, and his color had heightened. "Psyche, if you will not listen to me—"

"I have no intention of doing so," she told him, her voice calm.

"Then I must speak to this—this so-called marquis."

"I'm sure he will be delighted," she lied. "He went off to fetch me some punch."

"And what ridiculous costume is he wearing?" Percy demanded.

"He is—ah—he is wearing a set of mouse ears," she told him, swallowing a wicked grin. With luck, he would not latch on to David. She had seen at least half a dozen mouse ears on young men of different heights and complexions.

Percy straightened his stiff white collar and threw back his narrow shoulders, which seemed to put an alarming strain on the buttons that fastened his sober black coat over his round stomach. "I shall speak to him and demand that he give up his insane quest for your hand!"

"I'm sure he will be impressed with your logic," Psyche said drily. One more bit of insanity to make the ball complete, she thought.

Percy thrust himself into the crowd, treading on a queen's scarlet train without apology or a second look. The royal lady glared and rearranged her skirts. Somewhere, unseen musicians began a new tune. It was a waltz.

Psyche thought wistfully of the waltz she and Gabriel had never danced. As if her thought had conjured him up, Gabriel emerged from the moss, two glasses of champagne in his hand.

"Are you all right?" he asked, offering her a glass.

"Better." She took a sip of the wine. Almost at once, her stomach calmed, and with it, her disordered emotions. This was Gabriel of the laughing eyes and beautiful face; Gabriel, who always knew her thoughts and never failed to respond when she needed aid. She had met him only a few days ago, but it seemed she had known him all her life. He could not be a murderer; she could not believe it.

"They are playing a waltz," he said now, as if he too hungered for a close embrace.

Smiling, she handed her glass to a nearby footman and held out her hand. He disposed of his own glass, closed his fingers around hers and guided her toward the music.

In the second ballroom, dozens of couples whirled and swayed. They both paused at the edge of the floor and Gabriel put one hand on her waist. He pulled her close, and she followed his lead as they took a gliding step and were swallowed up by the smooth flow of the melody.

Somewhere, a violin trilled, and Psyche felt a shiver of chill bumps run up her bare arms. Or perhaps it was not the music at all, but Gabriel's nearness. She saw a vein jump in his temple and then her gaze dropped and she admired the incredible smooth curve of his cheekbones; he might have been sculpted from marble, like the Greek statues in her father's etchings. He was just as beautiful to look upon, but he was alive, tanned and laughing and strong. She felt once more transported into a dream—he was the man she had never thought to find, and he was here, holding her close.

He bent down to whisper, "Do you know that you are the most captivating lady here?"

She laughed. "Cinderella would be offended to hear you say that."

"Cinderella will have to be content with her band of mice," Gabriel answered, his blue eyes warm. He pulled her even closer, and Psyche hoped that the music would never end.

Then she saw something in the corner of her vision that made her breath catch in her throat.

Gabriel raised his brow. "What is it?"

"That man is watching us. He was in the other room a few moments ago. Did he follow us?"

"Perhaps he also came to dance," Gabriel suggested, but he swung her round so that he could see the man whose appearance had alarmed her.

She felt him stiffen. "Gabriel?"

"I know the face," he answered quietly. "He's one of Barrett's ruffians."

She felt a shiver of fear run through her. She didn't want to cause a scene, but if they were in danger . . . "What shall we do? Can we call for help?"

"David left the room—he decided to stand guard in the front hall. And Freddy is not here tonight; he refused to dress in costume, not that he's much of a fighter, anyhow. I believe we shall dance to the other side of the room and slip out one of the French windows onto the balcony." Gabriel twirled her expertly around two couples and toward the far side of the room.

Psyche clung to him tightly. Surely the man wouldn't dare to attack them in plain sight of the other guests? Then she looked past Gabriel's arm and saw another man in rough clothes come to join the first, and then another. Oh, God, how many were here? How had they managed to walk into Sally's house without the servants noticing?

The costumes, of course. Everyone looked so strange, who could tell what was only a disguise and what was not?

Gabriel had noticed the other men, too. He quickened his steps, and they were almost to the edge of the room when a rough hand grabbed Psyche's arm.

"We'll just share this dance, won't we, me lord," a coarse voice said.

Psyche tried to pull away, but the grip was too tight. She winced at the painful hold.

Gabriel pushed the man back, breaking the villain's grasp on Psyche. "Unhand her!" he said, his tone sharp.

But the other two men crowded in, and one put grimy fingers on Psyche, while two pushed Gabriel back. "We'll ransom the lady for a fair sum," one of the men boasted. "And you, sir, will have your throat slit in a back alley."

Several couples who had been gliding and whirling to the waltz tune paused, and a woman shrieked, while the other guests around them stared with wide eyes. Psyche struggled with the man who clasped her wrist, waiting for someone to scream, to summon help.

Instead, a ripple of laughter spread through the crowd. One man said, "What will Sally think of next?"

"I want to be kidnapped, too," a stout matron called playfully.

"Careful, Angela," her friend warned. "Your husband is so tight-fisted, he wouldn't come up with a tuppence for ransom." More guests laughed, and several couples resumed their dance.

They would be murdered right here, or swept away under the very eyes of the whole ballroom, Psyche thought in alarm. She pulled harder against her captor. "Someone, help us!"

But the guest closest to her, who wore a Roman toga, laughed and shrugged. "Too many for me to fight."

The other two ruffians blocked Gabriel's path. One of them pulled a small but lethal dagger from his waistband.

Gabriel's expression was fierce, and his eyes had darkened. If she had not already been so frightened, Psyche would have shivered at the look he wore. But he had no weapon, only a few flimsy gilt-colored cardboard arrows in the quiver at his waist.

Despite his outrage, he would be helpless before the knife, she thought, despair threatening to overwhelm her. So she was as surprised as their assailants when Gabriel whipped the cloak off his shoulders and wrapped it swiftly around his left arm.

The man with the knife, as if realizing Gabriel's intent, lunged with the sharp blade outstretched. Gabriel blocked the blow with his well-wrapped arm and at the same time, his right fist thrust forward, meeting the man's chin with a sharp impact that rocked him back on his heels. Dazed, the attacker dropped, hitting the ballroom floor with a thud. Gabriel leaned over him and delivered another stunning blow. The spectators around them squealed and clapped, as if it were all a show.

Idiots! Psyche had overcome her own momentary feeling

of helplessness. The man holding her stared at Gabriel in surprise, and his grip was less certain. Psyche plunged her elbow into her captor's side. Gasping with pain, he let go of her wrist, and she ran to Gabriel.

The third man hesitated, looking unsure now that the odds were more even.

Gabriel grabbed her hand. "Run," he said.

They did. At least she was not hindered by huge powdered wigs or long mermaid tails, Psyche thought as they fled through the laughing guests. Perhaps her costume had been well chosen, after all.

And Gabriel had shed his cloak and hat, and his trousers and boots were easy enough to run in. They pushed their way through the edge of the ballroom and paused long enough to take stock.

"Are there more of them?" Psyche asked, breathing hard.

"It's likely," Gabriel said.

Even as he answered, two more thugs came out of the crowd. One held a rough club, and both looked unshaven and dirty.

She felt Gabriel tense. "Get behind me," he muttered.

"Look out," she said, stepping back a little so as not to hinder his defense. "There's another!"

The big clean-shaven man who stepped out from the other side of the room wore slightly better clothes and a determined expression.

Strangely, Gabriel laughed. Psyche glanced up at him in surprise, then saw that the last man had stepped in front of their attackers and held up his fists. But he faced the thugs, not Gabriel.

"Get along with you, guv," he told Gabriel.

Gabriel nodded. "They will be well occupied," he explained while Psyche grappled with the surprise that this man was an ally, not an enemy. "I hired him from Gentleman Jackson's Academy. But it is time for us to leave."

They hurried down the stairs, and Gabriel waved to a footman, who approached and bowed. There was a quick exchange of coin, and Gabriel said, "Summon our carriage, quickly, and you'll get another of these. And bring the lady's cloak, and then remain beside her. Do not let her be accosted by drunken revelers."

His eyes bright, the footman hurried away.

"Don't leave me," Psyche said before she thought, reaching for his arm. She found she was shivering, more with shock than with cold.

He put his arm around her, and she leaned against his comforting strength. "I won't," he promised. "Where is David? We could use another good man, and the lad is strong for his age. Did he go back inside? We'll never find him now. There are too many people in this crush, and too many damned mice!"

The tightness in her throat seemed to strangle the laugh that tried to emerge. Madness, this night had been mad, from beginning to end.

She watched the crowd for signs of the men who had attacked them. She heard shouts of encouragement from inside the ballroom and looked up toward the landing to see that the impromptu round of fisticuffs was a hit with the guests, who still appeared to think this was all devised for their entertainment. Whatever would Sally say?

Psyche glanced uneasily toward the open double doors. No more assailants emerged from the cheering crowd. Yet Psyche felt a prickle on the back of her neck, as if vigilant eyes watched from the cover of the oddly garbed mass of guests.

"Gabriel," she whispered. "Do you think Barrett is here? I mean, I know that Sally would not have invited him, but—"

"But he could have walked in, disguised like the rest of us?" Gabriel muttered back. "I would not be surprised."

Psyche shivered. And the masquerade had seemed like such a good chance for a safe outing. Safe? She clamped down on a wave of hysteria.

The servant returned, bowing, and draped Psyche's cloak around her shoulders. "Your carriage awaits, my lord."

"Good, you may accompany us to the door." Gabriel

pressed another coin into the footman's gloved hand. "The lady is a bit giddy from too much excitement."

Psyche shot him an indignant look, but he met her gaze with a bland smile. Oh, very well, they had to say something to excuse their abrupt departure. The footman held open the door and they hurried out, almost falling over a prone body on the outside steps.

"David!" Psyche exclaimed. "Is he all right?"

Gabriel knelt to touch the boy's throat, lift one of his eyelids. "He's been knocked out. Here, get him aid at once," he ordered the servant. "We cannot stay."

The man shouted toward the open door, and another servant scurried out to assist.

Psyche lingered for only a moment to make sure that David was breathing evenly. "What about Sally?" she whispered to Gabriel.

"We'll make our apologies later," he answered absently.

"No, the villains—we can't just leave them here!"

He nodded and added to the footman bending over David, "There are some roughly dressed men who have taken advantage of the costume gala to slip inside and look for purses to pick. I'd round up some more servants to scour the crowd and get them out of your mistress's house before they do any more serious harm. They are the ones who must have attacked my friend here."

"Yes, my lord." The footman looked alarmed, but he handed Psyche into their carriage and then hastened back to help carry David up the steps of the mansion.

Gabriel conferred for a moment with the coachman, then took his seat beside her, calling, "Drive on!"

With a clatter of horses' hooves and a jangle of harness, the carriage pulled away from the house. Psyche took a deep breath. She hoped that David was not seriously hurt, but at least she could stop looking over her shoulder; perhaps they had left the danger behind.

"A good thing you had coin on you," she said. "I would not have expected you to be so prepared, especially in this costume."

"I never go anywhere without funds," Gabriel said, his tone noncommittal.

Psyche remembered his uncertain existence, his years of exile, and flushed. "Of course." She looked down at her hand and discovered a sticky dark stain. What? Then her eyes widened. Back in the ballroom he had shed the remains of his satin cloak, and now she saw a slit in his sleeve.

"Are you wounded?" The man with the knife had injured him, after all. She leaned closer to see his arm in the dim light, touching his ruined sleeve lightly. She felt dampness. The fine silk had been slit, and she could detect blood still seeping from a long gash.

"We must bind it up," she said, distressed. "You never said a word."

"It's only a scratch," he told her. He pulled out a linen handkerchief, and she wrapped it around the wound.

"Like the last cut was only a scratch?" Psyche frowned as she tightened the knot. "You are very nonchalant about having knives thrust into you."

"Why shouldn't I be when I have your heavenly hands to tend me, goddess." Gabriel wagged his brows comically. It wasn't easy to glare at him in disapproval, but she managed.

"When we reach home, we must wash it," she said, "so it doesn't turn septic."

He shrugged. "We are not going home," he said, his voice calm. "Barrett's men are growing too bold; we must give them the slip."

Psyche knew that her eyes had widened. She glanced out the carriage window and saw that indeed, they had already passed their own square. "But where are we going?"

"I think it's time I examined my new property," Gabriel said. "And I need a quiet place to lie low for a time, till my ownership is established and I can find a way to defeat Barrett once and for all."

"But isn't that the worst spot to evade Barrett?" She tried to grasp his audacious plan.

"From what the solicitor tells me, the scoundrel hasn't visited his former estate in years," Gabriel said. "He is a most indifferent landlord. And sometimes the obvious card is the most unexpected one to play. I will be vigilant."

A flicker of light from a streetlamp momentarily threw light into the carriage's interior. She made out an unexpected object tucked between his body and his shirt, a lethal outline clear beneath the thin fabric. Then the shadows thickened once again.

"What is that?"

But she knew the answer as soon as she spoke the words. It was the dagger that the first of Barrett's hired killers had brandished. Gabriel must have taken it away from the man after he had knocked him out; she had missed his action in the strain of the moment.

Gabriel raised his dark brows. "Never throw away a weapon," he murmured.

She remembered the old woman's gossip, the whispers from Gabriel's past. *They said he'd killed her....*

She was riding off into the darkness with an accused murderer as her only companion, and no one else even knew their real destination.

Eighteen

*B*ut she didn't really believe Gabriel could be a killer. Anyhow, her anxiety was premature. He seemed quite anxious to be rid of her.

"If they had not already discovered Sally's location, I should have left you there," he told Psyche as he stared outside at the dark streets. "But with the gang in the house, it hardly seemed advisable. What other friend or relative would you feel best about visiting?"

She had a sudden absurd vision of turning up on Percy and Uncle Wilfred's doorstep. She grimaced. No, having to explain her danger would offer too much support to all of Percy's warnings about Gabriel and his lack of authenticity. Besides, to be forced to listen to Percy lecture all day and to be too available for his amorous advances—no indeed, not even to save her life. And Aunt Mavis with her sour chatter—Psyche could not brook that idea, either. Despite her abundance of relatives, she could think of no one to whom she wished to turn in her moment of deepest need.

The fact was, she felt safest with Gabriel by her side. She had reached out to him instinctively in the ballroom. Although he was the one who had attracted the assailants in the first place, his presence made her feel most protected, and she did not want to part from him. It was illogical, but the strength of her feelings could not be denied.

"No." She shook her head. "I won't."

Gabriel turned to regard her through the dimness. He sounded concerned. "You need to stay out of sight, too, Psyche, for your own sake. Believe me—"

"I'm going with you," she said firmly.

Silence, then he spoke again, and she could not read his voice. "Psyche. My dear Miss Hill—"

What had happened to goddess? The formal title was a reminder of the great gulf that lay between them: he was a fraud, an impostor, and he had no right to remain in her company.

"We have no chaperon. It will cause your ruin—"

"If anyone in the Ton finds out," she finished calmly. "We shall have to be sure they do not. Besides, your enemies are entirely too persistent. They know where my house is, they know my family. No matter where I go in London, what if they find me again? If it's a choice between getting my throat cut and having my reputation tarnished, I think I should choose the latter."

He didn't answer. Did he hear her remark as a rebuke? She didn't intend it so; he had not asked for this life-and-death struggle.

Leaning her head against the squabs, Psyche closed her eyes and thought of her years of careful deferment to the strictest rules of decorum, of her anxious observance of all of society's edicts. Having a band of murderers after them made those concerns seem almost insignificant. Almost. . . . A respectable reputation was still essential for a woman of good birth. Had she not made that her touchstone ever since her parents' death? And now she had thrown it all to the winds. She should be distraught. Instead, like her costume, this turnabout made her feel strangely free.

"Are you sure?" Gabriel said at last, his voice still husky with emotions she could not identify. "You must understand that I cannot guarantee your safety, my dear."

"Yes, my mind is made up."

He made no comment—did he not wish her to come? Before she could worry about this, another thought struck. Circe and Aunt Sophie. She spoke her thought aloud. "Circe and my aunt will be anxious," she told Gabriel, "if we do not come home after the ball."

Gabriel nodded. He should have remembered her family. He was too accustomed to only looking out for himself, to having no one about who cared whether or not he came home. And the shock of finding that Psyche meant to remain beside him, despite the dangers, despite the pressing and more rational need for her to distance herself from his company—it awoke emotions that had been buried for years deep inside him.

Once, he had been cast off from all that he held dear, denied the refuge of his own home, rejected by those who should have flown to his defense. Vowing never again to be so trusting, so vulnerable, he had built up a wall of cynicism to protect himself from ever repeating such a crushing blow. He had built up his barricade brick by brick. Psyche had no idea how high that wall had become . . . or that she had shaken it to its selfish foundations, made the first crack in a battlement he had never thought could be breached.

Psyche was watching him, her expression anxious. Gabriel pulled himself together and called to the coachman. When the carriage pulled up, Gabriel hopped out and summoned a young street sweeper standing his post at the corner.

"Here, a coin for you if you deliver a message," he told the lad.

The youngster was ragged and dirty, but his eyes were alert. "Yes sir," he said.

"Tell the household"—Gabriel gave him the address and carefully described the house and square—"that Miss Psyche has been called away into Kent to visit a sick friend; they are to say little about her absence but not to worry. Can you remember all that?"

"Blimey, yeah," the lad agreed.

"I'm sure the footman will have another coin for you, if

you tell him I wished it so," Gabriel added. "Now, make haste."

The boy looked even keener. "I'll run all the way, gov'nor," he promised. With Gabriel's coin clutched firmly in his dirty hand, the boy took to his heels.

Gabriel returned to the carriage and signaled the coachman. It lurched a little as it again moved forward. A good thing he had put a good stash of blunt at the bottom of the silk quiver with its fake arrows, Gabriel thought. This costume had little in the way of useful pockets. But he was too accustomed to his life turning unexpectedly upside down to go out without having funds easily obtainable.

Psyche was watching him. He told her the message he had sent, and she nodded.

"Do you think he will find the right house?"

"With the promise of another coin as payment? I'm sure of it," he told her, wishing he had never involved her and endangered her orderly life. She looked so small and vulnerable. Her voice was still uncertain, and he wanted urgently to comfort her fears. He wanted her . . . that was the crux of it. And he was still trying to credit that she had elected to remain with him. She had stayed, in the heat of danger and difficulty, when she had every reason to leave him and protect herself. He could barely believe it was true.

"Do you not want me to come, Gabriel?" she asked quietly from the corner of the carriage.

They had reached the outskirts of London now, and the streetlamps popped up less often, so the interior of the carriage was darker. Fortunately, an almost full moon gave light to the coachman and the team, but it shed only a faint illumination inside the carriage. Gabriel could no longer see her face, it was lost in the shadows, though beneath her cloak, her white costume made a pale silhouette against the dark cushions. She sat very still, her hands clasped together in her lap.

Not want her to come? He would have sold his soul to keep her beside him forever. The sudden realization was blinding in its intensity. He wanted her beside him, he wanted her soft body beneath him—his yearning for her was so intense he did not trust himself to even take her hand.

The truth was, he loved her. He loved her. Gabriel had never thought he would love a woman again. But he loved Psyche with a heat and a depth that shook his whole concept of himself. She was beautiful in her soul as well as her body, intelligent, selfless, loyal, all those things he had thought did not exist in any female form. He had taken his pleasure often enough, enjoyed flirtations and trysts and hot-blooded joinings in tumbled beds and on sun-warmed sands, but he had not expected to love. He had not even imagined that the capacity for it still existed inside his hollowed heart.

He loved her.

Gabriel took a deep breath. He had not answered her question, and the silence between them had grown strained.

"Of course I want you with me," he said. She would have no idea how much truth the simple statement held. "But I must think of your well-being, Psyche. As I said, I cannot guarantee your safety."

He saw her relax subtly, the shape of her body losing its tenseness, and he heard her sigh deeply. She smelled of rose oil, and he wanted her so badly—

"I understand," she said. "But I have the right to make my own decision, Gabriel."

It was his turn to nod. He would not dispute that. But what she did not know, and what he did not yet dare to tell her, was that the danger existed not just from Barrett and his hired killers, but closer at hand. Who would protect Psyche's good name, Psyche's pure loveliness, from Gabriel himself?

The carriage rocked over a bump in the road, and the steady cadence of horses' hooves was the only discernable sound. Neither spoke, but the silence between them was pregnant with emotions so powerful that the air itself seemed to pulsate, like the blood in Gabriel's temple and the thundering of his heart.

The moon was waning by the time they reached the vil-
lage that lay nearest to Gabriel's hard-won estate. The carriage slowed and rolled at a leisurely pace through the quiet
lane. All the houses and the one tiny inn were dark and shuttered. All the residents seemed to be asleep in their beds,
quiet of conscience and easy of mind.

Gabriel wished he felt the same. Would Barrett think to
come after them here? Was Gabriel taking too much of a
gamble? If it had been only his own life he was risking, he
would have chanced it all without lingering doubts, but
when Psyche's well-being also depended on his choice, he
found he had much more reason to second-guess himself.

The hours of their travel had passed without conversation—he thought that Psyche had dozed in her corner of the
carriage. He had too much to think on for sleep to claim him.
He was taut with all the emotion that he had to suppress: the
worry for Psyche's safety that he did not wish to alarm her
with, the pent-up longing that he also did not wish her to
know. Sleep was a luxury he would not be granted.

It didn't matter. He'd had many sleepless nights in his
lifetime, many flights from danger. But for the first time, he
was fleeing toward something—his redemption, his personal victory, his chance to reclaim his rightful status.

He stirred, wanting to tell the driver to hurry. The first
sight of his new property, the property he would never again
risk in a card game, the property he meant to leave to his
sons and his grandsons. . . . When it was restored, it should
even be suitable to bring a wife to, it should be an almost
suitable haven for—he glanced at the quiet figure slumber-
ing in the corner of the carriage. For the most generous,
most courageous, most beautiful woman he had ever hoped
to find. He was not worthy of her, and he knew it. Did he
have any hope of claiming her heart?

He would do his damnedest. But he had to bring the estate back to some semblance of prosperity first. With Barrett
as its absentee owner, the place was bound to be shabby and
in need of polish and paint. But it would be done, and with
care. He would see to it, perhaps do some of it with his own

hand. He longed to have roots again, to have responsibilities, to prove that he was man enough to shoulder them.

They left the village behind, passed a last farmhouse or two, and the carriage picked up speed once more. Gabriel could hear the driver urging on the tired team. Only a mile or two, now, by his solicitor's directions.

When they turned off the main road into an overgrown driveway, Gabriel leaned out the window of the carriage door, trying to make out the first sight of the house that should be at the end of the drive. He could barely contain his excitement. His movement seemed to wake Psyche, though he had not spoken. She straightened, too.

"Are we there?"

He nodded, grinning like a schoolboy.

Psyche seemed to share his eagerness. "Oh, is it in sight?"

"Not yet." Gabriel had a sudden intense desire to see his new home for the first time without any witnesses, except for Psyche, of course, with whom he would willingly share any treasure. Something so important as reclaiming his lost birthright should be a private moment.

He called to the driver. "Pull up, if you will."

The carriage slowed.

"What are you doing?" Psyche asked, her tone puzzled.

"I want to examine my property for the first time without anyone nearby," he said, unable to adequately explain his mad jangle of emotion. He knew that his voice was unsteady. "I'd like you to come, if you wish, but if you are too weary—"

"No," Psyche said quickly. "I will stay with you."

He helped her out of the carriage onto the narrow dirt lane. The driver peered at them with sleepy eyes.

"Go back to the village and wake the innkeeper; ask for grain for the horses and food and drink for yourself," Gabriel told the man, handing him a half crown. "We shall interview the caretaker and look over the house. You can come back for us after you've had a short nap, just after the noon hour perhaps, and tell the landlord to have a meal waiting for us when we return."

"Yes, milord," the driver agreed, brightening at the suggestion.

There was a patch of open meadow just ahead where the driver was able to turn the carriage, his hands on the reins deft and sure. All of Psyche's servants seemed both capable and loyal, Gabriel thought. Perhaps because she, like her parents, treated them generously and with consideration. How many mistresses taught their kitchen maids to read or worried over an injured footman? Too bad his own father had never learned that lesson.

The carriage retraced its path, leaving them standing alone amid dark quiet woods. Gabriel hoped this was not a mad impulse. "We will likely have to return to the inn ourselves later," he told Psyche. "There is supposed to be a caretaker, but he did not answer my solicitor's letters. I'm sure the beds will be damp and unaired and the furnishings covered in dust cloths, probably not habitable until I can get some servants in."

She nodded and reached to tuck her hand inside his arm. "You are brimming with excitement," she said. "I can feel it, too."

He grinned, still drunk with exhilaration. "I have waited so long," he tried to explain. "I know it may not be just as I'd like, but as long as I can reclaim the land, refurbish the house . . ."

"Let us not waste another minute," Psyche told him, her tone almost as impatient as his. "Come!"

They hurried up the lane, stumbling a little in the darkness over the rough clods of dirt that littered the way, large trees again crowding the narrow strip of road. He would have to trim some of these trees, widen the drive, Gabriel thought. He would have a great deal of work to do on this place, yet the thought did not dim his sense of expectation but only made his ownership seem that much more real. A slight breeze stirred the leaves of the trees, and somewhere, a sleepy bird twittered. It was not far from dawn.

Walking rapidly, they turned one last curve and then the trees fell away, and the landscape opened up. He could make out the outlines of a sizable house, its silhouette dark against the skyline. Gabriel stopped for an instant, and Psyche, as if sensitive to his mood, paused also.

It looked like a handsome dwelling, better than he had dared hope for. There was a fine line of rooftop, a solid set of stone steps that led to the front entrance, and two ells reaching back on either side of the main house. The stables and other buildings were no doubt hidden around the back. Before the residence stretched a swath of overgrown lawn, and he caught a glimpse of a stone wall to the side—perhaps a formal garden.

Yes, it had the prospect of a fine gentleman's seat. Gabriel would no longer be a vagabond, a homeless gamester living hand to mouth, never sure where he would find himself at the next sunrise, the next sunset. This would be his home, won by his own hand. He would owe nothing to his father's bitter bequest, and that made the victory even sweeter.

He had come home.

Gabriel found that he could not speak—the lump in his throat was too big, and he feared that his vision had blurred. He blinked hard, not willing to reveal such unmanly weakness before the woman at his side.

Psyche stood quietly, giving him the privacy of the moment. She made no comment, and he blessed her for her perception and her containment.

At last he felt that he could trust his voice. "It looks reasonably well," he said. "Shall we go closer?"

"It's a very handsome building," she said. "At least, as much as we can see of it." Psyche glanced toward the east. The first faint touches of dawn lightened the darkness. While they had stood there, the ebony sky had faded to gray and then to lavender, and almost as they watched, a faint wash of gold and peach showed above the treetops. A bird sang, and then another, and another, the chorus slowly building. The sound was exultant, matching Gabriel's mood.

"I'm glad you are here." He reached to take her hand, his heart full.

Psyche smiled up at him, her face pale in the dimness but her eyes shining with a radiance to rival the rising sun. She gripped his hand firmly, and they walked closer to the house.

The front carriageway was almost bare of gravel, weeds thrusting through the once carefully combed drive. The stone steps had withstood the passage of time, but Psyche could see that the large windows were dark with grime and she made out one or two broken panes. She hoped that the interior was not in too bad a shape. Gabriel had his whole heart already committed to this place—she did not wish to see him disappointed.

They climbed the steps slowly. Gabriel seemed to be holding his breath. The daylight was growing brighter, and the birds in the trees now peeped loudly, a disjointed hymn of delight at the start of a new day.

Gabriel reached out to knock on the heavy wooden door. He rapped once smartly and then cursed in disbelief.

"Oh, no!" Psyche gripped his now slack hand in sympathy.

Beneath the impact of his touch, the door listed precariously, creaking as rusty hinges gave way. Then its own weight pulled it downward, and it crashed into the dark interior, sending up a cloud of dust that floated toward them, while the sound of the door's fall seemed to echo through the house.

Gabriel stood very still. Even in the pale early light, she thought that his face had blanched. Then he took a deep breath and stepped forward, treading on the dry-rotted wood of the door, which crunched beneath his weight.

"Gabriel, wait!" she called, but he did not seem to hear. He plunged into the house. Choosing her path carefully, Psyche followed.

The inside of the house would have daunted the most optimistic of new owners. Psyche looked around. The walls were streaked with damp, and the wooden wainscoting showed signs of rodents' teeth. The house smelled strongly of mildew and mold and rot. Psyche put one hand to her nose to block the smell and walked further, glancing into the first doorway.

It had once been a small morning room, but rooks had nested in the paneled shelves beside the empty fireplace, and spiderwebs festooned the old-fashioned chandelier so heavily that she could barely make out the outlines of the piece. She took one step inside. There was little furniture, and what there was had been left uncovered and was dark with damp and streaked with mildew. An empty outline above the mantel marked where a looking glass or painting of handsome size had once hung. It had been taken away, and the wall showed only the lines of dust attesting to its loss. Psyche took another step inside the chamber, then heard a skitter as of tiny feet. Shivering, she retreated to the hallway.

The other rooms she peered into seemed no better. There was a library, thankfully with few books left on the almost bare shelves, because those that remained were certainly ruined by damp and cold and neglect, not to mention by the mice who scurried away every time Psyche ventured into a room.

It would be a cat's paradise, she thought wryly, but as for Gabriel—she took a deep breath, then regretted it at once as she coughed on the dank odors. Oh, Gabriel, who had been so happy, so full of anticipation, who had entertained such high hopes for a new start. How could he bear such a disappointment?

She hastened further into the house as the brightening sunlight shone through dirty windows and allowed her a better view of the interior. Unhappily, more light did not alter her perceptions of the house. Everywhere, she saw damp and neglect—strips of wallpaper had loosened from the walls and drooped in sad fingers; cobwebs were thick in every corner, sometimes inhabited by dark shapes that scurried away from her passage and made her shudder again. And the track of small rodent feet made tiny trails through the dust on the floors, otherwise marked only by one man's footsteps.

"Gabriel, where are you?" she called.

She found him at last, sitting on the staircase that curved up to the upper floors, his face hidden in his hands. From the touch of grime that marked his cheek, the wisp of cobweb that adorned his dark hair, she saw that he had ventured even farther into the house, and from his silence, his bowed shoulders, he had found nothing to contradict the ruin of the ground floor.

"Gabriel?" she whispered.

When he raised his head, she was shocked by his expression. The spark of hope and happiness had vanished, and the bleakness of his face, his cheeks hollowed by shock, his eyes dark with a grief so deep that it cut her to the heart, made her take a shuddering breath.

"Gabriel, it will be all right."

He shook his head. "This was to be my home, this estate was to be the key to remaking my reputation, restoring my lost status as a gentleman, giving me back the life I should have had. And it is as empty as all my most foolish dreams." His voice was flat, so devoid of his usual intonations that she would have thought it belonged to a stranger.

"Gabriel, it is not so. Your dreams were not foolish." She tried to take his hand, but he waved her away.

"I had the presumption to think that someday, after careful stewardship, this would be fine enough that I could ask a woman of good birth to share it with me. It was to be the house to which I would someday be proud to bring my bride." He could not seem to look her in the face.

"It's nothing but a moldering ruin. Barrett has stripped it of every item with any possible value, and then he used the deed, with lies about the property's condition, as a stake in one final game. And no doubt he intended to continue using his 'estate' as bait for other gullible souls. Lies and deception, and I bought them all, I—who counted myself such a sharpster." He laughed, a harsh sound that cut her to the quick. "I was once again the most pathetic of fools."

"Gabriel, stop it!" she said, her tone urgent. She could

not bear the bitter anger of his words, nor the misery that she knew lay behind them. "It is not so bad."

"You think not?" He raised his gaze to meet hers, and she saw again how deep this blow had struck. "You would wish to make your bed with the spiders, spend your time with the rats and the mice who are busily chewing away at what is left of the foundations? Such good caretakers they are."

"Hush, my dear," she repeated, "It is in sad shape, I grant you. But the bones of the house are most likely sound; it has not been untenanted that long. You can still restore it, it will simply take more time than you had hoped—"

"And more money," he added quietly. "I shall have to go back to the gaming tables, and desperation does not make for a clear head. And if I lose the property itself, my only asset, where do I go then?"

She thought of Gabriel leaving England once again, returning to exile, of the wandering that had been his life, and she felt a wrench of her own. No, she could not allow it.

"I wanted this to be worthy of you," Gabriel said, so softly that she wasn't sure she heard him aright. "I wanted it to be clean and beautiful and good, like nothing has been in my life for so many years. I wanted to dust it off and polish it up and offer it to you on a velvet cushion. It would never have been enough, of course, for someone who deserves gold and diamonds and castles suitable for a queen. But I had hoped."

His voice trailed off into silence, and she saw how his pride had been shattered, how much anguish festered behind the facade of control he strained to maintain. It was a mask more concealing than the one he had worn for the masquerade—the night of playful deception that seemed so long ago, yet was only a few hours behind them.

It was time to put aside the masks.

"Gabriel." Psyche took his hand. This time, he did not pull away, but regarded her with an almost puzzled look, as if behind his shock and grief and disappointment, he could not think clearly. "I do not need elegant houses, nor gold, nor jewels. I need you, Gabriel. I need only your love—that is the greatest gift you can bestow upon me."

Unblinking, he stared at her for a long moment, then he laughed, an ugly sound of derision and desolation. "Do you think I would accept your love out of pity?"

"It is not pity—" She tried to interrupt, but he was not listening.

"Or that any man who cared about you would allow you to throw yourself away on a wastrel with a stained past and a cobweb-cluttered pigsty for a home? You are worthy of so much more than that, sweet Psyche, with your clear eyes and generous heart, which even all your icy decorum cannot conceal. How could I offer you such base coin?"

"Offer me your heart," she said, her voice soft but clear.

He was not sure that he had made out the sense of her words. How could she possibly consider loving a man so far beneath her? He had hoped for so much, and to find himself once more cast down upon a rubbish heap—the shock of disappointment made him almost mad with grief. He had wanted it in the beginning for his own selfish purposes, but lately he'd desired it even more for her, for Psyche, as a gift to offer the goddess who now held his heart in her keeping. Because of that, the regret was twice as hard to bear.

He shook his head, unable to believe in her words. "Never would I allow you to lower yourself so far." His voice was hoarse with pain and despair and a longing that he couldn't conceal.

She gazed back at him, her blue eyes hard to read. Her lips were pressed together—oh, if he could only kiss them open again, tease that full sweet mouth with his own lips, his questing tongue, taste her sweetness and teach her—

So much that he could have taught her about love and laughter and delight too deep for words. But only if the cards had fallen a different way. Not like this, with nothing to give her, no safe haven to offer, only this wreck of a house, which echoed the havoc of all his dreams.

"As soon as the driver returns, I will send you back to

London," he said, his voice dull with weariness. "You will be safer without me."

"And you?" she asked, her voice whisper-soft.

He didn't answer, not sure how he would go on. How many times could a man pick himself up, regain some semblance of self-respect, and try again? Worse, now that he had seen Psyche, loved Psyche, he would never be content to wander as a gamester with no reputation and no place in the world, with nothing to offer but his skill with cards, his face and his easy charm. Worthless, all of it.

Her eyes narrowed, and he heard her draw a sharp breath, as if she read something of the depths of his devastation.

"No," she said. "I will not leave you."

"You must," he told her, his tone flat and cold. "There is no need for you to be ruined, too. Go back home, protect your safety and your reputation. I will find Barrett and we will settle this fight, once and for all. I know now that I owe him even more enmity than I had thought."

The thought of Gabriel putting himself in such direct danger made Psyche sick with fear.

"No," she said. "I am staying."

"I will not allow it."

"You cannot stop me," she told him calmly. "That is . . ."

He waited, too weary to explain to her properly what folly all this was. But in his wildest dreams, Gabriel could not have predicted her next words.

"I shall play you for the choice," she said in a rush.

This time, despite his exhaustion, his brows rose. "What?"

"You mean to go back to being a gamester, yes? Then you might as well start now. We shall play to see who prevails. If you win, I shall go quietly back to London. If I win, I stay, and . . . and you will be my prize."

A long, stunned silence, then he cleared his throat. His voice was husky. "Psyche . . . goddess, you do not know what you are saying."

"Oh, I think I do," she said, her smile serene. "I think I know quite well."

In this nightmare of a house, still reeling from the shock, Gabriel found it hard to think. He could not believe her; she was a gently reared young woman of good family. True, her parents had been eccentric, but even they would not have allowed her so much liberty that she really understood—his gaze dropped to the smooth curve of her neck, the white hollow at the base of her throat that he ached to kiss. He couldn't think rationally. But one fact stood out, even in his bemused state.

"Psyche," he said gently, as if to a child. "I am a gamester. I play cards to survive. You think that you can best me?"

"I can try," she said, still strangely certain.

Perhaps it would be easier to humor her. He would beat her at a hand of cards, and send her on her way, with less cajoling and argument. However—

"We have no cards," he pointed out.

"I saw some in the library," she told him.

He shrugged. It was folly to honor any chamber in this house with such a designation, but he didn't waste his breath pointing this out. "Very well, let us see."

They walked together through the dusty hall and into the large room lined with bookshelves and wood panels and wide moldings that were likely quite handsome, if one could see beneath the veneer of dust. Sure enough, scattered in the corner of the room where perhaps a card table had once stood, playing cards littered the hardwood floor.

Gabriel shook his head, then bent to collect the cards. The stiff cardboard pieces were thick with damp and slightly warped, but more importantly . . .

"We cannot play a game without a full deck," he explained patiently. "I see only about two-thirds of the deck here." Shreds of the rest no doubt cushioned some rodent's den behind the wood panels of the room. "It is impossible."

"Then we shall draw from what is there," Psyche replied. "A simple game, which will offset your greater experience, at least. Pure luck, no more."

Once, he would have laughed and told her that Lady

Luck was his constant companion. Now, he knew how bitter such a statement would sound, and how false. Gabriel nodded, resigned. It was true that such an uncomplicated match would deny him the chance to outplay her, but nonetheless, he could not conceive of losing. Cards were the only thing in his life which seldom failed him.

He awkwardly shuffled the handful of warped cards, then placed the stack atop a dusty three-legged table, the only piece of furnishing left in the room. "Very well, draw."

For the first time, Psyche looked tense. She reached for the top card and smiled as she turned it over to show the faded colors of a jack of diamonds. "A fair draw."

"We shall do two out of three, of course," Gabriel told her.

She frowned, but when he drew a trey of spades, relaxed. "I win," she pointed out.

"Only the first round." He nodded, and she drew another card. The table, on uneven legs, rocked slightly at her touch. This time, she turned over a six of hearts, and Psyche's brows knit with concentration.

He drew the ten of diamonds. "My win," he noted.

Psyche bit her lip, then jumped at the rustle of small feet nearby. "Gabriel!" She looked at him in mute supplication.

Nodding, he walked across to one of the room's dim corners. Beneath a yellowed sheet of ancient newsprint and a few stray curls of dust, the rodent who had alarmed his companion darted away once more. Gabriel stamped his foot, and the mouse disappeared into a hole in the baseboard. The room was silent again, and he returned to the table.

"I have sent away our uninvited guest," he told her, his tone wry. "Draw, Psyche. The morning is advancing, and you need to be on your way."

"I have not lost yet." As if to prove her point, Psyche reached for the deck and turned over the queen of hearts.

Gabriel frowned. "Impressive," he admitted. Slowly he reached for the cards and drew a jack of spades.

"I win!" Psyche exclaimed. "I am staying, Gabriel."

Gabriel sighed. He had hoped to avoid a confrontation,

but the cards had failed him, too. On such a day, how had he expected anything else?

"It was a child's game," he said, his voice patient. "But this decision is not for play, it is most serious. You must risk neither your good name nor your person, Psyche. You have to return."

She shook her head. "Do you not honor your bets, my lord?"

"Don't call me that!" Gabriel said sharply. "There is no one here to impress, save the rats. It is too late for masquerades, now that we have seen the reality." He nodded toward the devastation of the house.

But Psyche looked only at him. She took one step closer, and above the sour smell of damp and mildew, he detected the light fragrance of her perfume. A smidgen of dust darkened one cheek, but beneath it, her fair skin was unblemished, glowing with the inner luminescence of an heirloom pearl. He wanted her so badly that his muscles ached. And— damn these stupid silk breeches—if she looked down, innocent or not, she would realize the intensity of his need.

The futility of the situation, of his dream, seeped into him like the mildew that coated the walls. He had been so damn close to having all that he wanted. He had been so close to having Psyche and being worthy of her.

Fate had trumped him in the final trick.

"It is done, Psyche." He spoke the words with quiet finality.

"You can't mean it." Psyche stepped toward him, but stopped when he retreated.

"But I do. This game is over and every gambler knows when to cut his losses and leave the table."

Gabriel turned and walked toward the library door. The once proud line of his shoulders slumped, looking defeated and tired. She could not bear it. Only a little while ago he had been so hopeful, so jubilant.

"But I won," she insisted softly.

He halted in the doorway but did not turn to face her. "I

said I will not hold you to such a ridiculous wager. You could not know what you are asking."

There was little else he could have said to make her angrier. Slightly aghast at herself even while she did it, Psyche picked up the warped deck and heaved it at him.

It felt fabulous.

Cards scattered everywhere, only a few actually hitting him on the back and neck. He turned and gaped at her before closing his mouth into a thin line.

"Listen to me and listen well, Gabriel. You are not going to tell me what I know and what I need and what I must do. I have done nothing else for years except abide by society's rules, propriety's dictates, and I am sick unto death of it." Her voice rose until it was a fair shriek.

He said nothing.

Psyche let her words sink in for a moment, and then raised her chin high. "You may be giving up, but I am not. I will get my inheritance, I will not marry Percy, and I will have you!"

He quirked a brow. "You think so?"

She nodded decisively. "Yes, I won you fairly."

He seemed to think that over for a moment before shaking his head. "Would that I could."

Infuriated with his arrogance, she pounded her hand on the rickety table, sending up puffs of dust. "You can!"

"Damn it, Psyche. I cannot!" He ate up the space between them with long-legged strides. He grabbed her upper arms in his hands and pulled her close. "What sort of man would I be if I were to make love to you, share your body and take your innocence, all the while knowing I would have to leave you?"

Psyche watched him, loving him even now when he was so angry. Want and need had stripped him of all his usual defenses. His azure eyes were naked of his customary insouciant charm and full of stark emotion.

"Sweet heaven, I want to love you so badly, what I would not give to taste and touch. . . ." He was so close. Each warm breath on her lips, each brush of his chest against hers made her need swell inside her to unbearable proportions.

Just when she thought he meant to embrace her and press his lips against hers, he thrust her away. Her hip bumped painfully against the table, but she stood firm.

"Why can't you simply freeze me out as you would Percy?" His voice sounded strained and tight.

She laughed weakly. "Because I don't love him as I love you."

Her declaration nearly sent him to his knees. It staggered him. This wonderful, incredible woman loved him. And that was when he knew he'd have to hurt her.

He made his smirk cruel. "My dear, you'll have to trust my vast experience when I tell you that what you are demanding has nothing to do with love and everything to do with lust."

Come on, darling. Slay me with a look, or cut me to ribbons, but leave so that I cannot ruin your life, too, he urged silently. He would not see her suffer disgrace because of him.

But improbably, the corners of her delectable mouth lifted. Her smile was slow and sure as she walked close to him. Laying her hands on his tense shoulders, she leaned in until her lips were a breath away from his.

"I love you," she whispered.

His smirk disappeared, and he closed his eyes tightly in an attempt to shut her out.

"I love you." Her voice grew steadier.

"Stop it," he ordered. Every line in his body went rigid as he strove to reject what she offered, what he so desperately wanted.

"I love you," she said firmly.

He opened his eyes. She saw the battle that was raging inside him revealed in their dark depths. "You mustn't," he pleaded, his voice achingly tender.

Tears welled in her eyes because she knew then that he loved her, too. She raised smudged hands and cupped his lightly stubbled cheeks. Turning, he pressed a fervent kiss into her palm.

She tasted her own tears as she laughed weakly. "I think it's about time I do what's right instead of what's correct, my love." Tracing the scar near his hard mouth, she adored him with her eyes. "You taught me that, you know." Leaning her forehead against his, she whispered her demand. "Now, teach me everything else."

Even knowing he wouldn't deny her any longer, she was unprepared for his arms clasping her so tightly, lifting her high against him. Their lips and tongues met in sweet battle, their breaths growing heated and short.

"As you wish, goddess," he said when at last he pulled away. "But no more instruction. For once, we must do this my way."

Her stomach tight in anticipation, she brushed her cheek against his with her nod. "I can do that," she said, her voice eager. She felt as well as heard his deep chuckle. She pulled back to scold him, but his sudden change of expression stopped her.

"I know I do not deserve you," he said.

Psyche opened her mouth to protest, but he held up a palm to silence her.

"But for a few hours, I want to pretend that this is our home, that it is worthy of you, that *I* am worthy." He closed his eyes and swallowed the lump that had lodged in his throat. "For just a little while, let me be the man you deserve." He lifted his lids, blinking hard, and saw his own tears reflected on her cheeks. "This brief time together will have to last me a lifetime."

Unable to answer, she gave him a watery smile.

"Psyche, my dearest." His voice trembled. He felt hesitant, unsure of himself, a boy again new to lovemaking, uncertain as to how to please. He lifted a trembling hand to her cheek but pulled it back before he could feel her warmth. Once he felt her skin, he did not trust he'd have the fortitude to stop. "I-I don't want to hurt you in any way. And if I stayed, I would. I always end up hurting those I love. . . ."

But Psyche would not allow him any distance. Capturing his hand, she raised it again to her cheek, brushing his fingertips across her smooth skin and down to the fullness of her lips. Rising on her toes, she kissed him, and the softness of her lips amazed him yet again. His mind might be bemused, his poise stripped away by the new emotions that had sprung up within him, but his body remembered. With a helpless moan, he kissed her surely, firmly, his arms pulling her even closer, and she relaxed into his embrace.

The kiss lengthened, and her lips parted, till he could taste the sweetness of her mouth and tantalize the softness he found there. He thought of other soft places waiting for his invasion, and his groin ached till he feared he would disgrace himself like a green boy. He pulled a little away.

She opened her eyes, her expression perplexed.

"When I love you, I want it to be as if we have forever," he explained, trailing his hand down the soft curve of her throat. Her pulse jumped, like a small bird fluttering beneath his hand. "It would take forever for me to have my fill of you."

She relaxed. For an instant, however, he had seen a trace of nervousness beneath her calm.

"We can have forever, my love," she whispered.

Instead of answering, Gabriel leaned forward with careful slowness and kissed her again.

His lips were firm and sure. Psyche thought she might float away, such was the aching sweetness of his touch. Then the kiss became deeper and more demanding, his tongue probing, and Psyche pressed herself against him, ready to meet his passion with the rising heat within her own breast.

Her eyes shut, Psyche became aware of the touch of his hand on her face, the slow soft movements of his fingers as he stroked her cheek. The light touch sent tingles of feeling through her, and when he dropped his hand to her neck, caressing the curve of her throat, then the hollow at the base of her neck, she felt prickles of sensation that made her feel as if her skin were on fire.

She waited, eager for his hands to move on, but Gabriel took his time, gliding his fingertips over her throat and shoulders and neck again and again until she trembled with eagerness, feeling as if she were an instrument on which he played a harmonious melody.

Psyche could not speak, she was beyond words. Where this stream of sensual joy would take her, she could not rationally predict, but thoughts were gone, only feelings existed. She felt as if she were falling into a morass of sensation—then she found that she *was* falling, or at least, Gabriel was carefully placing her back against the floor. He had untied her dark cloak and laid it against the dusty boards.

"I want to believe that this is our bed, and I am laying you down on scented sheets and down-filled pillows," he whispered huskily in her ear. She smiled at the image and raised her arms to him as he lay beside her.

"And this is not a dirty costume but a gown you have specially chosen to wear for your lover." With a sure motion of his hand, he slipped her tunic to her waist and pushed it further down past her thighs.

She made a soft sound of protest at the loss of his touch, but he moved his right hand up and caressed each one of her breasts in turn until the ripples of feeling again threatened to overwhelm her. With practiced fingers, he traced the curve of her breast. No man had ever touched her there—Percy's awkward fumblings during the times she had slapped her cousin's hand away could not be compared to this. But thinking about her cousin or any other man now was sacrilege.

Psyche arched her back, pressing her breast deeper into his palm. She had no desire to push Gabriel away. Her nipples strained, erect and tender, as if instinctively aware of the pleasures they were owed. Gabriel did not deny her. He cupped one breast in his hand, stroking it softly, teasing the nipple with a skillful touch. And while she breathed long sighs of pleasure, he leaned forward and she found to her surprise that he had pressed his lips to her breast.

She gasped as his mouth found her nipple, kissed it, surrounded it, gently manipulated the tender flesh until waves of pleasure ran over her like a warm tide from a tropical sea.

Was it possible to die of pure joy? She could not imagine how much more pleasure lovemaking could offer, if this brief interlude left her so charged with sensation—and then she found that she was woefully, joyfully wrong.

Gabriel lowered his head and kissed the soft skin of her belly, till she shuddered from the impact of his warm lips, and his hand cupped the sweet curve of her, touched the silky golden hair.

She stiffened, alarmed for an instant, yet the feelings in her belly were so intense that she could not push him away. She instinctively wanted whatever it was that Gabriel was offering, but she had no idea what it was.

Gabriel did. He would delight her in ways that surely few women had known before. His hand soothed her, incited her, opened her up to sensations that she had not even known existed, brought her to such heights that she almost could not breathe. Pressure swirled and built between her thighs as he held her prisoner with only the tips of his fingers. She paused, breathless, reaching for something she could not name but wanted desperately.

She sobbed his name in supplication. Gabriel smiled down into her flushed face in understanding and then replaced his fingertips with his mouth.

Psyche reared up in open-eyed shock, then the delicious sensation enveloped her. She fisted her hands in his thick hair and held tight as his hungry mouth devoured her secrets.

Gabriel slid his hands beneath her writhing hips and cupped her buttocks in his palms, burying tongue and lips into her. Gasps heaved in and out of her chest, and just when she thought her heart would surely explode, he gave a final caress with his clever tongue, and her heart and all else exploded into a burst of color and light. Her hips jerked and thrust, but Gabriel slid up her body and kissed her into stillness.

He watched her, taking all his delight in her pleasure, her surprised but passionate responses. She rested for a moment, looking dazed, her fair body a stark contrast against the dark cloak. During the lovemaking, her hair had come unbound and was twisted around her sweat-dampened body. Tendrils clung to her chest and cheeks.

"I never knew."

"I thought I knew," he said hoarsely, feeling his heart still pounding. "But I can see there is much that you can teach me."

Shaking her head at the absurdity of that, she realized she was completely naked and he was fully clothed.

"This will not do at all," she said in a seductive purr. Slight tremors still rocked her as she pulled at his shirt, needing to feel the warmth of his skin against her. Reaching down with urgent hands, he assisted her, yanking on buttons and ties until his chest was bare and his masculinity exposed.

Psyche's eyes widened at the proof of his desire.

He chuckled low in his throat. "Goddess, you do wonders for a man's vanity."

Looking back up into his face, she shrugged and gave a fair imitation of her usual icy disdain.

"Oh, no, you don't."

Just when her pulse had almost slowed to normal, he sent it rocketing again by pressing his hardness against her wet warmth, and at the same time, taking her mouth in a desperate kiss. When he pulled his lips from hers, he captured her chin in his hand.

Pressing the smooth tip against her, he held himself there at the brink of her opening until her lashes fluttered, and she focused her passion-dazed eyes upon him. His gaze captured her as surely as his heavy body pressing her into the unyielding floor.

"Pretend that I have a lifetime to worship you instead of only this one time."

Before she could challenge that utterance, he pushed into her wet warmth in one smooth stroke.

Psyche exhaled and tensed slightly at the strange sensation, but Gabriel seemed to anticipate her feelings because he ducked his head down to hers. Carefully, his breath labored, he pressed kisses to her eyelids and nuzzled in the rumpled curls at her forehead.

Pulsing with heat inside of her, he held himself still and let her adjust. It was all so new to her. On the edge of fright, Psyche opened her eyes again. She saw that Gabriel was watching her, his sea deep eyes tender, and his expression intent.

"Relax, my love," he told her, and then he drew almost out of her before pushing back in to the hilt. Psyche braced herself for more discomfort, but this time it was fleeting, and Gabriel's arms were comforting around her.

He kissed her lips very gently. "You are more dear to me than my life," he whispered.

Then he moved again within her, and this time there was no pain at all, only the wonderful sensations that had been growing through all his careful ministrations. He had incited an intensity of feeling through his touch and his lips that now his deep thrusts stirred into even more blissful passion.

Psyche felt waves of pleasure so intense they were almost pain. She could not bear so much joy—surely she would fall apart, disappear into wisps of vapor that would rise like the dew toward the morning sun.

Still Gabriel moved inside her, his pace quickening as her own response became more fevered. She felt joined with him at some elemental level, as if one skin covered both their bodies, one pulse labored in both their veins. They had been made one, and she would never again look at the world in the same way.

The waves were higher, deeper, but this time Psyche knew what to expect, and she wanted it desperately for herself and Gabriel. In characteristic fashion, she held back not at all, rushing headfirst instead to meet it. Psyche moved with him, pushed against the strong thrusts, pulled him closer, kissed him so hard that her lips felt swollen, then fell back again, barely aware of the hard floor beneath her. She could feel only the rising passion that surged and crested at last in an ecstasy beyond thought, beyond words, ecstasy that no poet had ever hoped to express.

She cried out, then felt Gabriel's whole body tense before he pulled himself quickly out of her body and emptied himself into the discarded sash.

He kissed her, then pulled her into the circle of his arms. They lay side by side, breathless with spent passion. She felt so alive that she thought she might hear the mice in their nests, the spiders scuttling along their silken webs, the stars making their own celestial music. Speech was impossible for some minutes. She was content to lay her cheek against his chest, feel the light sheen of perspiration that coated his tanned skin, hear his heart still beating fast, his breath at last beginning to slow, and to know that she had mirrored his responses with perfect precision. They were two parts of one whole.

"Pretend that instead of just leaving your body, I had instead come inside of you, that we had created a little life inside your womb." He laid a trembling hand on her belly as if shielding a life there; his voice was wistful. Psyche let the tears fall unhindered down her face and dampen her hair.

He brushed the tears away and tried to bring back her smiles. "You are a goddess indeed," he said, very low.

She smiled for him, though her heart ached. She knew him so well but did not know how to convince him that he was worthy of her love. Until he believed it, nothing she said would sway him. But this was no time for sadness. She rallied for him and injected a teasing note into her voice. "Don't be irreverent."

"Then you are the part of my soul that I have been lacking for so long." This time, his tone was serious; she knew he was sincere.

His breathing slowed, and she thought that he slept. He had had no rest through their lengthy carriage ride.

It was as well. She could not bear to hear more denials of their future. She had vowed her love to him, and she had meant it. True, Gabriel had been free for so long, his affections unfettered, his charm and face and perfect body the object of so many women's lust.

How could she expect to hold him?

She just would, that was all. She would not accept one interlude of perfect joy. That, she could expect, had in fact already been given. But she had no doubt that the future could hold much more.

She turned her head and gazed at Gabriel. Midmorning sun streamed through the uncovered windows, the grime filtering the bright light so that it fell on his prone body reverently, softly. She studied the strong planes and angles of his face, unsoftened even by sleep. She would have Gabriel, or she would have no man at all. Hands fisted at her sides, she breathed a silent plea.

"Please, allow us a future together!"

Nineteen

When they awakened, she still lay in his arms, at ease despite her nakedness. When his gaze traveled over her still flushed breasts, his open admiration was a benediction that she accepted without self-consciousness. So much had changed so quickly, and Psyche had changed, too. In some corner of her mind, she gave thanks that— whatever the future held—Gabriel would always be the one to have taught her about the physical side of love. She was sure that no one else could have opened her mind and her heart to the wonders of this passion, could have elicited such responses from her body, responses that had surprised even herself. No, she was glad that this had been the first time, with Gabriel, and it had truly been an expression of love.

They were both still sticky with a light sheen of perspiration, and she thought longingly of a warm bath, or even a chilly secluded lake into which they might plunge. Together, naked, feeling the water cool against fevered skin . . . that picture evoked images of lovemaking all over again. She blinked, amazed at the feelings that so easily reawakened within her.

Gabriel raised himself to one elbow and leaned over her,

gazing at her face, smiling at the spark of yearning that rekindled within her blue eyes.

"I believe I have created . . ."

"A monster?" She finished for him, a little fearful that these feelings were perhaps not normal, certainly not . . . respectable.

"Never," he said quickly. "A marvel, though not really of my creation. An awakening, I should say instead. An awareness of the passions I always suspected lay beneath your proper exterior."

He saw the doubt that clouded her eyes, and he kissed her very gently. "Rejoice, my love. You have been granted a rare gift, a gift that comes from your own honest heart, your own healthy body and mind. Some women take years to learn what you have already instinctively grasped, and some women never come to know it at all."

Some women never have a man who cares enough, who is wise and gentle and loving enough, to bring them to this knowledge, Psyche thought, but she did not voice her instinct. "So," she drawled after leaning in for a long kiss, "what made you finally succumb to my demands?"

"Honestly, I was afraid you might throw the table at me next." Gabriel laughed and ducked to avoid her mock-furious attack. He gently bracketed her wrists in his hands in expectation of her next swat. But instead, she lifted her face and they shared a long kiss, luscious in its sweetness, with warmth that rapidly grew—

And was never to flower into passion. Instead, a slight noise instantly stilled Gabriel. He paused and lifted his head.

Psyche had heard it, too. "A mouse?" she whispered.

"If so, it has two very large feet," Gabriel told her, his voice grim. "I believe it is time to leave this wonderful manse, my dear."

She rapidly pulled her simple tunic back over her head and into place, smoothing her hair as best she could and picking up her cloak and her sandals.

Gabriel also dressed quickly. He tossed the soiled blue sash into the ash-littered fireplace. They had disrupted the layer of dust on the floor, but there was little other sign that someone had been here. With his boots in one hand, Gabriel motioned for her to follow. She tiptoed across the dusty floor and waited while he peered around the door frame.

"It sounds as if they are at the rear door," he breathed into her ear.

She nodded again, not even asking who "they" were. Neither of them had any doubts, she was sure. Barrett would never give up; how long could they continue to elude his murderous thugs?

Which way? She looked the question at Gabriel, who seemed to be thinking. He glanced back toward the window, which was shaded by overlarge, untrimmed shrubbery. He motioned, and they ran lightly to the window.

Gabriel grunted as he pushed at the window sash, the wood swollen from years of neglect. At last it slid open, and he put his head through, glanced quickly around, then withdrew to help Psyche slide over the sill. He held her hands as she scrambled through, then dropped the few feet to the ground.

Psyche looked around as Gabriel followed her, jumping to the soft earth just beside her. The grass rustled and the bushes stirred; the slight noises seemed loud to Psyche's ears. Had anyone heard them, seen their escape?

A shout from the back of the house was her answer.

"Oy, they be getting away!" a hoarse voice shouted.

"Make a dash for the woods," Gabriel directed.

Holding her hand, he half-pulled her along as they both ran for their lives. Psyche pelted through the grass, wincing as her bare feet hit pebbles and stubbed against hard roots. Once, she almost fell, but Gabriel caught her and tugged her erect once more.

Men were racing after them; she could hear the crash of bodies through the undergrowth, see the shaking of limbs as she glanced back. She and Gabriel sprinted across the uneven ground. Soon, she was panting, but Gabriel never seemed to tire, and with his strong hand to urge her own, she was determined to keep up, to run till her lungs burst from the strain. She would not be the weak link, the cause of his capture, his death. Nor her own, for that matter. The thought of falling into the hands of Barrett and his hired ruffians left her cold with dread.

So she ran till her sides ached and her legs trembled and her vision was streaked with red. Only when she seemed to float in a daze of exhaustion, when she no longer could even make sense of Gabriel's words, when he had to take her by the shoulders and pull her to him in the shadow of a giant oak, did she realize that they had apparently outrun their city-bred pursuers.

"Rest for a moment," Gabriel whispered. "But do not make a sound."

She nodded, she had no breath left to answer. Her whole body was shaking, and she would have fallen if he had not held her against him, his hard-muscled body reassuring in her current state of weakness.

While her labored breathing slowed, Psyche strained to hear. The woods around them seemed empty again. She heard birds call, and in a moment a hawk shrieked somewhere in the skies above. The sound made her shiver. The hawk was a predator, angry perhaps because it had dived for a songbird and missed. Other predators roamed the forest today, just as angry, just as frustrated.

Had the men given up and turned back to the decaying manor? Or were they behind the next tree, waiting for Gabriel and Psyche to show themselves?

Psyche shivered. They could not stay hidden in the shadow of this tree forever.

Gabriel seemed to have the same thought. "If we can make it to the village . . ." he whispered into her ear.

She nodded. Her driver was there, with the carriage, and people who would witness and perhaps deter further attack. Gabriel scanned the clumps of trees closest to them, then nodded to her. Swiftly, but quietly, watching where she stepped, aware for the first time that her feet were bruised and bleeding and leaving a track that any shire-born hunter would likely be able to follow, she trailed Gabriel through the trees.

He was angling back toward the drive, she thought, or perhaps going parallel to it. They could not go too far into the woods and risk getting lost—they might even accidentally double back and walk right into the fox's den. Yet if they walked openly down the drive, they could be seen.

Even as she considered all the dangers, she felt Gabriel stiffen. "What?" she breathed. Then she heard it, too, the faint sound of horses' hooves. Barrett's reinforcements? Fear rushed over her, and she saw the grim set of Gabriel's jaw. He kept hold of her hand, but with his other, he reached inside his shirt and brought out the small knife.

She knew they would not take him, or injure her, without a fight, but Gabriel would be sadly outnumbered.

The noise came nearer, and Gabriel bent low beneath a leafy branch to make out the horse, or perhaps the team, that approached them; the driveway was only a few yards from their current hiding place. Then he dropped her hand and—to Psyche's shock—darted toward the approaching vehicle, yelling and waving his arms.

While she watched in astonishment, he looked back and motioned her forward. "Quickly," he called.

She ran to join him, then saw with a spreading wave of relief that it was her own carriage and team, her own faithful coachman, returning to collect them as instructed.

"Get in!" Gabriel pulled open the door so that Psyche could scramble inside. "We've been attacked," he called to the driver. "Turn at the first opportunity and make your best speed away from this place! When you get to the main road, I'll give you more directions."

The man nodded, and Gabriel jumped inside.

Psyche was still breathing quickly. "Where are Barrett's killers—did they see us?"

"I don't know, but we will soon outdistance them." Gabriel felt almost giddy from the release of tension. "Barrett is too low on funds to have a four-horse team or a well-sprung racing curricle. If they have the same gig they used before, it cannot keep up with your steeds."

Psyche nodded and drew a deep breath. Her cheeks had been flushed from the exertion of their mad race through the trees, but now her complexion was fading to its normal creamy hue. She reached back and pulled a twig from her tangled hair, trying to braid her locks into some semblance of order. In his mind's eye, he saw her hairpins scattered on the library floor where his eager fingers had tossed them.

Gabriel's brief elation faded, and he felt a new wave of guilt. How much longer would her safety be threatened by his enemies?

"Are we going back to London?" she asked, her voice quiet.

Gabriel considered. He had underestimated this group of villains more than once; he must not do it again. "No, they must be expecting that. They might have an ambush waiting along the road," he told her. "We will go south instead."

Psyche did not protest. She pushed her hair back and then brushed at the leaves that clung to her costume after their dash through the woods. "I will look a strange sight at an inn," she observed, but her tone was only mildly rueful.

How many well-bred ladies would have maintained their composure when faced with a sudden flight from a blood-thirsty gang, all the while wearing a disordered costume and little more? She had no baggage, no maidservant, and her reputation was in dire peril, yet her blue eyes were calm, her expression serene. She was a marvel, his enchanting Miss Hill. Gabriel gazed at her, love swelling inside him. She was unique, and she was his—if only briefly. He must keep her safe; next to that, nothing else mattered.

Even if he had to break a vow he had sworn to uphold all his life.

When they turned into the coach road, Gabriel conferred briefly with the coachman and then returned to the carriage. He sat quietly for some miles, keeping his gaze directed toward the countryside that flowed past outside the carriage window. This time, the demons that he wrestled with were uniquely his own.

The voices in his head were louder than the steady echo of the horses' rhythmic gait. "No whelp of mine will disgrace the family name in such a fashion! You disgust me. . . . No whining, dammit, this time you've gone too far. . . ." Gabriel's jaw clenched with the memories of old pain, anger that still simmered deep inside.

Psyche watched him, knowing she should demand more information as to where this mad flight was taking them. After all, it was her safety which hung in the balance, too. But the strange sense of contentment that had outlasted their few hours of passion lingered. However their future would unfold, whatever Fate had in store, she thought that perhaps it was important to savor each moment they spent together, even if it involved nothing more than rolling side by side in her carriage down a quiet road, the hedgerows filled with the chatter of birds and the rustle of small animals and all the other sounds of late spring in the English countryside.

She didn't want to think of the future, of afterwards when Gabriel might not be with her. Now, the carriage swayed, and she could hear the pounding of the horses' hooves and the occasional crack of the driver's whip swung over the team's heads to keep them alert, never touching their burnished chestnut backs. She was aware of Gabriel's presence in every inch of her body. His ridiculous costume would have looked absurd on anyone else, but Gabriel's easy poise transcended what he wore and made any outrageous outfit seem only a minor detail compared to his beautiful face and well-shaped body.

So she allowed her eyelids to lower till she could see only a glimmer of light, and she relaxed against the soft squabs, giving herself up to the gentle rock of the carriage. As long as she was with Gabriel, she would not fret over assassins or scandal or the threat of family outrage. Gabriel's presence, Gabriel's love, was talisman enough to ward off the dangers of the morrow.

When she woke, she raised her head from the cushion;

the swaying of the vehicle had ceased, and she heard a horse stomp its foot. She felt his absence at once, even before she glanced at the empty seat. Psyche bit back a cry. She was alone in the carriage, and the light was dim. Where were they? Where was Gabriel?

She peered out the small window, the glass dusty from their travels, and saw that the afternoon was advanced and the sky had clouded over. Before her she saw a high stone wall and a gatehouse. They seemed to be paused at the entrance to some large property. Gabriel was talking to the gatekeeper, and their discussion seemed animated, though she could not make out the words. The gatekeeper waved his arms, his voice shrill. Gabriel shivered once and fell silent, then he spoke more quietly, but she caught just a trace of his steely tone. At last, Gabriel appeared to prevail. The gatekeeper went to push open the large iron gates, and Gabriel climbed back into the carriage.

He was frowning. She looked toward him, her expression inquiring. He reached to take her hand.

"We will stay the night at an . . . acquaintance's house," he told her. "You will be safe here from Barrett's men."

Judging by the size of the wall and the intransigence of the gatekeeper, she found that easy to credit. But what old acquaintance was this, who kept such a large and secluded holding? The mysteries about Gabriel's past continued to mount. She thought of the old rumors of murder, but pushed the memory aside. He would tell her when he was ready. She would not be added to those who marked him guilty without any proof. Did she not know him better than that? She knew his heart was good, no matter how cynical the shell that he tried to hide it beneath.

So she refused to question him now, though curiosity stirred. But it was such a new feeling to have someone else looking out for her, someone else ready to make decisions after years of bearing so much responsibility all alone, that she found it strangely easy to put herself into Gabriel's capable hands. For now she would enjoy the comfort of having a comrade in arms to lead them into the fray, someone she would—could—trust completely. So she rode in silence, knowing that Gabriel's brow was furrowed with thought. She felt his tenseness, and she knew that Gabriel was weighing every danger, every possible ruse and defense and option, knowing with every instinct in her that he thought of her safety first, that her well-being was paramount. She would have trusted no one else so completely.

The wood they rode past was thick with towering, century-old trees, and once she saw a deer lift its graceful head from browsing on a patch of grass. The drive was neat and well cared for. At last the carriage rolled to a stop, and Gabriel, his expression wooden, opened the door and alighted, turning back to offer her a hand.

Psyche stepped down and looked around her. The house in front of them was enormous, a great pile of gray granite imposing in its formality, and strangely silent. No dogs barked, no servants could be heard calling to each other, no children laughed amid their play. She glanced toward Gabriel, but he was giving instructions to the driver, who nodded and flicked the reins, taking the carriage around back to the stables. The sound of the carriage wheels and the horses' hooves seemed loud in the unnatural stillness.

Gabriel offered her his arm.

"Do they know we are coming?" she asked, wondering if some lady was going to be upset by the unheralded arrival of two guests.

"No, but there is no shortage of guest rooms," he told her, flashing one quick smile. It did not lessen the tenseness of his jaw, however, nor the guarded look in his eyes.

"You are sure they will make us welcome?" she asked again, feeling unusually shy.

"Not exactly, but they will house us," he said grimly.

Before she could demand an explanation of that cryptic comment, she heard the front door open at last, and a footman emerged.

Gabriel took her hand and led her up the wide steps. "Greetings," he said.

The servant gaped at him in surprise. The man wore a

heavy wig and full livery, despite their isolated location, but he seemed a little dim-witted. "Um, the m-master's not at home," he stammered.

"He will be to me," Gabriel said calmly. He ignored the footman, who blinked at them in confusion, and led Psyche through the open door.

Inside, an elderly butler hurried up, waving his hands. "Here, ye canna come in like this, the master won't allow it. Out w'ye afore I loose the dogs."

Psyche paused in alarm. "We don't want to intrude," she said to Gabriel.

He didn't seem to be listening. "There are no dogs, McDuffie, he can't abide their fawning ways. Don't you remember how he drowned the stray puppy I brought home, the year I was eight?"

Psyche stared at her companion, her eyes wide. The tall, skinny butler looked as if he might faint.

"It's yourself, sir! Come back to the manse . . . I wouldna have credited it."

Psyche's curiosity was not just astir, it positively boiled, and she wanted desperately to pull Gabriel aside and demand to know where they were and what was going on. "Gabriel . . ." she whispered.

Gabriel was focused on the servant who was wringing his hands.

"But his lordship—he promised he would have ye horse-whipped if ye showed your face again after what ye said to him the last time—I dinna think—"

"Leave his lordship to me, McDuffie," Gabriel said, his voice strangely calm in the face of the servant's agitation. "I suppose he's in the study? I will speak to him. Oh, and tell the housekeeper to prepare two guest chambers and add two settings to the table for dinner. We will be staying the night."

Ignoring the man's stuttered protests, Gabriel strode down the hall, and Psyche roused herself to catch up with him. He glanced down at her. "I would spare you this interview if I could, but unless you want to wait in the drafty hall, I have no place else to put you. He will not have fires built in any room but the one he uses every day. And it's hardly fitting for you to huddle in front of the kitchen hearth." Gabriel smiled at her, but his lips were taut, and the expression seemed more like a grimace.

"Gabriel, where are we? I don't think—" Too late, they had evidently arrived at the study. Psyche bit back her protests.

Gabriel rapped sharply on the heavy oak door and then flung it open. The room was dark; a fire flickered on the hearth at the far end of the room, but no lamps had been lit even though the afternoon was overcast. Heavy draperies covered much of the windows, and the air smelled stale, as if the room were in need of a good turning-out.

Gabriel stepped inside. Psyche followed, feeling as if she were walking into a spider's lair. It did not reassure her that Gabriel nodded to her to remain near the door. She folded her arms and struggled with an impulse to hide herself behind a large sideboard. Gabriel walked on into the center of the room, then looked toward the hearth.

"Why in hell's name are you disturbing me at this hour? It's not dinnertime yet," a hoarse voice roared.

"We will be brief," Gabriel said. "I thought you would wish to know that you have guests for the night."

Silence, then from the shadows of the room, a figure stirred. The man had been sitting in a large wing chair pulled up to the fire, and Psyche could not see his face until he rose and turned toward them. She held her breath for an instant, then shook herself mentally. Why did she feel like a child whose book of tales had opened to reveal an ogre?

The man who took two heavy steps forward and stopped to glare at Gabriel was indeed impressive in stature. He was as tall as Gabriel and as broad shouldered, though his frame was massive, thicker through the waist. He had sandy hair and fair, freckled skin, and his features were not as pleasing. Of course, given the grimace of surprise and displeasure that twisted his face, it was somewhat difficult to judge.

"What the bloody hell are *you* doing here?" His tone, as well as his words, was deliberately insulting. Psyche gasped, but her indignation faded into shock when Gabriel answered.

"Hello, Father. I was sure your welcome home would be warm."

Gabriel's inflection was even, his expression politely cynical. How much effort each cost him she could only guess from the tension she sensed in his body. He stood very still, as if prepared to face a foe more dangerous than any they had so far encountered.

"Why should I welcome you? After the words you tossed at me when you left, what else do you expect?" The large man folded his arms, his initial surprise overladen now by anger and what Psyche suspected was a habitual scowl.

"I believe I said, 'What kind of father are you?' " Gabriel pointed out, his tone still almost casual. "Under the circumstances, it seemed a reasonable query."

"Damn impertinence," the older man retorted, his tone close to a growl. "After what you did—"

"Yes, but that is water under the bridge, is it not? An old argument, for another time. Just now, for reasons of our own, I am here with a lady, and we must stay the night. We will be gone again in the morning, and your peace will once more be unbroken." Gabriel turned away before the other man could answer.

His father? Gabriel had not even introduced her, Psyche realized, still bewildered by these continuing revelations. Why had Gabriel never said that his father was so wealthy? How had they come to such bad terms? The murder, the *rumored* murder of a well-bred lady—did it all return to that?

Without further discussion, Gabriel offered her his hand and she was relieved to slip out of the room. Gabriel closed the door behind them, and they found themselves alone in the hall.

"Gabriel—"

"Later," he said quietly. "I know you have questions."

Questions? She was overflowing with them. But he still held her hand and he guided her through the empty hallway—had the servants fled, totally nonplussed by the arrival of guests that she had to suspect was a rare occurrence? Psyche began to feel that the house was indeed haunted as in some fairy tale, a manse inhabited by ghostly denizens and at its dark heart, a pugnacious demon who snarled at any intruder.

She found that Gabriel was leading her down a side hall and out another door. Had he changed his mind, were they leaving already? But the relief of getting out of that unwelcoming house was palpable. Psyche drew a deep breath.

Gabriel did not speak. He led the way past a garden that was almost painfully neat. Not a weed dared to protrude through the formal beds, yet the whole effect was strangely sterile. Like the house, it was nominally well tended, but it had no heart. Gabriel paused long enough to pluck one early rose from a climbing vine, then walked on.

Psyche tried to conceive of a small boy growing up in such a bleak house, and she could have wept for the young Gabriel. What was his mother like? Surely she could not be so harsh and unfeeling as the man Psyche had just glimpsed.

"Gabriel?" She tried again to pierce the wall he seemed to have drawn up around himself. His brow was knit, and he frowned, almost unconsciously.

"In a moment," he said. "I wish to see—I'm seeking my mother."

Psyche pushed back the queries that threatened to spill over and followed him in silence, past the formal garden, past a kitchen garden filled with orderly rows of vegetables, where even the bean vines seemed to grow in straight lines. Why would Gabriel look for his mother here? Did she usually hide out in the gardens, was this her only refuge? With such a husband, it was easy enough to imagine.

But they continued walking, past an orchard where no single twig littered the grass beneath the trees, past tall groves. At last they came to another smaller stone wall, and inside the boundary she saw a family graveyard and in the center a small chapel of gray stone. Did his mother take refuge in prayer? The door of the chapel was closed. She expected him to walk that way, but he turned aside and led the way down the pebbled path, then paused a moment to look around him.

Psyche began to understand. Most of the headstones were weathered with age; some leaned at crooked angles. The Sinclairs seemed to be an old family. How had the current patriarch come to such a solitary existence?

Gabriel moved forward. She followed a pace behind him when he walked to a grave obviously more recent than the others. The small stone read simply, "Mary Gillingham," with the dates of the woman's birth and death. *Why Gillingham*, Psyche wondered, then a wave of empathy pushed aside inquisitive thoughts as irrelevant. His mother had died three years ago while Gabriel was still abroad. Psyche had also lost parents—she knew the aching grief. She felt a lump in her throat and she wanted to touch him, to offer him comfort. But Gabriel stood very still, his whole body stiff, and his thoughts seemed far away.

"The gatekeeper told me," he muttered as if to himself, "my father never bothered to try to send me word."

"Oh, Gabriel!" Psyche blinked hard against tears.

"A graceless stone, with no inscription at all," he went on. "Damn him, he couldn't give her even that. I shall have it replaced with a proper headstone."

Psyche put a hand on his arm. Gabriel's body was so rigid he might have also been carved from stone. Inside him, there must be enormous turmoil, pain and grief.

"She used to plead with him to have done, when he beat me," Gabriel said, his voice husky. "When he sent me to bed with no supper, she would slip up with bread and butter wrapped in her handkerchief. She tried to look out for me, but my father was too strong for her, too unfeeling."

"Your mother must have loved you very much," Psyche said, her voice low.

She felt him shudder, as with too much grief too long contained. "Perhaps," he said, his voice dull. "But she did not come to argue when he sent me away. I had thought she might have confronted him more openly just once, when it was so vital, but . . ."

"Perhaps she was too afraid," Psyche ventured, though her every instinct recoiled from the idea of a mother who would not defend her child, who would not at least try. In truth, she could not imagine any woman, certainly not the timid, gentle soul that Mary seemed to have been, prevailing against the brutal man Psyche had glimpsed in the study. What a life the poor woman must have had! And as for Gabriel—

"How did you stand it?" she asked, wondering how he had grown up to be charming and sympathetic, with such a brute for his only model.

As always, he seemed to know the direction of her thoughts. "In my earliest childhood, he was not quite . . . as he is today. He was always gruff, unaffectionate, but he was not so quick with his fists or with his curses. But—he thought that my mother had betrayed him."

"Oh, dear," Psyche breathed, not sure what to say.

"If she did, she had good enough reason." Gabriel's tone was grim. "But after that, he became obsessed with the thought that I was not his natural son. I look little like him, whereas my older brother has his nose and his sandy hair. I think I simply resemble my mother's family, but—the idea seemed a canker inside him. He became increasingly resentful, abusive to my mother and to me."

"He did not consider divorce?" Psyche dared to ask, trying to understand the embittered man she had glimpsed in the dark study.

"No, he has a morbid dread of scandal, so that later—" Gabriel paused and drew a deep breath. "My mother sent me away as much as she could. I spent long visits with my maternal grandfather. He was a gentle, scholarly man—much like your father, perhaps. Grandfather may have been my salvation. He gave me cause to believe in myself, despite my own father's rejection, cause to feel that I was not the total failure my father seemed to think."

She nodded. Gabriel bent, laying the rose he had plucked from the garden in front of his mother's headstone. Then he straightened and took a deep breath.

"I hope she did not believe the gossip. I never had the chance to explain—"

Psyche drew a breath and held it; would he confess at last the scandal that had sent him away from his home?

Twenty

"*H*er name was Sylvia Fowley, but all who knew her intimately called her Sylvie," Gabriel said, his voice very quiet. He continued to stare down at the mound of earth, not meeting Psyche's gaze. "She was a woman of two and thirty when I met her, petite and dainty as a butterfly, with soft brown hair and big brown eyes. I was visiting a friend from school—I took any excuse not to return home during the school holidays, as my grandfather had died by then. She was my friend's aunt by marriage. She seemed to enjoy my company at once, did not dismiss me as too young, danced with me at the Christmas ball, smiled into my eyes and touched my cheek. . . . I was captivated. No woman had ever treated me so. She whispered to me after the dance, invited me to her room after everyone was asleep. She and her husband had separate chambers, of course."

Psyche nodded and held her tongue, afraid to break the flow of confidences. She thought of a young and innocent Gabriel, a schoolboy entranced by an older woman, and her heart ached for the disillusion that must be coming.

"I was totally infatuated. I tiptoed down the hall at midnight, my heart in my throat, my body aching with new yearnings, and she was waiting. During our time together, she taught me about lovemaking, and fashion, and other worldly pursuits, and I was an eager pupil. I thought I would love her forever, but I did not expect her to remember me past that holiday. But she did. She wrote to me at school, she traveled to be near me, and she made sure to have me invited back for more visits. Our trysts continued, even though her husband was becoming suspicious. After some months, she told me he had threatened her, and she suggested that we run away together. She was prepared to seek a divorce."

Psyche raised her brows. How could a mature woman expect a schoolboy to defy convention, as well as all his family? They would have been outcasts in society.

"But what I had first taken for charming wiles became shrewd manipulation. Through her sulky tears and fits of temper, she had begun to order my every thought, my speech, my clothing, my habits. She wanted to choose my friends, and she wanted me to leave university. . . ."

Gabriel took a deep breath, then went on. "I loved my years at university, it was a way to get away from home, for one thing, after my grandfather's death, but I truly enjoyed the books and the tutors and the quiet atmosphere of learning. I had friends there; my tutors approved of my work. So as the weeks flew by, I felt increasingly overwhelmed by Sylvie's love, which appeared to have no boundaries. She was like a sweet-smelling flower that grows on a seemingly limpid vine, until the vine twines around you, constricting your very breath."

He put one hand to his face, then lowered it. "I gathered my courage and told her that I thought it best, for both of us, that we not invite the scandal of a divorce and the censure of society—which would have fallen more heavily upon her. Perhaps I was wrong, perhaps I should have been true to her, but—"

"Gabriel, how old were you?" Psyche interrupted at last, unable to bear the regret and self-condemnation she heard in his words.

"I was seventeen when we first—when we met," he answered. "Just past eighteen when I suggested that we part.

That interview was horrendous. She wept and screamed at me; she said I had ruined her, taken her honor. She flung a gold pin at me—one of many little fashionable gifts she had chosen for me, but this, she said, was special. This trinket was engraved with our entwined initials. She had engraved her own as *S. S.*, as if we were already married. While she broke china and tossed cushions about the room, she ranted hysterically. I had never seen this side of her. Finally, she told me to leave, and I did." Gabriel swallowed hard.

"I did not know—had not enough experience in the world to comprehend—that she was much more unstable than I had suspected. That night, she drank a whole bottle of laudanum, and she died the next day."

"Oh, my dear." Psyche put her hand again on his arm. She felt the shuddering breath that he drew, the way his whole body trembled at the memories.

"I learned before I left that she had had other young lovers—a collection, if you will. But it was I who broke her."

Psyche shook her head emphatically. "It was not your fault. You were only a boy."

"I must bear the blame," Gabriel argued, his tone dogged. "I kept that gold pin, until Barrett's hired killers stole it from my bags. It was a reminder to me that I should never give anyone or anything too much control. That other women might want me for my charm, my looks, but they would never be allowed to touch my soul, nor would they want to. I was marked for life, my reputation ruined forever, and I should never be allowed to ruin yet another woman's life, as my youthful adoration had destroyed Sylvie's, as my very existence had troubled my mother's, destroying any trust her husband had had in her."

Psyche stood mute, shaken by the depth of his guilt and pain.

"And my father—when he heard they were saying that Sylvie's death was because of me, that I had as much as murdered a delicate, overly nervous lady of good breeding—he told me to get out, that I was not fit, had never been fit, to bear the name of Sinclair. So I left."

"You cannot blame yourself!" Psyche insisted. "Sylvia was a grown woman with much more experience than you. She sought the affair, and she sought to control you. You did not even have a father to ask for advice as to how to proceed, only one who turned on you and railed at you without listening to your account of what had ensued."

Gabriel's eyes were shadowed still with the pain he had lived with too long. Psyche longed to kiss his brow and soothe his hurts. She held one hand lightly to his stubbled cheek. "You must forgive yourself, my love. Whatever blame you may wrongly assign to yourself, the lady is at peace now."

He looked down at her, his expression hard to read. "You do not hate me, now that you know my history?"

She stood on tiptoe to kiss his lips. Gabriel pulled her to him, pursuing the embrace with the fervor of a near-drowned man who has found a safe rock on which to stand. When at last the kiss ended, leaving her a little breathless, he whispered into her hair. "I could not bear to tell the story. I have told no one since the day I left this house, and soon after, departed England. My father had convinced me that Sylvie's family might demand my arrest, though I think now that would not have happened. They only wanted to cover up the sad circumstance of her death."

He had been in exile for no reason, Psyche thought, stunned at the revelation. His father's brutal anger and his own guilt had driven Gabriel away from every friend, every chance of aid. For years, he had fought his battles unaided, carried on his solitary struggle merely to survive.

But he *had* survived, he had prevailed, and the years of contention had burnished him like gilded steel. "You are stronger and wiser because of your pain, because of your journeys," she told him. "But, Gabriel, I think it is time now to stop running."

He held her close to him, and she leaned her cheek against his chest. Perhaps he did not wish her to see the expression on his face; he was too accustomed to fighting all his battles alone. That feeling she understood. But would he ever lower his guard and truly let her in? Still, he had taken a big step today, sharing the story of his boyhood scandal.

They stood in close embrace for long minutes, till Gabriel reluctantly raised his head and loosened his grip. "It will be dinnertime soon," he told her. "They keep early hours here, and you will wish to wash up a little."

Psyche looked down at the grass-stained linen costume, which revealed several rents and tears after their earlier flight through the woods. She could do with a lot more than soap and water, but without baggage, had no hope of more. She would not complain, Gabriel had enough to deal with in this house of brutal memories. Accepting the hand he held out to her, they turned back toward the big house. They had almost reached the side door from which they had emerged when a small, stout woman of middle years suddenly hurried out of the door.

"Master Gabriel!" she exclaimed, beaming. "It is you!"

Gabriel released Psyche's hand and took two long strides to swoop up the round little woman, lifting her into a bear hug.

Psyche smiled. She did not know who this woman was, but she was the first person who seemed happy at Gabriel's return, and so Psyche knew that she would like her, whatever her position or name.

The mystery was resolved in a moment. When Gabriel set the plump woman with the graying fair hair back on her feet, he turned to Psyche. "This is Mrs. Parslip, who was my nurse, and later became under-housekeeper. Mrs. P., this is Miss Hill, my . . . fiancée."

"How do, miss. My felicitations to you both. But I'm housekeeper now," Mrs. Parslip corrected him.

"I can't believe you stayed," Gabriel said. "With my father such a difficult master to please."

"Oh, he discharges me about once a week," the woman said, shrugging. "But I take no notice of his ranting. My family is all dead, you see, and I've nowhere else I really want to go. Besides, I'm the only one who knows how to make plum pudding just the way he likes it. So I stay."

"He's lucky to have you, I'm sure." Psyche held out her hand.

The housekeeper made a dignified curtsy, then touched Psyche's fingers, her own smile wide. "Such a lovely girl, my dear, even if I say it, who shouldn't."

Gabriel grinned. Psyche was so pleased to see him reunited with someone who cared for him that she could have hugged the little woman, too.

"Thank you. You must tell me all about Gabriel as a boy," she suggested.

Gabriel made a face. "Not the story about the chimney sweep," he urged. "And not the one in which I overturn a whole bowlful of jelly on the kitchen floor."

"But that's the best one." Mrs. P. chuckled. Her wide hazel eyes swept over his face, and she patted his arm. "I see you've had your share of difficult times."

"Is it so obvious?" Gabriel asked, raising his brows. But the subtle withdrawal did not deter the servant who had known him since childhood.

"Ah, it's written on your face, my dear. Your eyes never used to be so guarded. But I can see that beneath the handsome face still beats a kind heart. A fine man you've grown into, Master Gabriel. I always knew you would. I just wish your mother could have lived to see you return."

Gabriel's smile faded. "Yes." Abruptly, he changed the subject. "Perhaps you can help us, Mrs. P. We had to leave London suddenly, just as we were in the midst of a costume ball."

"So that's the reason you look like some deceitful Romany," Mrs. Parslip said, her tone composed. "Still up to mischief, are you, Master Gabriel?"

"Um, not exactly. But we could certainly use a change of clothes. If there are any of my old clothes left, I would make do with them, and for Miss Hill, perhaps a gown of my mother's?"

The housekeeper looked Psyche up and down. "Hmm,

yes. I had the garb safely put away with herbs to ward off the moths. It would have to be let out a bit there, and taken in a bit here, but I think I can manage. I'll see what I can find, and a pair of razors for you, too. Such a grubby lad he looks, and he never was one for untidiness," she confided to Psyche. "You come along to your chambers now. If you're late to dinner, you know your father will shout."

She sounded exactly as if she were speaking to a schoolboy, as if Gabriel were still in short pants and just out of the nursery, going down for his first grown-up dinner. Psyche smiled. She was thrilled at the thought of a suitable gown and the opportunity to dress properly for the evening meal. It would be bad enough having to sit at the table with that brute of a man who had—probably—sired Gabriel. They seemed opposites in every respect. Were the man's suspicions correct? Affairs among the Ton were common enough, and she knew nothing of Gabriel's mother. Or was the elder Sinclair a victim of his own dour imaginings?

They followed the housekeeper obediently up the main stairs and into a quiet wing of unoccupied rooms. Two bedchambers had been opened, hastily by the look of it, and a maid was still fluffing pillows in the room Psyche entered. She hesitated in the doorway, and, without meaning to eavesdrop, heard the housekeeper speak quietly to Gabriel.

"She tried to change his mind, you know, Master Gabriel. She begged him to let you stay."

"My mother? But she never appeared. When he told me to leave the house, I waited for her to come, but she never left her room."

In Psyche's chamber, the maid turned and blushed in confusion. "I—it's all ready, miss, and there's warm water in the jug and towels on the chest. Can I help you with anything?"

"No, thank you," Psyche said. The maid curtsied and departed, and Psyche shut the door, though she longed to hear the rest of the conversation in the next room.

Gabriel saw Psyche disappear into the bedroom, but he

hardly noticed. He was stunned by Mrs. Parslip's revelation. All this time, he had thought—

The housekeeper continued to speak, and she watched him anxiously.

"He shouted her down. They had a terrible quarrel—I never heard her scream at him so, not before or after. But he won out, of course. He was always stronger. Before you ever got in that day, he took her by the shoulders and marched up to her bedroom. He bellowed at her to compose herself; she was pale with weeping, poor lady. And then in the hall, he told her maid to give her a double dose of laudanum. Your mother didn't realize what she was drinking." The housekeeper's voice was sad.

"She was drugged?" Gabriel knew that his voice was hoarse; he could barely speak.

"Your poor mother didn't wake for two days. I feared she would die, herself. And by then, of course, you were gone. But she never lost faith in you, Master Gabriel. I promise you that. She spoke of you—to me—often."

"Thank you, Mrs. P.," Gabriel said, his voice husky. "And thank you for staying, so that she had one friend by her."

The housekeeper sighed. "I'll go now and see about the clothing. But you should know that your mother cared, Master Gabriel. You deserve that much." She curtsied and left the room. The door was still ajar, and he heard the sound of footsteps retreating.

Gabriel stood very still. He couldn't seem to make his limbs move, and the room was a blur around him. He heard a quiet knock on his door, and then a familiar voice said, "Gabriel, the poor little maid is so flustered, she forgot to leave any soap. Is there any here that I can— Gabriel, what's wrong?"

This time, it didn't even occur to him to hide the fact that his eyes had flooded with tears. He turned to Psyche blindly and muttered, "My mother—my mother did try. She did care, after all."

He felt himself sway. It was only this silly weakness in

his legs; he would be himself again soon. But Psyche showed no ridicule for his frailty.

"Oh, my love, of course she did," she said gently. She pushed a small chair closer and he sank into it. Then she stood by him and held him against her, his face pressed to her body, and Gabriel wept.

For a long time they stood thus, with Gabriel sobbing quietly, his face against her stomach. She stroked his dark hair gently and offered no intrusive words. Let the poison out, she thought, release the sadness and the pain—perhaps even the anger—at his mother's apparent rejection. Let it go. Otherwise, Gabriel might someday end up like the shadow of a man who lurked in the study, consumed by his own acrimony.

At last he fell silent and, after another long minute, drew a shuddering breath. "She was the only one who cared, you see, after my grandfather's death, except for Mrs. P., of course. To think that Mother too was so disgusted with me that she would not even say good-bye—it was a very great hurt."

"I understand," Psyche said, her voice quiet.

He straightened. His face was still red, and his eyes swollen. "I have kept you too long. You will want to wash up, and I must do the same." He sounded suddenly formal.

Oh, Gabriel, she thought. *Don't shut me out again.*

But then he smiled at her and said more softly, "Thank you, Psyche, love, my dear Miss Hill."

And she felt warmed inside. She touched his arm lightly and smiled, then returned to her own chamber. She had forgotten the missing soap. But the little maid was back, still blushing and anxious, with some rose-scented soap for her.

"I'm sorry, miss, I'm that flustered—"

"It's fine," Psyche assured her. "Thank you." When the servant departed after one more nervous curtsy, Psyche poured the now tepid water into the bowl and pulled off her grass-stained linen costume. It was a relief to wash off some of the grit of the journey and to make herself feel more presentable. She took down her hair and shook it out. Finding an ivory-backed comb and brush on the table, she brushed her hair and tugged at the tangles, removing a stray bit of twig that had clung to the tresses.

She was feeling much better already when a soft knock at the door made her snatch up a towel and drape it around her before she pulled open the door.

It was only the plump little housekeeper, her hands full of garments and—thanks be—hairpins! "I have brought my sewing basket, miss, and we'll just take a look at this gown and shift."

Psyche donned the clean shift, stockings, and then the gown. It was a very sober dark blue silk gown, the neckline filled in with a lace fichu, such as older ladies sometimes wore.

"Ah, you have no need of that." Mrs. P. removed the bit of lace. The housekeeper touched the soft fabric, muttering to herself and taking measurements with a piece of tape. Then Psyche removed the gown, and Mrs. P. took her needle and thread and took in the waist, which was too wide, and made a few more quick alterations. The little servant's fingers flew as her needle darted in and out; she was amazingly swift. Such was her speed that Psyche was soon back in the gown, with her hair twisted into a neat chignon. She gazed at her reflection in the looking glass above the vanity. The gown was not unbecoming, dark against her pale skin. She heard a loud gong on the lower level.

"Ah, dinner," Mrs. P. said, sighing with relief that all was ready. "And you look lovely, miss, if I do say so."

Psyche smoothed one straying strand of hair and then smiled at the housekeeper. "Thank you, Mrs. Parslip. You have been an enormous help."

The servant returned her smile. Moved by impulse, Psyche bent to kiss the woman's cheek. "And thank you for your loyalty to Gabriel," she whispered. "It is balm to his troubled soul, you know."

The housekeeper's eyes glistened, and she blinked hard. "I stayed because of that, because he might someday come back," she confessed, very low. "Poor boy. I'm glad he has a good lady, a strong lady this time, to love him. I will be happy to see him settled with a family of his own."

It was Psyche's turn to blink. If only she could be sure. . . . But the housekeeper's tone was approving. Psyche smiled again and cast aside her doubts.

"Now, mustn't be late to dinner," the servant warned.

Psyche turned obediently toward the door. She still wore her gold-colored sandals, but otherwise, she felt much more prepared to venture into mixed company.

Gabriel waited for her in the hallway. He wore a dark evening coat, white waistcoat, and tan pantaloons, and sported a neatly tied white neckcloth. He was clean shaven and looked much more his usual immaculate self. If there was a suspicious puffiness about his eyes, one would have had to look very closely to detect it. And there was something else, something almost intangible, yet evident in his eyes and bearing. His effortless charm had returned, but it seemed milder and lacked some of his usual cynical edge. Dare she believe that the new softer light in his lapis eyes might signal the beginning of healing?

"Very nice," she murmured.

He grimaced. "If I lift my arms too much, I think my coat will rip," he warned her. "It seems I have widened a bit since my university days."

She laughed. He had more muscle, no doubt, but having seen him naked, she would attest to the fact that his torso boasted not an ounce of extra fat.

"You look a vision," he told her. "The blue becomes you."

She smiled and took his arm. He almost made her forget the ordeal that was ahead of them. Together, they headed toward the big staircase. Downstairs lay the dining room and his tartar of a father.

As they descended, Psyche could almost feel the temperature falling. Gabriel's body grew more tense with each step. Beneath her hand, his arm might have been carved from the same granite that composed the big mansion. As they slowly made their way down, she glanced at the por-

traits that hung along the stairwell, old pictures of genera-
tions of Sinclairs. One small copper nameplate caught her
eye, and she gasped.

"The marquis of Gillingham? He is a relative?"

"Great-great-grandfather, that one," Gabriel observed,
his tone wry. "Was rumored to have locked his wife into her
room so many times the poor lady went mad."

"Good heavens. But does that mean your father—"

"Is a marquis. Yes, I'm afraid so," Gabriel said. "But I
have an older brother, you know, who is very much like my
sire and also disapproves of me, so the title is of little matter to me."

He had mentioned a brother earlier, she remembered. "Is
your brother . . . ?"

"Oh, he's the image of my father."

"Poor man," she said before she thought.

Gabriel laughed and wrapped his arm around her in a
quick embrace.

"Why is he not here?"

"He is like my father in temperament as well as appearance. They fight like mad dogs when they are together.
There is a smaller estate in the next county; my brother
spends his time there."

He had a brother, and a father who was a marquis. And
she had made him a fictitious marquis. The audacity of such
a trick of fate took her breath away. But there was not time
to comment on the incredible irony of it because now they
had reached the ground floor. They walked into the main
hall just as Gabriel's father emerged from his study. The big
man glared at them.

"Come along then, if you're determined to stay. Won't
have my dinner getting cold."

Gabriel simply nodded. Psyche thought the older man
looked disappointed. Did he still expect his younger son to
quail, as the boy might have done? She felt intense indignation at the many cruelties that Gabriel had had to endure.

They all walked in silence into the dining room. She felt
the reaction in Gabriel, the way his muscles clenched be-

neath her hand, but knew it was too subtle for his father to detect. How many bad memories did this house hold for its younger son?

This room was dark and gloomy, with thick draperies pulled across the tall windows, and the chandelier only half lit. Did this surly old man enjoy the darkness? It certainly suited his personality.

The table was of black wood, with thick Jacobean legs and heavy carving. The sideboard was massive and groaned with food. All this for one man? The kitchen staff had had little time to add dishes in deference to the unexpected guests.

But perhaps they had made an effort. The elder Sinclair frowned at the bounty. "Wasting my blunt on a scoundrel?" he demanded. "Can't think what they are about. I should fire the lot of them."

Psyche bit her lip, pushing back her angry reply only with great effort,

But Gabriel was no longer a small boy cowed with fear of his intimidating father. "Perhaps they have some sense of what guests are due," he said, his tone cool. "Scoundrels or not."

The footmen served the first course. Psyche was aware of how empty she was; she had tasted no food since the day before, and much had happened since they had left London. Even with her hollow belly, however, she found it hard to swallow. The tension at the table was thick. The food itself was only mediocre. Her own cook would have chopped off her own fingers before serving such thin sauces and over-done roast beef. The jellies were watery, and the horseradish sauce had lumps. Only the puddings were superb, perhaps Mrs. P.'s contribution. But the head cook seemed to lack her skill. In this house, with this master, with no mistress to guide the staff, Mrs. Parslip must fight a losing battle. Psyche was not surprised to find the service and the meal below par.

But she needed to eat; who knew what tomorrow would bring? She put another bite of beef into her mouth and chewed deliberately. She felt for Gabriel, who also ate very slowly. How much harder was it for him to endure this icy silence, the heavy animosity that glowered from every glance that the older man threw his way?

They made it through three interminable courses without speaking, and Psyche could feel the tightness in her shoulders growing. When the last course had been served, and they dabbled with a fruit tart that needed more cinnamon and less sugar, she wondered what on earth she was supposed to do when the dessert was consumed.

Normally, the ladies at the table would withdraw to the drawing room and leave the men to their brandy and cigars for a while longer. But Gabriel had said the drawing room had no fire, and it might even be draped in dust cloths. She supposed she could simply retire straight to her guest chamber. It would be more comfortable than remaining here, though she hated to leave Gabriel alone with this bully of a man.

The elder Sinclair put down his fork; she heard it clink on the china plate. "So. I have fed you. I think I have done what's expected of me."

"Expected of you?" Gabriel noted, raising one elegant brow. "Since when did you ever do what was expected of you? And how is my brother, by the way?"

"He is as usual."

"I'm sorry to hear it." Gabriel took a sip of his wine. "You may send him my felicitations, when next you speak, some year or other."

"Ha! At least he has not tarnished the name of Sinclair," his father barked.

"As I have? Yes, you did mention that a few hundred times before you threw me out."

"I had cause!"

The servants had left the dining room after passing the last course. Now a footman reappeared in the doorway, his expression nervous. "My lord, do you require more—"

"Away w'you!" the marquis roared. The servant slipped out again and shut the door hastily behind him, just in time to avoid the wine goblet that the old man hurled. It struck the wood, shattering with the impact, the shards falling to the floor with a sound of tinkling glass.

Psyche gasped, then held herself very still. She did not want to attract this despot's attention.

"You have no idea whether there was cause or not." Gabriel's voice rose, just a little. "You had no idea what I did; you listened to rumor and innuendo, and you were not willing to hear my accounting of the affair—of the events that had transpired."

The other man made a harsh, mocking sound deep in his throat. He reached for another glass—were his servants familiar with his rages?—and gulped down the wine.

"Although, I must admit, you never did listen to me, so I really should not have expected anything else." Gabriel selected a piece of fruit from the fruit bowl. Psyche admired his apparent calm.

"A pack of whining excuses you would have given me, worse than your mother, you were," his father snapped back. "Waste of my time. Never were any good, from the time you were whelped."

"The first time you told me that, and the next half dozen, I wept," Gabriel observed. He put down the pear untouched. "But I am no longer a child. I regret to inform you that I really have no interest in your opinions."

The older man's face darkened. "Mock me, will you? Poor manners and bad blood, no doubt about it."

"If you disparage your own bloodline, it is your judgment, and I must accept it." Gabriel's voice was steady.

Psyche felt genuine bewilderment. How could the older man feel such enmity for his own offspring? Even if he doubted Gabriel's paternity, how could anyone hate a small boy who only wanted to be loved and accepted? What kind of small-spirited person would take out his doubts upon a child?

Gabriel added, "As for my manners, my mother taught me those, and her father. A good thing; I would have fared very ill in the world if I had had only your impressive example to guide me."

"Aye, I can see how far you've come," his father snapped. "Come creeping back to your boyhood home dressed in such ridiculous fashion. Become a gypsy, have you? Reading palms and stealing from the back garden?"

"I hate to disappoint you," Gabriel said. "I will inform you when I hold that impressive position. In fact, I have not yet made my mark on the world. I suppose the acorn never falls far from the tree."

The other man snorted. "Don't blame your misbegotten weaknesses on me," he said. "Doubt I had anything to do with your pretty face."

Psyche wanted to shout at the man. She held in her instinctive protest with great difficulty, anger bubbling inside her like an overboiling pot.

Gabriel seemed to grow even colder. "A fortunate thing for us both."

"Humph. So what do you want, then?" The other man folded his arms; he seemed disappointed that he had not been able to provoke his son. "If it's money—"

"Never," Gabriel said, his tone flat. "My purse is not empty. However, I do need your gracious hospitality for one night. The lady and I will stay overnight and be on our way again in the morning."

For the first time, the older man turned to glare at Psyche. She stiffened. The leering expression on his face warned her what to expect from his cesspool of a mind.

"Lady? About as much a lady as your own mother, doubt me. How dare you bring your doxy into my house—I won't have it—" But this insult he was not allowed to finish.

Gabriel pushed himself back from the table and took three rapid strides, his long legs covering the distance between them before his father could complete his statement. He took the older man by the throat, pulled him erect, and held him as lightly, as dangerously, as if he were a striking asp.

"You have just insulted the two women, the two honorable women, who are the most dear to me," he said, his voice deathly quiet. "If you wish to live to take your next breath, you will swallow those words, and I will not hear their like again."

The other man struggled, but Gabriel's grip seemed like iron. Psyche watched and held her breath as the older man fought for his. His square ugly face turned bluish, and his eyes seemed to pop from his head.

Psyche began to shake. Surely Gabriel would not murder his own father. She made a noise deep in her throat.

"Gabriel, you can't!"

Twenty-one

*F*or a long moment, she thought he had not heard.
The older man struggled, trying to push Gabriel back,
but fifteen years had wrought more changes than simply
gray hairs and lines; the father's strength was no longer
equal to that of the son's.

"No, I will not become the same ilk as he," Gabriel
agreed, his voice husky with emotion. His gasp loosened,
and the man in his grasp drew a long shuddering breath.

Gabriel looked down at his sire. "You cannot beat me any
longer, Father," he said. "Now, mind what I said about the
lady. She is a lady, you may trust me on that. You have no
need to know her name. Because of a complicated plot
against us, she is in need of shelter and protection for the
night. That you will provide, and what poor excuse for ci-
vility you can manage, which I know will not be much."

He released the other man, who staggered back into his
chair, still gasping for air. It was a moment before he could
speak. Psyche heard the fire pop and, somewhere, a floorboard creaked. She wondered if the servants were listening
outside the door.

"I'll have you horsewhipped," Gabriel's father croaked.
"I'll have you hung!"

"I will hang only if I actually murder you," Gabriel said, his voice almost cheerful, as if the assault had released some of the simmering resentment he had harbored for years. "And I would not stoop so low. Nor will you horsewhip me because you no longer have the muscle, nor do any of the browbeaten, mistreated servants whose spirit is so poor that they are willing to stay with you. You will do as I say, and keep your mouth shut."

The marquis made a noise almost like a growl, but Gabriel ignored him. He turned to Psyche and bowed.

"My lady, may I escort you to your chamber?"

She was very glad to take his arm. When they reached the guest chamber, Gabriel said, "Lock your door. I do not think you are in any danger, but just—just to be safe."

Psyche's eyes had widened; she nodded. "I will." When she shut the door, she turned the key as he had instructed, but the room seemed very barren, very cold despite the small fire that flickered on the hearth. How had their parsimonious host agreed to the fire? Perhaps the extra luxury was due to Mrs. Parslip; the housekeeper seemed to have her own mind about how to treat Gabriel and his guest, Psyche thought, smiling a little.

But the faint lift of her spirits soon faded. It would be a long night, she thought, pulling back the bedcovers. Tomorrow, she would be more than happy to leave this place. She removed her gown and put on the old-fashioned white nightdress the housekeeper had left for her, then took down her hair, shaking it to release the last of the borrowed pins. Taking the comb from the bureau, she threaded it through her hair slowly. When the golden tresses were as smooth and soft as she could make them, she washed her face in the tepid water from the pitcher. Then she could put it off no longer. She had to climb into the high bed and pull the covers up to her chin.

She was lonely. Was that what Gabriel's lovemaking had done to her? Not only did her body yearn for newfound sensations, for his further instruction, not only did she ache to lay her cheek against his firm chest, but the bed was so empty without his presence that she could almost have wept.

There was nothing to be done about it. She knew that Gabriel would not come to her in his father's house. It would seem to confirm his father's distrust of his character, to reinforce the slanderous gossip that the marquis, the real marquis, had chosen to believe too easily and too quickly. What a sad thing to grow up with that bitter man for a father.

She remembered her own father, her mother, the laughter and the camaraderie that had filled their household. She and Circe had delighted in it and had thought it only normal. But compared to this bleak and unhappy house, Psyche saw for the first time just how richly she had been blessed. What's more, she had grown to girlhood witnessing the mutual respect and appreciation that her mother and father had held for each other. She had that example to draw from, had seen what a marriage could be between a man and a woman.

Her father had loved her, believed in her, as had her mother. They had never distrusted her; they had always taken her actions and her statements on faith. She had never had the burning need to prove herself that seemed to have helped form Gabriel's mind and heart.

No wonder the neglected house and overgrown property had been such a blow to him. Gabriel had planned to emerge from its acreage like a phoenix from the ashes of its sacrificial fire. He had to prove to his father, and to himself, that he was a man who counted, a man who could be proud of who he was. And until Gabriel learned that, until he believed it in his heart of hearts, he would never be content, she thought. No woman's love would hold him, not until he could trust himself.

Sighing, she shut her eyes, trying to will herself to sleep and thus pass the long hours till dawn. She hoped they would make an early start. The fire burned low, and the air became cooler. She snuggled deeper beneath the blankets and still could not capture the slumber that eluded her.

So when a faint cry sounded from down the hallway, Psyche heard it at once. She listened, wondering if her ears were playing tricks, then it came again. Psyche pushed back the bedcovers and sat up, her whole body tense. Who had cried out in such alarm?

She scrambled out of bed and relit her candle. Pulling a knitted wrap about her thin nightdress, she lifted the candlestick and headed for the hallway. With no thought of danger to herself, she unlocked the bedroom door and pulled it open just a little, peering into the hall.

She saw nothing but shadows, yet the cry came again. Psyche slipped out into the hallway, shivering with nervousness. Who was in distress?

The sounds came from next door. Gabriel? Who had dared to assault him in this house of ill memory? She tried to turn the doorknob. At first she thought the door was locked, but then it moved beneath her palm. "Gabriel?" She looked inside the darkened room, keeping her voice low. "Are you there?"

An inarticulate cry was her only answer. She slipped inside and shut the door behind her, then held the candle higher. Its faint light threw wavering shadows on the bedsheets, which heaved with the movements of the body beneath them.

"Gabriel, are you ill?"

She set the candle down on the nearest bureau and hurried to his side. Gabriel's eyes were closed, but he moved restlessly. She put out a hand, and he grasped it as if he were a drowning man. The strength of his grip made her gasp.

"Gabriel, it's Psyche!"

At last, to her relief, he opened his eyes. He seemed dazed, and he blinked at her in the flickering light. "Psyche?"

"Yes, my dear, you were having a nightmare." She touched his cheek gently, and he shivered.

"I dreamed my father had locked me in my room, and I could not get out."

This house evoked bad memories, she thought. No wonder he had not locked the door of his bedchamber.

"In my dream, I was a child again," he explained, as if afraid she would laugh. Psyche touched his cheek.

"But you are not a child," she reminded him. "And you have proven you are no longer in your father's power."

For a moment, she remembered the scene at the dinner table, and wondered if she should have reminded him of that painful incident. But to her surprise, Gabriel laughed softly. "No, indeed I am not. Not a child, because a child would not be thinking what I am thinking when I look at you in such lovely disarray. And not in my father's power, thank God, never again."

She felt self-conscious for a moment, then became aware that indeed, her bare feet were chilled and she had a tendency to shiver.

"Then take me into bed with you," she suggested. "Because the rug is thin and the floor is cold, and so are my feet." Psyche gave him a comically coquettish flutter of lashes. "As a matter of health only, of course."

He grinned, looking much more like his usual self, and pulled back the covers. "Anything less would be inhumane, indeed, my dear Miss Hill."

She climbed in beside him, content now that she could lean her cheek against his bare chest, and snuggled even closer beneath the warm coverlet. His body was hard and firm, and not the least childish.

He leaned down and kissed her, then ran his hand down the outline of her back. This was how marriage would be, she thought wistfully. A real bed, a quiet room, no one to disturb them. This bliss, this close companionship, every night if they wished. The delightful thrill of his touch—

Then he kissed her again, and Psyche happily surrendered all thought to his heated caress.

He hadn't meant to make love to her tonight, in this bleak bitter house. But the warmth of her skin affected him like dry wood on a kindling flame. Desire leaped, all his senses seemed intensified, and he wasn't sure he could manage his next breath.

Her lips parted in answer to his kiss, and he saw the

warmth of complete trust in her blue eyes—how had he ever thought her cold? Ice maiden, indeed. She was everything that was good and lovely and pure.

Damn. He should try—swallowing hard, he pulled away. "Psyche, it would probably be better if I took you back to your room."

"My bed is bigger?" Her blue eyes twinkled.

"No, you vixen!" Gabriel told her in mock censure. "You know that I should leave you to sleep alone. I will—I can endure alone the hell of old memories that this house holds for me. I am learning my own strengths, thanks to you."

She took away one of her hands—good, she was listening after all—but then he felt it touch his cheek. "Gabriel, I have no doubt that you can. But the point is that you don't have to suffer alone. I am here for you. Heaven or hell, I want to share it with you."

He could feel the whirlpool of his desire pulling him deeper and deeper into its yawning maw. Longing grew inside him, pulling on his limbs like treacle. He tried to be logical.

"You certainly aren't fit for hell. I, on the other hand, have been familiar with the nether regions—and my haunted memories—for years."

"It would be hell if you left me." Her voice was soft, and she still held her hand against his cheek.

"You are made for paradise, my dear."

"Then take me there again," she whispered.

She leaned into him. He felt the blood pounding in his veins, and the last of his self-control washed away with its pulsating tide.

Swiftly, he reached beneath the heavy covers and pulled her long gown up and over her head. Psyche raised her arms to help shed the nightdress, then pressed her soft, full breasts against his chest. Unable to resist, he lifted and shaped them with his hands while she nibbled delicately on his jaw and neck.

Psyche threw a long, silky leg over him and then pulled back in surprise at the feel of fabric.

"I thought you were as bare as I beneath these covers," she said with such blatant disappointment that he did not try to stifle his laugh.

"Habit, love. It's best not to be completely naked when you might need to leap out a window at any moment."

Her beautiful eyes narrowed in suspicious disapproval. "Jealous lovers?"

His lips twitched, but he managed not to give in to the grin. "Poor losers."

"Hmm," she considered. "A perfect nonanswer. One could infer that by poor losers you meant card players or that the jealous lovers were the poor losers. Knowing you, however, I—umhhf. . . ."

The rest of her words were muffled by Gabriel's laughing lips. But Psyche did not mind. Instead, she used her energies more pleasurably by pushing back the bedcovers, then ridding Gabriel of his breeches and tossing them to lie with her gown on the cold floor. Turning, she rose on her hands and knees and crawled on top of Gabriel's outstretched body.

"Tonight, I wish to see all of you, feel all of you." She sighed against his chest. With seeking lips, she discovered all the new and different textures of his skin. Silky flat nipples, tickly swirls of hair, sweetly hot skin over hard curves of muscle.

Her curious fingers trailed down his tightly ridged stomach until she grasped him in her hand, squeezing softly, then firmly. Shuddering with enjoyment, Gabriel silently blessed Psyche's distinctive take-charge attitude. He lay in pleasurable acquiescence beneath her for as long as he possibly could. But her naive touches—sometimes hesitant, sometimes bold—made it impossible for him to remain inactive for long.

Inflamed by her awakening desire, he could not remain passive. Reaching down, he grasped the back of her thighs and spread them so she was straddling his hips. Psyche sighed with pleasure at the feel of his rigid length pressing against her. Raising her head, she sought his mouth with her own. Before she could fall completely into the kiss, Gabriel pushed her up into a sitting position and with a slight readjustment of his hips slid deep inside her waiting warmth.

"Ohh," she breathed in wonder, throwing her head back at the glorious sensation. This time there was no stretching tightness, only undiluted pleasure. She gripped his hips firmly with her thighs as he rolled and thrust beneath her. Psyche gave herself up, following his lead in this most sensuous of dances.

She lifted her body a bit to change her position but stopped in delight at the sweet friction her movement caused and Gabriel's resulting groan of pleasure. Experimentally, she rose to the tip of his hardness and then sank down suddenly. Gabriel's eyes, which had been half-lowered and slumberous, flew open with heightened arousal.

Oh, this is heady stuff indeed, she thought.

She granted him no mercy as she raised and lowered herself by teasing increments, only giving in to his hoarse pleas when he grabbed her hips.

"Goddess, *please*." He groaned, trying to end the sublime torture.

Smiling the wicked smile of a woman reveling in her newfound power, she evaded his hands. But she had underestimated Gabriel's own power.

Eyes ardent with fevered passion, face tense with impending release, he touched the pad of his thumb against her swollen, tender bud just above their joined bodies. He fondled her once, twice, a third time, and she was plummeting over the edge of ecstasy into completion and Gabriel's grasping arms. Her body's clenching tremors sent Gabriel into his own magnificent release.

They lay still entwined, as Gabriel drew long shuddering breaths in and out of his lungs. He could feel Psyche's heart pounding against his, and nothing had ever felt so right. She raised passion-dazed eyes to his and smiled with such love, such trust.

It made the knowledge that he had to leave her that much harder to bear.

Later, when they lay in quiet repletion, limbs entangled and her hair cloaking his chest, she said, "You are not still desiring your father's approval?"

"No," he said too quickly, then sighed. "I suppose I would like his respect."

"But failing that, can you not respect yourself?" she suggested.

"For what?" he asked, his tone troubled. "For running away from the scandal I had caused?"

"You were a boy," she reminded him. Somewhere, a cricket rasped its nighttime song.

"But I am a man now. What have I done to be proud of?"

"You have returned, older and wiser," she shot back. "You have saved me from my greedy uncle and annoying cousin. You have stood up to your enemies, you have faced your old fears. You have faced your father."

"When I left, I said I would come back and force him to his knees," he said, very low.

"That was a boy's threat," she told him.

"So you do not think less of me, that today I allowed him to walk away?"

She leaned up to kiss the tip of his chin. "No, my dear, I do not."

He was silent for a moment, then he moved restlessly beneath her. "Older, yes, but wiser? Because I know how to win a game of whist, how to dance and shoot and handle a sword? Because I know how to charm a woman? Or at least, most women. You were not amused by my banter when we first met, as I recall." He kissed the top of her head.

She smiled into the dark; the candle had guttered out some time ago. "Even charm is a gift that can be used well or ill."

"You think I have used it well?" There was a glimmer of hope in his voice; funny how she could hear even more layers of meaning in his words when she could not see his face.

"Yes, I do. I have seen you make a plain woman feel beautiful."

"You think that is worth commending?" He moved his arm slightly so that he could stroke her cheek; his touch was soft and sure.

"I think it very commendable," she agreed. "And not a gift to be lightly dismissed."

He made a sound that was almost a sigh. "It seems little enough to me."

"But not to the woman whose day you have brightened," she countered. "You must let go of the memories, Gabriel, and also of your anger. You have a good heart, it must not be tainted by bitterness. You have courage and loyalty. These are valuable attributes."

"Funny," he whispered into her hair. "All those pleasing tributes I would have used to describe you."

She smiled, though he could not see. "Really?"

"Of course. And perhaps you, too, need to let go of your anger, the anger you feel for your parents." He said it very softly, and for a moment, she was not sure that she heard him correctly.

"I—angry? I most certainly am not angry!" She was about to argue further, when the truth of his words hit home. "Oh," she whispered, pulling the covers tight around her neck. "Oh, yes, why did I never see it? I fear you are right. I was so angry because they left me, because they died. Yet how can I blame them for that?"

His only answer was to stroke the soft curve of her back. And she knew that only she could decipher that puzzle. For a long time they lay, two halves of one whole, their bodies curved together, and eventually, she slept.

In the morning, Psyche woke in the other guest chamber to find the other side of the bed empty. She raised her head in alarm, then laid it back on the pillow as memory returned. He had carried her, half asleep and protesting, back to her own bed in the early hours of the morning. He would not embarrass her before his father's staff, she thought, smiling. Would they ever have the chance to lie late in bed, with no fear of awkward explanations? She would enjoy teaching him to lie abed until dawn was past, holding her close as they nestled into smooth linen sheets. Then she remembered that she might not have that chance, that despite everything, he might not stay, and a wave of grief threatened to overwhelm her. With an effort, she pushed it back. He would come to see clearly, she reassured herself. But she was wide awake now, and she sat up, stretching, and pushed the bedcovers away.

Dressing quickly in the same navy gown, she pulled her hair into a smooth knot and then made her way downstairs. She found Gabriel in the dining room and, to her relief, no one else except a nervous-looking footman, who served her.

Psyche took her seat and sipped her tea.

"Good morning, Miss Hill. Did you sleep well?" Gabriel asked, his usual mischief lighting his eyes.

Since he knew very well what had troubled her sleep, she frowned at him for an instant, before remembered pleasure softened her expression. "Tolerably well," she murmured, aware of the servant still hovering near the sideboard.

"Mrs. P. makes a nice sleeping draught. You should try it," Gabriel suggested, his blue eyes still laughing.

"Thank you, I will keep that in mind the next time I have a disordered night," she answered gravely. She saw him grin.

The footman offered her platters filled with sausage and kidneys and ham, eggs and porridge and toasted bread. Psyche filled her plate and ate slowly. She was, in fact, quite hungry. She looked across the table at Gabriel, whose gaze had shifted, his expression hard to read.

"What are you thinking?" she asked at last.

"My mother used to sit in that chair," he told her. "She would have liked you—she would have loved you, I am sure of it."

"I am sorry I did not have the privilege of meeting her," Psyche said, reaching across to touch his hand.

Gabriel nodded, but he did not answer. In a moment, he said, "I have told the servants to summon your carriage."

"Are we going back to London?"

He nodded. "The day is clear. We should be in the city by afternoon. I cannot think that Barrett's gang can keep up an ambush for this long. There should be enough traffic to spoil their plans and keep us reasonably safe."

Psyche could not honestly say she was sorry to leave this sad, empty house. When she had finished her meal, she pushed back her plate, and the footman jumped to pull her chair out and allow her to rise.

She nodded her thanks. "Should we—um, say our thank-you's to our host?"

"Our reluctant host?" Gabriel amended, his tone dry. "I suppose so."

With her hand tucked into Gabriel's arm, Psyche walked by his side down the hall and to the study door, where Gabriel knocked.

He waited for a moment, then opened the door. "We are leaving, Father."

Silence, then a noise that might have been a grunt. The wing chair was pulled up to the fire again, and the air in the room was too warm. Psyche thought how much this bitter old man was missing, through his inability to love or accept his sons.

"Thank you for your hospitality," Gabriel continued, his tone polite.

Still no answer. A coal popped in the fire, then Gabriel shut the door. Psyche was left with the image of the motionless man staring into the fire, a perennial scowl on his face, his form lost in the shadows. She had a moment of instinctive insight: somewhere deep within his heart of hearts, the marquis must believe himself completely unlovable, totally without worth, to be so unable to accept any affection, any friendship even, from those who by nature's law ought to be closest to him.

She looked up at Gabriel and for an instant caught an expression of grief on his face, then he recovered his usual air of poised urbanity and lifted his brows as he saw her gazing at him.

"I'm sure you are ready to leave this house," he said, his tone dry.

She nodded, but she pressed his arm as they walked to the outer door. Their carriage was waiting. Mrs. Parslip was there to curtsy and make her farewells. Regardless of the staring footman, Gabriel reached to hug the little housekeeper again.

"It was good to see you, Mrs. P.," he told her. "You made me feel like a boy once more."

The woman smiled. "I shall hope to see you again." She took something from the folds of her apron and put a small object into his hands.

Psyche couldn't help but look—it was a miniature of the type that fashionable ladies often had painted of themselves. She saw a lovely, sweet-faced lady with soft brown hair who bore an obvious resemblance to the man beside her— Gabriel's mother.

Gabriel had to clear his throat. "Thank you, Mrs. P." He was quite sure the housekeeper did not have his father's permission for this gift, but it meant the world to Gabriel. The small portrait would mark the beginning of his newly revised memories, the easing of old pain.

Mrs. Parslip beamed and curtsied one more time as Gabriel handed Psyche up. He took his seat beside her. The driver lifted the reins and the carriage rolled smoothly forward.

They sat in silence as the vehicle moved down the long drive, then Psyche turned to gaze in inquiry at her companion. "Was it helpful, this visit?" she asked quietly.

Touching the miniature, he did not pretend to misunderstand her. Indeed, some of the old bitterness, the long-standing anger, had ebbed. After they had made love, he had slept easily, and the dreams had not returned. He seemed to have turned a corner. He knew now that his mother had loved him. And to see his father as an adult was to see that he was not the all-powerful, all-knowing figure who had ruled Gabriel's childhood with an iron hand. And if his father was fallible, after all, then his assessment of Gabriel might be similarly flawed.

It was only because of Psyche that he had had the chance to understand these revelations, as startling as bolts from the heavens. Only because of Psyche had he returned to this house of bitterness, and because of Psyche, he now understood that he could be the man he chose to be, not the failure that his father had judged him, not a replica of his tyrant of a sire.

"I think you have released me from a decades-old curse," he told her.

She looked startled, then her eyes cleared as understanding dawned. "I am glad," she said. "We must all come to terms with our parents, I suppose."

It was his turn to be surprised. "What, my jackass of a father has taught you something, too?"

"Oh, yes," she said, thinking of the long, silent dinner they had endured, the glares they had received from the marquis when he deigned to look Gabriel's way at all. "You were right in what you said last night. I have been angry at my parents for a long time, for risking themselves in such a foolhardy experiment, for dying, for leaving me to raise Circe by myself. But staying in that house reminded me of the years of love and laughter and good times I shared with them, and how fortunate I was to have parents who valued me, who encouraged me, who accepted me for everything that I was."

Her voice quivered, and she had to swallow hard. Gabriel saw that her eyes gleamed with tears, and she blinked them back. "I still miss them; I always will. But I will also remember to be thankful for every day we had together."

He took her hands and held them close within his own; he wanted desperately to lighten the sadness that shadowed her face and to protect her from any further grief. It pained him more than he could say to think that he might cause her unhappiness if he left. But he also knew that he could do her more harm by staying.

Soon enough, he would be gone, back to foreign lands and high-stakes card games that might someday allow him new entry into the kind of life that Psyche deserved. He thought he had found his chance, with Barrett's property, but he had been misled. Gabriel knew that he must leave—he would never cheat Psyche of what she so rightfully deserved. Nor could he expect a woman like Psyche to wait for the years it might take him to retrieve his fortune. But what they had had was so precious, their stolen lovemaking so intense, so overpowering, that he would cherish it all his life.

No, despite the beginnings of new understanding, he could offer her too little. And the truth was that even if he had money and property, he was still not the man for Psyche, not the kind of sterling upright gentleman with an unblemished past whom Psyche deserved. For Psyche, the best would hardly be good enough, and he fell far short of that exemplary level.

Sighing, he looked outside the carriage. They had made the main road and had turned north toward London. Within a few hours, they would be back in the city, and he would have to come up with a way to dispose of Barrett once and for all, to convince the old villain to call off his hired gang and settle this man to man. Unfortunately, he had not the glimmer of an idea how this was to be accomplished. But he must think of something!

"Gabriel!" Psyche exclaimed.

A moment later, he saw what had caused her cry, and he called to the coachman to pull up the team. When the carriage rolled to a stop, Gabriel opened the door and jumped out, and Psyche leaned her head outside the vehicle to see what was going on.

The sight that had brought them to a halt was alarming enough. The sporty curricle that partially blocked the road had lost one of its wheels and now tilted at an angle toward the ditch at the side. Two horses stood amid the tangled traces, one shaking its head, the other whinnying softly; the animals seemed unharmed. As for the solitary occupant . . . now Gabriel understood Psyche's perturbation.

"Why, Cousin Percy," Gabriel drawled. "What on earth are you doing here?"

The rotund figure jumped up. Psyche's relative had been sitting on the side of the road, perhaps contemplating his next move. "Cousin!" Percy exclaimed in relief, staring at Psyche and ignoring Gabriel's comment. "I am relieved to see you well."

"I am quite well, thank you," Psyche answered. "You, however, do not seem to be so lucky. What are you doing here?"

"I came to assist you, of course. After you left town in such a precipitous fashion, I feared the worse!" Percy turned to glare at Gabriel, and his meaning was obvious.

Psyche sighed. "No, I have not been abducted, Percy. And how did you manage to upset your curricle?"

"It was not my fault," Percy protested. "A rabbit jumped out of the hedgerow, and my near horse shied—it could have happened to anyone."

"No doubt," Gabriel said, his tone dry. "And you didn't even bother to bring a groom with you?" The groom's seat on the skewed carriage was empty, as they could all see. "Or did you send him to get help?"

"No, of course I came alone. I did not want to broadcast the news of my cousin's sad disregard for the proprieties to the world! To go off alone with a man—" Percy's face flushed, and he seemed prepared to prose on forever.

"A man who happens to be my fiancé!" Psyche cut him off without ceremony. "Percy, neither my reputation nor my person needs your protection. You have no claim on me! How many times do I have to tell you that?"

"Until you wake from this sad infatuation, your comments are hardly to be trusted," Percy said, his tone stiff.

Psyche drew a deep breath, but Percy had turned to face Gabriel. "I should ask you to take me up to your estate, if you would, sir. I understand it is only a few miles from here."

Gabriel glanced at the man in surprise. It was true that the estate he had won from Barrett lay just ahead, but— "How did you know that?" he demanded, suspicion raising the hair along the back of his neck.

"Aunt Sophia told me you had gone into Kent after I demanded your destination," Percy admitted, looking complacent. "I made inquiries about large vacant estates. I could hardly let Psyche go off like this without coming to protect her good name, if nothing else."

Had he hounded the poor woman unmercifully? Her aunt must have been distressed enough by their sudden flight to have let the information slip, Psyche thought. Poor Aunt Sophie!

"My good name will be just fine, if you can keep your mouth shut," Psyche told him. "And remember, any scandal touching me will also reflect on yourself, Percy. I know how strongly you and your father feel about family honor."

"Didn't I just say that that is why I came?" Percy pulled himself up to his full height, bringing him almost to Gabriel's shoulder. "And having come this far only to support you, Cousin, I think a little assistance on your part is not too much to ask."

Gabriel glanced at Psyche. "I'm afraid you don't understand. I'm not refusing you hospitality, but the estate is in ruins. It has nothing to offer you. There is a small inn in the next village—"

"Do you think I could be seen in a public hostelry looking like this?" His tone outraged, Percy gestured to a small rip in his elegant sleeve and a slight sprinkling of dust on his pantaloons.

"But Percy, the house is empty. There is no housekeeper to repair your coat or dust off your garments," Psyche tried to help. "Truly—"

"I cannot believe you would refuse such a simple request!" Percy folded his arms, the picture of affronted obstinacy.

"This is a waste of breath," Gabriel said. "He will not stop talking long enough to listen. Perhaps we should indeed stop at my . . . estate . . . and show him its condition. We could at least leave his horses there till we can send some-one from the village to reclaim them."

"Is it safe?" Psyche whispered.

"I should think the ruffians would have given up by now. They have no reason to think we will return," he pointed out.

Psyche nodded. "Very well. Percy, we shall take you to Gabriel's property, and then on to the village where you can see about getting your wheel repaired."

Above all, she did not want him sharing the carriage with them all the way back to London; the thought of listening to Percy sermonizing, full of recriminations for her unmaid-enly conduct, was enough to make her shudder. And she and Gabriel had so little time left. She knew he was still think-ing of moving on; she could tell from the occasional mo-ments of quiet when he visibly withdrew into his thoughts, seemed even to forget her presence. No, they must get rid of her obnoxious cousin as soon as possible.

Gabriel and their own driver managed to extract Percy's horses from the traces. One seemed whole, but the other limped badly; both were tied to the back of their carriage. Then Percy stepped into the chaise, taking the first seat, where fortunately he faced the driver, with his back to Psy-che and Gabriel, who remained in the rear seat. This did not keep Percy from looking over his shoulder and addressing them often, however. They had to go at a very slow pace be-cause of the injured horse. Psyche was most glad to see the neglected driveway of Gabriel's property soon come into view. The driver turned the team, and the carriage rolled along through the narrow driveway, pulling up in front of the house.

It really had lovely lines, Psyche thought, imagining the house refurbished. If it were reclaimed from its neglect, it would be a most handsome dwelling. She lost herself in thoughts of new paint and wallpapers while the men got out of the carriage.

"Cousin," Percy called to her, holding out his hand to as-sist her.

She had not meant to leave the carriage, knowing their stop was to be brief, but it was easier to get out than to argue with Percy. She took his hand as briefly as possible and stepped quickly down to the weedy gravel.

"There, you see," she told her cousin. "There are no staff here to make you comfortable. We will leave your team here and go on to the village. It is a small place, and no one will remark upon your torn coat."

Percy climbed the steps and peered inside the open doorway. "If that is the case, what were you doing here, Psyche? You did not stay here—alone—last night?" He sounded horrified.

Psyche bit back a groan, and Gabriel frowned. "We did not stay the night here," he said, his tone sharp. "We visited a relative of mine, and we were suitably chaperoned."

As to that, Psyche bit back a grin, but she must not allow Percy to see her amusement. "Come along, Percy," she said. Really, her cousin was too provoking. Now he had wandered into the house, as if searching for some evidence of a secret love nest. She walked after him, determined to get him back in the carriage and headed to the village, so they could be rid of his irksome company as soon as possible.

Gabriel was still frowning Something was not right. Why did Percy seem so determined to inspect Gabriel's ruin of an estate? Was it just another bit of evidence to convince Psyche to give up her engagement to a man her cousin, with an unusual moment of perception, was convinced was a scoundrel? So be it. Gabriel knew that Percy, for all his inanities, was quite right about this judgment.

What were they doing, lingering inside the moldy hall? "Psyche," Gabriel called. "Are you ready to leave?"

He heard her exclaim, then Percy muttered a soothing word. Gabriel headed quickly up the steps. More mice? He walked through the doorway into the dimness of the hall, and before his eyes could adjust, he felt strong hands grab him from behind.

"Ah," a familiar voice purred. "Just as I hoped. Welcome to my estate, Lord Impostor."

Twenty-two

He was a fool, more than a fool.

Gabriel felt the awareness of danger pour over him, making his muscles taut and putting his nerves on edge, but it was too late. Barrett stood with a small pistol pointed his way as one of Barrett's hired killers pulled Gabriel's arms together and tied his wrists with stout rope. Another ruffian held his hand over Psyche's lips. Behind his grimy fingers, her face was pale with shock and fear. Percy looked merely smug.

Percy! Damn the coward, he had somehow joined with Barrett to lure them here. Damn himself for being lulled by Percy's impotent idiocy into believing him harmless. If they lived through this—which was most doubtful—Gabriel swore to himself that he would have Percy's head on a silver platter.

Psyche bit the hand that had prevented her from giving Gabriel any warning. The man who held her swore and waved his injured finger in the air. Psyche stared at her cousin in disbelief. "Percy, how could you? How did you even know—"

"Barrett came to me and explained," Percy said, his tone just as pompous as usual. "Since I wanted to rid you of your entanglement with this scoundrel, and since Barrett was able to tell me even more about his misdeeds—"

"*Misdeeds?*" Psyche's voice trembled with outrage. "*This* man"—she jutted her chin to indicate Barrett—"has tried to murder us more than once. Don't talk to me about misdeeds! How could you strike a bargain with him, Percy?"

"I wanted Tarrington out of the way," Percy said simply. "I know it is a shock to your feminine sensibilities just now, Cousin, but in time you will come to see the wisdom of my actions, and you will thank me for it."

Did he really believe this claptrap? Psyche stared at her cousin with horror, not sure she had ever really seen him before. He met her gaze calmly, his self-satisfaction unblemished. But he had always been selfish, had always thought only of himself, his wishes, his desires, and never of hers. Why should this betrayal be such a surprise? Percy might be too squeamish to murder with his own hand, but if someone else would do it for him . . .

"I will detest you for the rest of my life," Psyche told him, steadying her voice with great effort. "No matter how long or how short that may be. And I will never, ever, consider marriage with you, not if I die a spinster ten times over."

Percy shrugged. "You will change your mind," he said, his confidence undaunted. "Females do."

"Percy!" Psyche glared at him. "You are a fool."

He sniffed.

"What makes you think you will be allowed to live long enough to pursue this noble plan?" Gabriel asked the other man, keeping his voice low. Barrett crossed to the other side of the room and seemed to confer with his two hired killers. The man who had been holding Psyche released her at a nod from Barrett. "You really think that Barrett will leave any witnesses alive after he has disposed of me?"

Percy blinked. The idiot had apparently never considered this possibility.

"He wouldn't." Percy's smile faded just a little. "I agreed that I would say nothing—"

"And do you have any conception of the danger to which you have exposed Psyche?" Gabriel felt both disdain for Percy's stupidity and fear for Psyche, and the fear threatened to slow his thoughts. No, he must not panic. He needed all his wits about him.

Percy pursed his thick lips as if he mulled over Gabriel's words. Psyche glanced toward Gabriel, looking anxious.

"Do you see anything about with a sharp edge?" he whispered, testing the bonds that held his wrists immobile. The rope was new and stout, and he pulled against it without result. She glanced around the room, but only curls of dust and a few splinters of wood littered the floor. No handy knife revealed itself. The small dagger he had confiscated at the masquerade was tucked inside his coat, but he had no way to reach it, nor could Psyche, without the others seeing.

Barrett was striding back to face them; he had sent one of the men out of the room, heaven knew for what ungodly purpose. Percy looked up. "I say, Barrett, I think I'll just start back to London with Miss Hill," he said, his tone almost normal. The doubts that Gabriel had induced were beginning to work, but it was too late. Everything was too late.

Gabriel felt his chest tighten with fear and building anger. How dare Barrett plot to harm the woman that Gabriel adored, the lady who had imbued him with the courage to love again. Whatever else happened, he had to see that Psyche emerged from this danger alive and unhurt. He struggled once more against the ropes that held him. He thought that the knots slipped just a little, but not enough.

Barrett glanced at him warily, then looked back to Percy. "I'm afraid that won't be possible," the man said, his tone full of oily politeness.

"Why not?" Percy was sweating now. Droplets formed on his forehead, and his tone was not as sure.

"Because I fear that the lady would never be silent. She has formed a tendre for this rascal, as women usually do for a pretty face. They seem reluctant to realize the true nature of a man's worth." Barrett lifted his sharp chin and stepped closer to Psyche.

She shuddered. "I think I know your true worth," she told him, her voice commendably steady.

Sweet Psyche, who had the mettle of a lioness, Gabriel thought. He had let her down again by allowing Percy to lead them into this trap, and he would never forgive himself, for however many minutes he had left to live. He would deserve the deepest circle of hell for that foolish error alone.

Barrett snorted. "I should like to take the time to teach you otherwise." He leered at the smooth curves of her bosom. "Unfortunately, the longer we linger here, the greater the chance, however remote, that some passerby might notice that my hulk of an estate boasts occupants, and that is so unusual it might stir talk in the neighborhood. I fear we must dispose of these troublesome trespassers, and if a blaze should break out in an empty house, ah, well, the evidence will soon be destroyed." He turned his pistol toward Percy, who shrank back in alarm, and Psyche, who stood her ground, though her expression was somber.

Gabriel felt himself go cold. He stopped his useless struggle against the ropes and prepared to launch himself toward Barrett. He knew that he could not reach the villain in time, but it might give Psyche a few moments to escape.

Outside, wind gusted, and a branch from an overgrown tree rattled the window. Barrett jumped. Psyche glanced toward the window and her glance swept over the cowering Percy, who had gone quite white.

"This is all your doing," she snapped. She moved suddenly to strike his cheek, and everyone else, even Barrett, blinked in surprise. Her blow left a red imprint upon Percy's white face.

"C-Cousin," he protested. "I didn't mean—I never thought—"

Ignoring his words, Psyche pushed him with all her strength, and Percy jerked backward, hitting the window with a crash. He cried out as the splintered pane fell to the floor in jingling shards. Percy slipped down atop the splinters, his expression dazed.

Everyone else stood as if frozen by the sound of the crackling glass—everyone but Psyche. Throwing her hands to her cheeks in seeming horror, she dashed to where Percy lay slumped under the broken window. Bending, she yanked him into a sitting position.

"Dear God! What have I done? Forgive me, Percy."

Gabriel watched in confusion as she fussed over the dazed form of her cousin. Soothing and clucking over him, she drew her handkerchief out of her sleeve and whisked it over Percy's face and hands, which showed several small cuts.

Barrett smiled.

"Perhaps you have not made a conquest after all, Sinclair. Perhaps *all* your skills are getting rusty." He gestured to Psyche. "You should know better than to trust a woman," he taunted. "Weak things, they always side with the familiar. In this case, her family."

Psyche whirled to face Gabriel.

"None of this would have happened had you not made poor Percy crazed with jealousy. He only thought to protect my honor—the honor you stole from me in yet another of your casual seductions!" Her chest heaved with barely restrained emotion, and her cheeks had gone scarlet.

Barrett arched a heavy brow. "Oh, very good, Sinclair. I was almost disappointed in you. How unlike you to not sample such a lovely morsel. And after I kill you, it will be my turn."

Gabriel strained at his bonds, his hands aching to slam themselves into Barrett's face. This vermin had no right to breathe the same air that Psyche breathed, let alone speak of her in such a way. Psyche was neither weak or disloyal. He would not believe she could abandon him. Nor had what they shared been sordid or casual.

Psyche had been crouching beside Percy, but she stood slowly when Barrett stopped speaking. She faced Barrett with grim disgust. "You may have the final pleasure of killing this rogue, but not before I have my satisfaction."

Barrett's remaining man took a step toward her, but Barrett halted him. "No," he said slowly. "This could be entertaining."

Gabriel stared intently into Psyche's stormy eyes as she moved purposely toward him. Her lush lips were pulled into a firm line, her cheeks had faded to a dull rose. As she stepped closer, he saw the way she was holding the blood-stained handkerchief close to her waist. With the barest flicker of her wrist, she exposed what was cupped in the cloth.

Pride rippled through him in waves. What had briefly reflected the pale yellow rays making their way through the dirt-encrusted windows was a thick shard of lethally sharp window glass.

That's my smart girl, he thought, containing the grin that wanted to spread across his face. An answering twinkle echoed in her beautiful eyes for just a moment, accompanied by the most alarming amount of trust he had ever seen. It, more than any fist or weapon ever could, almost brought him to his knees. *She trusts me to resolve even this*, he thought wonderingly. The realization was humbling. He drew a deep breath; he could not disappoint her.

She stopped just in front of him. "So, you thought you could steal my heart as well as my reputation?" she demanded.

Gabriel tried to look suitably downcast; he felt the slightest whisper of sound as she sawed at the thick rope that bound him. Her hands were hidden from the others' sight by her body, and she continued to look him in the eye, her expression revealing only her feigned scorn.

"Miss Hill, you mistake my motives. . . ." Gabriel tried to play his part, while his whole body was taut with anticipation of his moment of impending freedom.

Psyche leaned even closer, and while one hand sawed at the rope, the other lifted to pause dramatically just in front of his face. "You, sir, are the cause of all this heartache. How many other maidens' affections have you trifled with?"

Despite the deadly peril of their situation, Gabriel had to fight hard to hold back a swell of mad laughter that bubbled inside him. What courage Psyche had—what quick wits. "Not that many . . . maidens," he answered after a thoughtful pause.

"You cad!" She swung the flat of her hand against his cheek, producing more sound than actual force. Gabriel blinked, though he had felt little pain. Behind them, Barrett cackled with glee, and his henchman guffawed. Even Percy, who had staggered to his feet at last, permitted himself a prim smirk. Her cousin had stepped back, closer to Barrett, as if to remind the mastermind that Percy was on his side, not a threat. Would Percy allow Psyche to die, too, if doing so would save his own misbegotten hide? Gabriel would not be surprised. The anger he felt fueled the resolution inside him. He strained against the ropes as Psyche's rough blade sliced at them, and at last he felt them give.

Only a thread of the rope was still intact, but he could not reveal that he was virtually free, not yet. Barrett had a pistol. Gabriel pressed his wrists together as he met Psyche's clear blue eyes briefly. A flicker of understanding passed between them. He thought that she understood; they had to play for time.

"How many other reputations have you besmirched?" As she continued her tirade, Gabriel watched Barrett from the corner of his eye. Barrett seemed to be enjoying Gabriel's denouncement. He stood several feet away from them. How could Gabriel cross that much space before Barrett could lift his pistol and fire? And with Gabriel dead, Psyche would be helpless. He would have willingly died here and now to save her, but it would be useless if she were left at Barrett's mercy, with no one but the faithless coward Percy to plead her case.

If only they could induce Barrett to come closer. Even as he thought that, Gabriel heard Barrett speak again.

"As entertaining as this is, I fear, Miss Hill, that we must bring this little drama to a close."

Psyche whirled to face Barrett. "How can you belittle my suffering? Surely you—as a gentleman—must feel incensed over the wrongs this man has done me?"

"Really, Miss Hill," Barrett purred. "A moment ago, you were calling me a murderer. I fear I have some doubts as to your motives—"

She threw herself at him, and Barrett raised his pistol in alarm. But Psyche paused just in front of him, to wring her hands in a most un-Psyche-like pose. "Please, you must have pity! You do not know what I have suffered at his hands."

Gabriel was almost forgotten. He was able to flex his arms and break through the last shredded filament of the rope. He had a sudden premonition of what Psyche meant to do, and it turned his blood to ice—*no, no*, he wanted to shout. *It is too dangerous!*

But Psyche was intent only on the villain who eyed her, his expression skeptical. "I fear that you could not be trusted to hold your tongue, my *lady.*" He made the last word a mockery, but no one seemed to notice, least of all Psyche. "It's nothing personal, you understand, just a natural inclination to tidiness and a keen attention to my own well-being."

Psyche sobbed and lifted one hand to her face, as if in despair. But the other hand, which still clutched the handkerchief with its sharp fragment of glass, flashed toward Barrett's throat.

Gabriel was already in motion, but Barrett swung the pistol toward Psyche, and as Gabriel threw himself at the man, he heard the pistol explode and smelled the gunpowder. He had his hands around the villain's throat now, and he grappled with the man, who was stronger than one would have suspected, his small frame full of wiry strength.

Psyche, where was Psyche? Was she hurt, killed? If she was, Barrett would not leave this room alive, Gabriel vowed. His desperation gave him strength, and in another moment, he had forced the other man to the floor. Gasping for breath, Barrett collapsed into a semiconscious heap. The just-fired pistol fell to the floor unheeded. As Barrett's coat fell open, Gabriel saw a matching pistol, the other half of the pair. He grabbed the loaded gun to thrust into his own waistband, then turned quickly to find Psyche.

She was holding the shard of glass to the remaining ruffian's throat; the man looked dumb with surprise and fear. Trust Psyche to keep her wits about her!

Weak with relief, Gabriel took out the pistol and pointed it at the man, so that Psyche could lower her hand, which showed the slightest inclination to tremble. He reached for her and pulled her against him with his other arm.

"Thank God you are safe," he whispered into her hair as she hid her face, for an instant, against his chest. "If you had been hurt, I would have gone mad with grief!"

"Hush." She raised her head, lifting her hand to touch his cheek. "We are both here, more or less sound, and—"

He glanced down and saw the stain of blood on her arm. "Psyche! You are hit!"

"Just a scratch, I believe you would say," she told him, calm once more. "But I think we should make a strategic retreat, do you not agree? One or more of Barrett's henchmen still linger about the estate."

"Yes." Gabriel lifted her forearm to inspect it; the bone seemed unbroken and the flesh wound appeared superficial; the trickle of blood was already slowing. He would bind the wound as soon as they left the building. He almost groaned at the thought of Barrett's plan to burn down the house—his house. For, despite everything, he still considered it his property. If he had been alone, he would have gone after the other henchman, but getting Psyche away from danger was more important.

What had happened to Percy? Gabriel looked about them and found Percy cowering on the floor in the corner, as far away from the gunfire and the ensuing struggle as he could get. His hands covered his face, and he seemed almost insensible with fear.

"Percy, get out of the house," Psyche said sternly. "It may be afire. And go back to London and put your affairs into order, because when I return, I shall have you arrested for attempted murder."

That made him drop his hands; his face was white. "Cousin, I never meant to harm you!"

"You think it excuses you that you were only going to assist in the murder of my fiancé?" Psyche demanded, her tone icy. "I doubt that the judge will agree."

"But, Cousin, please, I beg you. Think of the disgrace—"

"Think of the relief I will feel never to see your wretched person again," Psyche answered, unmoved by his pleas.

"Actually," Gabriel said, pulling the wretched man to his feet, "I think you should give him another chance, Psyche."

"What?" Psyche turned to stare, her expression perplexed. "You cannot be serious! After what he has done?"

"You could show magnanimity," Gabriel went on, "as along as Percy's father agrees that he will agree to your choice of husband, any husband, and will release your inheritance immediately."

Silence. Percy gaped, and Psyche's expression changed dramatically. "Brilliant," she whispered. "Yes, I think that is the only way you will escape the gallows, Percy."

Gabriel held back his laughter. He was not at all sure they had enough on Percy to put his head into a noose, but Percy himself was convinced, that was obvious.

"Cousin, I promise, I will speak to my father at once, just allow me to leave—"

"You have twenty-four hours," Psyche said, her tone as icy as it had ever been. "Then I expect my solicitor to receive the signed papers releasing my funds into my control."

"We will, Father will, I p-promise," Percy stammered, new hope apparently animating him.

"Get the sound horse from your team outside and ride to the next village; you can arrange transport there back to London," Gabriel told him. "Now, we had all best get out of here before the rest of Barrett's men reappear. Psyche, take the rope and tie this rat's hands."

She did, and then Gabriel motioned the ruffian to the far corner of the room. "Sit down with your back to us," he told him.

"But, guv," the man whined. "What about the fire? I'll roast like a spit capon."

"Your problem," Gabriel said, though he knew there would be nothing to hold the man inside once they were gone. "Just don't move as long as I can see you. Now, face the wall!"

Did he smell smoke? "Come along," he told Psyche.

She nodded, but she seemed to waver. She must be dizzy from loss of blood and the shock of her wound. Gabriel reached for her and steadied her, putting his free arm around her. She clung to him, and they moved slowly toward the door. Percy hurried along in front of them, not waiting to see about Psyche, as usual thinking only of himself. He disappeared through the doorway and out of sight.

They had almost reached the hall, too, when a faint scrape of sound from behind alerted Gabriel. But the warning came a fraction of a second too late.

"Gabriel! Look out!" Psyche shrieked.

But he was hampered by the weight of her, and she could not shift away in time. Barrett had regained his wits, and he launched himself at Gabriel. Gabriel staggered under the man's assault, then turned to meet his attack head-on.

Psyche tried to grab one of Barrett's arms, but he thrust her away with such force that she tripped and hit her head against the floor. She lay still, seeming stunned.

Barrett fought like a man who sees his own death just a step away. Hate glittered in his eyes, and he struggled with all his strength for the pistol. Gabriel tried to pull it away, but Barrett had hold of the pistol and he would not let go.

"Jake, get yourself here and aid me!" Barrett shouted to his minion, who still crouched in the corner.

The man looked over his shoulder, his expression fearful. Seeing the two men grappling at close quarters, he scrabbled to his feet, his hands still tied, and edged closer.

Gabriel would have two to fight if he did not finish this

quickly. He tried to push Barrett back, but the man clung to him with a single-minded determination to retrieve his pistol.

They fought blindly, and now Gabriel was sure that he could smell smoke. A shower of rain shook the window-panes and rattled the frame, and somewhere, he heard a horse whinny. Had Percy run away to leave them to Barrett's mercy? The little rat was consistent to the last.

Psyche had not moved. If she were seriously injured . . . Gabriel struck Barrett in the face, but the man had the strength of a madman; he hardly seemed to notice the blow. He twisted the pistol till the barrel pressed into Gabriel's stomach. If the man's finger reached the trigger—Gabriel struggled to turn the gun, but Barrett fought his every movement. For a moment, he thought he had shifted the barrel, but Gabriel wasn't sure if—

Then a blast of fire and pain exploded against his body. Gasping with pain, Gabriel felt his legs go weak, and he slumped to the floor.

He thought he lost consciousness for a moment; then someone was calling his name. He blinked, seeing red streaks against the black. Slowly, his sight returned; he still lay across the wooden boards, his clothes stank of gunpowder and blood, and—Psyche! Psyche knelt over him . . . she was all right.

"Get out of the house," he whispered. "Leave me. I think I am shot . . . get away before Barrett can—"

"Barrett is dead," Psyche told him, her cheeks wet with tears. "He shot himself instead. You are not hurt badly, Gabriel, though I feared for you at first. You caught some of the force of the igniting gunpowder; your shirt is ruined and I think your skin is burnt. But the bullet went into Barrett."

Gabriel forced himself up. He saw Barrett's body sprawled across the floor in a great pool of blood, the man's features twisted into one last snarl of surprise. "You—are you all right?"

Psyche nodded. "Come, we must get out of the house. I think Percy is long gone."

"What about Barrett's man?" Gabriel looked around, trying to assess any additional danger as he stood on shaky legs, Psyche holding on to his arm.

"He ran away, his hands still tied," Psyche said. "It was almost comical. And I have not seen the other ruffian."

"So he may still be about. Let us go and see if the coachman and carriage are still here." The most important thing was to get out of this building and away from any other henchmen. Gabriel was still alive—miracle of miracles—and Psyche was not seriously harmed. He gave silent thanks as he limped, with Psyche's help, toward the hallway.

The sound of steps in the hall brought them to an abrupt halt. Gabriel wanted to groan. In his current state, how could he defeat another assailant? He had to try.

"Get behind me," he told Psyche.

"No," she said, her voice calm. "We will face any peril together."

So they stood side by side, exhausted but resolute, and when the figure appeared in the doorway, both were silent with shock.

"Here you are, then," David said, relief lighting his face. "But you look a sight! Are you hurt badly, old man?"

"No," Gabriel said when he could speak. "See to Psyche. I thought you were injured. We left you unconscious on the steps of the Forsyth house. What are you doing here?"

"Oh, just a knock on the head, got a terrible goose egg still, but that's nothing. Circe told me to come," David explained, glancing apologetically at Psyche. "She had a notion you were in need of my services."

"But how did you know where to find us?" Gabriel persisted.

"I went to your solicitor, wrinkled the directions out of him, then rode hell-bent to get here. I've already doused a fire and tied up a couple of nasty-looking characters," he continued. "Thought it best to come in through the back entrance, you see. But where is Barrett?"

"David, you are a hero," Psyche said, her voice high with emotion. "Barrett is dead."

David looked past them to see the body on the floor; he whistled. "Hell's bells—oh, sorry. But never did a man deserve a bad end more."

Psyche shivered and held fast to Gabriel's arm. It could all so easily have gone the other way. It could be Gabriel lying there on the wood floorboards, a gaping hole in his chest, blood splattered about the empty room. *Thank you,* she thought, *thank you for sparing him this time. He has suffered enough.*

They walked out together. The shower of rain had stopped, only the occasional errant drop still fell. But their carriage was gone. Percy seemed to have appropriated it, with no thought at all as to their safety or convenience. David had his horse, which he offered to Gabriel. They helped Psyche up behind him to cling to Gabriel's waist, and David retrieved the uninjured horse from Percy's team.

"I don't know if he is broken to ride," Psyche worried as David prepared to ride bareback on the mount.

"Not to worry, never met a horse I couldn't stick to," David predicted, grinning. He vaulted up to the gelding's bare back, and although the steed tossed its head and threatened a kick or two, the horse soon settled into a bone-numbing lope.

Psyche looked back at the estate as they trotted down the driveway. Poor house, she was glad it had escaped a fiery destruction. It could be so much more, now that Barrett's claim on it was ended. Perhaps if Gabriel—no, one hour at a time. They were alive; she must count her blessings.

They rode slowly into the village and stopped at the tiny inn. There was no carriage to be hired here, but the landlord owned a small gig that could be used to start them on their journey, and he would send a hostler to retrieve and treat the injured horse they had left behind.

While Gabriel arranged for the gig and sent a message to the local magistrate about Barrett's criminal activities and untimely death, Psyche sat on the front bench beneath the cloudy sky—there was no private parlor and the common room was small and cramped and held several curious farmers who stared at this unusual influx of gentry—as she sipped some ale.

With David and Psyche to testify about Barrett's death, Gabriel should not be in any danger from the authorities, she told herself. He would be free now, free to take over the estate and restore it—slowly, if necessary—but without fearing an assassin popping up behind his back every time he let down his guard. And there would be no more need for his pose of the marquis of Tarrington. Exposing the fake title would cause a buzz among the Ton, Psyche thought wryly. But after all they had been through, she really was not concerned about a little gossip—or a lot. She would have her money at last, and she could hire the best teachers for Circe, allow her sister's talent to grow unfettered. And if Gabriel really left, she would be at liberty to attract all the suitors she cared to.

But the thought left her feeling empty inside. He had still made no promises to her, and she tried not to let that thought send her into despair. Wait till later, she told herself, later she would be able to deal with this. Return to London, reassure Circe and her aunt, rest and eat a decent meal, then they would all be able to make more rational decisions. She took another sip of the ale.

But when Gabriel came outside to find her, something in his expression alerted her at once.

"David will drive you back to London. You'll make the first part of the journey in the landlord's gig, a bit crowded, but it will serve," he told her. "You will be able to hire a chaise at the next town, and perhaps the services of one of the inn's maids to accompany you for the rest of the trip, to make it all look more respectable."

As if she were worried about propriety at such a time. Psyche felt her heart sink. "You are not going with us?"

He did not meet her gaze. "I think that since I am already closer to the coast, I will hie the other way. I need to repair my almost-empty pockets, and the gaming in Paris and Madrid should be heated this time of year. I will be too well known in London for any decent games after this episode becomes the latest *on-dit*."

"But your estate—" Psyche's lips had gone dry; it was hard to speak.

"I have not the money to restore it, just yet. I will take possession in a year or two, perhaps. The disrepair will hardly get much worse in that time."

A year or two, perhaps. . . . Psyche swallowed hard against the lump in her throat. *Perhaps*.

Gabriel glanced at her face, then away. He could not tell her the truth—that if he rode with them all the way back to London, witnessed Circe's happy cries that they were all safe, felt the lure of Psyche's company once more, the chance to fall into the easy routine of feeling himself at home, with family, he might not have the strength to leave. And simply to embrace Psyche again, to kiss her full lips and pull her willing body close to his—just the thought made his blood stir and the familiar ache reawaken. No, he had to do it now, while his resolve was fixed. Above all, he dared not touch her.

"I had thought that you—that we—" Psyche paused, as if not sure how to continue. "I can marry where I choose, now."

He could not leave her thinking that he did not care, no more false cruelties. She was too intelligent, anyhow, to believe them. "I feel only the greatest admiration for you, my dear Miss Hill," he said. "The utmost respect, the deepest fondness. But you deserve so much more than I can give you."

His voice faltered, then he summoned all his resolution and lifted his head to meet her gaze. "You deserve a prince among men, Psyche, not a make-believe marquis, a fake lord who has no reputation, no honor left to offer you. You deserve a man with an unsullied past. No matter how far I am able to make my way back, repair my life, some things will not change. I have thrown away my innocence, lost my good name, and I fear I will never be the man worthy of your regard, much less your hand in marriage.

"But you are the one I love," she whispered, her eyes glinting with unshed tears.

Gabriel felt his heart contract within him, and it was his turn to swallow hard. "I will treasure that thought every day that I draw breath. But for once in my misbegotten life, I will do the right thing. I will have the courage to walk away and allow you to have a better life, a more illustrious future than I could bestow."

She wanted to stomp her feet in frustration but stood still. "You are being a fool!"

"It would not be the first time," he agreed wryly. He yearned to lift his hand to her cheek, but he dared not touch that warm, flawless skin, or all his precious self-control would desert him. He took a step back.

"You will be better off without me," he repeated.

She met his gaze with stubborn resolve. "No," she said. "You may believe that, but I do not. But I will survive alone. I did not know that, for a time after my parents' sudden death, but I am stronger than I thought."

He felt a surge of pride in her. "Of course you are."

"But I will always love you, Gabriel," she said softly. "Always. Even as angry with you as I am right now, I will never deny how I feel."

The pain was almost too much to bear. Gabriel frowned, struck mute by the love shining from her clear blue eyes. She would forget him eventually, he was certain of it. With her beauty and her spirit and her courage, the men in London would make sure of that. But he would never forget this moment, nor the look in her eyes.

He would hold the memory to him many a lonely night and solitary day, but he would know that he had done the right thing, for once in his life, the noble thing. Psyche's well-being was more important than his happiness. After so many mistakes, he would find his redemption in relinquishing the one thing he wanted most in all the world.

Footsteps in the passage announced David's emergence into the sunlight. The younger man stopped, as if aware that he had walked into a private moment. "Ah, I'll just go round to the stables and check on the gig," he said. "Don't mind me."

"No, I was just going," Gabriel said.

Psyche reached out one hand, then saw that he did not trust himself to touch it. She nodded instead. "God keep you safe," she said, very low.

Then she kept her expression composed, although she bit her lip so hard she found later that it had bled, until Gabriel turned and walked away. And only when he was out of sight did she weep upon the lapels of David's blue superfine.

Twenty-three

He rode hard through the early hours of the morning, striding his hired steed and galloping out of the inn yard before the sun was well up. He rode through the rising mists that obscured the green fields, through the first bird-calls and then the rising cacophony of trills and warbles and less harmonious caws that greeted the rising sun. But he heard little, noticed little of the verdant pastures and golden grain around him, or the farmers in their fields harvesting the first hay, because his thoughts were centered on one thing only, on one woman only.

When he was an hour past Tunbridge and knew he would soon pass the entrance to his own bedraggled estate, Gabriel had a brief thought of stopping to inspect its condition, but he thrust the notion aside. It would hardly have changed much in a few weeks. It could wait. He had to get to London, he had to find Psyche. . . . Even now some callow youth could be bowing over her hand, eliciting the honor of an early morning ride in the park, lifting her up to her saddle. No one else should be holding Psyche, no other man's hands should encircle that trim waist or pull her close for an unbidden kiss—the thought made Gabriel curse a little and urge his tired horse onward.

But when he reached the drive that led to his own property, he slowed his mount despite his earlier resolutions. A wagon filled with lumber was turning up the driveway, his driveway. What would bring such a cart here? Had the driver mistaken his road? The weary horse beneath him snuffled into its reins, tossing its head. Gabriel hesitated, then turned his steed into the drive.

The lane showed signs of recent traffic, and the wagon lumbered steadily along. Gabriel tried to hail the driver, but the man seemed deaf to his call, so he followed, feeling increasingly more puzzled. In spite of the urgency that made him begrudge any moment wasted, he decided that he would investigate, very briefly. Had someone else claimed the estate? Was there some heir to Barrett who was contesting the deed? Had some band of gypsies made camp on the untenanted land? Someone must send them on their way.

The wagon rolled up to the front of the house, and Gabriel pulled up his horse just behind. But although two men came down to help the driver of the wagon unload heavy bundles of board, Gabriel's attention had been drawn to the house itself. He looped the ends of his reins around a marble statue that had somehow appeared in the newly weeded greenery at the side of the entrance, and then climbed the steps. The door stood open; someone had rehung it—or, perhaps, replaced it altogether—on shiny new hinges. Inside, he could hear the sound of hammering.

What in the name of— Gabriel stepped back to avoid a workman in a leather apron who hurried out, his arms filled with strips of wood.

"Sorry, guv," the man muttered, but he seemed to have no time to chat.

Gabriel frowned. He had to find someone in charge of this bedlam and find out just what they thought they were doing. Who had ordered this—this—he glanced around at the hallway, astonished to see how much change had been accomplished already. The walls gleamed under new paint and paper, and decayed parts of the wainscoting had been replaced. The first room that he glanced into had men working industriously. Sunshine glinted cheerfully through clean windowpanes, and the dust had been removed from the floors; there was no mouse in sight and the only sounds he detected were the banging of hammers. The house smelled of new paint and beeswax and soap and lemon oil. He could hardly credit it was the same derelict house that he and Psyche had walked into only a few weeks before.

Psyche—he had to get back on the road to London. He had to find her, beg her forgiveness, plead for another chance. . . . Gabriel hastened his steps, determined to have words with someone in charge and then return to his tired steed.

He almost walked past the library, as no sounds of obvious labor emerged from within. But as he strode past, he saw something from the corner of his eye that made him wheel swiftly to return to the doorway.

Astonished, he paused and stared. It was a vision, conjured up by his days and nights of dreaming of her, it must be.

The vision raised her fair head. Her eyes widened slightly, but she made no exclamation of amazement. "Hello, Gabriel," Psyche said. She sat in front of a handsome desk; papers littered the polished top.

For a long moment, he simply feasted his eyes on her face. Her fair hair was arranged much more softly than her normal tight knot. Her becoming soft pink gown was cut low across the bosom—too low, he decided, frowning briefly. She had never looked more delicately lovely or feminine. But he knew that "delicate" wasn't a completely accurate description. Psyche was strong—strong enough to watch him walk away and allow him time to get the truth through his own damned thick skull.

She looked recovered from their ordeal, but was it a vain hope to detect signs of strain around her blue eyes? She regarded him thoughtfully, yet she hardly seemed surprised.

Dear God, let her have missed me, too. Don't let her have changed her feelings about me.

He took a step inside, then another. Still, she did not speak.

"Can you forgive me?" he asked, his voice husky.

She looked down for a moment at the sheets of paper in front of her and folded her hands gracefully. "The question is, have you forgiven yourself?"

Silence. He thought about it before answering. "I think I have made a start, laid to rest some of the ghosts. And I did not think of my father at all, this time."

He hoped she would inquire just who he did think of, but instead she asked, "Where did you go?" She still sounded matter-of-fact, as if they had parted only a few hours before.

"I made it as far as Spain," he said, keeping his tone light with great effort.

"The gaming was not good?"

"Oh, it was, my pockets are much better lined, but the cards bored me," he told her. "And the weather there was bad this time of year."

"Too much sunshine?" she suggested, her tone dry.

"Too much heat," he agreed. "And I found I had lost my taste for paella and sangria, and I could not sleep at all at night. The crickets were too loud in the twilight, and the birds too shrill in the dawn. I had planned to go on to Italy, but I knew I should not like it there, either . . . because you would not be there."

She gazed at him, her beautiful eyes impossible to read. He felt the first stirrings of panic. She had never been so hard for him to decipher. Gabriel had to clear his throat. He felt as awkward as a green boy. "All I could think of was you; I saw your face in the first golden blush of daylight, and I heard your laughter when the church bells rang. You were always with me, but you were not with me, and I thought the ache of your loss might drive me mad."

"So you came back?"

Still, she did not smile. Perhaps it was too late. His heart lurched at the thought.

He nodded. "I am so sorry, Psyche, my dear Miss Hill."

"For departing or for returning?" Her tone was still detached, and she had not moved toward him. He thought he might die of the longing he felt to hold her in his arms. What if she told him to leave, to never return?

"For both, I suppose," he said, sighing, holding himself back with great effort. He took one more step to close the gap between them, and she watched him, her gaze solemn. "I tried for once in my life to do the noble thing, and I could not. I know I am not worthy of you, goddess, there is no way that I can change that much. But despite that, I cannot forget you. I cannot excise your image from my heart. And dammit, I don't want to!"

Gabriel stared directly into her eyes, offering himself as plainly and humbly as he knew how. "I am the man I am. I will never be a saint, but I will do my utmost to make you happy. Beyond that, I don't know what else to do except tell you that I love you."

She pressed her lips together, then they parted, so smooth, so soft—he yearned to kiss them just once more— no, to kiss them every day, every hour. She seemed about to speak, but Gabriel heard another footstep behind him. He looked over his shoulder, and Psyche lifted her brows as she gazed at the workman.

"Yes?"

"Beg pardon, miss, but where you want this 'ere mantel?" He gestured behind him, and Gabriel saw the handsome carved piece that two men were laboring to carry.

"That goes in the drawing room, the big room on the next level."

The men withdrew, and it was almost a relief to consider other questions. "What on earth are you doing here? What is all this?"

Psyche's lips twitched, as if she were fighting a smile. "Uncle Wilfred has released my money, and I have agreed not to implicate my cousin Percy in any criminal charges. So I decided to begin the renovations."

He blinked. "Psyche, Miss Hill, I cannot allow you to throw your money away on this wreck of a house."

"But I like this house," she protested. "And I have found,

Gabriel, that I have even more money that I had suspected. So I can afford to redo this house, our house, just as I like. Oh, and I have invited Mrs. Parslip to come to us as housekeeper. She insisted on giving two weeks' notice to your father, but she should arrive tomorrow. I hope that is satisfactory?"

"Of course," he agreed, feeling hope rise inside him with the force of a tropical hurricane. "But—does that mean you still—" Gabriel covered the last of the distance between then in two long strides and took her by her shoulders, lifting her to her feet and guiding her away from the desk. "Psyche, does that mean you will have me, flawed as I am? You will marry me?"

She smiled at him at long last, her face soft and content. "Since all the polite world thinks we are already engaged, that would be the most expeditious solution, don't you think?"

"The hell with *expeditious,*" he exploded. "I love you, Psyche! I cannot live without you. I tried, but—"

She lifted her lips, and he kissed her with a zeal and a passion that left them both breathless. When finally he raised his head, he had remembered another problem.

"Psyche, the Ton thinks that I am the marquis of Tarrington. How shall we account for that?"

She fit in his arms as if she belonged there, had always belonged there. She touched his cheek with one finger, tracing the line of his jaw. "Oh, I have already explained to Sally, in the strictest confidence, that you assumed a fictitious title to escape the ruffians who were trying to kill you."

"Which means?"

"Which means that by now, all of London will know the story and think it terribly romantic." Psyche laughed.

He kissed her again. "I don't suppose, along with the lumber and paint and new paper for the walls, that you brought along a special license?"

"You are impatient for the wedding?" She raised her brows, an impish gleam in her eyes.

"For the wedding night," he explained, kissing her temple and then the tip of her ear.

Psyche shivered with delight. "I'm afraid not. Circe absolutely forbade us to marry before returning to London. She is determined to be a bridesmaid. She was conferring with the dressmaker when I left, trying to design a gown that will give her the appearance of a bosom."

It was his turn to laugh. "You are all so confident. How were you so sure that I would return? Was my lack of resolve so obvious?"

Psyche looked thoughtful. "I found a collection of tracts in my library—on up-to-date methods of agriculture."

Gabriel hoped he was not turning red. "Umm, I just wanted to be a good landlord," he tried to explain.

She gazed up at him, her glance full of trust. "It gave me hope that you wanted to settle down at last and put down roots, hope that one woman might, indeed, be enough to make you happy."

"Oh, my dearest Psyche," he protested. "Since the day I first saw you, I have known there was no one else in the world that I could ever desire."

"Even when I'm old and wrinkled?"

"I shall love—and frequently kiss—every wrinkle," he promised.

"When I grow round with child?"

He stilled for a moment, awed at the thought. "I shall count myself the most blessed of men. And besides, I shall grow old, too, you know. An old weathered landowner, worrying about the health of his cows and whether the fields have had enough rain. Will you fault me for that, my dear Miss Hill?"

"Never." She touched his cheek, knowing that his handsome face would only grow more impressive with the years, but he would not want to hear that. She put her hand lightly to his lips, and he kissed her fingers. "I'm afraid we really must marry, Lord Gabriel Sinclair," she said, laughter bubbling again. "We have no choice."

Suddenly arrested, he paused, a question in his eyes.

She was annoyed to find herself blushing. "No, no, not—I mean, it seems to be the only way I can stop you from calling me 'my dear Miss Hill' every other breath. I must change my name. I shall be Lady Gabriel Sinclair, you know, after we are wed."

"I am only too happy to oblige," he agreed. "Although I could always call you my Queen of Hearts, after your fateful winning draw."

Her eyes suddenly twinkled with mischievous humor. "Oh, in that case I would be your Deuce of Clubs."

Confusion wrinkled his brow for a moment. Then understanding spread a grin across his travel-weary but triumphant face. "Why, you mean to confess that my very correct, very decorous Miss Hi—" He stopped at her warning glance. "That is, the future Lady Gabriel Sinclair, *cheated?*"

"Of course I did," she declared. "The moment your back was turned."

"Most improper," said Gabriel in dire tones.

Psyche rose up on her toes and flung her arms around his strong neck. "Oh, darling, I knew you'd be proud."

The kiss he gave her then could never have been termed "proper." And that, she decided, was just the way she liked it.

*Turn the page for a sneak preview of
Nicole Byrd's next novel*

LADY IN WAITING

coming soon from Jove Books!

Prologue

CALAIS 1822

*O*h, *dear God. She was going home.*

Circe Hill paced the Calais dock, pausing only to gaze across the heaving water of the Channel, toward England and a future she was certain she did not want. Overhead a gull called, raucous and impudent, and the slight stench of dead fish tainted the sea breeze.

Normally, the busy seafront would have delighted all of Circe's artistic instincts; normally, she would have been busy sketching the sailors as they toted barrels and boxes below deck, readying the vessel to lift anchor.

But not today. There was nothing normal about today. Today this same ship stood ready to push her toward home and a dreaded future. For two blissful years she had followed her childhood dreams, wandered amid Italian vineyards and French villages, sketching and painting, untrammeled, with no one except the long-suffering Miss Tellman to chaperone . . .

What was wrong with her, Circe wondered, not for the first time. *What proper young lady wouldn't love the idea of*

*a London Season? What proper lady wouldn't adore the
thought of invitations to the Ton's most tedious—er—exciting parties?* She was thankful no one was close enough to
hear her groan. The problem was that she was not and had
never been a proper young lady.

Only one thing, one *person*, would have brought her willingly back to the confines of London society, and she knew
he was still, forever, out of her reach. If only—a bustle of
movement nearby pulled her abruptly out of her thoughts.

"Attention!" Two men draped in dark cloaks and heavy
frowns accosted the French family whom Circe had noticed
earlier. Papa looked like a prosperous merchant, and Mama
was also sedately garbed, calling after her clutch of dark-
eyed children, which she and the nanny could hardly control.

Strangely, it was the young nanny the two men eyed, and
Circe saw Papa swell in indignation, and Mama frown. Why
were the officials interested in a mere servant?

Nearer to Circe, a petite young woman in a shabby trav-
eling cloak spoke timidly. "Signorina?" The girl stood
inches from the edge of the dock, her head lowered.

"Prenez garde," Circe said absently, "The wet wood is
slippery." Then she realized that the girl's salute had been
Italian, not French.

"It matters little," the girl muttered in accented English.
"I might as well throw myself into the deepest depths!" She
glanced up; she was very young, and Circe was shocked by
the desperation in her eyes. More than that—

"I've seen you before," Circe said slowly. "In front of the
bakery in Genoa, and later—" Circe gasped. "You were the
solitary young nun on the coach ride from Nice! You kept
your face down then, too, but I saw you look up. Why—"

The girl's brown eyes widened, and she made the sign of
the cross. "Do you have the Inner Eye?" she whispered.

Circe was startled into a laugh. "Of course not. I am an
artist, and I look at people's faces, bodies, the shapes of their
eyes—everything. Why were you dressed as a nun—"

The girl trembled, and Circe saw the two men in black coming closer. "Are you a thief?" she asked quietly.

"Oh, no, I swear it by the Holy Mother," the girl whispered. "Signor DuPree told me to follow you; he said you might help. Those men are Austrian Secret Police; they want me because of my father."

Her thoughts racing, Circe gazed at the girl. Her painting instructor had sent this girl? The men walked up, and one glance at their closed faces and cold eyes made Circe suppress a shiver. She had been on the Continent long enough to have heard of the Austrian Empire's notorious Secret Police and their equally infamous methods. She glanced down at the girl, whose face was now pale with fear.

"Comment vous s'appelez vous?" the man demanded.

"I am English," Circe said, though she understood his French perfectly. "My name is Miss Circe Hill, and why should you require it?"

The agent shrugged and glared at the girl in the shabby cloak, who looked as if she might faint. "Are you English, too?"

"This is my maidservant," Circe said, surprising herself as much as anyone. The girl's eyes widened, but she threw Circe a grateful glance, then looked down at her feet.

"I do not understand why you ask such questions. We are about to return home," Circe added. "I believe it is time to board; the captain will not wish to miss the tide."

Indeed, the French family had already disappeared inside, and Miss Tellman gestured to her from the deck.

"Are you an official of the French government? Because if not, I fail to see what right you have to delay me." She kept her voice icy, and to her relief, the agent hesitated.

"Come along, *Mary*," Circe turned away without looking at her 'servant.' From the corner of her eye, she could tell that the girl followed silently, her face still tilted down.

On board, they were swept up into the tumult of the ship leaving its anchorage. "There you are, Miss Circe," Telly said in relief. "I was afraid you would be left behind. Come inside, I have tea waiting in your cabin."

As Circe followed, she glanced back and found that the girl had disappeared. Recalling the stranger's earlier statement about throwing herself into the sea, Circe made an excuse and went to look for her. Outside, the thin figure in the well-worn cloak stood at the edge of the deck, face averted, gazing at the retreating shoreline.

Good, the mystery girl had done nothing foolish. But why was she a fugitive, fleeing so far from her home in the kingdom of Piedmont on the Italian peninsula? What had she, or her father, done?

Circe put her hands on the railing, bracing her legs as the boat dipped and the wind whipped her long skirts back against her body. Her thoughts returned to her own dilemma; how was she to manage a London Season? She didn't want to spend her time at boring balls and dinners. She had her art to focus on, all she wanted, all she needed. Really, it was.

She heard a muffled sob. "You are not alone, I will not abandon you." She moved closer to take the girl's hand. "What is your real name?"

The young woman blinked, and the flow of tears slowed. "Lucia—Luciana, if you please. Would you allow me to stay with you, to work for you, for a little while? I could save my wages and send them to my parents to help them escape, too. I am very handy with the needle." Hope dawned for the first time in the girl's brown eyes, and she clung to Circe's hand as if it were a lifeline.

"Of course." Circe squeezed Luciana's hand. "Now come inside and get warm, and let us get you some tea."

Shivering, Luciana followed Circe toward the cabins. Circe took a deep breath. Luciana's plight made her own worries look very small. Circe would help the frightened girl, and for herself, she would do what her sister asked. It was only a few months, then she would be back at her painting, and her heart—her heart would give up this foolish yearning for something it could never have. How hard could enduring one Season be?

It was just as well she did not know the answer.

One

No one had ever said Circe was beautiful.
But he didn't need a beautiful girl, only one who was well-bred and respectable. No one could deny Circe Hill's lineage, which was above reproach, and as for respectable—well, most of the time . . .

David Lydford, earl of Westbury, took the front steps of the elegant Mayfair town house with a bound, his hat at its usual jaunty angle, his morning coat hugging his broad shoulders as he knocked on the door. Impatience goading him, he rapped again before it swung ponderously open. An elderly butler gazed at him, his whole expression a reproof.

" 'Lo, Jowers," David said.

"My lord," Jowers intoned. "I regret to inform you that Lord Gabriel is out, and Lady Gabriel Sinclair is not at home to visitors." He began to shut the door again, but David put out one hand to hold it open.

"No, no, I know that, I just spoke to Gabriel at his club. I want to see Miss Circe. And I know she's back," David put in before the servant could try to deny the younger lady, too. "Gabriel told me, and I need to see her now, at once."

"But my lady is—" the butler tried to say.

"Not to worry, I'll show myself up." Ignoring Jower's

sputtering protests, David slid past him and headed straight for the stairs. "Knowing Circe, I can guess where she'll be."

He took the stairs two at a time, passing the first floor with its formal drawing room—as if Circe would be willingly found sitting primly in the drawing room like any normal well-bred miss—on past the level with the family bedrooms—on up a narrower flight to the old schoolroom, a room with large windows and a good array of morning light.

Important if you were a dedicated artist, as Circe most decidedly was. David tapped on the door, then pushed it open without waiting for a response. He saw just what he had expected to see, and for a moment the sight took him back six years, to the first time he had met Circe, all knobby knees and straight brown hair and those unexpected clear green eyes. He had once accused her of being a fairy child, with her strange air of knowing more than she should.

But her passion was painting, and she was, at this hour of the morning, hidden behind her easel and canvas, dabs of paint staining the coarse smock that protected her morning dress. As usual, Miss Tellman, who had once been Circe and Psyche's—now Lady Gabriel Sinclair's—governess and now served Circe in the role of companion, dozed in the other corner of the room in a comfortable chair, her knitting snarled in her lap.

"Hello," David said quietly, hoping that Circe was not so absorbed in her current work in progress that she would refuse to stop and talk. At the moment all he could see of her was a few wild strands of dark hair and an extra brush tucked behind one ear. Her face was obscured by the canvas that stood between them, and she did not bother to look up.

"I don't want any tea, now, thank you," she said absently. Her voice still had the clear bell-like tone that had always pleased him.

"Pity, that. I had my heart set on one of your tea parties." David grinned, tugging off his butternut gloves before tossing them carelessly onto a worn armchair.

The unexpectedness of his deep voice made Circe jump. Her brush clattered to the floor, leaving a broad smear on the already splattered cloth beneath her. Circe stared at the trace of blue-gray oil, knowing with absolute certainty that the man standing behind her easel possessed eyes of the same warm color.

Warily, she raised herself on her toes and peered over the top of the canvas. It was he, no mistake, looking so disgustingly perfect that she could have gratefully pulled the floor cloth over herself to hide. She knew how she must look right now. Hair flying in all directions, paint smeared over her brow or cheek, and, heavens, he'd never notice the bosom she had finally grown under her painter's smock.

And Circe knew that if it had been anyone but he, she would never have given her appearance a single thought. But it *was* David and therefore it mattered. Ducking farther behind her painting, she quickly swiped at her cheeks and smoothed back her hair. Little good it did, but it never hurt to try.

"What do you say, Circe?" David asked, his grin evident in his voice.

After a deep breath, Circe stepped from behind the protection of her canvas. *Say something witty,* she thought desperately. *And charming. Yes, charming would be excellent.*

"I never gave you a tea party."

Circe frowned, vastly annoyed with herself. *So much for charming.*

David laughed easily and a bit too confidently. "No, you were never the type for dolls and tea parties, were you, sprite?"

He should just tweak my blasted nose and be done with it. Circe gave up charm and settled for dignity.

"Not that I ever considered it a defect, my lord, but no. I had other interests."

Exuding sudden solicitude, David crossed to her and bowed formally. He then lifted her hand to his mouth, carefully planting a kiss just to the right of a white smear on her thumb. "My dear, you could claim a defect as soon as I could claim sainthood."

His bent posture brought their faces level; Circe studied

his handsome face. He was older, of course, the planes and angles of his face more defined. His dark chestnut hair was as thick and wavy, his smile as bright, his long, lean frame as dashing. Intriguingly, his nose was a bit off-center. Circe would have smiled at that proof of his misadventures, but she could not smile. There was something disturbing within the eyes she knew so well, a hint of weary unhappiness barely covered by his veneer of frivolity, echoes of old pain.

Circe drew her hand back and shook her head. "Don't do that, David."

He straightened and blinked in surprise. "I didn't—" He looked away a moment, collected himself and smiled again. "I beg your pardon, Circe. I am too used to a different type of lady."

Circe arched a brow in complete understanding. Surprised, David turned his laugh into a very unconvincing cough.

"Methinks you've spent too much time on the Continent, Miss Circe."

"And I think you've spent too much time in gaming halls and brothels."

David's eyes widened in disbelief. But a reluctant grin formed at the corners of his mouth. "A proper, young, *marriageable* lady," he emphasized the dreaded word meaningfully, "doesn't know of such places and wouldn't dare mention them if she did."

Circe could have stuffed one of her precious sable brushes into her mouth—paint and all. Why must she speak every word that entered her head? If she could shock David, she would give a society matron seizures.

Feeling completely hopeless, Circe sighed and turned back to her painting. "As I said earlier, I have other interests."

He stepped closer, observing the smooth line of her heart-shaped face as she deliberately averted her gaze. Was she being impudent, teasing him, or was she truly and totally disinterested? It did not bode well for his plan.

Glancing at the disarray of her brown hair, which had

been pulled haphazardly into a knot at the back of her
neck—she must be the despair of her lady's maid, David
thought—he took a quick peek at the oil-covered canvas that
stood on the easel.

It took his breath. It was a simple setting, a towering English oak with a smattering of daffodils and hyacinths
blooming in the grass beneath, and blue sky glimpsed between the green-leafed branches. On the grass, a woman in
a white gown sat holding a baby in her lap. You could not
see the woman's face as she bent over the laughing child,
but the whole picture radiated love and contentment and
ease, making him relax a little despite himself. Circe was
truly a genius with the brush, despite all the dictates of society that hindered a female artist from public acknowledgment. This deceptively modest scene was a masterpiece, he
told himself. He knew little enough about art, but any simpleton could see it. This should have been exhibited in the
Royal Academy, and if she had not been a woman—

Then she looked up once more, and he glanced at her
face. She had pulled off the smock and had tried to smooth
back her hair, which still strayed from its knot to soften the
pointed chin and heart shape of her face. Her skin was
smooth, if a little too brown from the sun for a fashionable
miss, and her eyes . . . her eyes were as still, clear and lucent
as a still green pond into which sunlight poured. . . . He had
a dim thought that this was a masterpiece, too, how had he
never seen that . . .

Then he gave himself a mental shake; it was only Circe,
taller now and more developed in figure, but much the same
as the child who had once sat on the stairs and quizzed him
about his lack of costume for a masquerade ball. And now
he needed her help.

"Tell me," she repeated. "What is so imperative that you
would interrupt the last minutes of good light?" Her tone
was reproachful, and he smiled, slipping automatically into
the easy charm that always softened women to his pleas.

But Circe shook her head. "David . . ." she warned.

"Oh, yes, sorry." He ran a hand through his unruly hair.

"Can we sit down, please? I feel like an errant schoolboy, standing here with my hat in my hands."

It was a feeling he had often enough with his only surviving parent; he did not care for it. Circe motioned to the wooden chairs that surrounded a battered nursery table. He held a chair for her—she smelled of linseed oil and turpentine—and then seated himself.

"It's my mother," he said.

Circe did not look surprised.

"She's on me to marry."

Circe lifted her delicately arched brows, and her green eyes were knowing. "David, she's been doing that for years, why is it so pressing just now?"

"She's never been this bad before," he protested, wounded that Circe would not accept the urgency of his plight. "She says she has contracted a lingering pleurisy and is likely to go into a decline." He rushed on before Circe could point out that his mother was always convinced she had one illness or another. "She says she will never see her grandchildren if I am not engaged at once and married before the fall. And she's giving me no peace at all!"

"So how am I to help? You already know all the eligible girls in London, and I have been away for years. Besides, you are surely not going to contract an engagement just to placate your mother." This time her tone seemed guarded.

"I can't deal with my mother just now," David said. The excuse about his mother was true enough, but it was hardly the whole story. However, David couldn't disclose the task his uncle had requested of him, nor its seriousness. Not many people would have considered him suitable for such a commission, so how could he refuse? But no one, absolutely no one, was to know; or national security could be threatened, not to say a dreadful scandal stirred up.

"David, you always have a lady on your arm," Circe retorted. "I don't see what I'm to do."

"Yes, but they're usually not the kind of lady that would do for my mother," David said.

"Oh, I see. You favor *chere amies*, or—what are they

called in England—light-o'loves?" Circe wrinkled her nose at him, looking surprised but not scandalized, which she ought to have jolly well been.

"Circe! You really must *pretend* to be shocked, at least," David admonished her. "But yes, just so." David was relieved that she understood. "So I thought I could do a bit of playacting myself, and you could help me, allow me to hang over you a bit. With my affections engaged, you can't see why I really don't want to be forced to squire some tongue-tied bashful miss around Almack's—"

"Whereas I always have something to say? Even if inappropriate?" Her tone was even drier. "David, you could 'hang over' any eligible young lady you choose."

David realized he could have been a bit more tactful. "No, I mean yes, you always say what you think. We've known each other for ages, Circe; we are old friends, are we not? And I don't want to break some poor chit's heart, y'know, who might misinterpret my attentions and think that I was really serious."

"Since you are such an eligible catch."

He grimaced. "Well, yes. And don't look at me like that; I can't help being an earl and single. It just happened."

Circe shrugged. "I suppose not. So I am to be your decoy, to keep your mother off your back while you pursue the beautiful actress."

He wasn't sure he liked her tone. "Yes, and it won't be all one-sided; I can help you, too, y' know, in your first Season. Gabriel said as much—" he paused, remembering that this was not to have been repeated.

Circe sat straight in her chair, alarm evident on her face. "What did Gabriel say? That you should take pity on me, on poor dowdy little Circe in her first Season?"

"No, no, not at all." David folded his arms, exasperated. Why was Circe taking a pet? She'd never used to be this touchy. Pity that girls grew up, he thought. Unless, of course, they turned into well-endowed actresses with flaming red hair and that "come-hither" glint in their eyes. With an effort, he pulled his mind back to the schoolroom. "He just said I could check up on you once in a while, lead you into an occasional dance. Thought you'd feel more comfortable with an old friend to speak to now and then. Is that so unreasonable?"

"I suppose no." Circe relaxed a bit, the bright flush of anger that had stained her cheeks fading.

Actually, there had been more to the conversation than that. "Psyche's having the devil of a time getting Circe to even agree to her coming out," Gabriel had told him earlier over a steaming cup of morning coffee as they both sat in the well-worn leather club chairs. "She's only interested in her painting, as you might remember. But Psyche thinks it important that she have at least one Season before she returns to her art. If you will help Circe, who has never bothered to practice any social skills, and try to guide her away from any disasters—you know her lack of regard for propriety—we'd be much obliged."

Since Gabriel had been his hero from the time David was in short pants, an older neighbor lad who had first taught him to fish and shoot and hunt and had allowed him to tag after him in the field, it seemed a small enough request. And then it had occurred to David that this could be to his advantage, too.

"You're not going to tell your mother that we are—are—" Circe's voice interrupted his memory.

"Lord, no." David almost shuddered. "You know my mother; she'd have the betrothal announcement in the papers before we even attended our second ball. But just a hint here and there that you might be considering my attentions could save me a lot of grief."

Silence again. Circe gazed out the window, and her thoughts seemed far away. Probably planning another picture, David thought, resigned. But before he had to remind her of the object of the conversation, she surprised him with her reply.

"Very well, I will assist you," she agreed. "But remember, it is only one friend helping another, David."